About the Book

A yearning for love and adventure evolves into a search for the meaning of life.

Tony had a passion for travel. What started out as an innocent pursuit for adventure took many turns: through love, tragedy, and disillusionment; and awakened his sleeping soul, setting him on a path of aspiration.

THE DIARY OF LADY X, a novel in two volumes, is filled with actual accounts. The story has appeal for a wide ranging readership who will find its characters to be engaging, and its story to be intriguing.

The Diary of Lady X

Volume I

Song
of the
Sea

by

Mursalin Machado

ARPress
45 Dan Road Suite 5
Canton MA 02021

Hotline: 1(888) 821-0229
Fax: 1(508) 545-7580

Ordering Information:
Quantity sales. Special discounts are available on quantity purchases by corporations, associations, and others. For details, contact the publisher at the address above.

Printed in the United States of America.

ISBN-13:	Softcover	979-8-89389-203-1
	Hardcover	979-8-89389-205-5
	eBook	979-8-89389-204-8

Library of Congress Control Number: 2024905303

Books in the series:

Volume I

Song of the Sea

Book 1

Song of the Sea

Volume II

The Journey Within

Book 2

Westward to the East

Book 3

Search and Be Found

Book 4

Journey Home

Who Was the Lady?

She was a small ship that had sailed

the biggest ocean in the world.

She was an innocent of twenty and

an actress.

She was a gifted dancer and artist

of the striptease.

She was a teenaged prostitute to keep

her family from poverty.

She was a mother and diplomat's wife

in need of love.

She was of the lowest caste and in love

with a man of the highest caste.

She was a woman of dignity looking to

the education of others.

She was lying half naked in a gutter in Calcutta

begging for money for her cremation.

She was a proud mother and still innocent.

Most of all she was a lady.

Om Shanti

BOOK ONE

Winter

    wind

      bites
      and
      pulls

    my

     tapping

  heels.

Listen.

The ships' whistles blow.

Song of the Sea

CONTENTS

PRELUDE

She was born in the fall of 1941 at a small shipyard in Sausalito on San Francisco Bay; a ship of only 312 feet in length and 41 feet in width at her midbeam. With a floating depth of just 14 feet and a flat bottom she could navigate into shallow waters when necessary. As a newly completed seaplane tender for the Navy she was christened *LADY* and given her first assignment. Her maiden voyage was to sail to Hawaii to join the U.S. Pacific Fleet at Pearl Harbor.

When the sun rose on the Pacific Ocean that December 6th, it was a beautiful Saturday morning with a sky of broken clouds. The *Lady* was north of the Hawaiian Islands at latitude twenty five degrees heading south and proceeding according to schedule.

At around six a.m. the ship's radar picked up a single blip that was heading in the vicinity of the *Lady*. Moments later the ship's lookout was able to recognize a small plane approaching the area. The ship's radio operator attempted contact requesting the plane to identify itself. There was no response. As the plane drew nearer, it looked like a reconnaissance plane with something under its belly, perhaps an extra fuel supply.

When the plane circled the ship it became clearly visible. It did not look like an American plane even though it bore an American insignia. And the object under its belly looked more like an oversized torpedo than a fuel pod. The ship's crew was immediately called to battle stations. Flying low to the water it approached the ship's port side with the blinding sun behind it.

By that time gunners were manning the ship's antiaircraft guns. The captain gave the order to fire at the same moment the plane opened fire with its guns. When the plane's pilot attempted to release the torpedo the mechanism malfunctioned. Gunfire from the ship apparently damaged the plane's flight controls as it passed over the *Lady*. The plane suddenly began to climb, then just as suddenly, did a crash dive into the water detonating the torpedo. An enormous explosion killed the pilot and crewman.

This entry for the ship's diary dated 6 Dec 41
has been removed by order #USNPH0937701

On the night of December 6th, with coastal lights looking like a string of pearls, a proud young *Lady* sailed into Pearl Harbor and took her place among some of the biggest and most awesome warships ever built.

After giving the crew orders to remain on board, the captain took the ship's log with him to headquarters to report the incident of that morning. The log's page for that morning was temporarily removed and stamped SECRET. The captain was told to swear his crew to secrecy concerning the incident until the Navy could have a chance to investigate the affair the following Monday. Upon the captain's return to the ship, he did as he was ordered and gave the crew shore leave until Monday.

During the calm and quiet of early Sunday morning, December 7th, the sky became filled with what seemed like a wrath from hell. Japanese dive-bombers and planes carrying torpedoes appeared as if from out of a nightmarish dream. The attack came in two waves. After only an hour and a half most of the ships that were anchored in the harbor lay either wasted or damaged, with over two thousand men killed.

For some reason, maybe because of her small size or her location, the *Lady* received only minor damage. Machine gun bullets had entered her across the starboard side and front of the bridge shattering windows, and starting a fire that was quickly extinguished. She also received a coating of fuel oil and debris from a nearby explosion.

Despite the ship's gruesome appearance, she was still afloat. One curious thing was that a bullet had hit the ship's bell at such an angle as to put a slanted gash just after the word LADY. When the mark was discovered during a damage check, someone of the crew had the idea to cross that gash with a line making it into an X, and to refer to the ship as *Lady X* in respect of her loss of innocence during those cruel events.

A short time later the ship was converted to a torpedo (PT) boat tender with *LADY X* painted on her stern. She was sent to the Philippines where she later assisted in a crucial rescue mission.

Chapter 1

YOUTH AND ADVENTURE

After the end of World War II most of the U.S. Navy's ships were retired to what were referred to as Moth Ball Fleets: a form of floating storage where they awaited further use. The Lady lay at anchor at such a facility north of San Francisco Bay for sixteen years. In 1962 she was completely refurbished and recommissioned in San Francisco to serve the U.S. Coast and Geodetic Survey Department. As a survey ship she was assigned to explore and chart the contour of the floor of the Pacific Ocean and to analyze its waters. So an addition was made to her name. Painted on her stern was the following:

Lady Explorer
San Francisco

Dressed all in white, she was no longer a relic of the past. After participating in the International Indian Ocean Expedition of 1964, she was given a new assignment that was to begin in January of 1965. She was to chart the ocean floor between the Hawaiian Islands and the Aleutian Islands of Alaska.

Because her basic design included a flat bottom she would be vulnerable to the occasional rough seas she had to encounter. With a crew of sixty men, she would be a tightly packed ship but very worthy of the task at hand.

The first week of that January, the *Lady Explorer* was at her home port to complete her crew before sailing. The place was on the Oakland side of San Francisco Bay. She was tied to a dock near a place called Jack London Square. The engraving on the ship's bell still read as it had since December of 1941:

U.S.N.

LADY *X*

1941

A young man, Tony Lewis, heard from a friend that the ship would need a few new crew members for her next oceanic cruise of four months in duration. He was told that applications from men with limited experience would be considered. Tony, tall and trim at twenty-six, had an almost insatiable passion for travel. The thought of signing on for a cruise in the Pacific excited him.

It was midafternoon on a beautifully clear and calm Sunday when Tony saw the *Lady Explorer* for the first time. He liked her small size and design. She could have been mistaken for a Coast Guard cutter painted white as she was.

He stepped onto the gangplank leading from the dock to the ship. When the subtle movements of the water lifted and lowered the ship, the gangplank also moved. He slowly walked up and sensed he was entering another world, the immense world of the sea with a life and mystery all its own.

When Tony stepped through the gangway a crewman standing watch greeted him with, "Welcome aboard, sir. How can I help you?"

"Hello, I'm here to apply for the next cruise."

The crewman informed him, "You need to go to the captain's cabin. Just go through that passageway and it will be the first cabin on the right."

"Thanks a lot, friend."

As soon as Tony entered the narrow passageway he became aware of the closeness of the space around him. On such a small vessel, every room and passageway needed to be of minimum size. Also there were the persistent odors of paint and diesel fuel.

Tony found the captain's cabin with someone inside, "Excuse me, are you the captain?"

Sitting at a desk was a middle-aged man dressed in a tan officer's uniform. He spoke with only the faintest hint of an English accent. "No, actually, the captain has gone ashore. I'm Henry Jenkins, the first mate and officer on duty. Perhaps I may be of some assistance."

"My name is Antony Lewis. I was told that you are signing on new crew members."

"Well, yes, in fact we are. We still have two positions open."

"Oh, great," Tony said with a sense of relief.

"One with the deck force, and one as quartermaster surveyor."

"Deck force and quartermaster surveyor?" The titles were new to him.

"The first is merely the deck crew that is concerned with the maintenance of the ship. The position of surveyor involves operating depth recording equipment. For that there is an exam that you will have to pass in order to qualify. The pay will be the same for either. We also require a copy of a recent medical examination, a record of any military service, and proof of citizenship."

"Fortunately, a friend told me what I would need so I have those with me."

"Well then," the first mate handed Tony some papers. "You'll need to fill in these forms, of course. If you have any related experience, be sure to include that in the application." After Tony began filling in his forms the first mate informed him, "Our basic work week is eight hours a day, seven days a week while at sea. The weeks run Monday through Sunday. We are at sea for three weeks at a time followed by seven days of shore leave in Hawaii. That will be followed by another three weeks at sea, then seven days off in Hawaii, and so on, until the end of this assignment."

Tony thought out loud, "Twenty-one days on, and seven days off." He looked up from the forms. "Did you say Hawaii?"

"That's correct." Then with a smile, the first mate asked, "Still interested?"

Tony thought to himself, *Are you kidding?* He tried to look business like, "Yes sir, I'm interested."

"Oh, blimey, I nearly forgot. The ship's doctor needs an assistant for one or two hours each morning, depending. How would you feel about that? You're not squeamish, are you?"

"Not at all." He was delighted.

Jenkins had taken a liking to him and was quite pleased as well. "The doctor's assistant duties will be carried out by the person who fills the surveyor position. Just give me the documents I mentioned, and fill out the paper work. After you have done that I'll give you the surveyor examination." He motioned Tony to a tiny desk in a corner. "You may fill out everything there."

After Tony had completed the application forms and the special exam, Jenkins took a few moments to look over the papers before commenting, "I don't think there will be anything to worry about. I see here that you are twenty-six and have never been married."

"That's right."

"It's just as well. These long cruises do damage to any marriage." Then Jenkins informed him, "The exam you've completed will be given over to a testing center in San Francisco. The results will be radioed to us before we reach Hawaii. So, unless you've changed your mind Mr. Lewis, for the first three weeks you'll be with the deck force." He paused to see if Tony would reconsider; which he did not, "Congratulations."

Tony felt elated. "Thank you, sir. To be honest, I thought this would be more difficult."

"You seem suitable, and we are sailing tomorrow."

"You said I'll be with the deck force, what will I be doing?"

Jenkins explained, "Well, that all depends on the bosun's needs and your abilities. It could be anything from maintenance and painting to steering the ship." He glanced at his schedule for the next day. "We will be sailing after lunch. Everything in your application seems in order, so you should report for duty in the morning before seven. Captain Reiger will have a contract waiting for you to sign."

"That's great, but I need to go back to the city to get my things. Will I need to be back on board tonight?"

"It will be better for us if you are, I'm sure, but it's not necessary."

"Then I better leave if I'm going to make it back in time to get some sleep."

"Very well, then." With the test and application still in his hand, Jenkins noticed, "I see here that you've spelled Anthony without the *h*. Isn't that the German spelling?"

"You're right, sir. I changed the spelling when I was in West Berlin."

"Ah, Berlin. If you would allow me to be curious, whatever for, the change in spelling, that is."

"No, I don't mind. I had a lady friend there who, when she first said my name, called me Antony. I never liked the sound of Anthony, but when I heard her pronounce it that way for the first time . . . , it just felt right somehow, so I adopted it."

"I'm sorry lad, I don't mean to pry. It sounds as though there may be an interesting story there. Perhaps as time goes by you wouldn't mind sharing it with me. I'm a bit of a romantic myself."

"Sure. I'd better get going. Thank you very much, sir." He started to reach for the door.

"When you return, there will be someone to show you to your quarters." The first mate reached across his desk to shake Tony's hand. "Welcome aboard, Mr. Lewis."

"Thank you, sir."

Tony made his way back to the deck and walked down the gangplank. His nostrils became filled with the scent of salt sea air blowing across San Francisco Bay with the afternoon breeze. He had a feeling of lightness, the way he felt after something very special had taken place, the way he felt when he traveled in other countries—a feeling of anticipation, excitement, fear, and wonder. It was a feeling of being really alive.

Maureen

Tony caught a bus crossing the Bay Bridge to San Francisco. From Market Street he walked up Montgomery to the edge of North Beach. Because he wanted to live near City Lights bookstore and what remained of the Bohemian area, he had rented a room in an old run-down rooming house.

The sun had just set. He climbed the stairs to the dimly lit fourth floor. He tried to open the door to his room, but it was latched on the inside.

A gentle voice came from the other side, "Who is it?"

"It's me."

Recognizing his unmistakable voice, Maureen unlatched the door. At twenty she was a wisp of a lass with long light brown hair framing a face that was both unique and beautiful. With disappointed love in her voice, she said, "You were gone for so long. I came back from rehearsal at around three thirty. I thought you'd be here."

"I didn't find the ship until nearly three o'clock."

She was almost afraid to ask, "So how did things go?"

"Just great, I signed on."

Even though his passion for travel was one of the things that attracted her to him she was suddenly overcome with sadness, "Oh god, that's what I was afraid of."

He held her in his arms; she seemed frail and vulnerable. "It's all right, love. I'll only be gone for four months."

"Four months! That means you won't be back until May. When will you leave?"

"Tomorrow."

She moved back from him with a look of hurt. "I knew this was coming, but I always put it to the back of my mind." She turned toward the bed and picked up an artist's sketchpad.

"What time tomorrow?"

"The ship casts off after lunch."

She objected, "But I'll be at work then. I won't be able to see you off."

He tried to sound sorry, "I know, love. The officer who signed me on said it would be best if I slept on the ship tonight, so I—"

"Tonight!" She couldn't believe what she was hearing. She dropped the sketchpad onto the bed and grabbed his arm with her other hand. "Do you want to sleep there tonight?"

"No," he answered as he embraced her.

"Do you have to stay there tonight?"

"I don't think so. He just said that—"

She placed a finger across his lips and spoke with a gentle plea in her voice, "Then stay with me."

He spoke in a half whisper, "I do have to begin work at seven, so I need to leave at around five to make—"

She gently touched his lips. "Don't worry, I'll wake you."

Without disturbing their embrace they moved against the bed then fell across it. They entered into a place where no one else existed. There was a slow and sweet exploration of each other's essence as they made love. His restless nature became quelled when their bodies seemed to melt into one flowing stream.

Sometime later she lay asleep in his arms. Her scent, that incense of her being, acted to revive his passion. But she slept so peacefully that he thought not to disturb her. He lay there looking out the window at the ever present Coit Tower atop its hill. Centered in the window it seemed placed there for his viewing. With her gentle breathing to coax him, he closed his eyes. With the feeling that the whole world lay before him, he drifted off to sleep and dreamed:

He was a great sea bird flying alone over a blue-green ocean. Far below he could make out a tiny group of islands. The largest island had a smoldering volcano. He descended toward it and could feel an intense heat for it was about to erupt, and engulf him. He began to shake and heard a voice calling from far away, "Wake up, Tony! Wake up!"

Abruptly pulled from his dream, he said, "What's happening?"

Maureen had been shaking him to wake him. "It's almost five o'clock."

"Oh, wow, I'm not going to have enough time."

"Don't worry. I'll make some tea while you pack your bag."

The smell of freshly brewed tea filled the room as he dressed and packed. "If I can get a taxi I should make it okay. You don't mind keeping some of my things at your place, do you?"

"It'll be okay." She was feeling sad as she poured tea into his cup for the last time. "Here's your tea, my love."

"Thank you. It's suddenly strange that I'm going. I'll miss you. I have to go, you know. It's as though something inside me is making me do this."

She tore the top sheet from the sketchpad. As she folded it she put something in it. "I wrote you a poem. Promise you won't read it until you're under the Golden Gate Bridge." The bridge across a great expanse of water had become a symbol for them both.

"I promise." He put the folded paper into his shoulder bag and finished his tea. "I have to leave now."

"Don't forget this." She handed him his black beret, the one he had worn since a friend gave it to him in Spain.

He embraced her, and for a moment they just clung to each other. They kissed as lovers have since the beginning of time, sweet with love but sad with parting. Just for a second he nearly changed his mind. After they let go of each other, he hurried down the hall.

She called to him, "I don't have an address for you."

"Don't worry, I'll send it when I write you."

"Bye, I love you."

"And I love you." By then he had reached the bottom of the stairs. "Bye, love."

Her voice seemed to come from far away, "I love you."

Outside the building, daylight began to push away the night. He had no trouble getting a taxi.

"Where to, buddy?" asked the cabby.

He wondered if he was doing the right thing; should he stay with Maureen? Marry her, raise a family, and live happily ever after? Or travel the world over, not knowing what to expect? The cruise would be finished in four months. Then he told the driver, "Jack London Square."

"You're as good as there." The cabby turned down the flag on the meter, and they were off.

It was six thirty a.m. when the cab pulled into the parking area nearest the ship. Tony paid the driver, then leaped out of the taxi, and bounded up the gangplank. This time there was a different crewman standing watch, a black man about Tony's age.

"Welcome aboard, sir. How can I help you?"

"My name is Antony Lewis, and I've signed on to join this cruise. I'm sorry I—"

"Ah, Mr. Lewis. We were expecting you last night."

"Sorry, I just couldn't make it back till now."

"Don't worry, man, everything is cool." Just then another crewman appeared on deck. "Hey, Willy. Can you keep an eye on things for me while I show Mr. Lewis to his quarters?"

Tony interrupted, "You can call me Tony."

"Tony to his quarters."

The crewman answered, "Sure thing, mate. But you'll need to make it quick."

"Quick as a wink." They disappeared as they went below to the crew's quarters.

"Is *mate* your name or was he just using a sea term?"

"You know, I'm not sure which it was but Mate is my nickname. Jerry Jones is my real name." From the narrow passageway, they entered a tiny cabin with sleeping bunks for four men. "Here we are, that will be your bunk." He pointed to a top bunk that had exposed plumbing only two feet above it. One of the pipes was for hot steam and had someone's laundry draped over it.

Tony tried not to be sarcastic. "Nice. What about my gear?"

The crewman pointed to a locker at the end of Tony's bunk. "This one is yours. You need to get into your work clothes because you're due at the bosun's locker in a few minutes."

Tony was puzzled. "Where is the bosun's locker?"

"There's a workshop on the fantail. You can't miss it."

"The fantail?"

"Yeah, you know. The stern, the tail end of the ship."

"Oh yeah, sure."

"Say, friend, you ever work on a ship before?"

"No, but I was a passenger on a freighter a couple of times, crossing the Atlantic."

"A passenger crossin' the Atlantic, that's not going to get you very far with the bosun. Better not tell him that. He likes to have men with experience."

"I thought it didn't—"

"Make any difference? It does to him. I'll help you till you catch on, it won't be hard. Just don't let on. We're both with the deck crew, but I'm standing watch until eight. Look, man, are you going to be all right, because I have to get back?"

"I'll be fine."

"Okay, but don't be late. Whatever you do on the *Lady,* don't be late."

"The lady?"

"The *Lady Explorer,* man!"

"Right, don't worry friend, I won't be late. Thanks a lot for your help."

"Later, man. Be cool."

"Later." Then under his breath, he muttered, "The *Lady*, sounds nice."

Seven o'clock came and Tony was on time at the bosun's locker. The deck crew all received their assignments for the first three weeks at sea. All, that is, except Tony. The bosun was unimpressed by Tony's idea of work clothes: a pair of Spanish boots, green denims, and a red plaid shirt. The fact that he had never crewed on a ship before was something the bosun found hard to accept. He told Tony to report to the purser to acquire some proper work clothes. He loaned Tony a book on seamanship and sent him to a nearby shop to buy a bosun's knife, all before lunch. Tony was to study the book and be ready for work the next morning.

After lunch, the harbor pilot *Albatross* came alongside the *Lady Explorer* to ease her away from the dock and to escort her as far as Alcatraz Island.

Above the ship's main bridge was an open deck known as the *flying bridge*. From there the ship could be steered when in port, for better visibility.

Captain Laurence Reiger and Johan Dutchman, the chief bosun, were standing on the flying bridge with Henry Jenkins, and a crewman at the wheel. The captain was a slender, gray-haired, steely-eyed man who seldom smiled. He had a slight German accent and wore a neat full beard that gave him a distinguished look. The bosun was a hardy man who had spent most of his life at sea. His weathered face was in sharp contrast to that of the captain's.

Jenkins was standing near the port side railing not far from the crewman at the wheel. On the main deck were the second mate and four crewmen at the bow, stern, and port side. On the dock were two longshoremen ready to cast off the lines. The ship's diesel engines had been running flawless since before lunch. All was ready. A line from the stern of the pilot craft had been tied to the bow of the *Lady*.

After conferring with the harbor pilot through his walkie-talkie, the captain nodded to the first mate who called out, "Raise the gangplank, and cast away all lines!"

A little boy was standing next to a building on the dock with his mother. With both hands he held a toy boat that looked like a replica of the *Lady*. He watched wide eyed at the spectacle before him.

The captain spoke into his walkie-talkie, "All right pilot, ease her away." The line between them creaked and wept water as it tightened. The *Albatross* moved the *Lady* away from the dock as gently as could be.

Jenkins said to the man at the wheel, "There is something very majestic about a ship moving ever so slowly away from its resting place, about to challenge a merciless ocean. Don't you agree helmsman?"

Moved by Jenkins's words, the man could only say, "Aye, sir."

Once she was well away from the dock and the other ships moored to it, the *Lady* let go of the line between her and the pilot boat. She then relied upon her own power and the man at her wheel as the *Albatross* lead the way.

The little boy and his mother faded in the distance waving goodbye to someone on the ship.

Tony made his way to the bow. Since he had no duties he was free to go almost anywhere on the ship.

The *Lady* left the docking area far behind as she followed the *Albatross* and approached the San Francisco-Oakland Bay Bridge. She glided under the seven-and-a-half mile long bridge, passing Treasure Island, and headed toward Alcatraz Island.

Once they were passed it, the *Albatross* gave one long, two short, and another long blast from her steam whistle as she swung around and headed back to port. The *Lady* issued a thank you blast from her whistle. She was on her own and approaching the sometime turbulent waters of the Golden Gate. By then the captain, along with the others, had gone one deck below to the main bridge to control the ship. Since the tide was high and the surface calm, the ship traveled at three-quarters speed.

Tony had been leaning on the rail of the bow, full of awe at the whole experience. As the *Lady* drew near to the Golden Gate Bridge, there was a strong breeze coming at him. He turned his back to the wind and pulled an envelope from his jacket pocket. He opened it and took out the folded sketch paper. Inside were a tiny pressed flower and a drawing of Maureen, Tony, and Coit Tower. Within the drawing were these words:

As I stood in the rain,
You whispered to me,
Of sunshine.
M.

He looked out to sea with misting eyes, hearing her voice, and feeling her gentle warmth. Two long blasts from the ship's whistle brought him back to earth. He looked up just in time to see the Golden Gate Bridge as it passed overhead. "Well, I guess it's too late to change my mind." He filled his lungs with sea air, held it, then he released it with a sigh. The bow of the *Lady* gently raised and lowered as she rode upon the open sea.

MEANWHILE

Tony had been gone for about a week. Even though Maureen missed him terribly, she was beginning to feel accustomed to being alone in her Nob Hill one room apartment. She soothed her longing by writing each day in a letter that she was putting together for him. Like a diary it was a day to day account.

One day Maureen received a phone call from a guy named Cliff. He was from her old circle of friends up in Eureka, California, and was a sort-of folk singer that accompanied himself with a guitar and harmonica. His voice had a world weary quality that was appealing and made his songs work more than his playing. He had just arrived in San Francisco to check out the coffeehouse folk music scene. He needed a place to stay for a few days while he looked for a place of his own. It was okay for him to stay at her place as long as it was for no more than three nights. He could sleep on the floor in his sleeping bag and leave his things there during the day while he looked around.

On the third night he played a long session at the Coffee and Confusion in North Beach. Maureen had accompanied him with her own sweet singing voice. Afterward they went back to her place for his last night there. It had been a workday for her so she was feeling extremely tired. Cliff was still feeling wound up from performing and from the uppers he had taken earlier. He produced a bottle of wine that he insisted she share with him. "Come on, Mori," he said, his voice more raspy than ever, "it's to christen my new career in Frisco."

She had already drunk some gin at the coffeehouse from a bottle he kept in his pocket. Her voice became very weak and she seemed to be fading when she said, "Cliff . . . if you're going to . . . stay in the city . . . it's San Fran . . . cisco."

"All right. Big fuckin' deal. San Francisco then. Come on, have a drink with me."

She didn't want any more to drink, but she was too tired to argue. After a little more wine she passed out on her bed still dressed, as he droned on about his future career and the faults of the competition. She had lain back when she went out. When he realized that she had fallen asleep, he just went silent. He was sitting on a pillow on the floor in front of her. He just sat there contemplating what lay before him.

Cliff had changed since Maureen first came to know him. He was no longer the honorable person he once was, and this was putting him to the test. He had acquired a way of justifying any solution to his needs. He thought she really ought not to sleep in her clothes so he reached forward, clumsily knocking over the wine bottle, then as carefully as he could he unlaced, then removed her sandals. As he did so he began to feel a warm sensation pass through him.

Cliff reasoned that since he was sitting nearer to her feet then it would follow that her skirt should be next. He began muttering to her, "Didn't yer mother ever tell ya that ya shouldn't sleep in yer clothes? That's not very nice, ya know." The skirt was very long with buttons in a row from the knees to the waist. He began with the bottom button and carefully worked his way up. As he neared the top buttons his hands began to shake a little. It was all he could do to undo the last one. But after he did, he slowly and carefully opened the skirt. He was so overwhelmed by passion and instinct that nothing could have stopped him.

Chapter 2

CALM BEFORE THE STORM

When the *Lady Explorer* reached the area near Hawaii, she turned north to begin charting the ocean floor in a grid like pattern between Hawaii and the Aleutian Islands of Alaska. The crew had become tolerant of the humidity and smells that were produced in such a small ship. After the first day or two the most susceptible of the crew were no longer becoming seasick. The rhythmic motion of the ship's rising and falling with the waves eventually became soothing. The ship became a kind of aquatic rocking chair.

It was an unusually warm day for late January. The sea was totally calm and as smooth as glass. The air was still and odorless, except for the faint smell of salty decks, the ever present diesel exhaust, and wet paint. It was a perfect opportunity for some much needed recreation and exercise. The ship's anchor was dropped onto a shallow plateau, and a makeshift diving board was set up on the fantail. Some of the crew, wearing bathing suits, dove into the refreshingly cool water with excitement.

Captain Reiger and the chief bosun were on the flying bridge. They stood together watching the swimmers in the crystal clear water. The bottom, with its carpet of marine life, was clearly visible. The bosun asked, "How deep do you make it, sir?"

"No more than fifteen feet," said the captain. "Fortunately, the tide is at its lowest. Much less and we'd be stuck on the bottom. You wouldn't think we were in the middle of an ocean, would you Dutch?"

The bosun remarked, "That's what worries me, Captain. Every time I see one of these eroded mountaintops just below the surface, it worries the hell out of me. If we get caught around here during a storm, we could come crashing down onto one of these underwater plateaus."

The captain reminded the bosun, "That is precisely why we are here, Dutch, to find and chart them before that happens. However, I just received word that one hell of a storm is coming toward us." He scanned the horizon with an experienced eye, "According to the report, we can expect it to hit sometime after midnight."

The bosun became very uneasy. "After midnight tonight, sir?"

"Tonight, bosun. Sparks just received word of the storm and is checking for more details now. What is the matter? You seem a little nervous. You've experienced storms before, haven't you, Dutch?"

He remembered something from his past, "Yes sir, it's just—"

"Just what?"

"Well sir, the ship I was on before this one lost two men during a storm in the Atlantic. They were my men."

"I see. How did it happen?"

The bosun looked out over the water as he recalled. "It was a very rough one, hurricane force winds, thirty and even forty-foot waves. Two of my men were on the starboard side securing a line that had come loose from a tarp on a hatch cover, when a wave came right over the ship from the port side. They must have gone over the rail. Someone said there was a cry for help, but the wind was howling so much you couldn't be sure. They were never seen again."

"You shouldn't blame yourself, Dutch. It was an accident."

"Yes sir, it was an accident." He thought to himself, *An avoidable accident.*

The bosun's eyes followed a swimmer going toward the ship's bow. There he saw a shirtless crewman stripping paint covered rust from the railing with a length of chain. The bosun said to himself, "That should teach him to keep his mind on his work."

Covered in sweat and rusty paint dust, Tony had been at his task all morning. Although a part of him was immersed in his own ethereality another part was heard muttering, "What crap! No wonder it was so easy to get hired onto this ship."

The bosun called down to him, "Mr. Lewis!" Tony looked back at the flying bridge as the bosun continued, "Yeah, you. You look as though you could use a good wash. Strip down to your skivvies, and jump over the side with the rest of the crew."

Tony asked, talking to himself, "What skivvies?" then called back, "Whatever you say, chief." He took off his clothes then disappeared naked over the side.

The bosun said in disbelief, "What the hell?!"

Tony came up for air with swimmers all around him. "Man, does this ever feel great." He ducked under and swam toward the shallow bottom that he had seen while working. He touched the different plantlike animals to see how they felt. It was like being in a garden on some other world. There was an odd looking fish following him around that had the motion of flying rather than swimming. His vision was so blurred he didn't recognize it but he was sure it was watching him. The need for air drove him back to the surface. He emerged gasping for air, right in front of Pete, the bosun's number-one assistant. His sudden appearance scared the daylights out of Pete.

"Jesus Christ! Man, what in the hell do you think you're doing? I thought you were a shark."

"Sorry, boss man, I was on the bottom and got a bit desperate for air. Gosh, if I look like a shark maybe I should—"

"Listen, wise guy, just watch what you're doing. Say, aren't you wearing anything?"

"No. As a matter of fact the bosun told me to—"

"The bosun, my ass, you don't come anywhere near me with those bare buns of yours or I'll put 'em to good use."

"Go to hell." Tony swam off toward the ship where he met up with Mate. "Man, isn't this just the day for it?"

Mate was pleasantly surprised, "Hey, Tony. What's happenin'?"

"I don't know which is stranger, the fish or the people."

"Did I just see you and Pete together?"

"That guy's a creep. And his boss is not much better."

"Yeah, man, I know what you mean. They're an odd pair all right."

An officer appeared on deck with a bullhorn, "All men return to the ship to prepare for lunch at eleven thirty hours."

Mate said, "I'm ready for that."

"I think it's lamb chops today," Tony said as he reached for the ladder.

"Hey, man, did you lose something?" Mate was referring to Tony's nakedness.

Tony laughed, "Oh yeah, I forgot."

"Let me go up first. I'll give you my towel so you can put it around yourself."

"Good idea. Thanks."

Water had just begun to lap against the side of the ship when the first mate appeared on the gangway of the main bridge. He looked up at the captain who had been observing a sudden formation of clouds on the horizon. "Sir, we've just received a radio message about the storm."

With a look of concern the captain asked, "Yes, Jenkins, what does it say?"

"That the storm is four hundred miles north-northwest of here, sir, and heading our way at approximately thirty knots per hour. Also they are reporting accompanying winds in excess of one hundred knots per hour."

After a moment's consideration, the captain said, "In that case, there's nothing we can do but turn into the storm at the appropriate time and ride it out. Have Sparks radio the coast guard at both Alaska and Hawaii giving our present position and the approximate location of where we expect to reach the storm. From midnight tonight keep in constant radio contact."

"Aye, aye, sir."

The captain said to the bosun, "After lunch, have your men make the ship secure. And make certain that the launches and life rafts are ready for use." He looked up at the sun. "We should have enough time to prepare before dark. I must work with our surveyors to find an area that is least hazardous for us to meet the storm."

A half hour into the meal break an announcement came over the ship's intercom, "Now hear this. Now hear this. All members of the deck force are to report to the bosun's locker at twelve thirty hours. All others are to report to their departments." The announcement was repeated, then, "That is all."

In the crew's mess most of the men had finished eating and were having coffee. Tony and Mate were sitting at a table with Willy and Chuck, from the deck crew. Willy, a man in his late thirties, loved to play his concertina and sing sea shanties. Chuck, not long out of high school, was nineteen but looked more like sixteen.

Willy said, "Well, lads, it looks like we're in for a bit of action tonight."

"Probably not the kind of action I could use," retorted Mate.

Chuck said, "I overheard the cooks talking about a storm, a big storm. I think they said tonight."

Mate said to Willy, "If that's right be sure to keep your concertina dry. Maybe you can write one of your sea shanties about it."

Willy said, "That surely is a coincidence. I've been working on a song about a storm, you know."

"No kidding?" Chuck remarked.

Willy added, "Maybe I'll get some fresh ideas."

Again the ship's intercom called out, "Now hear this. Now hear this. The watch for the next twenty-four hour period are to report to the bridge at twelve thirty hours." The message was repeated.

There was tension in the air as men scurried from one end of the ship to the other to report to their duty sections.

On the bridge the men who would be standing watch until the next afternoon were being briefed on what to expect. Some of them would have the duty of steering the ship.

Jenkins had been giving the briefing, "We should feel the full impact of the storm at around three a.m. Those of you whose watch begins at midnight be sure to get as much sleep as possible before your watch. You will need to be well rested and very alert. Once the wind has reached a significant speed the ship will head directly into it in order to avoid capsizing. Beginning at ten o'clock tonight every member of the crew is required to wear his life jacket even if he is in his bunk asleep."

Just as the watches were receiving their instructions, the last of the deck crew arrived at the bosun's locker to receive theirs. After the bosun explained the situation, he added, "It's going to be our job to make the ship secure and keep her secure during this storm. So plan on being very wet. There will be no exceptions to the wearing of life jackets."

Pete, who was standing next to the bosun, chimed in with, "And if any jerk goes off to sleep or isn't wearing his life jacket, it'll be his ass."

Tony whispered to Mate, "I wonder how he means that."

"All right, listen up," the bosun continued, "This ship carries two launches and eight life rafts. Now with a sixty man crew, should we need them, the launches and rafts are going to be very crowded at best. Since the men who are on watch now aren't here I'm splitting the rest of you up into four teams of two each. Pete and Chuck will be team one. You will make secure the area below deck from the engine room aft. Team two, George and John will take care of the area below deck forward of the engine room. Team three will be Tony and Mate.

You will have the forward half of the main deck including the life rafts, and the forward half of the upper deck including the flying bridge. Willy and Bill will be team four. You will make secure the after half of the main deck and upper deck including the two launches. Are there any questions?"

The chief bosun paused for a moment then added, "You are all expected to stand by your areas until the storm has passed. Just remember this ship is going to be thrown about the ocean like an empty bottle. We'll probably get the piss knocked out of us. Go to your assigned areas now, and make sure everything is secure until you hear the dinner bell. After dinner get some sleep. Then at twenty-two hundred hours all hands will be on duty. Any questions?"

Bill, in a voice that sounded of too many cigarettes and too much alcohol asked, "Hey, chief, who'll be wakin' us tonight?"

The bosun replied, "Pete has the pleasure of that duty. Any more questions? Then lay to. I'll be making the rounds to check your progress."

"Yes, sir."

"Aye, aye, sir."

"You can count on us, chief," said the men as they quickly made their way to their assigned areas.

Tony, Mate, Willy, and Bill stepped on to the main deck. As the bosun's locker was located on the stern of the ship, Willy and Bill began looking for anything that might be standing loose and need securing while Mate and Tony proceeded to the midship.

Bill grumbled to Willy as he went, "What a waste of fuckin' time. There's nothin' that needs doin' here."

"Yeah, and if the good ship *Lady Explorer* goes down tonight do you think you're going to swim back to Honolulu? Well, nothing to say?"

"Ah, fuck off," mumbled Bill.

"Listen, you old boozer, you're going to help me check the launches to make sure they're ready, or I'll throw your bloody ass over the side and tell 'em you slipped. And you know they'll believe me."

Bill had nothing to say to that, he just made a face and shrugged his shoulders. He then pretended to be looking for things that needed doing.

Meanwhile, amidships, Mate asked Tony a question that occurred to him before, "Hey man, do you suppose those two jerkoffs are gettin' it on with each other?"

"Who are you talking about?"

"The bosun and that asshole Pete."

"Beats the hell out of me. Do you know something I don't?"

Mate said, "Well, you know how Pete is, about boys and butts?"

"The bosun ain't no boy. But now that you mention it I have noticed Pete watching him walk away longer than usual."

"You got it. So what do you think that is?" pressed Mate.

"Okay, so the two scumbags are gettin' it on. So what?"

"Only that tonight, during the storm of the century, while you and I are out trying to keep our asses from gettin' washed overboard, Pete's goin' to be nice and cozy with young Chucky down below in the fantail."

"What's your point?"

"That's the smoothest riding part of the ship. And besides, Chuck's going to need a chaperon to protect him," urged Mate.

"Don't worry about it, the kid will have to look after himself. We have plenty to worry about with two decks and the flying bridge to keep an eye on." They found a few things left behind by the morning's swimmers but otherwise, Tony observed, "The main deck is looking good to me. We can take these things with us to the mess later. Let's check on the life rafts next."

They went up a ladder to the upper deck. There the rafts were held in place by quick-release straps that looked as though they hadn't been opened in years. The rafts were standing on edge next to breakaway railings. They were on both sides of the cabin that housed the surveyor's chart room with its depth recording equipment.

Tony asked, "What are we checking for on these rafts?"

"To make sure they're secure, and that we can get them loose in an emergency." He struggled with one of the straps, "I'm not having much luck with this one, how about you?"

"The same, I can't get this one to come loose either. Not surprising, with so much salt on everything. Some penetrating oil might help."

Mate suggested, "I left my gloves in the bosun's locker so why don't I go there for the oil and my gloves?"

"Sounds good to me, grab a couple of rags too."

"Okay, man," replied Mate as he made for the ladder.

"Meanwhile I'll mark the ones that need loosening up."

One of the straps Tony tried broke, then one of the breakaway railings was stuck and wouldn't open.

After a while Mate returned, wearing his gloves and carrying the oil and rags. "No one was there, but I got what we needed."

"Thank you, my friend." Tony took the oil and squirted some into every joint of the rail. "This sucker won't budge. Give me a hand with this thing."

"Hey now, lads!" The shout came from where the launches were located. "Hey!" Willy walked to where Tony and Mate were struggling with the railing. "You look like you need a hand."

"Great, man, good timing. Just grab a hold here," Tony said as he pointed to a part of the railing.

"Maybe one of you could give Bill and me a hand with the launch locks? We can't get 'em to budge. Working with that rummy is like being on your own."

"Sure thing." They struggled with the railings. It took all three of them to break one loose. "Have you ever seen so much rust where it shouldn't be?" Tony asked Willy.

"Well, she's been around a long time," Willy told them.

"How long?" Mate asked.

"Since '41. The *Lady* saw action in the Pacific."

"You mean during the war?" Tony asked.

"Hell, man, she was at Pearl."

"Pearl Harbor?"

"That's right. She got shot up a bit too."

Tony and Mate both felt a new respect for their ship. "Maybe some of this penetrating oil can help loosen things up a bit for you guys as well," suggested Tony. Then to Mate, he added, "After we get through helping them we can check the life rafts on the port side."

They followed Willy back to where the launches were secured.

Bill was sitting on the deck under one of the launches. He had just finished taking a swig of rum from a bottle when he heard them approach. As they reached the launches, Mate saw Bill quickly stuff the bottle into his jacket.

Mate asked, "Hey, Bill, something just fall into your jacket?"

Bill was taken by surprise, "What are you talkin' about?"

"I'm talking about that bottle."

"Mind your own business, boy."

"Who are you calling boy, you old rummy?"

Bill's face grew even more red than usual, "Why you fuckin'….."

Tony broke in, "Hold on, we came here to lend a hand, so let's do that." They were able to help despite Bill's sullied objections.

Slurring half his words, Bill informed them, "We don't need your fuckin' help." Then to Mate, he said, "I'll deal with you later."

"In your dreams you will," was Mate's response.

After a while the sky had filled completely with clouds, and the breeze had become a wind. Tony and Mate had finished helping Willy and Bill with the locks and were working on the remaining life rafts. Mate complained, "You know that asshole Bill is an accident looking for somewhere to happen."

"I know, man. I just hope I'm not around when it does. Don't let him bother you. That's just the rum talkin' when he goes on like that. Be thankful he's not your roommate."

Mate said, "Maybe you're right, but something about him gets on my nerves. And besides he stinks of boozer sweat and who knows what else."

"Yeah, I know." Tony continued, "Now, have you noticed that most of the joints and hinges we've had to deal with haven't been greased in a long time?"

"Hey now, what kind of bullshit is that?" replied Mate.

"I reckon the chief bosun hasn't been keeping up with things," Tony said.

"Maybe he and Pete haven't had time," suggested Mate. "Damn! We still have the flying bridge to secure yet."

Just then the bosun appeared as if from out of nowhere. With a slight scowl on his face, he asked, "Are you men having any problems you can't deal with?"

Tony wondered what the bosun might have overheard, "Yeah, chief. We're having a problem with some of the locks and latches not opening without a real hassle."

"I don't understand how that could be."

"We had to use penetrating oil to get things to open up, what with the salt, and the rust. It's as though they haven't been touched in years."

"And may I ask, Mr. Lewis, just what are your qualifications to make such an observation?"

"I don't have any qualifications, but that's the way it looks to me."

"Well you're wrong, Mr. Lewis. These things have been checked on a regular basis by Pete. And the records show it."

Mate spoke up, "He's right, chief. We've had a hell of a time getting some of the strap releases to open up. And most of the hinges on the breakaway railings wouldn't budge without penetrating oil and help from Willy."

"All right, Mr. Jones, I'll check with Pete to see what he has to say about this. Meanwhile continue to do as you were assigned. We're running out of time. If anything goes wrong it'll be your responsibility. Do you understand?"

"Okay, chief," they both answered.

With a peeved look on his face, the bosun disappeared down a ladder as they continued their work.

Mate reminded Tony, "We'd better hurry up if we don't want to miss chow."

Tony responded with a thoughtful, "Yeah, we'll make it."

SAVED BY THE RUST

The *Lady* encountered the storm at one a.m. By three a.m. the storm had built into one of the worst of its kind with winds over eighty miles per hour, and waves in excess of fifty feet high, all in total darkness. The scariest of amusement park rides would have been mild in comparison. A huge wave crashed into the bow lifting it high into the air, then just as suddenly a liquid valley appeared below her. She plunged down into it with a great jolt, and then was tossed from side to side.

Tony and Mate were on the forward section of the upper deck, windblown and very wet. They were slipping and gyrating to the movement of the ship while trying to hold fast to the railing, but shouting and clowning around like two kids really enjoying themselves.

Tony felt elated just to grab hold of the ship and ride with her. He shouted to Mate through the howling wind, "I love it!"

"What?" Mate shouted in return.

"Hey, man."--*whoosh!*--"All right! Do you think she can make it?"

As they were tossed about, Mate struggled to reply, "You worried, man?"

Tony said with difficulty, "Well, I'm just"—*splaashh!*—"just thinking." He started to slip, "Easy now!" He continued, "She's into her twenty-fourth winter, right?"

Mate shouted back, "Is that a question or what?"

Just as the ship rode down into another liquid valley, Tony shouted at the top of his voice, water running down his face, "Well, do you think she can"—*spray!*—"can make it through this storm?"

Mate patiently replied, "Hey man, relax."

"What?!"

Mate strained to be heard, "Relax! When she was"—*jolt! crunch!*—"was in dry dock the bosun said there was plenty of rust to hold her together." As another wave raised her up again, he added, "She'll be all right."

Tony bellowed in disbelief, barely able to hold on, "Rust?! What do you mean, she'll be all right?"

"Willy said that she's a stubborn old girl." Mate shouted just as the bow started another descent, "Hold onnn!"

On the deck where the launches were located, Willy was working alone. Bill had gotten sick earlier and had to go below. Willy was struggling with one of the hold-down straps that had become loose. He was barely able to stay on his feet, "Bloody hell, I need some help with this."

The *Lady* rolled to one side causing the weight of the launch to loosen the strap even more allowing the bow of the launch to come off its support. Fortunately, safety chains attached to the launch kept it from moving too far, but far enough to give Willy a nasty knock on the head, causing him to fall, then slide across the deck. The railing saved him from going overboard.

The launch tossed to and fro against the strength of the chains. A very groggy Willy struggled just to make his way back to the bosun's locker in the hope of finding help to secure the launch before it became wrecked.

In the ship's galley, the cooks had been trying with great difficulty to prepare hot food and coffee for the men on duty. There were broken eggs scattered everywhere. Hot cereal was running down the stove and all down the side of one of the cooks.

In the bosun's locker, Willy found the bosun and two other men. They returned to the upper deck as quickly as possible where the four of them were able to secure the launch. Willy's aching head was more than he could bear so the bosun sent him off to check with the ship's doctor in the sick-bay.

On the upper deck, Tony momentarily tried to shield himself in a corner near the bridge. He withdrew a cigarette from a waterproof packet, then turning his back to the wind and spray, he managed to light it. It was the sign of a true sailor, or so he thought. He called out, "Arr, me hardies. Shiver me timbers then. Time to hoist the Jolly Roger."

Mate was bewildered. "I don't believe this guy!"

At the apex of the ship's rising into the air upon another wave, it just as suddenly plunged down again. A cry came from the galley as a large urn of hot coffee overturned on to one of the cooks.

Mate tried to warn Tony, "Look out, man, hold on!" But it was too late. Tony had disappeared behind a curtain of water as in fact the entire ship was overcome by a giant wave.

Chapter 3

WASHED ASHORE

Tony was lying on a beach with gentle ripples of water reaching for his feet. He was on his back with his head turned to one side. There was some sand on his face and torso and seaweed around his feet. His eyes were closed, and his mouth was open as if he were unconscious. In the distance, a voice could be heard calling him, "Tony! Tony! Hey, man. Come on, wake up. Do you want to drown? The tide's coming in," pleaded Mate.

Beach sounds began to seep into Tony's awaking ears. Clad in his bathing trunks, he had been snoozing at the water's edge on Waikiki beach surrounded by the usual array of bikini clad beauties. As he opened his eyes to the brightness of the sun, he mumbled, "Umm. I guess I fell asleep." He turned his head to escape the sun's glare only to come face to toe with a lovely pair of ankles, calves, and thighs. "Sure a nice view from here."

"Amen to that, brother," responded a reverend Mate.

"Hey, Mate," Tony paused, still appreciating, "when do we next set sail?"

"After the *Lady*'s been repaired, probably in another six days. The storm gave her one hell of a pounding. As for the launch the Navy is going to give us?"

"Yeah?"

"It'll be ready by then, too."

"That's great," Tony said, "but staying out on the ocean for three weeks at a time sure gets old fast."

"It sure does that."

"So tonight, we'd better go where the action is, right?"

"Right on, brother. There sure as hell won't be any where we're goin' a week from now."

Tony squinted up at the sun. "What time is it?"

"Time for you to get a move on if we're going to do some serious boogyin' tonight," was Mate's encouraging opinion.

After going into the water to rinse off Tony dried with a towel. "You know this island better than I do. What would you have in mind, oh great leader?"

Mate was getting dressed. "Well, man, I know some groovy places on Hotel Street."

Tony frowned, "Now there's a name for you, *Hotel Street*." Reaching for his clothes, he asked, "What kind of places?"

"Places where a body can dance for one thing. And places where you can meet a fine woman," encouraged Mate.

Tony pressed on, "And after we've gone dancing with our fine women, a place where we can get some fine food?"

"The finest our money can buy!"

"Well then, Mate, let's head back to the *Lady* and get ready."

Once fully clothed, they left the beach. Tony spotted a pay phone. "Hold on a minute, I want to try to reach Maureen again. She didn't answer the phone last night. It's a couple of hours later there. Maybe she was too tired to answer."

"I hope everything is okay."

Tony produced a handful of change from his pocket. "She might be home from work by now."

Meanwhile Mate went over to the curb and tried to catch the attention of a taxi driver. He looked back at Tony who was talking into the phone with an odd expression on his face.

After only a minute Tony hung up. He joined Mate and told him, "What a strange call that was."

"Was she there?"

"That part's even stranger. A guy answered the phone then

gave it over to her. She sounded kind of weak and said she wasn't well enough this morning to go to work. She didn't feel up to talking and asked me to wait till the end of the week to phone. When I asked who the guy was she sounded kind of vague saying he was a friend from up north. She also said she sent me a letter, by way of our home office in San Francisco. I told her I hadn't gotten it yet."

"Maybe you'll get it before we pull out of here next Monday."

"I have an odd feeling about that call. It was like talking to someone that I hardly know, and I know her really well."

They got into a waiting taxi and went back to their ship.

SLEEPING LADY

The *Lady Explorer* was tied to a special docking facility just west of Honolulu to undergo superficial damage repair. Her port side was to the dock with her bow pointing westward. The repair was expected to take no longer than her seven days in port.

The late afternoon breeze was rich with the smell of a freshly washed island. The chief bosun was standing outside the bridge enjoying a fresh pipe full of tobacco. He watched as a taxi approached the ship from the road.

The taxi stopped just short of the gangplank. Tony and Mate stepped out of the car asking the driver to wait for them. As they walked up the gangplank the watch called to them, "Hey, you lucky guys, I saw you two soakin' up the sun at Waikiki."

Mate said, "And it was nice. But now we need to freshen up before we head out. We're going to check into a little night action."

Tony said, "Mate says he knows where some really great places are. Maybe you can catch up with us later?"

"I wish," then in a lowered voice the watch told Tony, "The chief's on board so be cool."

"Thanks." The two went below to their quarters then headed for the showers. While in adjoining stalls Tony started humming to the droning sound of a generator coming through the bulkhead.

After a few minutes Tony asked, "Hey, Mate. Have you ever thought of going to India?"

"What?"

"I said, have you ever thought of going to India?"

"India! What would I want to go there for?"

"It's a very spiritual place. The people pray all the time, have a lot of religious holidays, you know, things like that."

"You're kidding me, right? Pray all the time?" He put some shampoo on his hair. "If I want religion I can go to church."

Tony continued unabated, "Speaking of church, there are those who believe that when Christ was between the ages of fifteen to thirty, he was in India and Egypt."

"Hey, man, what are you trying to do to me? Here we are gettin' ourselves all sweetened up for the night life and you're talkin' religion, and prayin', and who knows what else."

Tony withdrew the topic for the moment. "Sorry, Mate, it was just something that came to me."

"That's okay, man, I just want to maintain my intended direction." He turned off the water and began drying himself. "Say, I just thought of something you might like. A little later on, maybe we can head out to a place I know about on the edge of town. You're going to like it, man. They have, would you believe, gospel singers in the cocktail lounge."

Tony perked back up. "Wow! That sounds pretty far out. Why don't we go there first?"

"No, we'll save that for last. First we find some energizin' food."

"Whatever you say, you're the navigator on this cruise."

"So let's put on some threads and split this place."

Then Tony remembered, "Oh, man! I forgot about the taxi."

All preened and dressed in their best casuals they raced
past the watch at the top of the gangplank.

The watch said, "That taxi's going to cost you a fortune."

Mate shouted back as the gangplank clamored under
his feet, "Hey, brother. Do you want us to bring somethin'
back from Waikiki?"

"Yeah, about five foot six with long hair."

"Say what?"

"You heard me!"

CRUISIN'

In the dusk following the sunset the clouds resembled the
rippled sandy bottom of a gentle stream. Their whiteness was
edged with golden hues. Tony looked out of the taxi window
above the very tall slender palms that reached into the sky and
felt as though he was looking into a dream world.

The taxi suddenly came to a halt. Honking the horn and
cursing, the driver continued on after nearly hitting another taxi
that had pulled in front of them. Tony and Mate were stunned.

Mate asked, "I hope you're taking us somewhere to eat?"

The driver said, "If you like fish, the Ocean Breeze is the
place for you."

"Groovy, man, let's check it out."

They passed the marina filled with yachts. A big pink hotel
came into view followed by more hotels sitting right on the
beach, totally blocking a view of the ocean. Then they came to
Waikiki beach. The taxi made a U-turn and pulled to the curb
opposite the beach in front of the Ocean Breeze.

Tony and Mate stepped out of the taxi and looked at the
sign displayed near the entrance. Tony read aloud, "'Food and
drink fit for a seafarer.' Well, that's us." They went inside a

dimly lit room filled with huge fish aquariums containing some very exotic fish.

Mate joked, "Hey, man. If the *Lady* had gone down in that storm, are these the kind of fish that would be eatin' us?"

"You're too big for them to deal with. Probably a shark's belly would be your new home."

Mate became serious, "Don't say that, man. I hate sharks. Have I told you about the nightmares I have with sharks comin' after me?"

"No, what happens?"

"Well, they're just about to get a mouthful of me. That's when I always wake up."

A sleek looking cocktail waitress approached them. She was wearing a fashionable long Hawaiian dress with a slit high up one side. The two men completely forgot about the fish.

"Hi, my name is Cheryl. Would you like a table or would you prefer to sit at the bar?"

Mate said, "The bar's fine with me."

Tony was pointing, "If you don't mind, Mate, I'd like to sit at that table near the fish tank."

"That's cool with me, man."

"Good," said the waitress, and she led them to their table.

After they had seated themselves Mate started looking through the menu. The fish in the tank near them fascinated Tony.

"Can I get you something to drink while you're looking at the menu?" Cheryl asked.

Mate said, "I'll have a Bloody Mary, please."

Tony smiled. "Nothing for me yet, thanks."

The waitress inquired, "I don't believe I've seen you in here before?"

Mate said, "You got that right."

Cheryl asked, "Well, if your name's Mate, what's his?"

"Tony. Tony's my name, pleased to meet you." He extended his hand to hers and briefly held it ever so gently.

Cheryl looked at him for a second, almost as though she sensed something different about him. "I'll be right back with your drink." She sauntered back to the bar.

Mate remarked, "I still can't get used to shaking hands with a woman."

Tony said, "I wasn't shaking her hand as much as I was just holding it. It's nice, kind of like a touch of magic."

"Man, you're somethin' else."

Tony said, "Those long dresses sure are nice, and with that slit all the way up one side. Hmmm, really far out, man."

"Hey, man, the girl's lookin' groovy."

"To me it's mellow. Look at it this way, like the beach here. Most of the women wear those tiny bikinis that show far more than they hide. After a while they all look alike. Appealing, sure, but not really interesting."

Mate interrupted, "Well, they sure as hell look interesting to me."

"Well, maybe *interesting* isn't the right word." Tony continued, "Have you ever noticed that when a woman isn't showing you her body, but kind of hides it away, she's more interesting?"

Mate, gently shook his head. "I'm not sure what point you're trying to make, but go ahead."

"I guess the word I'm looking for instead of interesting is *mysterious*. A woman who has a bit of mystery about her is more interesting to me than one who just lets it all hang out."

Mate objected, "Come on, man, this is 1965, not 1935."

"You're getting me all wrong, Mate. I guess what I'm trying to say is there's more to a woman than what you see."

"Okay, all right. I agree, and I disagree. There should be more to a woman than what you see, but most of the ones I've been out with can't think past their own looks."

"How do you know? What did you do to find out?"

In his defense, Mate answered, "I talked to 'em."

"What did you find out?"

"Not a lot."

Cheryl returned with Mate's drink. "Are you sure you wouldn't like a drink before dinner, Tony?"

"Not before, thank you, but maybe after. How did you remember our names, did you write them down?"

"No, I'm just good with names. I have a pretty good memory. Studying all the time has got to have something to do with it."

"Studying?" asked Mate.

"So you're going to college somewhere?" Tony asked.

"I'm a student at the University of Hawaii."

Mate said, "I don't believe it."

Tony said to Mate, "Just what we were talking about." Then to Cheryl, he asked, "What are you majoring in?"

"Religions of the world."

Mate, "I don't believe it."

Tony, "You said that."

Mate, "Not religion again."

Cheryl, "What do you mean?"

Mate, "Nothin', it's just that earlier, when we were back on the ship gettin' ready to go out, Tony started layin' some trip on me about religion. I don't know what brought that on."

Tony, "The vibrations."

Cheryl, "Vibrations?"

Tony, "Of the bulkheads, those are walls to you land lovers. A generator was running on the other side of the bulkhead making it vibrate."

Cheryl, "I still don't get it."

Mate, "I don't either, so let's change the subject."

From behind the bar the bartender was wondering why Cheryl was neglecting her other customers so he called to her, "Cheryl, would you come here for a moment, please?"

She excused herself, "I'll be right back."

"My man," said Mate, "if we're goin' to be doin' any dancin' tonight then we had better eat and move our young selves off down the road. So why don't we start by checkin' the menu?"

Tony nodded in agreement. As they delved into the menu, Tony observed, "I don't see any trout here."

Mate said with surprise, "Trout?"

"Yeah, for some reason I feel like having rainbow trout."

"You're in Hawaii, in the middle of an ocean, and you want rainbow trout?"

"What's wrong with that?"

"Oh nothing, nothing at all."

Tony felt the need to relate an experience he once had. "Listen, man, once when I was hitchhiking across the States, I stopped in a restaurant in Colorado Springs. On the menu were mountain oysters. I liked oysters back then so I had some."

Mate started laughing, "Mountain oysters?"

"That's right, Mountain oysters. There was something kind of odd about them but they tasted pretty good and I liked 'em. So what about that?"

Mate was still laughing and pointing at Tony.

Tony couldn't figure him out. "What in the hell are you laughing at?"

Mate swallowed back his laughter. "Those weren't oysters, you dope. Don't you know what mountain oysters are?"

"Well, what are they then?"

Mate half whispered so no one else could hear, "Balls, man, sheep's balls. They're just called mountain oysters. Get it?"

Tony began to feel very stupid, "No shit, man?"

"No shit, brother. You were eatin' sheep's balls."

Cheryl returned to their table. "I'm sorry I had to leave you. Have you decided what you would like to eat?"

Tony sounded a little uncomfortable, "I think I'll have that drink now."

She said, "Sure, what's your pleasure?"

Tony felt the need for something strong. "A Singapore Sling."

The Ocean Breeze had been slowly filling with customers. Tony had decided against eating flesh of any kind so he settled for a salad, whereas Mate happily downed a dinner of swordfish.

After some conversation with Cheryl who became quite busy, and talk of meeting her again, Tony and Mate made their way from the restaurant. By the time their taxi pulled away from the Ocean Breeze the night sky had grown dark, and there was the sound of night birds overhead.

Mate asked the native Hawaiian driver, "Hey, brother, do you know where the nightclub called the Sleeping Lady is?"

The driver chuckled, "Are you kidding? If I had a dollar for every time I took somebody there I could buy half this island."

"Well, if you take us there now I'm sure there'll be more than a dollar in it for you."

The unimpressed driver had a dry smile. "How can I resist a deal like that?" So off they went to the Sleeping Lady.

SOUL FOOD

As their taxi drew near to a club on the outskirts of town, Tony and Mate were able to read the huge neon sign on the roof, it read:

*The Sleeping Lady * Burlesque and Comedy*

Tony was also able to see the marquee over the entrance to the small adjoining building that read:

Now appearing—The Mother Jean Gospel Singers.

The taxi pulled to the curb. Mate stepped out and headed straight for the main entrance of the burlesque hall. But Tony walked toward the cocktail lounge annex and called to him, "Hey, Mate. Let's go in here first, I love gospel singing. I mean, a man has got to look after his soul, right?"

Mate turned in his tracks, "Right on, brother. The ride over has made my mouth a little dry."

Inside they found a small intimate cocktail lounge with a low stage along one wall. A piano was on one end while an organ sat on the other, with three female singers standing in the center. Mother Jean sat near one end of the stage where she kept a watchful eye on the performance.

Near the opposite wall stood a rectangular shaped island of a bar tended by a tall attractive woman.

Tony and Mate eased up to the bar and settled themselves onto adjacent stools at one corner. There were other customers seated at tables.

Although the atmosphere was calm, the music was stirring. If not for the fact that Tony was in a bar room, he could close his eyes, shut out the smell of smoking, the odor of the alcoholic beverages, and believe that he was in a church. Occasionally someone would feel moved to say, "Hallelujah," or "Amen," and he would feel something inside himself leap with joy.

Mate was feeling joy for a different reason.

The Korean barmaid was wearing a low cut flowery dress and a strand of white tropical flowers down one side of her long dark hair. She greeted them with a warm, "Good evening."

"Hi," Mate chimed.

Tony said, "Hi, nice music you have."

"Thank you. They're a popular group here. My name is Kim. Your faces are new to the Sleeping Lady lounge. Would you like something to drink?"

Mate was obviously taken by the barmaid's beauty. He just looked at her without talking, as if she hadn't said anything.

Tony looked at Mate then smiled and gave the barmaid a wink. "Well, I would like a rum and soda, please."

"A rum and soda it is." She looked straight into Mate's eyes as she asked, "Would you like something to drink?"

Mate acted as if he had waken from a dream, "What? Oh yes. What have you got?"

Kim had just a hint of a smile. She wondered if he expected her to name off every known drink, "Whatever you might require, sir."

He didn't know what to say to that.

As if from out of nowhere, a tall tan mulatto beauty appeared at the bar and settled onto one of the stools not far from Tony. She had long legs and was modestly dressed. The two women gave one another a warm greeting.

"Hi, Kim."

"Melina, dear." Turning back to Mate, Kim asked, "Made up your mind yet?"

Melina and Tony exchanged friendly looks as Mate answered, "Yeah, I'll have a scotch and soda, please."

Noticing their mutual interest Kim asked Melina, "Have you two met before?"

"I'm sorry to say we haven't," Tony answered for her.

"Well then," encouraged Kim. As she started making drinks she asked, "How was your day off?"

Melina had a graceful air whenever she spoke. "Real nice, I went shopping and found a beautiful pair of sheer long pants with a leopard print."

"That sounds pretty sexy," said Kim.

"Oh, it is, but it's lined with tan material. It has a matching scarf and looks great with a black blouse of mine."

As Kim began mixing the second drink, she asked, "Sounds real nice. Where did you find it?"

"At that little shop just down from the museum."

"The Museum of Art?"

"That's the one."

"That's a neat little shop." Kim turned toward the guys with the completed drinks in her hands. "Time to drink, would you like something from the kitchen?"

After taking a sip from his drink, Tony answered, "No thanks, we just ate."

Still taken by Kim's beauty, Mate added, "Maybe later, dove."

Melina swung her legs around and slid off the stool. "Guess I'd better get busy."

As Melina moved away, Tony asked Kim, "Does she work here?"

"Oh, she sure does."

Tony watched the motion of her body as she walked toward the tables. He noticed a flowing movement that he'd noticed all too seldom before. To himself, he said, "I'll bet she's a dancer. If not, she should be." He lit a cigarette then inhaled and exhaled slowly as he contemplated his new acquaintance.

The sound of the Mother Jean Singers doing a soft and lilting passage began to fill the air. With the charm of Melina's subtle beauty and the inspiring magic of the Mother Jean Singers, Tony's mind began to float off into a mist of memories:

After returning from Europe he was invited to a church Easter service as the guest of a lady friend. The choir was singing about the life and suffering of Christ. He had heard the songs before but something profound was going on deep within him. It was as if he was experiencing their reality for the first time. His chest became filled with a feeling of profound sorrow and love. His eyes began to fill with tears, and the crying became uncontrollable; much to the dismay of his companion. The children in the pew in front of them thought he was amusing. It happened each time the songs were sung. Tony's friend was so embarrassed she couldn't wait to leave. When they were leaving the church at the end of the service, the pastor greeted him with great enthusiasm. He acted as though his sermon had really hit home, which wasn't the case at all. Tony's friend didn't see him after that, so to avoid any similar incidents in the future he decided he shouldn't attend any more church services.

"Excuse me, is something wrong?" The sound of Melina's voice broke into Tony's trancelike state.

"Pardon? Oh, no." He pretended, "I seem to have something in my eyes. I think maybe the lime in my drink."

"There's no lime in your drink," interjected Kim.

"There isn't?"

"No."

"Well, maybe I—"

Melina handed him a tissue, saying warmly, "Here, try this."

His fingers barely touched hers as he accepted the tissue. He became immediately aware of the softness of her fingertips and her beautiful hazel eyes. "Thank you, maybe it's the smoke from my cigarette."

Melina thought he was probably feeling sad about something. She sat on the stool next to him. "What's your name?"

"Tony. Melina is a beautiful name. Where is it from?"

"Well, there's a little story behind it. Do you mind?"

"Not at all."

"I'm not sure why, but my mother said she named me after a planet."

"I've never heard of a planet named Melina."

"Neither had I, but that's what she said."

"Maybe it's in another solar system."

"Maybe, but she did say that it was very mysterious."

"Your mother sounds pretty hip."

"She was. She was into astrology and music; she loved to dance. Do you like to dance?"

"Yes, I love to dance." He was feeling more at ease. "But I don't think we can dance to this music." He felt his attraction to her grow stronger.

"No, you're right. I only meant in general."

"What time do you finish work tonight?"

The tone of her voice again grew soft as she answered, "Eleven o'clock, why?"

"I'm not familiar with Honolulu but if there is an after-hours place, would you like to go dancing after work?"

She put her hand on his and said, "I'd love to."

"Great!"

The Mother Jean Singers started the next song so softly that Tony had to call to Mate in a half whisper. Mate had been talking to Kim and hadn't taken his eyes off her.

"Hey, Mate. Do you want to go dancing with us?"

Mate was suddenly distracted, "Say what?"

Still in a half whisper, "Do you want to go dancing with Melina and me after she gets off work?"

Mate, who had been straining to hear Tony, said, "Sure thing, brother." Then looking at Kim, he asked, "Do you want to go dancing with us?"

"With the three of you? Sure, that sounds like fun."

Without warning, there was a sudden crescendo of piano, organ, tambourines, and voices as the singers almost shouted, "Sing hallelujah. Sing hallelujah!" At that point all eyes and ears were on the Mother Jean Singers.

As the evening progressed they each had the opportunity to talk at length with the new object of their interest. The time just flowed gently by until eleven o'clock when the ladies finished work. After Melina and Kim had freshened up, they left the Sleeping Lady with Tony and Mate in a taxi bound for the dance clubs on Hotel Street.

AFTER HOURS

Mate was sitting in the front of the taxi while Kim and Tony were in the back with Melina between them. Tony was very aware of Melina's leg and hip pressing against his. He just sat quietly savoring the experience.

The taxi pulled up to the curb in front of the Jolly Roger with a marquee that read: *Blues and Bop, Where You Can Dance Your Heart Out.*

When the foursome entered the club the band was on a break, so the music was disco style. Surprised, Tony asked Mate, "Hey, man, I thought you said there was going to be live music?"

Mate reassured him, "Don't worry, this place is the coolest. My man over there is just filling in for the kats while they're on a break. You know, man, probably out takin' some smoke."

"But of chorus."

Kim spotted a table at the edge of the dance floor, "Can we sit over there?"

"Sounds good to me, dove. I'll be with you in a minute." While the others made their way to the table, Mate went over to the disc jockey. After a brief conversation, he handed the DJ a five dollar bill before returning to the others at their table.

A cocktail waitress was taking their orders when the DJ began a soft romantic dance record. Tony was inspired, "Melina, may I have this dance?"

"How can I resist?" Holding hands like two children, they walked to the middle of the dance floor. Some other couples followed close behind, but Mate and Kim remained at their table.

Tony and Melina held one another for the first time. The music began with a slow undertone, but a quick over-beat came in about a third of the way through. The dancers could choose to dance slow or move faster. Tony and Melina began to dance with a slow and sensual movement, melting into one another as if in a dream state. They gradually changed into a faster tempo, each improvising their own response to the music and each other. The feeling between them was so connected that no matter what movement one of them did the others would flow naturally from it. When the piece ended they walked back to their table. Some customers who had been watching them dance applauded softly in appreciation.

Kim was impressed. "That was nice, you two."

"He's good!" said Melina.

"Aside from the fact that I love to dance, Melina really inspires me."

"Not bad for a white boy," joked Mate as he gave Tony a special handshake.

Sitting at the bar, smoking cheap cigars, and looking very out of place were two rednecks wearing brown combat boots, tight jeans, Hawaiian shirts, and sporting military GI haircuts. One said to the other, "Looks to me like we came to the wrong fuckin' place, Jack. These people don't know which race they belong to."

"You're sure as hell right about that, Jim," remarked Jack. "What do you say we pay up and get the hell out of here?"

"And maybe we can find a cabdriver who knows where we can find some good ol' down home music instead of this here jungle bunny shit. Right, Jack?"

"Right!" They paid their bill and left.

When the DJ played *Shotgun* Mate grabbed Kim's hand and led her quickly to the dance floor. When he improvised some dance movements, she couldn't match his flexibility or energy, but she maintained a rhythmic motion that gave Mate a focal point to return to.

"Go, man, go!" encouraged Tony from their table. "All right!"

"Amen. Man, he surely can move," added Melina.

As the song came to a sudden end an inspired Mate exclaimed, "More, man, give us some more. That just got me started." Mate was holding Kim by the waist as he tried to get the DJ's attention. But the DJ was turning off his equipment. When Mate saw why, he lit up.

The band slowly entered onto the small stage. When the drummer sat behind his drums, there was a thump as he adjusted his position to the bass drum pedal. Another musician slid on to the bench next to the keyboard of an electric organ, turned a couple of switches, tickled the imitation ivory keys, and made an adjustment or two. At the same time a tenor saxophone player went to the front of the stage and stood at the microphone preparing his reed. Last but not least, a heavyset man positioned himself at the back of the stage with his huge bass violin. He applied resin to the bow then used it to tune the strings.

Mate and Kim had returned to their table. Still holding his hand, she told the others, "Did you see this guy dance?" Then to Mate, she cooed, "Sweetheart, you're going to have to teach me some things."

Mate nodded his head in response, then motioned toward the stage. "Look at those kats, dove. I've got the feelin' we're in for somethin' mellow." The bass began with the first bars of

Doodlin, and then the sax took a couple of bars, followed by the organist. All the while the drums maintained a gentle tempo. Mate finally said, "Wow! These guys are so cool."

"They're definitely of the cool school," said Tony.

Melina asked, "Well, gentlemen, what are we waiting for?"

Kim said, "Mate, I think it's time for a lesson."

They began doing a slow form of the swing, a fast dance step that can be very graceful when done slowly. They were the only couples on the dance floor while the others just listened and watched, voicing occasional praise to the musicians.

When the piece ended they returned to their table amid some gentle applause for both the music and the dancers. Mate remarked to Kim, "Dove, you did just fine without any help from me."

"The swing is one of my favorite steps," she said.

Melina looked into Tony's eyes. "You know, I'm having a wonderful time."

Tony felt like he was floating. Looking into her eyes, he said, "Why don't you come to the beach with us tomorrow?"

She hesitated just a moment before she answered, "I'd love to, but I have some things to take care of before work."

He sounded disappointed when he said, "Oh, you have to work tomorrow night too?"

With a demure look, she replied, "Well, I have to earn my keep." Melina and Kim exchanged glances across the table. "Anyway, early tomorrow I have to drive my roommate to the clinic for his appointment. And I may have to stay there for a while."

Tony's heart sank just a little, "Your roommate is a guy?"

She was sorry she had to tell him. "Yes, he's more than a roommate." She wanted to be honest with him, "Actually, he's my ex-boyfriend."

A crummy feeling moved into his stomach, "If he's your ex then why is he still your roommate?"

While Mate was also waiting for the answer, Kim wondered how Melina would handle it. Melina continued, "This may seem a bit odd, but I feel I should look after him out of a sense of duty, at least for now."

Tony strained to ask, "Do you still love him?"

As she placed a hand on his, she said, "No, I'm sure I don't. You see, when I first came to the islands, Bruno, that's his name, looked after me and helped me to find my first job. Also at first we really hit it off."

Tony made an attempt to be sympathetic, "What happened?"

"Well, in a single word, drugs."

"Drugs," Tony repeated as both he and Mate gave an understanding nod.

"He had been dealing for some time, but then he started using the stuff himself." She reached for her drink.

Tony cautiously asked, half afraid to hear the answer, "What about you?"

Again wanting to be honest with him, she replied, "With marijuana I've been more of a social smoker than really being into it. Otherwise I don't smoke, and I don't drink much alcohol either."

Tony was beginning to feel a sense of relief. "So what's happening with . . . Bruno at the clinic?"

"He's been very sick. It's the side effects of drugs on his body and the use of dirty needles." Her eyes had become glazed with tears at the telling of her story, "Injuries he's done to himself while under drugs."

Kim added, "He's in a bad way all right. He was looking like death warmed over the last time I saw him. Melina is a saint to look after him the way she does."

Melina continued, "You know, I'm trying to do as much as I can for him, especially because he helped me. He has been improving, but it's becoming really difficult for me."

Kim suggested, "Melina dear, you need to give him over to somebody else."

"He's becoming so dependent on me though."

Tony asked, "Does he have any relatives here?"

"His mother, but she can barely help herself," said Melina.

Kim interjected, "And you're supporting him."

Mate thought to himself, *And the plot thickens.*

Tony said to her, "I would like to help as much as I can but I feel handicapped only being around a few days a month."

Melina was touched by his offer. "That's very kind of you and very sweet. I'm afraid Kim is right. It's becoming more than I can manage."

All four of them seemed in quiet contemplation. Then Mate asked, "Is anybody hungry?"

Kim suggested, "Melina dear, you and I have to get started early tomorrow so why don't we ask these nice young men to take us home?"

Tony put some money on the table in front of Mate, "Take care of the bill while I go out to find a cab."

"Right on, brother."

After Tony hailed a taxi he and Mate returned Melina and Kim safely to their apartments. They returned to the *Lady* where they had no difficulty sleeping through the remainder of the morning.

Chapter 4

CROSSWINDS

It was the voice coming over the intercom announcing lunch that roused Tony and Mate from their deep sleep. After throwing cold water on their faces they appeared in the crew's mess to partake of some nourishing ship's lunch.

Mate was obviously in a good mood while Tony seemed in deep contemplation. It wasn't until they were about a third of the way through their meal that one of them said something. Mate started off with, "Have you ever been playing a game of poker and be more or less losing when, for no apparent reason, you get a lucky feeling? You know, a real light feeling?"

Without lifting his head but with raised eyebrows, Tony looked up at Mate and said, "No, not really."

"Well, that's the way I'm feeling. Lucky, like I'm about to get something."

"You wish. And I'll bet I know what that something is too."

Mate, with a half smile and half grin, said, "You might. Say man, what's your plan for today?"

Tony thought for a moment and then said, "I've got a letter to mail. After that I thought I'd spend the rest of the day at Waikiki. What about you?"

"I've got a dinner date with Kim. We're going to a Korean restaurant that she likes. Maybe we can ride in together. I want to buy a lei for her. She loves flowers."

"A lei for her and a lay for you, sounds reasonable."

Mate frowned, "I'm not sure how you mean that, brother."

"That's all right. You can check the spelling later."

After lunch and a shower they made their way into Honolulu by bus. Tony mailed a letter to Maureen at the main post office, then they rode another bus to Waikiki. Mate went off to look for flower shops while Tony headed for the beach. On the way he stopped in at a pharmacy to buy some suntan lotion.

He found the section with the lotions and was looking for the one that would give the darkest tan, when a very familiar voice behind him said, "Hi! What a surprise."

He looked around and to his surprise there was Melina standing just behind him. He felt a sudden blush come over him and said, "Wow, this is great!"

They hugged, but as Tony attempted a kiss on the cheek she turned toward the counter nearby. "Bruno, look who's here."

Tony's insides suddenly shriveled up. Bruno was tall with shoulder length blond hair. He had a deep golden tan as only blonds seem capable of. He looked every bit the surfer that he was, wearing worn cutoff jeans and straw sandals.

Melina seemed happy. "This is Tony, I told you about him this morning?"

Tony thought to himself, *This morning? And what happened to looking like death warmed over?*

She introduced them. "Bruno, this is Tony. Tony, Bruno."

Bruno just said, "Yeah, man."

Tony managed a, "Hi." Neither of them seemed interested.

Melina was too pleased to notice. "We just came back from the doctor. Bruno's picking up a prescription. He's improved a lot." As Bruno returned to the counter, Melina asked, "But why are you here?"

"What? Oh, yeah. I'm on my way to the beach, and so I stopped here for some suntan lotion," he said in a flat tone.

Melina noticed a change so she asked, "Are you all right? You seem a bit off."

He felt really stupid so he lied, "No, I'm okay. Maybe I should have gone to bed earlier."

She moved close to him, and in a half whisper that he could feel on his ear, she said, "Maybe you should have."

Just as Tony's sails began to fill with air she glided away toward the door where Bruno, prescription in hand, was waiting. On their way out the door Melina waved goodbye while Bruno gave him a nod and a, "Yeah, man."

Tony was left standing in the middle of the isle holding his chosen bottle of dark tanning lotion and feeling like a guy who was all dressed up with nowhere to go.

A short time later, Tony walked on to Waikiki beach and looked around for a vacant spot among the usual array of sunbathers. To his surprise he saw the waitress from the Ocean Breeze. She was just as nice in a white and black polka-dot bikini as she was in the long dress she had on the day before. Her dark hair was back in a single braid. Near her head was an open bag containing textbooks and notepaper. Near that was a portable radio with classical music playing. Because her eyes were closed against the bright sun, Tony thought she might be asleep. He called to her softly, "Cheryl . . . Cheryl."

As soon as she opened her eyes the sun blinded her. Shading her eyes with one hand she said, "Oh, hi. How are you?"

He moved so that his shadow could shade her face. "I'm fine, thanks." Then he asked, "Mind if I join you?"

"Not at all, that would be great. It's Tony, isn't it?" she asked as she reached for her sunglasses.

"Yes." He opened his shoulder bag and took out a beach towel, then spread it on the sand next to her. "This is the second coincidence today. Oahu is smaller than I thought." He slipped out of his sandals, trousers, and shirt. His solid black bathing suit resembled a pair of shorts. He sat down beside her and began to apply the tanning lotion.

Responding to his last remark with a smile, she added, "The longer you're here the smaller the island gets."

He recalled, "You know back on the mainland, people think of Hawaii as some kind of paradise, far away from it all with unlimited space." He pondered the thought for a moment.

"Well, they're right on the last two points except that the unlimited space is water. Is this your first time here?"

"Yes, the ship I'm working on will dock here one week each month for three months then it will return to Oakland, California. The entire cruise is for four months."

"So altogether you're only here for a total of twenty-one days?"

"Yeah, I guess so."

"What do you do during all the other weeks that you're not here?"

"We're out at sea charting the ocean floor. It's actually quiet interesting. At least that's what I've been told."

Cheryl looked puzzled. "So you've been told?"

Tony explained, "Beginning with our next trip I start two new jobs: helping the ship's doctor in the morning and as a surveyor in the afternoon."

"That does sound interesting. By the way, where is your friend?"

"You mean Mate? He's shopping for a lei for his dinner date."

"That's nice. They are lovely, aren't they? You know they're sometimes made with orchids. Have you worn one yet?"

"Not yet," he didn't mind admitting.

"Oh, you should. It's not just a girl thing to wear a strand of flowers. It's kind of like a bit of that paradise that's mostly gone from here."

"Yes, I've seen a lot of guys wearing them, but I guess I see it as more of a tourist trip."

Cheryl informed him, "Yes, it's also a tourist thing, but it's part of a culture almost lost. When there were only islanders, and when life was innocent and beautiful."

Tony again reflected for a moment then slowly repeated, "Innocent and beautiful, they imply freedom and happiness, don't they?"

Cheryl continued, "Of course that was before the non-islanders came here, a pretty long time ago. You know if you have a chance you should try to get to the other islands. There are tour boats you can take, or you can fly over to one."

Tony reiterated, "I'm not much of a tourist. I mean I'd hate to end up in a group of Hawaiian-shirt-and-lei-wearing, camera-carrying, gawking tourists."

Cheryl agreed, "I know exactly what you mean, believe me. But you can catch one of the water buses over to the islands, and then go your own way."

"That sounds okay. Any particular island?" he asked with real interest.

"Well, for someone wanting to get away from it all, I would suggest Maui."

He agreed, "Maui it is then." After a pause, he added, "When would you like to go?"

"When would I like to go?" she repeated with a knowing half smile, half frown. "As in when I don't have classes, and when I'm not working, and when I don't have papers to write? And when you've nothing to do for seven days?"

"Yes," was his simple response while he held his breath.

Looking into his eyes she thought for a moment then answered, "I don't know. I really don't know."

He picked up a real sense of rejection, and from someone who was smarter than he. "I'm sorry. I guess I went a bit over the top."

Sensing his hurt she tried to soften the effect. "Maybe just a bit premature. You're a nice guy and one who can probably be trusted." She stood up and put on a wraparound skirt. "You know, even when I come to the beach to relax and get some sun I have to bring my textbooks with me. I have so much reading to do."

"Are you leaving?"

"I have to go home and get ready for work. You see, I have very little time to enjoy life. It's my choice, for now." As she began gathering her things, she said, "Oahu is small and for some people it becomes boring and isolated. After a month or so those people leave never to return. After your one-week-each-month visits are over you may be gone never to return. I live here and will for some time yet. Can you understand?"

He was touched by her words. "Yes, I think so."

She reassured him, "So we can be friends?" Now ready to leave for home she reached down to put her hand on his. "I hope I'll see you soon."

Hiding his disappointment he said, "So do I."

Then she asked, "By the way, what's the name of your ship?"

He said, "*Lady Explorer.*"

Cheryl repeated, "*Lady Explorer.* That sounds kind of neat. I bet there's an interesting story behind that name."

"There is."

"The next time we meet you'll have to tell it to me."

"I will."

"Bye." As she moved on, she urged, "Go for a swim. It will make you feel better." Smiling at her own words she added, "You'll see there are plenty of fish in the sea." She waved as she disappeared among the people on the sidewalk.

Tony slowly stood up and put his loose things into his bag. "Plenty of fish in the sea, eh." He made his way to the water's edge, zigzagging his way through the maze of sunbathers who were spread out like so many seals crowded together on the beach. To himself he said, "Looks to me like most of the fish are beached." He entered the calm, waveless water and waded out a quarter of a mile before the water became more than waist deep. He could see little fish swimming around his legs in the crystal clear water. He began to swim about then dive under, staying down as long as possible.

He saw an endless variety of fish, the kind he had only seen in the tropical fish shops back on the mainland. He swam for some time before leaving the water to return to his towel for a nap.

By late afternoon the beach crowd had begun to thin out. Tony got dressed and gathered his gear into his shoulder bag. He went over to the outdoor mall, named International Market, for a snack and a beer. The place seemed strictly for tourists. Hardly any of the people working there were native Hawaiians. The café he went into had a cook and waitress from Samoa. Not long after he settled into his cheeseburger, fries, and beer, who should walk by the window but Willy; wearing a broad hat made of straw. Tony leaped out of his seat and ran out the door, "Hey! Willy. Where're you going?"

"Tony! I'll be damned. I'm looking for a beer and some chow, in that order."

Tony motioned to him, saying, "Come on over here, the beer's on me."

Willy was pleased. "Well now, that's kind of you, matey."

He sat at Tony's table as Tony said, "I haven't seen much of you since the storm. I heard you had a very nasty knock on the head."

Willy doffed his hat to reveal a bandage atop a rather large bump. "Hey, I think that damned launch thought it was a baseball bat and my head the baseball. It must have been tryin' for a home run because it nearly put me past the rail." With that he burst out laughing and Tony with him.

Tony said, "I've never really been into the game, but you do make it sound interesting." They laughed again.

But that time Willy felt the pain of it. "Oh blimey, it hurts to laugh so much. It was paining me so much yesterday that I never left the ship till this morning."

By then, Sharon, the waitress was standing at their table. "Hi. Would you like to order?"

Willy answered, "I sure would, my dear. I would like a bottle of that Japanese beer there and a pastrami sandwich. And would you be so kind as to bring me the beer while I'm waiting for the sandwich, dear?"

"Of course."

"Thank you, love." Then to Tony, he spoke, "Fancy running into you like this. I've been driving around all day looking for something to do till sunset." As he talked, Sharon put a glass in front of him and filled it from a bottle. "Thanks, love."

Tony said, "Well, it seems this is the small world of Oahu. You're the third person I know who I've run into today."

"Right, small it is," added Willy. "Wait till you've been here a while, it gets smaller."

Tony finished his burger. "So what happens after sunset?"

"That's when the store closes."

"What store is that?"

Willy was served his sandwich. "Thank you." He then went on to explain, "I've been to these islands a number of times now. And in that time I've made the acquaintance of some artists, musicians, and singers. You know, like-minded people, like myself. Well, there is a little country-store-by-day coffeehouse-by-night sort of place up at the north end of the island near Turtle Bay called the Crosswinds. It's a place where the likes of us tend to gather after the day is over to discus or sing about the ways of the world."

Tony exclaimed, "Man, that sounds great. I spent many a night in the coffeehouses of North Beach in 'the city' when I wasn't in the jazz clubs. Some of my friends are folk singers and musicians."

"Well, then you'll love it."

"I never would've thought there'd be that scene here," said Tony.

After taking a long drink from his beer, Willy added, "Well, it's not quite like it is back in Frisco, you see."

Tony cringed as he repeated the word, "Frisco?" Like many who have lived there he was proud to have been a part of a city with such unique qualities.

After an awkward moment Willy corrected himself, "Sorry, matey, San Francisco." He ate his way through the pastrami sandwich and continued, "It's a very different world here. At the Crosswinds you'll have a mix of people who live off the land, or who dive for the fish they eat, even some hard core surfers, as well as folk artists, but rarely a Hawaiian. They don't tend to like us Howlies as they call the non-natives."

Sharon returned to their table and asked, "Would you like to have something else?"

Tony said, "I could go for another beer. What about you?"

"Not to be rude but I want to start for the Crosswinds. It's about an hour from here."

Tony asked, "How will you get there?"

"I've rented a car for the week. If you don't have any plans for tonight, why don't you come along?"

"That's not a bad idea." Then to Sharon, he said, "Cancel that beer for now. I'm going off with my friend here."

Sharon asked, "Will we see you tomorrow?"

"More than likely," Tony said as he paid the bill for them both.

Once outside they walked over to where a station wagon was parked along the curb. Through the windows Tony could see a duffel bag and a rolled up sleeping bag. "Look's like you're going on a trip."

"I'm going as far away from the ship as I can get. And if I see Bill anywhere, well, God help him."

"Amen to that," said Tony as they got into the car.

Once the car was moving Willy headed north for the Pali Highway, which would take them over the nearest range of mountains and then to the eastern coast of the island. Tony asked, "Have you heard how the cook's doing, the one who got scalded?"

"Yes, as a matter of fact. When the ship first arrived at the dock there was an ambulance waiting. It rushed us both to the hospital, me for an X-ray, and the cook for his burns. It turns out they were very serious so he'll be spending sometime at the naval hospital. He won't be sailing with us on the next trip, maybe the one after."

"That's a bummer. What about your head?"

"They couldn't find anything." They both laughed.

Tony was looking out the window at everything that passed by, "This place is so nice, especially at sunset."

Willy took his eyes away from the road for a moment and remarked, "It tickles the eyes all right, the way the ripples in the clouds get a golden edge to them."

Tony said, "Almost as if they are burning."

Neither of them said anything for a while. After about fifteen minutes they approached the Honolulu Academy of Arts. Tony could see some banners hanging from poles near the building. They announced a concert of Indian classical music being performed that weekend. "Wow! Slow down a minute. Can you pull over in front of the museum?"

"Sure." Willy slowed the car and parked near the entrance. "What did you see?"

"I'll be right back." Without explaining, Tony leaped out of the car and hurried up the steps into the entrance. After a moment he reappeared with a small poster in his hand and got back into the car. "Okay, let's go."

As they drove away, Willy asked, "So what's all the excitement about?"

"Ravi Shankar, the man is my idol."

"You mean he's here? I've heard his music, it's fabulous. What did you find out?"

Tony read through the notice, "Hang on a sec." He read half aloud mumbling to himself, then, "This is really far out! He's performing here at the museum this Saturday and Sunday night!"

"That's fantastic. I can't imagine a musician who hasn't heard of him," added Willy. "Do you want to go back for a ticket?"

"Not yet. I'm not sure if I can get this lady I just met to go with me along with a couple of friends."

"Well, you can include me if you don't mind."

"Sure, that would be great."

The car traveled over the highest section of road that crossed the mountain range approaching the east coast. Willy pulled
the car into one of the observation parking areas. When they got
out of the car, Tony was struck by the spectacular view. It was
vast and limitless. Even the island seemed but a speck in the vast
ocean. The wind that came from the windward side was brisk
and very clean, smelling of ocean mixed with vegetation.

They got back into the car and continued on until they came
to a fork in the road. They took the road that eventually joined
the coast road. Tony was almost in a dream state as he watched
the passing surf beneath a darkening sky. Mixed in it were tiny
phosphorescent creatures. When the surf broke onto the beach it
looked as though it was making sparks. Barely visible were the
little sea birds that ran up and down the wet sand following the
movement of the water's edge. They were looking for little
creatures to eat, until it was too dark for them to see.

"It won't be much farther."

Tony was almost startled by Willy's voice, "What's that?"

"We're getting closer to the Crosswinds. Were you asleep?"

"No, I was just watching the activity along the beaches. You
know, I never get tired of looking at the surf."

"Have you ever done any surfing?"

"Aside from a little body surfing, it's never interested me."

Willy confided, "Well, I gave it a try once during my first
trip to the islands."

"Great, how did it go?"

"Not so great. The board and I went down, then it shot up
into the air. When it came back down it hit me on the side of
my head, knocking my neck out of place."

"Oh, man."

Willy finished his story with, "That was the last time I sat my
tail on a surfboard." He drove the car into the unlit parking area of
what looked like a little country store. "Well, here we are."

They left the car and walked inside. The interior was divided by a wall woven from palm leaves. The right half was set up like a mom and pop country store with groceries and other goods. The left half was like a coffeehouse with a small kitchen. It had broad tropical windows that opened on to a sheltered patio. On the walls were signed photos, paintings, and a communal notice board. Most of the tables looked to be made of driftwood. Tony wandered outside. There was a large metal and wood sculpture on the patio, along with a tiki god carved from a palm tree. He thought of it as a mix between Monterey's Cannery Row and a Hawaiian beach community.

Tony looked up at the sky and at the light of the moon coming through the lower clouds and some remaining sunlight reflecting off the much higher clouds. He saw that the clouds were moving in different directions. He was observing the phenomenon from which the Crosswinds got its name. When it became too dark to try to figure it out he rejoined Willy inside.

The store had closed by then and Jim Brown, one of Willy's old acquaintances wandered in from the patio drinking from a large glass of iced fruit juice. Jim was surprised and delighted when he saw Willy. "Hey, Willy! Man, I haven't seen you in ages."

Willy was surprised too. "Brother Jim, how long has it been?"

"God, I don't know. Over a year?"

"Or two. I want you to meet one of my shipmates. Tony, Jim."

They shook hands, and Tony greeted him with, "What's happenin'?"

"Any friend of Willy is a friend of mine." Then referring to the concertina he asked, "By the way, did you bring your ax?"

"It's in the car," Willy replied with a smile.

"Mary, oh, you don't know her yet. There's a young lady named Mary, plays an autoharp and sings her heart out. She might be here tonight. She said she wants to go to San Francisco and try the folk music scene."

Tony told Jim, "I just left there. I was living right in North Beach."

"That's great, man. Maybe you can help her out," suggested Jim. "She's really a nice kid."

Later on in the evening, Willy was playing his concertina and singing from his collection of sea shanties when Mary came in. She recognized the melody he was playing. Without a word she opened the case she was carrying, took out an autoharp, and began to strum it in accompaniment. What a delight it was to here Willy's voice and the two instruments together.

When Willy finished, Jim introduced Mary to them. Afterwards, she followed Willy's set with a delightful round of bright cheerful songs. Her singing voice was very childlike. When she was finished she and Tony discussed the folk music and coffeehouse scene on San Francisco's upper Grant Street. Tony also gave her the names and phone numbers of like-minded friends in Sausalito and San Francisco who might be able to help her.

As the night wore on, Tony got into a very philosophical discussion with Emanuel Ruiz, a traveling poet guitarist from Brazil. He was on his way to Japan to explore the Zen approach to music. He was also considering going on to India. He was hoping to earn enough money in Japan teaching guitar to support his travels. They were discussing the lyrics from a song that had been performed. Tony was saying, "You know, Emanuel, from what I've seen, one man's fantasy can be another man's reality."

"Yes, this is very true," agreed Emanuel, "and the reverse is true as well. I have turned many of my fantasies into reality." Tony added, "You know, when I'm traveling, I feel really alive. When I step onto a new place I feel like I'm passing through a kind of portal, like I'm going from reality through fantasy into a reality that just grew bigger."

"That's a very interesting way you just put that, 'Passing through a portal,' where the new experience gives you a new understanding. Now on a different level think about this for a moment: From the realm of all that is, where universal knowledge resides, knowledge of anything can pass through one of many pathways, when the mind is quiet, receptive, and uninfluenced by any outside influence."

Tony recalled, "There have been moments in music when that has taken place for me, especially when I'm playing my guitar or piano alone, late at night. After playing for a while, and I'm improvising it's as if a vale begins to lift and a world beyond begins to present itself."

Emanuel said, "Indeed you are very fortunate for that experience has eluded me." And so the conversation continued until Emanuel excused himself to return to Honolulu.

The Crosswinds was to close at midnight. Willy told Tony, "I'm going to sleep in the back of the station wagon. I'll use a blanket I brought, so you can use my sleeping bag if you want."

"That sounds good to me. It's such a nice warm night, and quiet. I'd like to sleep somewhere on the beach."

Jim told the pair, "I can put one of you up for the night."

Mary apologized, "I wish I could help, but I'm staying with friends down the coast myself."

Willy said, "That's all right. This is why I rented a wagon."

Tony added, "I was looking forward to sleeping on the beach anyway. It's really okay."

Jim asked, "See you all tomorrow night?"

"Sure thing," answered Willy.

"Hopefully." Mary was not too sure.

"Maybe." Tony hesitated to commit himself.

After looking in the semidarkness for a likely spot to put the sleeping bag Tony found a flat place to sleep between the rocks, about forty feet from the water's edge.

In the dark hours of the morning, he was roused from his sleep but couldn't tell if he was awake or dreaming:

The wind was blowing swiftly, but he could not feel it. Although it was dark everything was plainly visible. There was, standing in the water before him, a giant over three hundred feet tall. It had hair that was like flowing water and seaweed combined. It wore radiant minerals and indescribable materials as ornaments. There were fish and sea animals of every kind leaping out of and into the water all around it. Its eyes were radiant with the mysteries of the deep and beyond. It was looking directly at Tony and talking in a voice that caused him to tremble with fear. Tony thought to himself, 'What terrible thing is this?!' Energy swirled in the air all about the being. Instantly the being answered in a language that Tony did not know, but he still understood the meaning. Each time it spoke, the surf became more pronounced. "I am the giant of the sea, and the custodian of the oceans. The secrets of the sea are with me." The being filled his chest with air, then looking at the landscape behind Tony, let out the air with a force that uprooted the trees and structures as effortlessly as one would blow feathers from a tabletop.

Tony felt the chill of the wind as sand blew around him. He could see the sand but not feel it. Again the voice filled him with fear, as he understood the being to say, "The winds are my companions. Together we are a force with no equal." Tony was blown into the water where a whirlpool appeared, taking him down into the depths. Spread out before him in every direction, were human skeletons and the remains of ships from every period in time. Again the voice said, "Not long ago you came close to being among these. The choice was not yours and is not." Suddenly he was again on the Lady Explorer at the height of the storm. He had both hands on the rail, with the freshly lit cigarette still in his mouth. The cigarette was blown from his mouth by the turbulence in the air, "Hey, man!" He opened his mouth in astonishment when he saw a wave so massive that it totally engulfed the ship.

She listed to one side then rolled over and went down. In the total darkness, men trapped inside the ship were shouting as they tried to open hatches to escape. But not for long for as the Lady headed for the bottom every area with air left in it collapsed from the enormous pressure of the sea around her. Tony gasped for air but his lungs filled with water. Then he was outside his body and saw it slowly drift toward the surface as a hungry shark was attracted to it. He felt utterly hopeless. A thundering voice filled the void, "In the arrogance of your youth do not assume that you are immortal." He was back in his body as the shark charged with its huge mouth open to begin feeding on him. At that same moment a whirlpool again formed but this time in reverse sucking him up and away from the shark and casting him onto the beach.

Trembling, he opened his eyes. He was very wet and saw that the spot between the rocks where he was sleeping was beginning to fill with water as the early morning tide nearly reached its peak. It was about six a.m. when he found higher ground. With his wet sleeping bag spread out beside him to dry, he laid on the dry sand to reflect upon the dream. An unusual and sudden gust of wind blew the sand onto Tony and his sleeping bag. He thought he heard the sound of laughter coming from the ocean. Eventually he drifted back to sleep.

After about two hours he was awakened by a pair of seagulls fighting over something. He turned on to his back and shooed away the gulls. Blinking the sleep from his eyes, he put his hands behind his head and stared up at the clouds. They were moving in different directions and so had to be at different altitudes. He remembered that something similar occurred with the currents of the oceans.

Leaving the sleeping bag behind, he wandered along the water's edge exploring the occasional tide pool. The morning air was crisp and refreshing, but after sleeping as he had on the sandy beach in a bag that became wet, he felt the need for a bath.

When he reached a small beach that was secluded by low cliffs, he stripped down to nothing and waded into the water to do a bit of bathing. Off in the distance, maybe two hundred yards out, he noticed some activity but couldn't tell what it was. When the water was waist deep he sat on the bottom and began scrubbing himself. The saltwater did a fair job of washing away the grimy feeling, but it became awkward when he tried below the waist while sitting.

As he went into deeper water the subtle swells became more pronounced. Each wave lifted his feet off the now rocky bottom. This gave a very nice sensation at first, but when the bottom was suddenly not there, a very uneasy feeling came over him. He realized that he might have just stepped off the edge of the island. If it was true then the bottom could be as much as two thousand meters down. He completely forgot about bathing when he realized that the current had been taking him away from the shore. He became worried and tried swimming toward the beach.

He had already drifted some distance and didn't seem to be making any progress. He thought he could see someone on a cliff so he began shouting, "Hey! Hey! Can you help me?" But there was no response. "Hey! Can you help me? I'm caught in the current and can't make it back to shore!" There was still no response.

Then the person came into view pointing and shouting, "Look out there! Out there!"

Tony turned to look, "Oh shit, no!" Coming toward him, cutting its way through the water at an amazing speed was a dorsal fin. Overcome with real fear and the realization that he could do nothing, he became motionless and just stared as the creature closed in. When it made contact, there was a dull pain in his stomach. He acted instinctively, rapping his arms around its head. In no time at all the creature had pushed him back into shallow water before swimming away. A dazed Tony realized that not a shark, but a dolphin had just rescued him. In just minutes he had gone from bathing, to nearly drowning, then to thinking that he might be eaten alive. He was stunned.

Eventually he regained his composure enough to put on his clothes. He found his sleeping bag which had dried in the sun. He laid on it long enough to get some much needed rest since he was feeling exhausted. So many things were going through his mind: the vivid dreams he had, the storm at sea when the *Lady Explorer* almost went down, the events of that day, and how all of those things seemed to be related.

After about an hour and a half, Tony made his way back to the Crosswinds. Willy's station wagon was nowhere around. Inside the store he bought a sandwich and a soft drink. There was a message from Willy waiting for him. It read, 'Tony, I tried to find you but didn't know where to look. Mary phoned to invite us to lunch. Sorry, mate. See you later this afternoon. Willy.' Tony took his lunch to the patio area and wrote a note, 'Willy, you can't believe what happened to me today. Really far out! I need to get back today so I'll see if I can catch a ride to the ship. Give my greetings to Mary, and I'll see you when you get back. Tony." He left the note with the couple running the store and then went out to the road where he had no trouble catching a ride back to the docks.

Arriving back at the ship before dinner, Tony checked in the crew's mess where the mail was posted. He had a letter from Maureen. He sat quietly at the end of one of the long tables, and just looked down at the letter for a moment before opening it. He savored her handwriting, the way the tops of the letters all leaned to the left instead of the right. And the way she placed the stamp upside down to symbolize her love. It had been a month since he last saw her, since he last heard her compelling voice, since he last enjoyed her aroma, her touch. He brought the letter up to his nose, but he could barely detect a hint of feminine odor. It smelled more like a hundred mail sacks. Using his bosun's knife he carefully cut it open and sniffed the writing paper, "Ah, that's more like it." As he read it he began to feel as though she were with him.

About two thirds of the way through the first page, he exclaimed, "What?" He read that part of the letter over again. In it she told him about Cliff getting her drunk and having sex with her after she passed out. When he told her about it the next morning, he wanted her again. She said she had only thought of him as a friend and wouldn't let him. He said that he was sorry, blaming the alcohol, and begged her to let him sleep there until he found a place. Days later she began feeling sick so she went to her doctor. The tests she was given showed that she might be pregnant. She was confused and didn't know what to do but really needed Tony's understanding and support. At first he was dumbstruck then angry. Finally he became sympathetic and felt like a brother to her. He said to himself, "That must be the jerk that answered the phone."

"What's that?" responded a steward who was preparing the tables for dinner. He thought Tony was referring to him.

"What? Oh no, sorry. I was thinking of someone in this letter, someone who thinks with the wrong head."

The steward chuckled, "Oh yes. Too many guys like that."

Tony went to his locker to get his writing paper and an envelope. In the bunk under his, George was smoking a miniature cigar and reading an article in one of his girly magazines. He had a vast collection. In Tony's opinion George only had one head and it wasn't to be found on his shoulders.

Tony returned to the crew's mess to write Maureen a reply. It was a sensitive letter expressing his support and platonic love. He stressed the need to have Cliff out of her place and how, if he were there, he would see to it. With their group of friends he was sure she would be all right.

After dinner he caught a ride to the post office in Honolulu. He hoped the late night airmail would get his letter to Maureen before he phoned her Saturday or Sunday. He walked to where he could catch a bus to the Sleeping Lady. When a bus pulled up and opened its door Tony hesitated. The driver asked if he was going to get on. He told the driver he had changed his mind, so the door closed and the bus drove off.

He just stood at the bus stop, wondering what to do. He thought to himself, *Maureen knew I was leaving, knew I wanted to travel. We talked about this and she agreed that I should do it.* He kicked the bus signpost. "Damn it! Why am I feeling guilty?" He took out a cigarette and lit it as he started walking to the Sleeping Lady. Talking to himself he said, "It was understood that we had our separate lives. She wanted her acting career in the city, and I wanted to travel. I must be a jerk, otherwise why do I feel like one?" He lit another cigarette. "Isn't it ironic? That creep, and a friend of hers at that as much as raped her and I feel guilty." He threw the partly smoked cigarette into a puddle and plodded on with both hands in his pockets. "Pregnant. What a bummer of a way for that to happen. What a shitty way for that to happen."

He had a long way to walk and so a lot of time to think with some time to calm down. By the time he reached the nightclub where Melina worked he had become a bit more sociable. He was certainly in need of some sympathy. The marquee over the entrance announcing the Mother Jean Gospel Singers was a welcome sight indeed. The sound of their music reached his ears before he reached the building. When his hand touched the door to push it open, he was full of anticipation to connect with Melina.

Once inside, the atmosphere of the room—the dim light, the air heavy with cigarette and cigar smoke, the overwhelming music and singing—all seemed to surround him. He saw Kim working the bar, but he didn't see Melina. He had an empty *Now what?* kind of feeling in his stomach. He went over and sat at the bar. Kim gave him a friendly, "Well, hello."

"Hi, Kim." He made a feeble attempt at sounding up.

"We missed you last night. Melina said she saw you yesterday."

"Yeah, at a drugstore."

Kim noticed that his recollection sounded a little flat. "With Bruno. She thought that maybe that was why you didn't come in last night."

"Because of Bruno? Not really," he half lied.

"Can I get you something?"

"Melina—"

"Melina?"

"I mean, have you seen Melina?'

"Are you all right, Tony?"

"It's a long story. I've had the most unusual day of my life."

"Well, Melina's here."

He only half believed her. "Where?"

"She went off to the ladies' room to powder her nose."

"No shit?" Embarrassing even himself he apologized, "Sorry. I don't know what came over me."

Kim was very understanding. "Tony, just relax. She will be back any minute now. In fact, don't look now, but here she comes."

Melina appeared wearing a beautiful long dress and a warm smile, "Hello, stranger. I missed you last night."

He was unable to speak for a moment then he began, "I went up north with a friend. To a place called the Crosswinds."

"I had a surprise for you, but I'm afraid it's wilted now."

"Wilted? You mean flowers, for me?"

"I actually had a lei made for you, didn't I, Kim?"

Kim affirmed the fact, "Oh yes, it was very nice."

Melina said, "I've heard of the Crosswinds. It sounds like an interesting place."

Kim asked, "Isn't it a grocery store by day and a coffeehouse by night?"

"That's the place, all right." Tony added, "One of my shipmates invited me up, I really dug it. I met some great people there. After it closed I slept on the beach."

"Sounds fantastic, I love sleeping on the beach," said Melina.

"Listen to this," with the gospel singers and music for a background Tony began telling them about his very real dream and the experience of being saved by a dolphin. The story was interrupted periodically when the ladies had to tend to customers. He finally finished with, "And that all happened this morning."

Melina was very moved, "God must love you because he sure is looking after you."

"That's for sure," remarked Kim. "If I'm standing in the water and anything that looks like a shark fin heads for me, I'll probably die of a heart attack."

Melina agreed, "You and me both, dear."

Kim was amazed. "A dolphin, isn't that something?"

Tony remarked, "Well, in old sailors' tales you hear of things like that." Then he said to her, "By the way, I haven't seen Mate since yesterday afternoon."

She said, "Oh, he's okay. He had something to do tonight, but he said he'd be by before closing. That should be pretty soon because we close in half an hour."

There was an unexpected squealing sound coming from the sound system on stage as the gospel singers packed up for the night.

Tony repeated, "Half an hour?" Then to Melina who was cleaning off tables and getting them ready for the next day, "Melina. I was hoping I could—"

Just then Mate almost fell in the door as he tripped over his own feet, "Damn! Well hello everybody."

"You made it just in time, Mate dear," Kim detected that he may have had a little too much to drink.

"Tony, my man, this is an exceptional surprise."

Tony went over to him. "Mate, it's good to see you. It seems like you could use some coffee."

"You know brother, you could be right." Easing himself onto a stool, he asked Kim, "My dove. Do you suppose I could have one of your mellow cups of the black elixir?"

As she placed a hand on his, she said, "If you mean coffee it's as good as in the cup."

In a truly appreciative tone, Mate answered, "Thank you, my lovely lady."

Melina had nearly finished with her preparations. She reminded Tony, "I think you were about to ask me something."

"Yes. I was hoping I could see you home?"

"That would be nice of you. Would you mind stopping for a bite? I'm kind of hungry—starving actually."

Tony brightened up. "You know I could do with a bite now that I think of it." He spoke more softly, "But even more than that I need to talk."

"Sure."

Kim told Melina, "You two, go ahead without us. I'm feeling kind of tired. I'm going to have Mate take me home. And then I'm going straight to bed." She gave Melina a wink.

Melina acknowledged, "I think I understand."

After closing, the two couples went in separate taxis to their different destinations. Tony and Melina arrived at a Japanese udon house. Once inside they took a table by a window. After ordering they sipped green tea while they waited for their food.

They were looking at each other's reflection in the window when Melina said, "You seem to have a lot on your mind."

He turned to look directly at Melina. He began telling her as much as he could about Maureen's predicament and how it was affecting him. "I'm feeling more like a brother who's responsible for her welfare."

She was quiet for a moment before asking, "Why didn't you marry her when you were with her?"

His sense of guilt reeled from the question as if it had been struck a blow. In his defense he said, "I don't know, I think marriage scared me. In fact I know it did. Once when the subject came up we both felt uncomfortable. It was like something you did later in life when you were ready to settle down and raise a family."

When the waitress brought their order Tony noticed she was wearing a wedding ring, and wondered if she had any children. Just then Melina began to struggle with the chopsticks so Tony placed a pair in his right hand to show her, "Here, like this."

"Thanks." Melina addressed what he had said a moment before, "I don't think two people should get married unless they love one another, and are prepared to commit to each other for the rest of their lives."

"Right. At this moment I am into traveling, and Maureen is committed to a career in acting." He was convincing himself as well as telling Melina, "So we are basically headed in opposite directions."

"I can relate to all of this. I'm committed to my dancing. The work I'm doing at the Sleeping Lady is only a step on a long road. There's little opportunity here, I'm lucky to get what I can. Being from my race doesn't help either. I don't want to be a novelty; I want to be the main attraction."

Tony suddenly felt small in comparison. What kind of goal was it to just want to travel, wandering from place to place?

She continued, "That's why I'm planning to go to Los Angeles, and hopefully New York after that, where the sky is the limit."

He was impressed, "You know, Melina, you just left me in the dust."

"I don't think so. Your travels are bound to lead to something fruitful. It all depends on you. And besides, if it weren't for that I wouldn't have met you."

He felt reassured. "Listen, I'm sorry for being so gloomy. There's a concert Sunday at the museum. Would you go with me?"

She asked, "Do you mean the Ravi Shankar concert?"

Surprised, he asked, "Yes, have you heard of him?"

"I love his music."

"Great!"

Then with a confidential manner she told him, "You're not going to believe this."

"What?"

"I was going to ask you if you wanted to go to the concert with me." She began to laugh.

"Really, you're not kidding me?"

"Really."

"Well, that means only one thing."

Reaching across the table she took his hand in hers, "What does it mean?"

"That if we don't go to the concert together we may be in big trouble."

"You're right, we better not take any chances." On that note they both began laughing.

The waitress again came to their table. "Would you care for anything else?"

They looked at each other, "Just the bill please." When they went to the register to pay, Tony noticed a photograph of twin girls pinned to a little notice board. It was their waitress who took his cash so he asked her, "Are those your twins?"

With a sense of pride she answered, "Yes, they sure are."

Melina said, "They're lovely."

"Thank you. They just had their fourth birthday a week ago."

Melina asked in amazement, "They must keep you pretty busy?"

"Oh yes, but my mother and sister help me a lot, otherwise I couldn't do it on my own."

Tony found himself fumbling in his pocket for some extra change. He left a larger tip than he normally would.

Outside they got into a taxi and headed for Melina's apartment. On the way her presence melted away his anxiety and for a few short moments the two of them were all that mattered. When they arrived he saw her to the door. She had a smile that was colored by disappointment. In a soft voice she said, "Good night. I have a busy day tomorrow, starting early." They embraced nearly melting into one another and kissed good night. "See you tomorrow night?"

"You bet." He was feeling light headed as he walked back to the waiting cab.

It seemed like a long ride. Sitting in the backseat alone, he felt uncomfortable and unsure of himself. A little while before, with Melina there, the inside of the cab had been filled with an intimate magic. Now it was empty and impersonal.

While he was walking through the night air from the taxi to the ship, his head began to clear a bit. Once on board he made his way to his favorite spot at the bow. He lit up a cigarette and leaned on the rail looking out across the bay. The quiet, the aroma of the island, and the calm of the water seemed to combine to quell his uneasiness. It had been a day he would not forget. Feeling very tired he said good night to the watch and headed for his bunk.

Chapter 5

WHAT'S WRONG WITH ME?

Tony had been in his bunk asleep for some time when he became restless. He was dreaming:

Maureen was lying naked on what appeared to be a doctor's examination table. Her hands and feet were bound to the sides of the table. Instead of a doctor three shadowy forms appeared; one from her head, one from her heart, and one from her feet. They had a form like hers and stood around the table along with a larger, darker form that was nothing like her. She looked right into Tony's eyes. He could see that hers were filled with fear. She pleaded with him, "What should I do? I'm so scared." He couldn't open his mouth. He felt paralyzed. The forms turned to Tony and smiled grotesquely. She began to cry out as they reached into her womb and struggled to pull out the contents. When they succeeded they had a tiny glowing form like a microscopic star. Unable to move she pleaded, "No! Please don't!" but they went into a frenzy. Then Tony cried out, "No! Stop!" But he was too late for they had begun to pull the glowing form apart, tearing it to shreds. Then the light was no more. The forms, exhausted but pleased, returned to where they had come from. Maureen was sobbing uncontrollably, "Why didn't you help me?" Tony, still frozen to the spot, was groaning and struggling as though he were chained. He suddenly became jolted by something.

"Are you okay? Hey man, are you okay?!" Johnny, the watch for the night had shaken Tony by the shoulder to wake him.

Tony was wet with perspiration, "I couldn't help her, I couldn't move."

"You couldn't help who? What are you talking about?"

Tony recognized the watch. "Johnny! Oh, man. It must have been a dream. What a nightmare I was having?"

"You were groaning loud enough to wake the ship. Maybe it was something you ate."

"I wish that's all it was." He began to relax a little.

Johnny tried to reassure him, "Well, try to go back to sleep. Nightmares don't usually come back after you wake up."

"I sure hope you're right. Thanks a lot, friend."

"Good night."

"Good night." He rolled on to his right side and drifted off into a peaceful, undisturbed sleep until nearly noon.

Tony managed to shower and shave before making it to the crew's mess in time for lunch. Once he had his tray of food he sat at a table with Chuck and his friend, Rob, from the engine room crew. Rob was a tall healthy looking guy of around thirty. He seemed to have become like a big brother to Chuck.

Tony placed his tray on the table. "Hi, guys. How's it going?"

"Okay, man," Chuck answered, "how about you?"

Tony gave a conditional, "All right."

As Rob was eating he added, "Johnny told me you had a rough night."

"Johnny?"

"Well, you know, we're both in the engine room so we share the same quarters. We're also good friends."

"Oh yeah, that's right. Well, I had a nightmare that still has me feeling a bit strange."

Rob looked over at Chuck then suggested to Tony, "We're taking a trip into the hills and any rain forest we can find. You're welcome to join us. The mountain air might be just the thing for you."

Tony was interested, "How are you going to get there?"

Chuck answered, "Rob has rented this really neat little car with no sides."

Tony wondered aloud, "No sides?"

Rob added, "And it has wicker basket seats and a flat top with a fringe around it."

Tony asked, "You mean like an old surrey? I think I've seen one or two from a distance, they look like fun."

Rob again said, "That's it. Want to come along?"

"Well, it does sound like a good idea. Okay."

When they finished their lunch, Tony changed into his boots. They went down to the area where the cars were parked and there waiting for them was a very small snub nosed powder-blue and pink Renault sedan with the sides and top removed. The flat canvas top had blue and pink stripes plus a fringe made of white tassels.

Seeing one up close for the first time Tony was amazed, "You must be kidding. It looks more like something from a carnival."

Rob told him, "These were the only cars this one place had. They are a lot cheaper than the cars at the other places."

Chuck added, "I think it's really cool."

Tony objected, "It'll be cool all right, like at night with no sides. And what about when it rains?"

Chuck pleaded, "Ah, come on Tony, this'll be fun. How often does it rain anyway? I mean like real rain?"

He seemed so enthusiastic Tony didn't want to disappoint him. And besides, he thought it did look like a fun car. So with a smile, Tony asked, "Do we get to take turns driving?"

Rob answered, "Sure. Would you like to drive first?"

"Maybe after we get out of town a bit." He didn't want Melina to see him driving it.

Rob got behind the wheel, "Okay, get in and buckle up."

Tony got into the backseat then informed Rob, "There are no seat belts."

"Then just hold on because here we go." The little car slowly began to move out of the parking area and onto the street.

At a stop light Tony lit a cigarette. After a couple of blocks, the wind blew the ashes onto his black pants. When he tried to brush them off they left gray smudges. "Hey Rob, can I send you the cleaning bill for these pants?"

Rob turned to look, "What do you mean?"

"Cigarette ashes." Then as an ash blew into his eye, "Damn!"

"Oh, sorry about that. But you'll have to admit, the fresh air is great."

Chuck reminded them, "I love it. It's almost like being on a motorcycle. You can hear and smell everything."

Along the way they stopped for a six-pack of beer to keep in Rob's cooler. They took one of the main roads up through the middle of the island until they reached the base of the Koolau Mountains. Once they took the car as far as it could go on the final unpaved section of road, they left it and began their trek by foot into the lush rain forest. Rob carried his cooler, while Chuck had a bag with potato chips and the like. Tony wasn't taking anything except his cigarettes.

They soon became surrounded by lush vegetation. The afternoon sky was barely visible through a canopy of fern palms.

They followed a stream and as they did the air gradually became filled with a damp fog. Eventually the fog ended when they came to a waterfall. Facing the pool under the falls were vine covered trees that rose majestically into the air. The leafy parts of the vines hung from the trees and looked like a kind of wispy garment that danced in the air flowing with the up draft from the waterfall.

Tony said, "This place is like a paradise," and sat on a moss covered rock. The cushy moss was comfortable, until the moisture passed through the seat of his trousers. He quickly stood up pulling the trousers away from his backside. With his head held up, he expanded his nostrils to fill his lungs with the fragrant air. He held it in for as long as he could before releasing it. "The air here has a kind of richness to it, don't you think?" Again he filled his lungs.

Rob sat on his cooler as he said to Chuck, "A smoker wouldn't usually notice that, so coming from one, I'd say there's still hope."

Chuck said, "Being a nonsmoker I wouldn't know about that."

Tony wasn't paying any attention to them.

Rob stood back up and knelt in front of the cooler as he opened it. "Are you gents ready for a cool one? One of the guys working in the galley gave me some little cans of vegetable juice and fruit juice. I also have a couple of sodas."

Since there wasn't a dry place to sit, Chuck just squatted, sitting on his heels as he answered, "I'm ready for one of those beers."

Since Rob knew that Chuck would work off the alcohol hiking he said, "Okay, but only one. Tony?"

"Not yet, thanks"

"Okay." Rob handed Chuck a can of beer along with an opener.

The two opened their beer in turn making the familiar popping sound in the background, while Tony bent down to scoop up a handful of water from the large pool. First he sniffed it. "Hmmm," then tasted it, "Ahh." Again he bent down using both hands to hold the water. He brought it to his mouth and drank. "I think this is the best water I've tasted in my life."

Rob said to Tony, "I had a feeling coming up here could be good for you. And we're just getting started. Hey, Chuck, how about one of those bags of chips?"

"Sure thing, Rob."

"Thanks a lot, my friends, it's just great here." Tony looked into the crystal clear water. "I don't see any fish in here."

"I don't think there are any freshwater fish here. At least none that nature put here," Rob said looking at both of them.

Chuck just shrugged his shoulders, "Why not?"

Rob said, "Well, to make a complicated story very short, they never evolved."

Tony was looking rather puzzled. "Well, you would think that as this island is old enough, some would have evolved by now."

Then Chuck had an idea. "Maybe they did, but maybe something or the natives ate them all."

"Maybe, but then that would actually make things more complicated." Rob gave them a little background. "This island has been here over three and a half million years. It evolved from a volcano, as did all these islands. Everything else that started here came from somewhere else. The first humans have only been here since around 400 AD. They came by canoe and brought things from their former home islands. Things like fruit plants, pigs, and so on."

Tony said, "You seem to know a lot about these islands."

"A little bit, natural history has been a real interest of mine for some time now. That's why I signed on to the *Lady* for this cruise."

The minute amount of alcohol in the beer had gone quickly to Chuck's brain. He dropped his empty beer can onto the lush carpet beneath his feet and stepped on it as he told Rob, "I finished my beer and chips. Are we goin' much farther?"

With an obvious frown on his face, Rob produced a plastic bag. "Here, put your empty can and bag in this, Chuck."

Taking Rob's frown as an objection, Chuck explained, "I was just tryin' to flatten the thing out first, honest."

"Good. Now we can go into the forest a little farther, but we'll have to stop and return to the car by sunset." He put the plastic bag with its contents into the cooler. "Is that okay with both of you?"

Tony said, "It's fine with me, I'd like to see some more."

"Yeah, me too," was Chuck's enthusiastic response.

"Then let's be off." With that they stood up, adjusted their clothing a little, and continued on with Rob leading the way.

They spent the remaining two hours exploring, then agreed to make a similar trek a month later.

Back on the ship, Tony showered then put on something casual but nice. He wanted to save time so he skipped dinner and sped off in a taxi bound for the Sleeping Lady.

Inside the lounge the gospel group had been on their break. Melina was wondering if it would be a good time for her to take one also. When she saw Tony walk in she had no doubt. She motioned him over to a corner table where they would be inconspicuous.

"Hi, hon." She took his hand and gave it a gentle squeeze as they sat together at the little cocktail table.

"Melina, you're beautiful." The nightmarish dream of that morning had left his thoughts, and now there were only memories of the rain forest. He turned his hand to hold hers, "I've had the most incredible day today."

"Really? Because you didn't phone me today I was afraid that you might not be all right. I'm glad you're here. So what did you do?"

"Two of my friends from the *Lady* took me to a rain forest at the base of a mountain range that I forgot the name of."

"The Koolau Mountains?" she asked.

"That sounds familiar. Have you been there?"

"Oh yes, I love it. But when I want to get away my favorite place is Maui."

He recalled, "Someone else suggested Maui to me."

"It's an incredible island. You can explore the forest, scuba dive, or just sunbathe in a cove."

"Well anyway, the place we went to today was a mind blower for me. I mean we walked through fern palms that were huge. And what beautiful flowers, you would love them."

"I know, and I do love them."

"And the air . . . I thought the air on the island in general was great until I breathed the air of that forest. It was so full, so . . . I can't describe it."

Melina knew exactly what he meant. "You know hon, living here so long I think I've gotten spoiled. But if I try to remember what it was like back on the mainland, especially in the cities, it seems so terrible compared to here. I think people there have even forgotten what air should be like."

"I think I must have forgotten. But this was my first time in a rain forest. It's not the same as the woods or the seaside. It really is a different world."

"Hon, I have to go back to work soon. Have you had anything to eat?"

"No, I came here as soon as I showered and changed."

"If it's not too late I might be able to get you something from the kitchen."

"That would be great." He suddenly had an apprehensive feeling. He held her hand a little tighter, "But don't go yet."

Sensing that something was troubling him, she said, "I won't. What's the matter, Tony?"

"I don't know. I'm just feeling a little strange all of a sudden." He was feeling a sense of impending loss. But he didn't know of what. He thought that maybe it was to do with his guilt feeling over Maureen. To reassure her, he said, "It's nothing, maybe I'm hungrier than I realized."

"Listen, I'll just have a quick look. I won't be long, okay?"

"Okay."

Melina hurried off to the kitchen. She returned with a chicken sandwich she put together with some potato salad. "Here you are, hon, this should keep you until I get off, then we can go for a meal." She placed the food in front of him.

He smiled when he saw what she had brought him. "This is really good of you."

"Do you want something to drink with this?"

"A glass of red wine seems about right. Do you have any?"

"I think so." She went over to the U-shaped bar and asked Kim, "Hon, is there enough red wine left for Tony to have a glass?"

"I wondered who you were keeping in that dark corner." As she looked for an open bottle, she said, "Here it is. There's a little more than a glass left." While she poured some into a wine glass she asked Melina, "How is he?"

"Okay, I guess. He's feeling a little odd."

Kim handed her the glass. "Here, this is pretty good. He should like it."

"Thanks, dear." She returned and placed it on the table by Tony, then sat with him for a minute. "Kim thought you would like this. There's only a little more left."

He took a sip. With a look of contentment, he said, "Very nice. It has that hint of walnut kind of flavor that I love."

The Mother Jean Gospel Singers were returning to the stage.

"Listen hon, I have to get back now. Are you going to be okay for a while?"

"The more I talk to you the better I feel."

After she returned to her work he started to eat. As the music began to work its magic he contemplated the fate of Maureen, his attraction to Melina, and the sudden apprehension of loss.

It was sometime later and just before closing. Tony was at the bar talking with Melina, Kim, and Mate who had come in an hour earlier.

Mate asked him, "Did you say the Shankar concert is Sunday night?"

"Yeah, at eight o'clock, it would be nice if the four of us went together."

"Sounds cool with me, man. What do you think about it, Kim?"

"I don't know anything about the group or their music, but I'm willing to try something different if you guys like it."

Melina reassured Kim, "I'm sure you will like it. Just watching them play is an experience in itself."

"That's great. We can work out the details later." Even though Tony was feeling pretty tired he asked, "Does anyone feel like going to the Jolly Roger for a little while?"

Mate said, "I can dig that."

Kim responded with, "But not for too long, honey, my feet are not going to last much longer."

"She's right about that, boys," Melina added. "This is almost the end of our work week and we work on our feet."

Tony said, "We don't have to dance. We could just listen to the music and have a little to eat."

Mate agreed, "Yeah, that's all. It's a mellow band."

After closing they bundled into a taxi and headed for the Jolly Roger. This time they all squeezed into the backseat. By the time the taxi arrived at the club each couple was so entwined that it was hard for the cabby to get them interested in getting out so he just left the meter running. The sound of the meter clicking off every few seconds brought the foursome to their senses.

Inside the club the air was thick with cigarette and cigar smoke. The musicians were on stage playing while the dance floor was crowded with couples. Some of the dancers looked as though they had been dancing for hours; they were so soaked with perspiration. Melina and Kim excused themselves and went to the ladies' room to freshen up while Tony and Mate found a table.

When the girls returned from the rest room they noticed one of the many small posters on the walls. It was a notice for a dance contest the next night. When they arrived at their table a waitress had also arrived to take their order. Melina asked the guys, "Have you seen the poster for the dance contest?"

They both answered excitedly, "No! Where and when?"

The waitress informed them, "Right here tomorrow night. There's a signup list at the register."

Mate leapt up. "I'll be right back."

"Me too." Tony joined him.

The waitress moved on to another table. With concern in her voice, Kim told Melina, "I don't know about you but I don't feel up to a dance contest. Working tomorrow night is just about all I've got left in me."

Melina agreed, "I feel the same way you do, dear, so don't feel guilty. Besides, we both have to work until eleven."

"That's right, we couldn't be here before twelve anyway."

Mate and Tony returned with Mate looking really disappointed. "Well, we didn't make it. They're booked up for tomorrow night. Damn!"

Tony added, "Yeah, they're only allowed so many couples on the dance floor at one time." Then with a smile, he added, "But we are signed up for the next one a month from now."

Mate who wasn't smiling included, "The only problem is that the contest is at ten o'clock."

Melina spoke up, "We both have to work until eleven, Tuesday through Saturday. And then it still could be another hour before we could be on the dance floor."

Tony didn't want them to feel pressured. "We know Saturday is not a good time for you," he said, then jokingly added, "Maybe Mate and I can dance together."

"What?" Mate couldn't relate to that idea.

Kim had an idea, "Maybe I can get Linda to work for me that night. I bet she wouldn't mind an extra night."

Melina had an idea too, "I have a girlfriend who loves to dance. You know her, Kim. Her name is Billy. She's a great dancer."

Since Billy was also very sexy, Kim asked, "Are you sure you want to ask her?"

"For this dance contest she's the one." Also Melina was sure Tony wasn't Billy's type. She was only interested in men with lots of money. "I only hope she's available."

Mate was very touched by what the girls were trying to do. "It would mean more to me if I could win this contest dancing with Kim."

She began to melt with those words. "That's so sweet of you."

He took her hand and kissed the back of it. "And besides, I can spend all that day massaging those lovely feet and legs of yours."

Her voice became more demure, "If you do that then we might forget about the contest."

Tony, already sitting next to Melina, tried to move a little closer. "Those two seem to be working things out okay. You know, sweetheart, I'm really not that concerned about a dance contest. I just thought it would be a fun thing for us to do. When I realized that it is on your work night I just let it go."

"But you said you signed us up?"

"Just in case things change, so you don't need to ask your girlfriend Billy. I'll still come to give my support to Kim and Mate, though."

The waitress returned to their table. "Sorry I had to leave you, but we're so busy tonight."

Tony said, "Yeah, you're really packin' 'em in."

"I think they're mostly here to practice for the contest. Also this band is very popular. Can I take your order now?"

After ordering a round of drinks and some snacks, they made plans for the concert on Sunday and discussed getting together Saturday for an outing to the walkthrough aquarium on the east coast of the island. Melina declined the outing since she had a prior commitment. They only stayed at the club for another hour before leaving in two separate taxis for home. Tony reluctantly returned to the ship.

After breakfast Saturday Tony went to a car dealer near the docks and rented a convertible for the next two days. He drove across Honolulu to the area where Kim's apartment was located, a small two story building surrounded by eucalyptus trees.

He parked the car then went up a stairway to her apartment. When he knocked, Kim opened the door to a neat and nicely furnished place. "Come in, hon, we've been expecting you."

Mate was in the kitchen pouring a cup of coffee. "My man, can I get you a coffee?"

"No thanks. Guess what, Mate? I've got this great convertible waiting for us outside."

Kim said, "I saw it. It's beautiful. Have a seat, I've got a surprise for you."

Tony sat on the couch. "What kind of a surprise?" Then his mouth dropped open.

Into the living room walked a beautiful creature wearing shorts and a blouse that was tied with a knot in front. "Hi, hon. I was able to reschedule my appointment." Melina sat beside him on the couch. Tony was speechless. "Say something," she urged.

"Can you stand back up a second?" Tony asked. "And turn around slowly?"

Watching from the kitchen, Mate had thought Kim's legs looked great in shorts, but Melina's were unbelievable. Under his breath he said, "What a trip."

As Melina stood in front of Tony, he commented, "You have got the most beautiful legs I have ever seen."

Mate agreed, "She definitely has the legs of a dancer."

Coming out of the bedroom, Kim commented in admiration, "You should see the rest of her."

Melina quickly sat back down and complained, "You guys are embarrassing me."

Tony apologized, "I'm sorry, but I just hadn't expected you to look so good."

Melina looked a bit puzzled, "I'm not sure how to take that."

Kim interceded on his behalf, "I'm sure he means that in the best way possible."

Melina relaxed, "Maybe I was being overly sensitive."

Tony was still in awe. "There's so much of you that's special that I'm afraid to touch you."

Melina whispered in his ear, "Don't be afraid."

Mate, who had excellent hearing, motioned to Kim. In a half whisper he said, "Dove, can you help me find something in the other room?" The two disappeared for a moment.

Melina's beauty intimidated Tony. Her mouth was still close to his ear when she said to him, "There's something about you that is very strong, and yet beneath it you're quite shy. That's a combination I find irresisti . . ."

He quickly turned his head and pressed his mouth to hers. The intimidation and shyness were overcome by passion. They were both overwhelmed by it. But mindful of where they were, they slowly released their hold on one another and were sitting quietly whispering words of affection when Kim and Mate reentered the room.

Kim was the first to speak, "We'll take my cooler to keep the food in. I made sandwiches and Melina brought over some fruit and nuts."

"I've got the sodas, and Kim is bringing blankets," Mate added.

Looking into Tony's eyes, Melina said, "Then let's go, hon."

"We're as good as there, sweetheart." Tony stood up with the car keys at the ready.

Mate told him, "Come on, man, give me a hand with the cooler and the other stuff."

When they got outside to load the car, a red and ivory '55 Chevrolet Bel Air, Mate exclaimed, "Man, where did you find this jewel?"

"Isn't it a beaut'? I've wanted one of these ever since they first came out, but I couldn't afford one."

"How long did you rent it for?"

"Until we leave on Monday. I'm hoping one of the girls can return it."

The things were loaded into the car, and once every one was in they were on their way to the windward side of the island.

The sun occasionally shone through the broken clouds. In the open convertible, the wind was invigorating. Some jazz was playing on the car radio. Melina was snuggled up to Tony in the front seat. He thought the moment was like an unbelievable dream and wondered why he was so blessed. The other two were in the backseat with Kim pointing out the sights to Mate. They were four contented people.

It wasn't long before the aquarium appeared in the distance. Melina's soft voice informed Tony, "There it is hon."

After parking the car in the lot they left some things in the trunk and went through the main entrance. A stairway led them down to a transparent glass passageway that took them through the water along the bottom.

Tony exclaimed, "I've never been in an aquarium like this. It's fantastic, like being under water with the fish."

"Hey, look at that!" Mate became excited by a huge manta ray gracefully flying overhead.

Kim told him, "You know, dear, they can get to be so big that a man could ride one."

"Not this man," he affirmed.

"I could dig it," said Tony, "if I had an Aqua Lung."

Melina saw something, "Look there, hon." A pair of dolphins would mate as they swam along, break apart, and mate again.

"Now that's beautiful," Kim said as she and Mate walked arm in arm.

Smiling, Mate said, "It looks like dolphins are very hip animals."

Melina added, "Can you imagine what it must be like to have such a free and natural life?"

They went through the whole aquarium. Even though they found it to be extremely interesting they became restless to be on the beach.

As they were walking back to the car Tony told Melina, "This is a very nice aquarium. Thanks for bringing us here."

Mate agreed, "It's a very trippy place."

Melina said, "I've always liked coming here. It's so far removed from the scene at the club."

Tony wondered what she meant by the scene at the club.

Mate had a suggestion, "Tony," as he gave a knowing nod toward Melina, "later on, why don't you let me drive back to town? Then you can enjoy the scenery."

"That sounds like a plan to me. Doing the driving doesn't let me do much of that."

They returned to the car and drove on to the beach.

The place that Melina had chosen had a broad expanse of rocky beach with patches of smooth white sand. The men carried the heavier things from the car while the women took the rest. In one of the sandy patches they spread out a couple of blankets and placed the food on the middle.

Since everyone was wearing a bathing suit under their clothing it wasn't long before they shed their outer garments. They applied suntan lotion to their partner, more to keep from getting burned than for a tan. But each time the sun showed through the clouds it became very hot.

They went into the mild surf to cool off and become refreshed. Because the bottom had abrasive rocks in places, they had to be careful. They were doing the usual horsing around when Mate rammed his big toe into a jagged rock, so he and Kim left the water to nurse his foot. Tony and Melina were in just above their waist, holding each other close. He couldn't believe how good it felt to just hold her. When the more subtle waves, raising and lowering, rolled past them they rose with them then gently bounced on the bottom. It was an incredible sensation for them both. He was licking her on the neck ever so gently as if to remove the saltwater. The sensation was making her very aroused, causing tiny goose bumps on her skin.

He recalled something she said earlier, "You said something earlier that made me curious."

She was licking the saltwater from his shoulder, "What was that, hon?"

"When you referred to the scene at the club?"

"Oh, you know, the way some customers can make me feel really bad at times." She began kissing his ear.

"I've always found the atmosphere in there to be so mellow, especially when the Mother Jean Singers really get going." He pulled away from her just a bit, and then fell backward pulling her to him as they drifted into shallower water.

"Oh, I agree. I meant the other side," as she pretended to be a vampire and playfully went for his throat.

"The other side of what?" he asked. And as he did he felt the composure of her body quickly change.

She thought to herself, *Oh my god, I thought he knew.* She said, "I meant the other side of the club, the burlesque hall."

They were now sitting cross legged on the very shallow bottom facing one another. "Sorry, I didn't know you served drinks on both sides."

"I don't." Almost afraid to say it, while trying to maintain her dignity, she said, "I'm a dancer on the other side."

He said nothing for a moment as the reality of what she just told him went from his mind to his heart. He awkwardly scooted along the bottom to sit beside her. He put his arms around her and held her as close and as tight as he could. He could feel her anxiety, her hurt, and her fear. He held her for a long time hoping to draw away those feelings. After a few moments a slightly larger wave caused them to lose their balance and topple over becoming completely bathed for an instant. They both began laughing a laugh that came from deep within. They both felt a great sense of relief.

On the beach Kim had been feeding Mate her well prepared food. "Hey you two, you better come up here before he eats it all."

"You just take your time." Mate reassured them, "Nothing to worry about. There's plenty for everyone."

Tony and Melina soon joined the other two. To protect themselves from getting sunburned they needed to apply more suntan lotion. Melina asked Tony, "Hon, when you finish can you put some lotion on my back? I can't reach it."

"Sure thing, sweetheart. Would you do the same for me?"

"But of course."

Mate and Kim had been listening to some rhythm and blues on the radio, and relaxing while Mate told her about his youth in Oakland, California. "I used to dance a lot when this music was popular. I was a sophomore in high school when it really started to take off. I wasn't old enough to go to the clubs, but there was either an R&B concert or a dance party somewhere every weekend. I even won some dance contests."

"I'm not surprised, honey, there's magic in those feet of yours," Kim said with sincerity.

"I started taking dance lessons in modern dance but when some of the guys at school found out they wouldn't leave me alone, calling me names like 'sissy' and 'queer.' We had a couple of fights, but I'm ashamed to admit I eventually quit the dance class to avoid the constant harassing."

Before Tony could rub lotion onto Melina's back she laid face down on her towel and asked him to undo the straps of her top so he could apply the lotion to her back unimpaired. He very carefully untied them and slowly applied the lotion. He said to her, "You know something, sweetheart? If heaven is better than this I don't think I could handle it."

"You certainly have a way with those fingers. I'm getting a heavenly feeling myself. Turn around, hon, and I'll do yours."

After he finished her back he retied the straps and gave her the bottle, whereupon she began rubbing the lotion onto his back while he laid face down on his towel. She heard him barely whisper, "Lordy, lordy, I do believe I've died and gone to heaven." Eventually they got around to eating, but Kim and Mate had drifted off to sleep.

As the afternoon progressed the sun became very low. It was nearing the time for the girls to return to work. They dressed themselves and loaded everything into the car. This time Mate was driving the convertible with Kim snuggled up beside him.

They hadn't gone far when the music on the radio became Miles Davis playing *So What*. In the backseat with Melina, Tony said, "I haven't heard that piece in years. Listen to that man's tone. Talk about magic, he has got to be a musical mystic, just as Ravi Shankar is with Indian classical."

Melina observed, "You know, Tony, you talk like a musician sometimes."

"I wish I was. Maybe if I had stayed somewhere long enough. But I like so many different kinds of music. Tell me, Melina, what kind of dancing do you like to do the most?"

"Like you I like all kinds of dance. From a very early age I wanted to do ballet more than anything, but by fourteen I was too tall. Then modern and interpretive dance became my favorite. Of course you haven't seen me dance yet. For the dance routines that I create I use music I record from albums."

"I can't wait to see you dance."

Looking unsure of herself, she said, "I'm so afraid you won't like it."

Kim had been sitting with her head lying on Mate's shoulder when she overheard this part of their conversation. She couldn't contain herself any longer. She turned to Tony, "Dear, let me tell you something. Very simply put, Melina is the only dancer they have. The others are just strippers."

"Kim!" Melina protested.

"It's true, they move around a little bit and take off their clothes. Now how difficult is that? When she's out there something different and very special takes place."

"Thanks, darlin', that's so sweet of you." Melina had always been a modest person.

"When am I going to see you do what you do so well?"

"Well, from what I can tell the next time your ship comes back to Oahu it'll be during one of the weeks I dance," Melina said.

"But that's a month from now. I could go crazy from the strain of waiting," said Tony, as he imagined the sight of such a beautiful creature doing her dance.

Without taking his eyes off of the road, Mate called back to the others, "Man, I know I would." He was hoping to increase his friend's chances.

Melina had an idea but kept it to herself. With a subtle smile she told Tony, "Well, hon, I guess you'll just have to wait."

Tony snuggled up to her putting a hand on her knee. He moved his hand around to the back of her knee, then with his fingertips he gave subtle caresses to the tender skin. When he began to nibble and kiss her ear she got little goose bumps all over her body. Then just to tease her further he talked softly into her ear with his best theatrical voice, seeming to be a much older man of culture, "Although I've been told by those around me that you are an intriguing practitioner in the mysteries of the dance, and even though I can see that you are a most beautiful woman, I cannot help but wonder what kind of mind you possess?"

"Right now? A dirty mind." She was both playing along with him and being honest.

"Excellent," was his sincere reply.

They burst into laughter as she started to tickle him. "Think you're pretty smart, don't you? But that was good. Where did you learn to talk like that?"

"I studied acting in the city, I mean San Francisco, for a couple of years. That was how I met Maureen. Then I did some little theater in Germany and England while I was traveling around."

"You haven't told me about this before, have you?" She was curious. "So what happened?"

"I have this overwhelming desire to travel. I mean I love acting. And in front of an audience, the most incredible connection takes place. And I love music. When I play there's a very spiritual connection that I experience. But like I said the need to travel is overwhelming. And being in a foreign place is very stimulating. I've never felt more alive."

Melina thought for a moment. "It almost sounds like a kind of addiction."

"I never thought of it like that. I'm sure an addiction to anything could be pretty disruptive to your daily life."

Melina had a second thought. "Maybe *addiction* is the wrong word. Maybe what you have is an obsession."

"Maybe, at least it's something I can gain from as opposed to an addiction where you only lose." He hoped so anyway.

"I guess you're right as long as you don't lose sight of your acting or your music." She also hoped that he was right.

Tony and Melina grew silent as they each contemplated the direction their lives could take.

It was five when their car arrived at Kim's place. Kim remarked, "It's a good thing we don't have to be at work until six o'clock tonight." As she and Mate took some things out from the trunk of the car, she said, "Come back as soon as you can to pick us up."

Tony and Melina had moved to the front seat. Tony reassured Kim, "Don't worry, dear lady. We'll be back faster than you can say 'flibberdeegibbalmdabippittybop', you have my word." Kim was left with a puzzled look on her face as they sped away to Melina's.

Her place was not far away. Tony parked the car by the front and helped her carry some things to the door. He had never been inside. Because he didn't want to bump into Bruno, he waited in the car while Melina went in to shower and dress for work. While he was waiting he put up the car's top then listened to the radio while he smoked a couple of cigarettes. It didn't take her long to get ready.

In no time they picked up Kim and Mate then drove to the Sleeping Lady. After dropping the women off, the guys returned to the ship to grab a bite to eat and freshen up. They were actually feeling a bit groggy after so much time in the sun so a cold shower was just the thing.

The plan was to meet the ladies after work. They had a bit of time so they decided to take in a movie. When the show finished Tony had to wake Mate up so they could leave, but on the way to the Sleeping Lady Mate fell asleep again.

After Tony parked the car in the parking lot, he gave Mate a shake. "Come on man, it's time to stand tall. Kim is expecting you. I bet the girls must be worn out. Imagine having to work tonight?"

Mate got out of the car and shook himself all over to wake up. "I have to admire them for working tonight after being in the sun all day. Do you realize how lucky we are to have hooked up with those sweet ladies?"

"I'm beginning to," admitted Tony as they walked. "Ready?"

Stopping at the door, Mate answered, "I could be a bit sharper. Let's go."

They walked through the door and entered into the magic of the gospel singers just as they were in the final chorus: "It's a miracle, He can heal the sick, He can do anything. All you have to do is ask Him. Let me tell you what God can do."

Kim was behind her bar, and Melina was getting things ready for the next shift. After the singers had finished, the group began to put their equipment away. Tony and Mate sat on stools at the bar.

"Hi, sugar," Mate said to Kim.

"Hi, lover, you can't believe how tired we are," Kim told him as Melina walked over to them.

Melina greeted Tony, "Hi, hon. I'm wasted. How are you two doing?"

"I would say that the sun has done a real number on all of us. Mate and I went to a movie, and he slept through most of it."

"What did you see?" Kim asked.

Tony answered, "A slice-em-up, so you know he must have been tired."

Melina asked, "What's a slice-em-up?"

"A Japanese samari movie."

"And you call them slice-em-ups?" Kim asked in surprise.

"They have a lot of duels with razor sharp swords," Tony explained.

Mate went off to the men's room as the lights of the room came on full. The remaining customers prepared to leave as one lone cleanup man began by putting the chairs on the tables. With a small push broom he began to sweep the floor, while absentmindedly mumbling to himself. When he came across something stuck to the floor he would dig at it with a dinner knife.

Tony said to Kim, "I bet he's glad his day is almost over."

She informed him, "It isn't, he's just starting his shift. Then when the show next door finishes he cleans all of that, and that can be a mess."

"What a bummer. So when does he get off?"

"I think it's around eight. He said that when he gets home his kids have already left for school."

"He has a family?"

She continued, "That's not all."

"What do you mean?"

"Because he doesn't earn much money doing this he has another job that he does from six till ten before he comes here."

"Damn, when does the poor guy see his family?"

"On the weekends, if they're around. He's having problems with a teenaged son."

"I'm not surprised."

Kim told him, "You know, a lot of people, especially from the mainland, think we live in some kind of paradise here. But there are people here who have a rough time of it. Just like anywhere else."

Mate returned from the men's room. "I had to go throw some water on my face. Sorry, dove, I don't know why I'm feelin' so wasted. But the water helped a lot."

Melina was standing between Tony and Mate. She put her arms around both of them as she looked at Kim. "Well, dear, it looks like the best thing for all of us is to go straight home and rest up for our big day tomorrow."

Kim agreed, "That sure is the way I feel. We had a busy night, and my feet are killing me."

Tony said to both ladies, "Mate and I agree that you are two fantastic women. How you can do as much as you do is amazing."

Kim said, "What is amazing is what I can do when I have to."

Melina added, "What is also amazing is that Kim is having us all over for lunch tomorrow."

Mate said, "I guarantee I'll be rested for that."

They had all assumed they would do something that night, especially since the guys were due to leave in only another day and a half. Ironically they were all too tired, so when the ladies were ready they left.

After dropping Kim off, they drove to Melina's. While they were at the door kissing good night, Melina told Tony that she had told Bruno to see if he could move in with his mother. Tony felt his heartbeat quicken for a moment. He was deep in thought as he and Mate returned to the ship for some much needed sleep.

The following morning Tony and Mate slept through breakfast. After they were up and ready they took the car into town, stopping along the way to buy a bottle of good wine to take with them.

As they got nearer to Kim's, Mate informed Tony, "I don't know about you but I feel like takin' it real easy."

"You don't seem up to your usual ready-for-anything self lately. What's happening, man?"

"I don't know for sure, but I think I've been bit by the bug."

"And which bug would that be?"

"The lazy bug."

Tony reminded him, "Well tomorrow, at seven a.m. it's back to business as usual."

"Yeah, you're right about that; and for the next three weeks. Man, I'm going to miss Kim. We better make the most of what little time we have left."

"You know, I haven't seen Willy since I went with him to the Crosswinds."

"Why do you need to see him?"

"He said he'd like to go to the concert tonight. Actually he could still go on his own. He knows when and where it is."

"Don't worry, he might have something important to do."

As the car neared Kim's place Mate asked, "Aren't you going to pick up Melina?"

"She lives close enough to Kim to walk over, and she has a car. Sometimes it's not running though. Anyway she's probably been at Kim's for the past hour or more working with her to put this lunch together. I think we're in for a real treat."

After parking the car they went upstairs to the apartment. When Kim, with white flowers in her hair, opened the door, the aroma of pan fried trout greeted them. Tony exclaimed in amazement, "I don't believe it! Is that trout I smell?"

Melina came out of the kitchen wearing an apron, "It sure is, honey." Then she gave him a hug and a kiss hello.

After a wonderful meal they were enjoying coffee and listening to some relaxing music. Melina suggested they go to one of the parks for a walk then added, "There's usually a Hawaiian craft and art fair going on at the Kapiolani Park around this time of month."

"That is a good idea," Kim agreed. Then to Mate, "Let's do that. You don't mind do you, hon?"

"Sugar, whatever you want to do is fine with me."

Tony thought Mate was starting to sound like a married man. When they finished their coffee they left for the park.

They arrived at the park and slowly walked through it, enjoying the many works along the way. At one crafts table in particular, Tony and Melina stopped to take a closer look at the work of a silversmith. "Melina, look at these." He was pointing out a tiny pair of silver ballet shoes.

"They're gorgeous." She asked the craftsman, "May I touch them?"

"Yes, of course. Allow me." The young man took the tiny silver shoes out of the case and handed them to her.

Sensing a kind of magic she handed them to Tony and said, "Feel these. Aren't they special?"

He only held them for an instant before placing their frail silver chain around her neck. He asked the smith, "How much do you want for them?"

"Forty-five dollars," he replied.

Melina told Tony in a soft voice, "They're too expensive."

Tony insisted, "They're you, I only wish they could be gold."

She looked in a mirror. "Tony, they're beautiful. Something tells me they're going to bring me luck."

After Tony paid, the man gave him his business card. The smith was a pale complected man in his early twenties with freckles and very curly red hair. "I see your name is Bill Younge," Tony commented, then jokingly added, "You don't look like a native of Hawaii."

The smith agreed, "I'm not, but I am part Cherokee."

"Really? So am I. Your work is beautiful. Thanks a lot, my friend."

Melina was very pleased, "Yes, I love them. Thank you so much." She took one of his cards and put it in her bag. After some brief conversation they continued on. One of the places they encountered along the way was a maker of leis. Melina thought it might be a good time to give Tony one. She asked him, "Hon, I want to get one of these for you if it's okay?"

To her surprise he answered, "Sure, that would be nice."

"Great." She picked one with mainly blue flowers that would go well with his brown shirt and placed it around his neck, "It really becomes you."

Tony confessed, "You know, I wasn't into wearing a lei before. I thought they were just for tourists, but someone explained to me the symbolism of wearing flowers and how it relates to the history of the islands. Besides, I think this place is beginning to grow on me."

Melina had to confess, "Well, believe it or not, I felt the same way when I first came here. I wanted no part of anything touristy. Now, after I've been here for a while I love it all."

Kim and Mate suddenly appeared from wherever they had gone. Mate observed, "Well, look at who just got leid!" That was followed by a little laugh.

Not grasping Mate's double entendre, Tony mumbled, "What are you talking about?"

Mate came back with, "That's all right, man. Like you said before, check the spelling."

Then Tony got the joke.

Kim said with a note of surprise, "Melina, I never noticed that pendant before. It's lovely."

"Tony just bought it for me, and I love it." Putting her arm through Tony's she asked him, "Did you feel what I felt when I first held these little shoes?"

"I felt something, like a light, clear, like a happy feeling. They felt like you."

Kim told Tony, "You know, those blue flowers look so nice on you. Welcome to Hawaii."

He seemed to be resigning to it all, "Thanks."

Mate chimed in, "Hey, man, you look like one of the locals."

"Okay, don't overdo it. By the way, Mate, where are yours?"

In a soft sweet tone, Kim asked Mate, "Darling, let me pick one for you?"

"Dove, when you sound like that how can I resist?"

Tony thought to himself, *This guy is hooked.* Then he said, "There's not a lot of time left. Let's find a place to go for a snack?" Luckily they found something to eat there at the park.

THE CONCERT

Sometime later they arrived at the art academy with enough time to get seats in the front row. The concert was being held in a square courtyard surrounded by the building. Chairs were set up in rows on the grass and facing an open corridor that was raised about three feet above the ground. Midway along the corridor a section extended out enough to act as a stage.

Not long after they arrived, Mate recognized someone and told Tony, "Hey, look who's here."

Turning to look back at the people still arriving, Tony saw Willy with Mary, the singer they met at the Crosswinds. He motioned them to two empty seats behind him. After they had seated themselves Tony introduced everyone. He said to Willy, "This is great. I was afraid you were going to miss this."

Willy told him, "The whole thing is far out, matey. Mary is a fan of Ravi Shankar too."

Then Mary added, "And I have a friend who goes to his school in Bombay."

Tony agreed, "That is far out." He turned to Melina and said, "This is going to be so fine."

She said to him, "It sounds like your world is growing smaller. I'm so glad we all came. It seems this is going to be a special moment for all of us." They sat quietly and just held hands as they waited.

When the lights were adjusted to concentrate everyone's attention to the stage the audience became quiet. In the middle of where the musicians were to sit was a very small incense holder with some burning incense sticks. Since this form of music was spiritual in nature the rising smoke was meant to be symbolic of prayer rising to heaven. Ravi Shankar was the first to arrive with his sitar, followed by his tablaist Alla Rakha, and lastly, the accompanying tamboura player. After sitting near one another on the stage they greeted the audience. Mr. Shankar first tuned the tamboura then his sitar. Then Mr. Rakha tuned his drums to the sitar. Being both a gifted musician and a teacher, Mr. Shankar gave a brief demonstration of the instruments followed by a description of the music and then the pieces they were about to play. Each piece had either a masculine or feminine nature and was to be played at specific periods of the day or night.

The music began with the hypnotic droning sound of the four stringed tamboura. It established both a foundation and an ethereal atmosphere. The sitar began exploring the mood and personality of the piece as if it was coming out of a deep sleep. Tony closed his eyes and became aware of the influence of the tonal subtleties. Slowly he became less concerned with all else around him. He seemed to go into another level of awareness, like a soul floating freely within its own consciousness.

As the sitarist developed the character of the piece, it seemed to surround the audience in a mist of peace and serenity. When it became more melodic and rhythmic, Tony imagined himself moving about in a slow sensual dance. Still holding Melina's hand he imagined her joining him. The tablas entered emphasizing the rhythm and enhanced the mood and personality by introducing a second voice, that of the drums. As the rhythm increased in tempo so did the expression of the dance in Tony's mind. Melina was having a similar experience. This awareness continued throughout the piece becoming more profound and ever uplifting. Eventually the exchange between the sitar and tablas became akin to that of two lovers during love play.

In both their imaginations Tony and Melina became like two birds darting to and fro, then stopping, then swirling, becoming as one, and then separating. They soared high into the sky, becoming again as one, then dove down toward the sea, touching the water, and becoming two again. The exchange between the two instruments triggered a playful teasing between the two imaginary birds that flew up and down in a spiral around each other.

In Tony and Melina's imagination they transformed back into themselves dancing in the air. At times their dance became more dignified as the two lovers courted one another. As the music went, so flowed their imaginations. There was a point when the two forces of male and female went off into ecstasy to remain for some time exploring the many facets of each other. Then another spiral led to a climactic crescendo. The two forces melted into a state of rest and tranquility.

After a moment of quiet, the audience burst into applause for a stunning performance. Sitting motionless, Tony and Melina were overwhelmed. Near the end of the applause they began clapping out of a sense of duty but by then the others were standing. They stayed seated and just resumed holding hands.

Melina asked the others, "Was that as incredible for you as it was for me?"

Willy answered as he conferred with the others, "It exceeded any possible expectation." Finally the applause ended.

During the next few minutes the musicians retuned to their instruments, then Mr. Shankar announced the next piece. The concert went on in this way for another two hours. At the end Tony and his friends could only consider retiring for the night.

After the concert Mary took Willy back to the ship in the station wagon while Tony drove the others to Kim's apartment.

Inside the apartment Kim prepared a pot of chamomile tea for everyone. She asked Mate and Tony, "What time do you two have to get back to the ship in the morning?"

Tony answered, "We start work at seven in the morning." He hesitated, "So sometime tonight would probably be best."

Mate added to that, "But we still have some time before we have to leave, right?"

"I sure hope so," Kim said as she gave them their tea.

Melina took two cups handing one to Tony, "And I'm returning the car for you so that's taken care of."

"That's right, so everything's just groovy," reiterated Mate.

Tony had settled onto the couch with Melina. He didn't know why but he felt apprehensive about staying the night; and he knew Mate wanted to.

After Mate and Kim disappeared into her bedroom, Tony and Melina slowly dissolved into one another, kissing and caressing; tenderly at first then gradually becoming more passionate. The elements of time and place were quickly forgotten.

They carefully removed each other's clothing while kissing and caressing. Even so she sensed that something was holding him back. With his eyes closed for so long he seemed to slip into a dream state, when he imagined Maureen's voice from his nightmare, *'Why didn't you help me?'* He became confused and felt his passion begin to wilt and leave him as the inevitable drew nearer. When Melina's beauty lay before him in all its glory, Tony was not ready for the ultimate embrace. When she pulled him to her with a demure, "Oh, Tony," he couldn't understand what was happening to him.

When he didn't attempt to enter her she whispered to him, "What's wrong, hon?"

He thought to himself, *Oh god. Not now,* then whispered to her, "I don't know. I'm sorry, but I don't know." But he knew.

Instead of Melina, he had visualized Maureen lying there waiting for him. He closed his eyes to stop the image. Instead, he saw Maureen tied to the doctor's table. He was so overwhelmed with guilt and doubt that his naked body became cold and unresponsive.

In a sympathetic voice Melina whispered, "It's okay hon, maybe you're just tired." But she couldn't help wonder if it might have been something about her that put him off. She had offered him her greatest gift; her entire self. Having that rejected was causing her to feel somehow at fault.

"Maybe you're right," he lied. He felt so embarrassed and so inadequate. This would have been their first time, but now? As they both put on their underclothes Tony tried to make light of the situation, but she could tell he was upset with himself.

She tried to comfort him, "Really hon, it's not that bad." She reached for a folded blanket at the end of the couch. "Here, put this over us. It seems to be getting a little chilly."

"Thanks. You're so nice and I'm so stupid."

"Shh," she said, placing a gentle finger on his lips. They laid quietly on the deep couch with the blanket over them. With the pillows removed there was quite a bit of room. Since they were very tired it wasn't long before they drifted off to sleep, each thinking their own thoughts.

At five a.m. the sound of an alarm clock came through the bedroom door like the unwelcome siren of a police car. After a few moments, the door was opened by Mate, wearing only a towel. He was feeling pretty good, in contrast to Tony who could have done with a lot more sleep. He called to Tony, "Hey, brother. It's time for us to get movin'."

With great effort Tony responded, "Wow, man. What's the time?"

"It's about ten past five."

"What'll happen if we're late?"

"Don't worry, man, we'll make it."

"Okay, I'm getting up." Then to an awake but also very sleepy Melina, he kissed her on the eyes then the tip of her nose, her chin, and finally her lips. "I have to start getting ready to go. I think I know what happened to me last night. I'll tell you as much as I can on the way back to the ship."

Then fully awake she said, "It's okay hon, really."

"I have to tell you."

"All right, but we need to hurry."

The next hour was spent washing and dressing. Kim put together some food for the guys to eat in the car. Before they knew it they were in the car and on their way. So Tony could talk to Melina he asked Mate to drive. In the backseat while finishing his snack, Tony told her about the nightmare he had of Maureen three days before and how he was haunted by it last night. "I hope this helps you to understand what happened to me. What worries me now is how to keep it from happening again."

She kissed him on the cheek, "Oh Tony, I do understand. The odd thing is that I was afraid that it was me."

"What do you mean?"

"You know, that there was something about me that you didn't like. Or because I'm part Negro."

Very touched by her words, he was saddened by her insecurity. He saw things differently. "You're a variation on a theme. And you're lucky because you look like you have a great tan."

"I don't mean the outside, I mean the inside."

"Inside you're beautiful. As far as color goes we're all just a variation. Besides I wouldn't care if you were green." As he poked at her he said, "Actually a bit of green here and there might be nice, like frosting on a cake."

She grabbed his finger and said with a laugh, "You're tickling me."

He had a sudden urge to make love to her, but he became motionless. He hugged her and said softly, "It's my problem, and I'll have to work it out somehow."

Meanwhile Mate and Kim had been in quiet contemplation in the front seat. It was six thirty when their car pulled up to where the ship was tied. Mate was the first to get out followed by Tony and Melina as she got behind the wheel. Tony asked her, "What are you going to be doing Monday three weeks from now?"

"Why, are you asking me for a date?"

"I might be."

"You might be?"

"I am."

"I think I'm going to be sitting in my car parked right about here."

"That's great because I'm going to need a ride to your place."

An impatient Mate tried to pull him toward the ship, "Come on, man. We've got just enough time to change for work."

Tony gave Melina one long kiss goodbye, then he ran up the gangplank behind Mate. They both waved as they disappeared below.

There were similar scenes being acted out as other cars had brought men back to the ship at the last minute, some already dressed in their duty clothes. Sitting in their car waiting for the ship to leave, Kim said to Melina, "The next three weeks are going to go by really slow."

"They sure are, hon."

"You know, I try to be careful with the guys from the ships, but this time I think it's happened."

"You mean love."

"I mean serious love. Marriage, babies, the whole works."

"But it's only been a week, girl."

"What about you?" Kim asked.

"I don't know. I think he's really special, but I need to know someone for a long time before I start thinking about marriage. What about your parents? Won't they flip out if you marry a black man?"

"I don't know, but he's such a sweet guy they're bound to like him."

"Don't be too sure, and don't be so hasty. Having fun with somebody is one thing, but living with somebody for the rest of your life is something else again."

"I know you're right, but I can't seem to think straight."

"Look, dear, just give it some time. And introduce him to your parents as a friend at first. It can't do any harm."

"You're right. Maybe a three week break will be a good thing."

Chapter 6

BACK TO IT

Mate and Tony changed and reported to the bosun's locker just in time. "Mr. Lewis, you're no longer with us. You're to report to the chart room for quartermaster surveyor duties."

"Thanks, chief. See you later, Mate." Tony quickly made his way to the forward section of the ship where he went up a ladder.

The chart room was above the main deck and just beneath the bridge. He entered through the hatch on the starboard side and was greeted by two junior officers dressed in tan uniforms, "Good morning. Mr. Lewis?"

"Yes sir, good morning."

"I'm Philip Brown," as he extended his hand, "just call me Phil."

As Tony shook his hand, he said, "Pleased to meet you, sir. Sorry I'm late but I reported to the bosun's locker for work."

The other officer replied, "That's all right. We weren't sure if you knew about the change. Anyway my name is Thomas Wait." He extended his hand. "You may call me Tom."

"Pleased to meet you, sir."

Ensign Brown informed him, "From today we'll work from eight till five. You have also been assigned to work with Dr. Christian. Tomorrow morning you will report to the sick-bay at eight o'clock for training with the doctor. You'll be back with us after lunch. You'll be with the doctor one hour each morning and whenever he needs your help. This morning we'll be training you in the use of the depth recording equipment and you'll be with us the remainder of today."

"Yes, sir. What time do we sail, sir?"

"In about ten minutes. Is someone seeing you off?"

"Yes, sir."

The ensign told him with a smile, "Well, in that case I think you can take a break until we're under way. There's not much we can do until then anyway. Is that all right with you, Tom?"

"It's quite all right with me."

"Thank you, sir, sir," he said as he looked at each of them in turn then exited through the door way. He thought to himself, *Oh brother, what a change from the deck force.*

Because the stern of the ship was nearest to the parked cars, Tony made his way to the rear of the ship then went up to a platform that was just above the stern; there he could stay out of the way. When Melina saw him she and Kim left the car and went near to the ship. By then the lines from the ship to the dock had been cast off and a small tugboat was pulling the *Lady* away from the dock. The pilot boat *Gypsy* was waiting to lead the *Lady* to just beyond the docks where she would be left to head out into open waters.

Mate was part of the deck crew and was busy at work on the deck securing lines. Once again Tony was the only one with nothing to do during these moments. Once Mate had done with the lines he stood at the stern just below Tony as they waved farewell to the ladies. The women watched as the ship grew smaller and smaller until the men were no longer discernible. Likewise the men were watching the women grow fainter until a harsh voice reminded them of other things.

"Hey! Mate, you've got work to do," growled the bosun.

"Okay, chief." He quickly ducked into the bosun's locker.

"I guess I'd better get movin' too," Tony said to himself then returned to the chart room.

Once the *Lady* was past the marking buoy she was again on the open sea. Even before that the men were aware of the familiar rhythmic up and down, and side to side motion of the ship. After spending some time on land there were always a few men who took a little longer than others to get back their sea legs. So a few would usually experience a short period of motion sickness. Once they became accustomed to it the motion became almost soothing.

Back in the chart room Ensign Wait was teaching Tony the use of the depth recording sonar equipment and how he was to relay that information to the two officers. Using sound bouncing off the ocean floor the depth recorder continuously printed out a graph that actually formed a profile image of the ocean floor. Tony was to relay the depth readings to them. In turn they were to apply the data to their map-like charts. These would eventually be used to form navigation maps and topographical maps of the ocean floor. The two ensigns were also to take water samples from different depths. The work promised to be interesting, and Tony found the two junior officers pleasant to work with.

From the morning coffee break until the late afternoon, Chuck was assigned to repaint the launch given to the ship by the Navy at Pearl. It was to replace the one damaged by the storm. Along with other maintenance duties Pete was to oversee the painting. Since the entire surface of the launch was navy gray they needed to change it to white, the color of the *Lady*, and to paint the name *Lady Explorer* on its stern. It needed an overall light sanding by hand before painting. The job was expected to take about five days.

After lunch Chuck was still sanding the outside of the hull with about a third of that done. The mid-February sun had been shining through a clear atmosphere so he was a bit dehydrated and sweaty. There was a thin layer of gray lead-based paint dust on his skin and hair. Pete had been too busy to check on Chuck's progress before lunch.

Pete eventually appeared and asked, "Chuck, how's it going?"

"Okay, except I sure am thirsty."

"Didn't I give you a dust mask to wear?"

"No."

"I guess I forgot. You need a mask, that paint is loaded with lead."

"Lead?"

"Yeah, I'll fetch you a jug of water and a mask. I'll be right back." Looking at the work, he asked, "Have you done the other side?"

"Just what you see."

"Hmmm, that's not much."

"This is hard to do with these overlapping planks."

"You've got to get the shine off of everything so the new shit will stick to it."

"I'm doin' the best I can, Pete. I'm really dried out. Can I get some water?"

"Just hang on, I said I'd get it. We might be heading into some weather in a day or two so you've got to get movin' on this."

"How about some help?"

"I think the chief's thinkin' of sendin' Bill up here tomorrow."

"Bill? That guy is useless."

"That's not for you to say, and stop your whining." Pete disappeared down the ladder near the bosun's locker. After about fifteen minutes he reappeared with a large metal paint bucket containing a dust mask, a jug of water, a mug, and some more sand paper. "Here, try this, it might work better. The paper you've got is too coarse."

Chuck poured himself a mug full of water, drank it, poured another, and drank that. He dampened a rag to wipe his face and put on the mask.

Pete pressured him, "Come on, Chuck, try the paper I just gave you."

"Okay, just a minute." He folded the paper and tried it. "Hey, this is totally different, a lot better." Then with a frown he asked, "Why didn't you give me this paper before?"

Pete didn't answer. He turned the empty bucket upside down, sat on it, and lit a cigarette. He watched from behind as Chuck worked. He didn't say anything at first, he just watched Chuck move back and forth as he put all of his energy into his sanding.

When Chuck realized that he was being stared at he got an uncomfortable feeling and asked, "Is something wrong?"

"No, you're doing just fine. Tell me something." Chuck just kept working as Pete continued, "Did you meet any girls in Hawaii?"

"Not really."

"Why not?"

"I don't know. It just didn't happen, I guess."

"Did you spend a lot of time with Rob?"

"Yeah, so?"

Pete accentuated his next question, "Do you have a thing for older guys?"

"He's my best friend. What do you mean a thing?"

Pete went closer to the boat and pretended to be checking over Chuck's work, "You know, Chucky, if you play your cards right you could have an easier time of it on this cruise."

"I don't understand. You're not making any sense."

"I recommended you for this job. When the chief was trying to decide on someone for it I suggested you because you're young and have a lot of . . ," he lingered over the words as his eyes went down Chuck's body, "unspent energy."

Not seeing Pete's look, Chuck said, "Well, thanks for the recommendation."

Surprised, Pete said, "You really don't get it."

Suddenly the bosun's head appeared above the ladder, "Pete! I've been looking all over for you. I need your help below in the engine room, pronto."

"Aye, aye, chief." Then back to Chuck, he quipped, "Think about it kid." He disappeared down the ladder leaving a puzzled Chuck.

At the end of the day's work Tony, Mate, Chuck, Rob, and Willy were sitting together for dinner in the crew's mess. They were discussing their first day back at sea and all wished they were still in Hawaii. No one had any real complaints except Chuck, who said that Pete had been acting odd and bitchy with him after lunch. He told them how Pete would sit behind him and just watch.

Mate said to Chuck, "You know what's wrong with that asshole, don't you?"

"I'm not sure."

"He's after your butt, man."

"So?"

Willy told Chuck, "Literally, he means Pete is into boys' butts."

Chuck's face turned red, "No shit. I must be stupid. That's why he was talking that crap to me."

Rob asked him, "What crap was he talking to you, Chuck?"

"Stuff like, why I hadn't met any girls and asking if I had a thing for older men. He said if I played my cards right I could have an easy time of it."

"That bastard!" blurted out Rob.

Tony added, "That jerk is a first class creep."

Mate said, "I'm standing watch at the helm this time out, so I can't be much help."

Rob told Chuck, "You're just going to have to stand up to him. If he gives you more hassle than you can handle go to the skipper. I don't think the bosun's going to be any help."

Mate reassured him, "You've got the four of us to back you up."

Willy said, "I don't think anybody on this ship really likes him. I think the bosun just finds him useful."

"Thanks a lot, guys. I think it's going to be okay, now that I know what he's up to."

That night some of the crew turned in early since they hadn't had enough sleep the night before. Tony was one of those, but before retiring he intended to go to his favorite spot at the bow. To aid the vision of the helmsman at night there were no lights from the bridge forward to the bow. They steered by the compass while another crewman stood watch keeping a sharp eye out for anything that might appear ahead. They were also aided by radar.

After changing into dark clothing Tony made his way to the bow where he loved to sit with his feet hanging over the edge. As the bow cut through the water like a giant knife, the displaced water shot up and out. Often the water would take on the appearance of sparks shooting back due to the phosphorescent sea creatures in the water. The sky was filled with a blanket of stars. The thrill of these two spectacles combined with the sensation of sitting on the bow's edge would give him goose bumps and his imagination would run rampant. He could be sitting on the edge of the world. He wondered, if he fell would it be into a dark abyss, or would he fly up into a sky with endless new worlds to explore? He passed many nights in this way.

After breakfast the following day Tony reported to the sick-bay to begin his duties with the ship's doctor. "Good morning, sir. I'm Antony Lewis."

The doctor seemed to be in his early thirties, had blond hair, and was thin like Tony. "Oh yes, Mr. Lewis. Pleased to meet you. I'm Dr. Christian. John Christian."

"How do you do, sir?"

"Quite well, thank you. I read your application and noticed that you have done a bit of traveling."

"Yes sir, throughout the states, Thule, Greenland, and Europe. I also worked in a factory in West Berlin."

"Really? That's fascinating. This is my first time away from the mainland. I would love to be able to travel myself. You must tell me more about your experiences."

"Yes sir, I'd love to."

"I think you'll find this fairly easy and I hope not too boring. Should there be a need for my services you'll act as my assistant. Each day after today you will familiarize yourself with the location of everything in this room, then seeing to it that every item is clean, neatly kept, and ready for use."

"Yes, sir."

"Now as you can see I have a fair collection of medically related books. Feel free to look through them."

"Oh, thank you sir. There are a couple of areas I would like to look into."

"Oh really, what might they be?"

"Male sexual dysfunction is one."

"Not something we're likely to encounter at sea, but I do have a book that thoroughly covers both male and female sexuality and sexology, if you need some insight into the psychological aspects of the problem."

"That sounds like the right book."

"And what is the other area of interest?"

"Weight, I need to gain some weight."

"Now there's an area where I could use some help as well. The best way to start helping you though is with a thorough physical examination to determine why your weight is as it is."

"I've never been much of an eater."

"I see. Well, all that aside, the first priority you have before you as my assistant is to make sure you understand the use of first aid." The doctor took a small book titled *First Aid Manual* from his desk. He motioned to a chair near the bookcase, "You can sit there if you like. Study this book thoroughly. After the morning coffee break we will go over the methods to be used. Then after lunch you'll report back to the chart room."

"Thank you, sir." He sat in the chair and quietly studied the manual. Since he had learned first aid while in the military sometime ago, he used the manual to refresh his memory.

After the break, Dr. Christian tested Tony's knowledge of first aid and gave him a complete physical as well. The doctor was very pleased with the results and was confident that Tony would do well as his assistant in an emergency.

Later that night there was a poker game going on in the crew's mess. Tony watched for a while and was tempted to play, but he remembered an old adage that went: 'If you can't afford to lose then don't play.' Tony always seemed to be short of money for some reason. Probably because he never thought about it until he really needed it for something. But Mate won a hundred and twenty dollars before he quit playing.

Tony went back to his quarters thinking that he might write a letter to Maureen then decided to wait a while longer. The area was so small there was no room for a chair, only the two double bunks and four narrow lockers. He ended up in his upper bunk hoping to read himself to sleep.

An electrician named George occupied the bunk below Tony. George seemed to spend every evening in his bunk reading girly magazines and paperback books. He was also a devout smoker of cigarettes and little cigars. That combined with George's occasional bout of gas and one could understand Tony's difficulty in falling asleep. The ventilation system was circa 1940 when functioning. If he tried to sit up in his bunk in order to read he would come into contact with the plumbing, including steam pipes, suspended above him. So the only function his bunk could serve was as a place to sleep. If Tony lay on his side trying to read, he would become uncomfortable, try to sit up, bang his head against a hot pipe, cuss, lay on his other side, become uncomfortable again, and so on. Meanwhile, in the bunk below him, George was in hog heaven. When Tony confronted George during the previous month's run George insisted that he had a right to smoke until ten p.m. Afterwards it would take an hour for the air to clear and Tony to fall asleep.

The next morning in the mess Mate sat down to breakfast with Tony and asked him, "Hey, my friend, what's with those red scratches on your forehead?"

"The pipes."

"The pipes?"

Willy, who was already sitting there began to sing an Irish favorite, "The pipes, the pipes are calling . . ."

"You know, above my bunk."

Willy continued, "Oh Danny boy, from glen to glen . . ."

"Oh yeah," Mate recalled, "you got a bum deal on that bunk,".

"Thanks, Willy. That's a great song, but the situation with my bunk is rotten."

Willy suggested, "Maybe you can switch with someone."

"Who would want that setup?"

"Good question," Mate agreed.

Willy added, "I've got an idea, remember the cook who got badly scalded in the storm?"

"Yeah, he ended up in the burn unit at the hospital at Pearl."

Willy continued, "And they put him up in a barracks near the hospital for at least a month so he can heal."

Mate chimed in, "Brother, you are saved."

Willy added, "And I think he had a bottom bunk."

Tony perked up, "You just made my day. Who do I talk to?"

"Try the purser, I think that's his department."

"Thanks a lot, Willy."

"Well, at least for this run. You may have to give it up for the next one though."

Little by little, Tony's situation on board was improving.

Later that day Tony spoke with the purser who agreed to the switch until the cook would rejoin the ship in a month. So after work he made the change, locker and all.

During the first night he discovered that the kitchen workers got up at four a.m. so they could have breakfast ready by six. Even so having a bottom bunk and breathable air was a blessing.

Toward the end of the first week Tony had completed all of the chores the doctor had given him. While looking through the doctor's collection of textbooks he came across one on sexology. He looked through it until he found a section on male disorders and there he read: "If a man is experiencing emotional stress and/or intimidation or pressure from his sex partner sexual dysfunction more commonly in the form of *erectile dysfunction* may occur. For this problem counseling is recommended."

Tony thought to himself, *In other words, he can't rise to the occasion.* Then out loud, "Well, at least I know why. The next question is how to fix it."

The doctor had just walked in, "I beg your pardon?"

"Sorry sir, I was talking to myself."

"I think I heard that something needs to be fixed. I hope you haven't broken anything."

"Oh, no sir, it's nothing like that. Maybe you can help me figure something out."

"I will be happy to try."

Tony described the situation with Maureen, the nightmare about the abortion, then his problem his last night with Melina.

Dr. Christian went right to the heart of the problem.

"It's not that difficult to see what you are doing. Basically you are holding yourself responsible for something that you are not. To put it another way, what happened to your friend in San Francisco was not caused by you."

"But you see, sir, I feel that if I hadn't left her this jerk wouldn't have had the opportunity to do her the way he did."

"Not necessarily."

Tony was puzzled, "What do you mean, sir?"

"He did her, as you put it, the way he did because of his character. If you had never left he still could have taken advantage of her as he did. Perhaps in another environment but similar circumstances under the guise of two friends working together to help one another combined with too much drinking."

"I can see how that could happen."

"As for your leaving her, that was something you had both agreed to. If you were still there would you be keeping her constant company?"

"No. In fact we lived in different parts of the city. Sometimes she would stay with me and sometimes I would stay with her. But there were plenty of times when she wanted to be in her own space and just do her own thing."

"Can you see now how you actually have no responsibility in this matter?"

"I think so."

"And whatever she decides to do about the pregnancy is entirely her decision that you will have to accept."

"Yes, it sure looks that way now."

The doctor asked, "So how does all this make you feel now?"

"Like a ton of mud had just been lifted off me. It's been on my mind almost all of the time."

"With the feeling of guilt out of the way your problem will have vanished into the air like so much smoke."

"I hope you're right. If I could talk to Maureen in person . . ."

"Look at the time. You need to return to the chart room."

"Yes sir, thanks a lot for your help Dr. Christian."

Later during dinner in the crew's mess, Chuck was relating another encounter with Pete. A few days after the work began; Chuck was putting the final touches to the launch when Pete appeared.

Chuck said, "He came over to me as I was finishing up and started telling me what a great job I had done and how clever he thought I was, and would I like to join him for some rum and cola he had stashed to celebrate. I told him I wasn't interested in his rum or him and that if he didn't stop trying to do his thing with me that I was going to go to the skipper."

"Good for you. What did he have to say to that?" Willy asked.

"He said to me, 'Why I don't know what you mean,' and hasn't bothered me anymore."

"You just have to stand up to him. Bullies are like that."

"Thanks for your advice, guys."

They gave him an approving nod. "You'll do all right, kid."

After dinner there was a movie in the foc'sle at the bow. As many of the crew as could fit in the confined space were there, including Chuck and Pete. But Pete acted as though Chuck was invisible. It seemed that the matter between them was closed.

By the middle of the second week out Tony had settled into the routine of his two jobs. After finishing work late one afternoon he went up to the deck above the chart room to enjoy a cigarette. He was leaning on a railing beside the radio room that was just behind the bridge, and watching the activity of some whales far in the distance. Sparks, the radio operator, joined him for a bit of fresh air just upwind of the cigarette. Sparks was a pleasant person and the sort who wouldn't mind sitting alone in a tiny room for hours at a time day after day. Tony asked, "How long have you been with the *Lady*, Sparks?"

"Ever since the Navy gave her to Coast & Geodetic Survey, back in '62."

"So you were with her when she went to the Indian Ocean."

"That's right, The International Indian Ocean Expedition of 1964." He looked as though he was transported to another time, "It was a fabulous cruise."

"I'll bet."

"I was still pretty bummed out over John F. Kennedy's assassination so the Indian Ocean did much to quiet my feelings and just accept the things I have no control over."

"How does that work?"

"I don't know, determination I guess. But it still pisses me off when I think about it."

"Yeah, I'm hip."

"Did you know Kennedy skippered a PT boat in the last war?"

"He did?"

"PT is for pursuit/torpedo. After Pearl got hit by the Japs the *Lady* was converted to service torpedo boats instead of seaplanes. In 1942, just before the Japanese took the Philippines, General MacArthur was evacuated from Guadalcanal by a group of four PT boats?"

"No kidding? I never knew that."

"They were the fastest boats afloat. I've always wondered if the *Lady* serviced Kennedy's boat. That information would have been in the ship's diary, you know, but the skipper would have entered the boat only by its number: PT 109."

"That would be far out. Listen, Sparks, I just remembered something you'll appreciate. About two months after President Kennedy was murdered I was in East Berlin to visit the mother of two of my friends. I rode the S-Bahn, that's the rail system, through the city to the fringe area where she lived. The train was full of students in their late teens. They seemed like a fairly happy carefree group much like me at the time. In that moment I felt I could easily have been one of them. I found the home of my friend's mother and was met by a family friend named Klaus. Late that night while we rode the train back to Check Point Charley, Klaus told me that he as well as many of the East Berliners, was greatly saddened by the death of John F. Kennedy. Remember his visit to West Berlin not long before that when he said that like all free men of the world, he was a Berliner?"

"That's right, and the Berliners went wild."

"According to my friend in East Berlin they went wild there too."

Sparks said, "Thank you so much for that story. He was a good man. Now then, what do you know about the *Lady*?"

"Only that she got shot up during the attack on Pearl Harbor."

"She has a history to be proud of." And as Sparks told Tony the story of the *Lady Explorer*'s past he could tell that Sparks was proud to be a part of her. Tony stood in awe of his many revelations. Sparks finished with, "I'll probably stay with her until they kick me off."

Tony was awestruck, "So they renamed her *Lady X*. Incredible. I've got to see that bell." They had both forgotten about the time. "Hey, I'd better make it to the mess or I'll miss chow."

Sparks told him, "I'll be in the radio shack. One of the kitchen crew will bring my dinner."

"I'll see you later. Thanks for telling me about the *Lady*."

"Enjoy your dinner."

A couple of days passed. The ship was near the end of a southern sweep and not far from the Hawaiian Islands. Sparks received word that a light sea plane would be flying to the *Lady* to deliver a sack of mail the following morning. Any outgoing mail would be picked up at that time. That night the ship was quiet as most of the crew were busy writing letters.

The next day the *Lady* reached the rendezvous place at the appointed time. She stood motionless as she awaited the plane's arrival. When it came into view the *Lady*'s crew let out a loud "Hooray!" She sent out the launch that Chuck had prepared, to meet the plane. The old launch looked like new. They exchanged mailbags, and somehow a couple of cases of beer and cigarettes were included with the incoming mail. They were a surprise gift from the skipper. Along with word of the mail pickup was news that he had just become a grandfather.

At the end of the day's work there was a mail call. Mate had a letter from home and one from Kim. Tony had one from Maureen and one from Melina. Down in the crew's mess for dinner, Tony was sitting at a table with his unopened letters in front of him. Not knowing which to open first he wondered if either could affect his life from then on.

Mate placed his tray of food opposite Tony, sat down, and asked him, "Aren't you going to open your mail?"

"Yeah, eventually."

"What's the matter?"

"I'm not sure. Maybe I'm afraid of bad news."

"Bad news, there could be good news too, you know?"

"It's just that having them both in front of me like this . . . makes me feel like I'm about to chose one over the other."

"Haven't you already?"

Tony didn't want to accept that, as what he had done. Then as if asking himself, "Have I done that? Or is this just the way things have gone? I'm starting to feel guilty again. I don't know what to do."

Mate encouraged him, "Come on, man, open the letters. I'll help you. Take the one you've known the longest and open hers first. Sound fair?"

"Sounds fair." So he opened the one from Maureen first.

"You forgot to smell it," Mate reminded him.

"Yeah, okay." He sniffed it and carefully considered the aroma. "Not the usual pink. It smells more like blue flowers."

"Blue? How can you tell the color?"

"Here, you try it then." He held it near Mate's nose.

With a surprised look on his face, "You're right. It does smell like blue flowers."

A crewman sitting near by gave them an odd look.

In the letter Maureen told him that she was against having an abortion and that she had decided to have the baby adopted. She knew a young couple that would be interested. She said she wasn't as distraught as she was in the beginning and had accepted the situation. She understood his need to travel and had always accepted it. She said that she had a very strong premonition that he would be gone much longer than he thought and only hoped that he wouldn't forget her by the time he returned.

When he finished her letter he got up from the table without a word and stepped outside. He went to the railing and watched what was left of the setting sun. He had the sad feeling that something was ending. "I'll never forget you." He lit a cigarette and paced restlessly about until he finished it.

When Tony returned to the crew's mess Mate had finished eating and was waiting for him. "Are you okay, brother?"

Tony sat in his chair. "Yeah, I'm okay." He contemplated the remaining letter for a moment then picked it up.

"Don't forget to smell it," Mate again reminded him.

He peered up at Mate as if looking at him over imaginary glasses. He gave it a sniff. "Hey, this smells of red flowers."

"Man, what are you talkin' about? Let me smell that." Tony handed it to him. He sniffed it. Then in disbelief, "Now how do you get red flowers from this?"

"Just kidding, but it does smell mighty nice, you'll have to admit that. Now, if you don't mind I'd like to read this in the privacy of my very own world."

Undeterred, Mate answered, "I'll grab some dessert."

While he was gone Tony read Melina's letter. She basically told him how much she loved being with him and enjoyed the things they had done together, especially the concert. She also told him that Bruno had moved in with his mother. She had a surprise for him and was counting the days till his return.

Mate returned with his dessert and one for Tony. "Good news?"

"There's no bad news. Bruno is finally out of her place."

"Well, isn't that good news?"

"Yeah, pretty good. Thanks for the dessert."

"You're welcome. So is that it?"

"Pretty much, nothing earth shaking. Oh, I forgot, she's counting the days till my return."

"That sounds pretty good to me."

"I'm just feeling pessimistic, I don't know why. How was your letter from Kim?"

"She's crazy about me, what else?"

"Plenty else, I'll bet."

"Maybe, I'm about ready."

"I wish you all the best. You make a great couple."

"Actually, I'm a little scarred."

"Well, you've only known her six days."

"Yeah, I know, but that's not what I mean. What if her parents don't like me?"

"There's always that possibility with anybody. You just have to grit your teeth and press on."

"Yeah, I guess you're right."

"Anyway man, give it some time." He wondered why it was always easier to give advice than to know what to do for yourself.

"Living the way we are now, time seems all screwed up. Say, later on do you want to join me and some of the guys for a game of poker?"

"No thanks, it's not my scene. Sparks has a portable shortwave radio I can borrow. I'm going to take it up to the flying bridge and see if I can pick up some music from Asia."

"I can dig it."

"I'm just going to lie there and contemplate the stars until it gets too cold."

"You better tie your leg to something."

"Why is that?"

"If you start to levitate I wouldn't want you to get blown out to sea."

"What if it's toward Honolulu?"

"Hey man, if that happens I'll be right behind you."

They both had a good laugh at that.

One night during the last week out Willy was just finishing a shift of steering the ship while standing at the helm. When he stepped outside the bridge he heard what sounded like Chinese music coming from the flying bridge. He climbed the ladder to the open area above him. On the deck he saw Tony lying on his back with arms and legs out stretched, with a radio near his head. In the dim light Tony looked as though he was unconscious. Willy called out to him, "Hey! Tony!"

As if coming out of a dream Tony lifted his head to see who was calling him. "Yeah?"

Now beside him Willy asked, "Are you all right?"

"Willy! It's you. Yeah, I'm fine. I lie like this to become totally relaxed." He rolled over onto his right side propping his head on his right palm.

Willy sat cross-legged opposite him, "I was scared you were a goner."

"You know I was thinking about something you must have thought about a lot."

"What's that, my friend?"

"We float around out here for three weeks, with not much to do at night but think about it all. Then for one week we cram as much of life as we can into those seven days."

"You're right, I have given that a lot of thought. We end up over compensating in that one week."

Tony asked him, "What are we learning from this, Willy?"

"Well, we definitely get a different perspective on time. I think the most important thing I've learned is that one has to be careful not to get into a situation too easily because of a shortage of time."

"That makes sense. So how do you deal with it?"

"Time can be a very tricky factor if you feel you don't have enough. It just depends on how you look at it."

"And how is that?"

"If you don't think you have enough time and you tend to make bad decisions, try saying to yourself that you have more than enough time then just wait it out. Eventually you'll make the right decision. Otherwise you'll almost always make a mistake you'll regret later."

"I can sure relate to that. Nearly every time I've made quick decisions about important things they turned out badly."

"Exactly, is that what's going on with you now?" asked Willy.

"Yes, a bit. But it looks like it's happening big time with Mate."

"When women are involved it's so hard for men to be objective and patient. Waiting is probably the toughest thing of all."

"For a lot of us," Tony admitted.

"For all of us," Willy replied.

"It won't be long now before we're back on our little island in the sun. Just the thought gives me a restless feeling."

Willy admitted, "I know what you mean. Even though I've done this 'returning to land' number a thousand times I still get a bit nervous just before I arrive."

"It sounds a bit like stage fright."

They became quiet as each one entered into his own thoughts, and the Chinese music began to fade into the night.

Chapter 7

THE DANCE

Tony was suddenly awakened by the blaring sound of the fire alarm attached to the bulkhead of his quarters. It was five seventeen a.m. when he leapt out of his bunk and into his clothes. He made his way as fast as he could to his assigned area while passing or bumping into other crewmen doing the same. He quickly arrived at the sick-bay just after the doctor had. Over the intercom came a request, "This is the bridge, sick-bay report."

"Bridge, this is the doctor speaking. The sick-bay is in good order with all equipment functional, sir."

"Sick-bay stand by . . . . Bridge out."

Tony asked the doctor, "Do you think there's a fire?"

"I don't know, but I haven't smelled any smoke. Have you?"

"No sir."

After about five minutes there was an all-clear signal over the ship's intercoms. "This is your captain speaking. This has been a drill."

The doctor commented, "Thank God for that."

The message continued, "Thank you for a job well done. As you may recall from our last safety drill I said we would have the next drill when you least expect it. I'm sure you can appreciate my helping you to get an early start for our arrival at Honolulu this morning. Again, I thank you. All stations were well prepared. Now enjoy your breakfast and the coming week, you deserve it."

"Well, that certainly was good news." The doctor reminded Tony, "Should you have a need to get into the sick-bay during the next week the purser has a duplicate key. I'll be flying home for a few days. Thank you very much for your help. I hope you have a good week off."

"Thank you, sir. You have a good visit with your family."

Dr. Christian told him, "Don't worry, Mr. Lewis, I'll secure the sick-bay before I leave." "Aye, aye, sir." They shook hands then Tony went to breakfast.

It was around six o'clock when the highest point on Oahu came into view from the port bow, while the island of Kauai had been visible fifty miles to starboard for some time. Tony strained his nostrils, but the only odors he could detect were from the ship and the sea air.

With the help of Sparks Tony was able to send a message to Melina letting her know that they expected to tie up at the same dock around ten a.m. He was sure that she would contact Kim with the news.

Soon the scent of the island was in the air. There was a distinct odor of green plants and flowers. In the final two hours before the *Lady* was due to arrive she followed the outline of the Oahu Coast from Kaena Point, down past Barber's Point and Pearl Harbor to a docking area opposite Sand Island.

During that day's watch, Mate had been at the helm, but after the Aloha Tower had come into view he was relieved of his watch by another crewman senior to him to prepare for the arrival of the harbor pilot. When the *Lady* was approaching Sand Island the small tugboat *Jenny Girl* pulled alongside so that the harbor pilot could come aboard. Once aboard, the pilot took over the helm of the *Lady* as the tug escorted them into the docking area. Tony had been ready for hours. He was topside, keeping out of the way. He watched the pilot and tug skillfully turn the *Lady* around in the confined space and place her along side the wharf at her regular berth.

Mate had been standing by in the bridge in case he would be needed. Once the lines from the ship to the wharf were secured, he quickly went below to shower and get ready to go ashore.

Tony was standing topside when a feeling of anticipation welled up in his chest. He saw what he hoped to be Melina's car leave the street and enter the parking area. When the car parked in the same spot it occupied when they set sail he could clearly recognize Melina and Kim in the front seat. He had the urge to shout but waved both of his arms enthusiastically instead. Melina gave a *beep, beep* on the car horn. She and Kim left the car and walked to the ship. Melina was looking very streamlined while Kim was wearing a flowery summer dress. They were also filled with anticipation. "Alright!" Tony called to them, "Hey! You look great. I'll go below and tell Mate you're here. He should be ready in a few minutes."

The sun reflected off her silver pendant as Melina called back to him, "We're taking you out to lunch. I hope you're hungry."

"Oh, we are," he said, "in more ways than one." He disappeared below and went to Mate's quarters carrying a small shoulder bag. "Hey, man, they're here!"

"They are?!"

Tony was excited, "That's right, man. And Kim is looking mighty fine in a pretty dress."

"Oh my god." His hands became jittery so that he could barely tie his shoes. He stood up. "How do I look?"

"You look great. Wait a minute, let me fix your collar." The collar of his shirt was half up and half down under his jacket collar so Tony adjusted it. "There, let's go." Mate grabbed his small duffel bag. When they appeared at the top of the gangplank the ladies were waiting at the bottom. The guys nearly ran down the plank with Mate almost tripping on the last step.

After a restrained hug and kiss hello, they got into the car with Mate and Kim sitting in the back, and Melina driving. There was a tiny gift wrapped box on the front passenger seat. Melina told Tony, "That's a surprise for you, hon." He thanked her as he turned it over in his hand trying to guess what it was.

Kim told Mate, "I have so much to tell you. I had hoped you could meet my parents, but they've left to visit relatives in Korea and won't be back for another three weeks."

Mate had a feeling of relief. "That's too bad, dove. I really wanted to meet them." He thought a small fib was often best.

She said, "I'm really sorry, but you still can when you come back in a month."

As Melina drove the car onto the street Mate said, "That's cool; it'll give me a chance to work on my Korean."

Distracted from his inspection of the little box, Tony asked, "I didn't know you wanted to learn Korean."

"Just a little, you know. Hello. How are you? Glad to meet you. Stuff like that, just to begin with."

"So how's it going?" Tony asked.

"I haven't started yet. I'm hoping to find a book on it while we're here this week."

Kim said, "Don't worry, honey, if you don't learn any Korean it's really okay. My parents speak very good English."

Melina said, "That's very nice of you, Mate."

"It's all his idea," Kim assured them.

Mate added, "I know a couple in Oakland. My friend's wife is from Korea so he took classes to learn her language. Naturally she took classes to improve her English. Their kids are learning both English and Korean."

Melina asked, "Is he a colored man?"

"No, he's French and English," answered Mate.

Tony asked Melina, "Why did you ask that?"

"I don't know."

"Well, good luck, Mate," Tony said, returning to his little box, and gave it a light shake.

"It won't break," Melina told him. "Give up?" She pulled the car into the parking lot of Hook, Line, and Sinker, a unique looking restaurant specializing in seafood. The front of the building was in the shape of an old fishing boat's bow. "Well, here we are. Tony dearest, why don't you open your present in the car?"

He carefully removed the wrapping, opened the box and, "Wow! This is really something. It's very nice, Melina."

"Let's see," said Mate, followed by, "Woe! That is beautiful."

It was a gold and silver pendant on a thin gold chain. The pendant was a ship's anchor in gold, entwined with a silver rope. It was very striking. Melina said, "Here hon, let me put it on you." As she did, "Remember Bill Younge, the goldsmith who made this?" pointing to the silver pendant Tony had given her.

"Sure, he was a neat guy."

"I had him make this for you. Doesn't he do beautiful work?"

Tony just asked, "Can I kiss you now?" In the front seat of the VW beetle it was not easy but they managed.

Because the car had no back doors Mate said to Kim, "Now I know the meaning of captive audience."

Melina said to them, "Really, let's leave our little cocoon and enjoy some lunch."

After they were inside and had ordered their food they discussed the things they would like to do in the coming week, especially the dance contest. Melina told them, "After work Saturday I'm getting a lift to the Jolly Roger to meet up with you. I might be there by eleven thirty at the earliest."

Mate asked her, "Is there any chance you could be there before the dance contest is over?"

"Not really, I'm dancing from eight to eleven all this week."

"You should consider yourself lucky, Mate," Tony jokingly told him. "You might get beat."

"Yeah, right," laughed Mate.

"Oh, I nearly forgot," Kim said, "there's a concert of classical Balinese music and dance at the museum Sunday night."

Tony responded to that news, "Fantastic, I've never seen the dance, but I've heard the music on a friend's album. It is out of sight." Mate told him he had never heard the music, but he would not mind going to check it out. Tony said, "Just imagine very early Milt Jackson with brass xylophones, cymbals, and gongs with the musicians all sitting on the floor."

"Now that sounds far out," Mate agreed.

"It's a real gas, man, you'll dig it." And so the conversation went until they finished their lunch.

It was mid-afternoon when Melina took Tony to her apartment. As they climbed the stairs she asked him, "You haven't been in my place, have you?"

He remembered why, then answered, "That's right."

"Well, I've made some improvements." She opened the door and went in. She had prepared well for this moment. Her favorite flowers were fresh and subtly placed. There was an oval Oriental rug on the teak floor of the main room. On it sat a low table in front of a couch covered with a soft fabric. On the table was a dish made from a sea shell, with dates, coconut pieces, and dried pineapple in it. There was a light odor of incense in the air even as a gentle breeze came through the open sliding glass door that led onto a veranda. Melina suggested, "Hon, why don't you warm up the stereo and tape deck? I have some music tapes I'd like you to hear. Then just make yourself at home while I make some mint tea."

"Sure." He turned on the sound system then went over to the low table where something had caught his eye. It was Kahlil Gibran's *The Prophet*. He picked it up, "Have you read this?"

Melina entered the room carrying a box with tapes of her dance music. "I've read it more than once. It is so beautiful, and I refer to it often. Have you read it too?"

He admitted, "No, but it's on my long list of books to read."

The kettle in the kitchen started to whistle. She handed him the tapes. "Here, play this one first while I brew the tea."

He opened the tape deck and carefully placed the chosen reel in place. He ran a length of leader through the head to the blank take-up reel. "What speed is this tape?"

Melina brought in a teapot and cups. "Seven and a half, the sound is so much better. Can you figure out the sound system?"

"Yes, it's one of my hobbies." He savored the aroma of his tea then sipped it, "This is lovely."

"I really want your opinion of the music. Listening with your eyes closed might help."

"Only if you sit next to me." The music began to play.

"I will, but first I have to get your second surprise ready. Now close your eyes."

"Second surprise?" Then, "I like these sounds already."

She left the room. "The surprise is too big for the car."

"Too big for the car?" He momentarily opened one eye to sneak a peek but only saw the leaves of the banana palms blowing gently outside the veranda. He couldn't imagine what she was up to. "You shouldn't have gone to so much trouble. Nice music though."

Melina had just prepared her second surprise. She was wearing a black and gold mask like those worn at a sixteenth-century French masquerade ball. It covered just her eyes and nose but had a piece of black lace from the mask to her chin. Her raven black hair was held in a ponytail by a gold ring.

She wore a totally sheer violet and gold silk top with full sleeves but no front. Her breasts were barely hidden beneath a sheer white and gold silk bib. Over this was a black and gold lace vest. Her waist and stomach were bare. From below her navel she was wearing only a pair of sheer violet and gold full pants that were tight at the ankles. Over this was a sheer black and gold full length skirt. On her feet she had a pair of violet, black, and gold slippers.

"Just relax, hon. I'll be with you in a second." She lit a little cone of incense and placed it through the doorway into the room. "You can open your eyes now." Still in the other room she quieted herself and prepared to begin her dance.

Tony savored the exotic aroma of the incense. "This music is so mellow." The late afternoon sky was turning golden outside the glass door and cast a golden light into the room. By then he was almost in a dream state.

Without a word Melina gracefully floated into the room as if on a magic carpet. Tony was dumbstruck. She danced as though she was communing with the source of the music. Also her dance took on the appearance of expressing a conversation with the music. Her movements were improvisational, Oriental, and exotic at the same time. Tony became totally absorbed in her. When she was near the glass door, the light made a golden silhouette around her body. When she was away from it, the golden light shone through her costume reflecting off her tan skin.

Tony was fascinated by her dance and knew that he was witnessing something profound. The music went from slow fluid melody to more sensual rhythms. She removed the black vest. The sheer white bib only accentuated the shape and beauty of her breasts with their dark pointed peaks. He was becoming increasingly stirred. The sheer black skirt was the next to go. Her body had become visible as if through a mist. Now her dance was to him. He never had his passions aroused quite like that before.

She came near him and took his hand, attaching his fingers to the bottom of her bib, nodding to him. He pulled on it but not hard enough. She teasingly danced away from him then returned to give him another chance. She nodded again. He pulled harder and off it came. She pulled away, removed her mask, and returned to him. She moved her hips and breasts invitingly from side to side in a circular motion near his face. When she danced away he didn't think he had ever seen anything more beautiful.

His blood was boiling, and his heart was pounding. Again she danced near him touching her fingertips to his lips, then glided away. Her dance became more provocative. She came near him again, touching her finger tips to his lips and down along his neck to his chest. Leaning forward she offered her breasts to his lips. Her dance ended and another kind of dance began. In that dance he had no trouble taking the lead.

Melina's remaining garments quickly fell to the floor accompanied by his. Just as when a fire has been lit, and the wind is right, the blaze will spread throughout, gaining in momentum. Nothing can stop it until the fuel is spent.

And so it was for the rest of the evening until late when they fell into a final sleep.

In the morning she slipped out of bed while he slept and went into the kitchen to prepare a breakfast. She put on a bib apron that was hanging on a door. In the bedroom Tony woke and realized that she was absent. Hearing sounds coming from the kitchen he got up, put a towel around his waist, and went in. Melina, wearing only the bib apron, was a sight to behold. "Good morning," he said as he went over to her.

She turned to see him. "Good morning yourself."

He hugged her. Kissing her neck, he said, "I think I'm cured."

"I'm not a doctor, but I think I just qualified to agree with that." Their kissing became more passionate. She attempted to put the spatula from her hand onto the counter, but it fell to the floor, as did his towel.

He reached around her back untying her apron, saying, "I can't get enough of you." Soon they were locked in the ultimate embrace, standing with her back against the counter.

Afterward they lay on the couch just long enough to recover. She said to him, "Remember the dolphins at the aquarium?"

"Sure," wondering why she was asking.

"You don't suppose you're part dolphin, do you?"

He hesitated at first not sure of her meaning. Then with a laugh, "You might be on to something, I sure like the ocean."

"Among other things," she laughed.

"The vision of you dancing, sweetheart, is still very much in my mind." He began caressing her back.

She put a hand on his chest and pretended to push him away. "You better take a break, Mr. Dolphin if I'm to get breakfast ready. I'm going to have a quick shower. You can have one while I make breakfast. Okay?"

"Okay." When she went off to the shower he couldn't help notice the movement of her body. He thought, *If ever there is poetry in motion that has to be it*. He found his cigarettes and lit one.

After a late breakfast they made themselves ready to meet with Kim and Mate for a rendezvous at the beach.

The foursome spent the afternoon at Waikiki, lazily enjoying the quiet of a Tuesday. The sky had broken clouds with an occasional sprinkle that was not enough to protect one's self from. While Tony and Mate played in the crystal clear water, the ladies avoided the sun under a beach umbrella. They wanted to conserve their energy because they had to work later.

Kim asked Melina, "What are you two going to do after Mate takes me to work at five?"

"Tony is taking me for some Japanese sushi."

"That sounds okay but wouldn't it be more romantic at your place?" Kim asked with a smile. She hadn't heard anything yet of Tony's stay at Melina's.

"That's the reason I'm having him take me to dinner. If we go to my place before work I'll never make it to work."

"Really? It sounds as though his problem has gone away," Kim added with a questioning smile.

"Very much so, dear, very much so."

"I see. You know what they say about men who like sushi, don't you?" Kim said with a smile.

"I don't believe I do."

Kim whispered something into Melina's ear.

Melina couldn't help smiling. "Well then, there must be a lot of men who like sushi." With that they both had a good laugh.

Just then Mate and Tony returned from swimming, dripping wet. As they reached for their towels Mate asked, "Now what are you two laughing about?"

Tony sat down next to Melina. "Yeah, let us in on the fun."

Kim said, "It's nothing for your ears. It was just girl talk."

Melina added, "You know, feminine matters." The girls started laughing again.

"Oh come on, tell us what it is," they booth pleaded.

The girls stood firm, "No, sorry. It's too personal."

"Okay, we give up." Mate asked Kim, "What time do we need to leave to get you to work on time?"

"Pretty soon, lover, I need to go home to freshen up." She gave Melina a suggestive wink.

Mate said to Tony, "Well, my man, am I going to see you at the Sleeping Lady later on?"

"Yeah, Melina doesn't start work until eight so we're going out to dinner first. I might see you after that."

"Sounds good to me," Mate said as he and Kim gathered up their things and started for the car which Mate had rented that same morning; a cream colored '52 Cadillac convertible.

Tony said to Mate, "Maybe tomorrow you can let me look at that car?"

Mate agreed, "Whenever." He and Kim said their goodbyes.

Tony told Melina, "You know, I had a Caddy rag top just like this one, a '50, when I was in high school. I sold it and got a '53 MG. I even got a G.I. haircut. Driving that car with the windshield down flat was the only way, unless the weather wasn't good enough. What a contrast. I wish I still had them."

Melina asked him, "What car do you have back home now?"

He answered, "The Muni, none other than the San Francisco Municipal Railway. I have a whole fleet of buses, streetcars, and cable cars at my disposal."

Puzzled, she asked him, "How come you don't have a car?"

"Before I left for Europe in '63 I sold everything for travel money."

Melina wondered briefly what she was letting herself in for.

After the meal of sushi Tony took Melina to work in her car. She had everything she needed for her performance at the club, except her tapes that she always took with her. He left the car in the parking lot then went into the lounge to visit with Kim and Mate. But Mate had gone off to do some errands for Kim. Since Tony had drunk some saki with his dinner earlier, he drank only soft drinks at Kim's bar. It was difficult to have a conversation with her because she was so busy making drinks.

Tony had been at the bar for an hour when a lull in business gave them a chance to talk.

Kim asked him, "How do you feel about watching Melina dance in front of a room full of men?"

"You know, I'm not really sure. I am kind of uneasy about it."

Kim told him, "Dancing is probably the most important thing in her life. Even though burlesque is not what she is willing to settle for she's grateful that it gives her a way to experience her art and earn a living. And it accepts her."

"You know her very well, don't you?"

"We know a lot about each other. When she first came here we hit it off really well. We've become the best of friends and so she has confided a lot in me."

"That's great."

"She was so unsure of herself at first. Her experience next door and here has worked well for her. It's making her stronger, and preparing her to move on."

Tony said, "She told me that she needed to go to either Los Angeles or New York to learn more because she has hopes for the modern dance theater."

"Yes, she wants to study further. Imagine what a great teacher she could be someday?"

"I've never seen any woman dance with such mystique."

"When she first started dancing here she was so vulnerable that places like Los Angeles and New York would have eaten her alive."

"I know exactly what you mean. I think I'll go watch her."

"Will I see you later?"

"I don't know." He slid off the stool and went out the exit of the lounge and into the entrance of the burlesque hall.

At the entrance to the club a very large Samoan was sitting on a bar stool checking IDs. Tony showed his driver's license, paid five dollars at a little ticket window in the wall, then went in. The place was large, dimly lit, and nearly full. The air, or what was left of it, was heavy with cigarette and cigar smoke, and the accompanying smell. He didn't want Melina to know that he was there so he sat along the back wall on a bar stool to help him see above the heads of those in front of him.

A scantily clad cocktail waitress took his order, a soda this time, as his stomach was feeling a bit off. There was a music combo on the stage to the right. Talking into a microphone at center stage, a middle-aged man dressed like a down-and-outer was doing a vaudeville comedy routine. He managed to get a few laughs before a long pole with a big hook at the end came out from the wings. It went around his neck and pulled him back into the wings. It was just part of his act.

The band did a drum roll, followed by the master of ceremonies speaking into the microphone. He sounded like a carnival barker as he announced, "Ladies and gentlemen. Here she is, all the way from Baton Rouge, Louisiana: the beautiful, vivacious ... *Jessica.*" The band began playing some jazz number as a dancer strode onto the stage; and she was a beauty. She wore a lacy light summer dress, long lace gloves, high heeled shoes, and carried a summer umbrella also of lace. She relied on the band for her music, but dancing was not one of her attributes.

She did a simple routine, a gradual tantalizing striptease, leaving only the mandatory G-string and pasties, the self adhesive discs about the size of a half dollar, depending. She had a body that was beyond any reasonable man's wants, but she was not a dancer. At the beginning she was a little boring, but as more of her began to appear the audience took notice. By the end they were hooting and whistling and throwing wadded-up paper money onto the stage. She gathered up her money and was gone.

She was followed by a pair of jugglers, complete with burning torches. Jugglers always seem to hurry on, hurry through their act, then hurry off.

The MC returned to the microphone, "Ladies and gentlemen, here she is, all the way from cold, freezing Anchorage, Alaska: the luscious . . . *Wanda*. When things warm up, this lady knows how to take 'em off." Again the band played a jazz number followed by the appearance of Wanda. She came out dressed like a milkmaid carrying a pail and a stool. She managed to do some dance movements as she approached the center of the stage, put down the pail, sat on the stool, and commenced to mime milking a cow. As she did she became increasingly warm and so she had to remove more clothing, finishing with only the G-string and pasties. She gathered up her clothing in one arm and rather ungracefully bent over to pick up her money, facing away from the audience. The cat calls and whistling that followed rose to a new level with more money being thrown.

The comic was back with some different jokes, before the hook removed him again. When the band began to leave the stage Tony wondered if it might be time for an intermission, but the MC spoke into the microphone, "Ladies and gentlemen, here she is. All the way from the exotic and mysterious island of Manhattan: the beautiful . . . *Melina*."

Tony's heart skipped a beat. Her special music came through the speakers above the stage as he was momentarily taken back to the dance she had done for him. The room was quiet except for an occasional, "Come on, come on," from a drunk or two. Tony was momentarily annoyed and noticed the smell of spilled beer near him. Once Melina appeared, she again absorbed him. She was wearing a costume similar to the one of the day before except a different color and without the mask. Also she had the mandatory G-string and pasties beneath it all.

Not far from Tony someone called out, "Hey, baby," again pulling him from his reliving of the day before. By the time she removed the first garment most of the audience was fully enthralled by her presence. Her magic was in the fluid way she moved. Nothing else mattered. They realized that they were watching a dancer strip, not a stripper dance. Melina used the dance to express herself first and to earn a living second. The magic she possessed was out of place there, if only because no one else had it. Tony could see that she no longer belonged there and in effect her gift was being degraded.

By the finish she had completely stripped off all but the G-string and pasties and was doing an improvised modern dance.

Someone near the front slurred out, "Come on, mama, take it all off." Tony wanted to run down to the front and hit the guy in the mouth. Then another guy off to the side said for all to hear, "Now, I want some of that." Tony's annoyance and anxiety were building in proportion. Somewhere near the back wall there was a dispute between customers. When Melina finished she gracefully stooped down to gather the money that was all over the stage. Right next to Tony, the drunk who had spilled the beer said, "Look at that ass!"

"Hey, man!" Tony exclaimed to the guy. He slid off his bar stool to confront the guy. As he did so, he stepped on the spilled beer and slipped. He reached out to grab his stool for support but it tipped over causing Tony to fall to the floor.

The drunk looked down at him, speaking with a slur, "Don't you think you've had a little too much to drink, buster?"

Tony was sitting on spilled beer. Without help he tried to get to his feet. A rather large Samoan bouncer appeared. "I'm afraid I'm going to have to ask you to leave, sir." He had been told to take care of a disturbance at the back of the room and thought Tony must be part of it.

Tony was standing but having difficulty maintaining his balance on the wet floor. He didn't understand what was going on. "What? Hey, this guy was saying crap about my lady friend. I slip and fall and you want me to leave?"

The bouncer didn't see any lady friend. He quickly looked Tony over and saw that his trousers were wet and dirty with a cigarette butt stuck to the backside. And there was a smell that included beer coming from his clothes. "Yeah, that's what I said. You need to leave. You are creating a disturbance. Now you can leave on your own or I'll have to remove you. What'll it be, mister?"

"I can't believe this. Don't worry, I'm going." He walked to the exit followed by the bouncer. "You're really making a mistake."

"Good night, sir," said the bouncer as he closed the door between them.

Once Tony was outside in the bright lights of the parking lot he saw his clothes for the first time, "Damn, what a mess." He not only looked nasty but his clothes smelled, and he felt nasty. He was going to go back into the lounge to talk to Kim but when he saw how dirty he looked he decided to return to the *Lady* for a shower and change of clothes.

He returned to the ship in Melina's car. Once on board he thought of the different world he had just come from. He imagined the *Lady* was like a spaceship taking him from Earth out to the peace and quiet of outer space; and that each place where the ship docked was like another planet.

Since Melina wouldn't be finishing work until eleven he took his time. He shoved his dirty clothing into a bag bound for the cleaners, and put on a pair of sandals.

After dressing he went up on deck, for a cigarette and to reflect on the past two days. He went to the bow, away from the dock. It was a typically quiet midweek night with the air fresh and crystal clear. From miles away he could see tiny lights and their reflections on the water. Most of the seagulls were asleep but one was watching him. He thought of how tranquil the sleeping birds were. The next morning they would all be at their routine: scurrying for food, eating garbage and anything they found dead, pecking at one another, making a terrible racket, and crapping on everything in sight. That was their job, like any animal, they only did what they were supposed to. But what was he supposed to do? That was the ultimate question.

He was listening to the sound of tiny waves lapping against the *Lady*'s hull when he heard the *toot! toot!* of a boat's horn in the distance. He thought it amazing that so much had happened in the past two days, from the moment he stepped off the ship Monday until then. The thought almost made him dizzy. But he knew that something was very wrong. He had given in to his passions again, and again something was wrong. *What? Why?* He thought he knew what, and maybe some of how, but not why. He lit another cigarette, inhaled deeply, and looked up into the sky at the stars as he exhaled the smoke. The stars were momentarily shrouded by the smoke. He wondered if the answers to why might come from there, from beyond his own ability, his own limitations. And once the smoke within his mind had cleared . . .

"Melina! I nearly forgot," he blurted out. He hurried off the ship and to the car. He was supposed to be meeting Melina in the lounge.

Tony arrived at the Sleeping Lady, parked the car, and dashed in. When he sat on the hard stool at the little bar he realized that his wallet with his money inside was not in his back pocket. He sat next to Mate and hardly had time to say hello when Melina entered from next door. She was in a good mood and wearing a lei. She said hello to everyone. She was carrying a second lei that she put around Tony's neck along with a kiss on the cheek. "Hi, hon, have you changed clothes?"

He didn't want to spoil her good mood. "Yeah, you could say I got spilled on. I went to the ship to clean up, and I only just got back. Thanks for the lei, it's real nice."

Mate commented, "I wondered what happened to you, man. I haven't seen you all night."

Kim reminded him, "Honey, when Tony was here you were out doing me a favor."

Mate told him, "Sorry I missed you, brother."

Melina asked Tony, "Did you see me dance? I looked for you, but the light in the hall is so dim and the stage lights are so bright that it's hard to see anyone in the audience."

He hesitated to answer at first, "Yes, I saw you once. You were beautiful, and your dancing was like magic. Then there was this spill so I had to leave." *No lies so far*, he thought.

Sounding disappointed, she asked, "Where were you sitting?"

"Along the back wall."

"No wonder I didn't see you. There seemed to be more noise than usual tonight. But I'm pretty good at concentrating on my dancing so I shut out a lot of the distractions."

"You do?"

"I have to, otherwise I couldn't deal with it. I'd probably have to quit."

Kim said to Melina, "I hope you weren't planning on doing something with us tonight. We were really busy and I'm wasted."

"No, no plans." She gave Tony a hopeful look, "Not yet."

Tony was feeling a little tense and just said, "Well, shall we go then?"

Melina took his arm, "Are we all getting together tomorrow?"

Kim answered, "How does a late lunch at my place sound?"

"Sounds lovely," Melina said.

"I'm going to bake something special."

"Sounds excellent to me dove," said Mate.

Tony agreed, "I can hardly wait."

Melina said, "We'll see you tomorrow then."

And with that Tony escorted Melina to the car. Once inside he informed her, "Before we do anything else I need to get my wallet. When I realized I might be late meeting you I forgot all about it and left it on my bunk aboard the *Lady*."

She said, "It's quite a ways, why don't I give you some money until you get it back?"

"Thanks, but the main problem is that it has my ID in it and other things I need."

"You're right, we should go get it then."

Tony started the engine and headed back to the ship. Melina was in the passenger seat with her left hand and arm on the back of his seat. As they drove along she gently massaged the back of his neck. He began to feel more at ease. "Something happened, actually a couple of things happened to me tonight."

With concern in her voice, "What happened, hon?"

He described the events in the burlesque hall as best he could complete with his impressions.

"Oh my god! They threw you out?"

"That's right." He tried to be as sensitive as he could to her feelings but couldn't help revealing his distaste for most of what he saw, heard, and smelled. "Your talent is being wasted on that lot of slobbering drunks."

"Working there has helped me so much."

He asked, "Is there nowhere else you can work dancing?"

"Are you kidding, on this island? There's another nightclub but not as nice as the Sleeping Lady. It doesn't have anything like the lounge next door where the Mother Jean Singers are."

"The lounge is not bad, even uplifting. But next door, it's filled with sleazy men, and all that smoke. I didn't know what a pigsty the floor was until I slipped and fell onto it."

In defense of the club she said, "This may have been an off night. It's not usually so bad, I'm sure."

"After tonight I find it hard to imagine it being much different."

"Remember a month ago, we were at the beach near the aquarium? You first learned what work I do?"

"Yes, I remember."

"You were very understanding and nurturing."

"I felt a sense of love and compassion for you."

"And now?"

"I still do, but the place you are dancing in is bad news." They had nearly reached the ship. His voice was beginning to sound strained, almost irritated. "And getting used to it is only going to degrade the gift you have."

The car entered the parking area near the ship. Melina was feeling a sense of frustration and confusion. "Well, what can I do? There is no other professional dancing on the island other than the hula dance shows."

"Then you'll have to leave the islands."

Melina had become quite irritated. "That's not as easy as you think. Also, I happen to like it here. I can't just hop from place to place the way you can."

He parked the car near the ship. He softened a bit, "Yes, I know. But if you want to go on, to further your career as a dancer, you're going to have to figure a way to leave here."

As Tony was getting out of the car to go to the ship, Melina got out on her side. She went around the car to the driver's side and gave him a hug. "I need to go home alone. I'm very confused right now." She kissed him lightly and said, "Okay?"

"Yeah, sure." He felt his face become flushed.

"Call me?"

"Okay." He watched her get into the car and slowly drive away. When her car was completely out of sight he turned and very thoughtfully walked to the ship. Seeing the *Lady* quietly sitting there at that moment reminded him of something different. It was like a big white mother duck waiting for her little ducks to return from playing in the mud. He stepped onto the gangplank with the subtle movements of the water rhythmically lifting and lowering the ship. He carefully walked up the plank and was suddenly taken back to the very first time he had done so. He remembered the smell of the wind coming across the bay from San Francisco. When he reached the end he stopped. "That's it!"

He startled the crewman standing watch, "What's that?"

"San Francisco, maybe she'll have a chance in San Francisco."

"What in the hell are you talking about?" asked a dumbfounded night watch.

"Everything's okay, I was just thinking out loud."

The night watch was accustomed to crewmen coming back to the ship late at night a bit on the drunk side. "Maybe you could do with some sleep."

"You're probably right. What time is breakfast?"

"From eight till ten and cold cuts from twelve till two, while in port."

"That sounds good to me," as he started down the steps to the next deck. "Don't worry about me, I'll be okay. Good night."

"Good night."

He went to bed, but after only three hours he was awake again, unable to go back to sleep. He was afraid he had hurt Melina's feelings. Their new relationship had so much potential. Unable to get back to sleep he lay in his bunk until seven.

After dressing he went into the sick-bay just to see if things were still in order. That done he went to the crew's mess for some bacon and eggs. In the dining room he ran into Rob and Chuck who were just preparing to leave on an excursion by boat to the island of Maui.

Rob told him, "You're welcome to join us. The place is like a paradise."

Chuck added, "I haven't been there before, but everyone I've talked to said that it is just great."

Tony excused himself, "I'd really love to. I've heard nothing but good things about it too. But I have some very important things to sort out. When are you coming back?"

Rob told him, "Since it's Chuck's first time I thought we'd just make a day of it. We'll be leaving from there around dark."

Tony asked, "You like jazz, don't you?"

Rob said, "I sure do."

Tony told them, "Well, there's this all night club called the Jolly Roger."

"Yes, I've heard of the place," Rob recalled.

Tony continued, "In the evenings they have disco dancing, and dancing to a rhythm and blues band most nights. But from ten or eleven o'clock, on some nights like tonight a jazz group will do a few sets."

Chuck said, "That sounds really cool, but I'm not twenty-one."

Tony reassured him, "That's okay because they serve food. When you two get back from Maui and if you have any energy left you should check the place out. Mate and I should be there late tonight with our girlfriends so you can meet them."

Chuck said, "That sounds cool."

Tony continued, "You'll like it Chuck, if you like dancing. They really get it on there. You might even meet some women."

Rob said, "The place sounds better all the time. I guess it will depend on if we have any energy left when we get back."

Chuck was more enthusiastic, "The club sounds great. I sure would like to meet a girl, so I'll keep some energy in reserve."

"I hope you both make it. I'll keep an eye out for you." Tony finished his meal and went below. He made sure he had what he needed, especially his wallet. He left the ship and caught a bus to Honolulu.

Once he was in town, he phoned Melina to apologize in case he had hurt her feelings. He had, but she was also sorry for losing her temper. Because they were expected at Kim's at around two o'clock, they arranged to meet at a small café by one thirty.

There was a light rain falling when Tony found the Cup and Saucer, the café where he was to meet Melina. He found a booth by a window so he could watch for her while he waited.

He watched the traffic and people go by. Overcome by a lack of sleep he started to doze off when he was jolted wide awake by a crashing sound. He looked up at the waitress who had just dropped the metal spoon for the tea he ordered onto the table. He became aware of a radio playing the song, *'It Ain't Me, Babe.'*

"I'm sorry, sir. I hope I didn't startle you."

Just a bit unsettled, he said, "What? Oh, that's okay. I must have drifted off for a minute." The lyrics of the song seemed stuck in his mind as he looked up at the clock over the door. Melina was late so he glanced up at it every few minutes. It was one forty-five when Melina drove up and parked her car. He got up when she came in, and after a kiss hello they sat in the booth next to one another.

She told him, "Sorry I'm late hon, but there's been a change in plans. Remember Kim was going to bake something special?"

"Yeah."

"Well, something went wrong with her oven and it got ruined."

"That's a bummer."

"So we're going to meet them at the udon restaurant at three o'clock. She is so disappointed."

"That's a real shame. Listen sweetheart, I have been thinking so much about last night."

"And so have I," she said as she leaned against him a little more.

He said, "I know your situation here is not an easy one. And I can understand how you love it here."

"Yes?"

"I had an idea last night. What do you think of giving San Francisco a try? It's not so dog eat dog as it is in New York or L.A., the city has a lot of soul. And the surrounding Bay Area is huge."

"You know, hon, it's not that I'm against the idea. I have heard some good things about a modern dance scene forming there. It's going to be so difficult for me to give up these islands."

She ordered a tea as they continued to discus their situation and where they wanted to go with their lives. Melina seemed more in touch with the direction of her life than he did with his.

It was close to three o'clock when they drove into the parking lot of the udon restaurant. Mate and Kim had arrived just ahead of them. They got out of Mate's rented car and walked over to Melina's car. Mate said to Tony, "Man, what a day this has been."

Kim greeted Melina, "Hi, hon. I'm sorry about this." Then after lowering her voice, she asked, "How are things with you two?"

Melina gave her a reassuring look.

Tony suggested to Mate, "Why don't you show me your car before we go in?"

"Okay." Mate and Tony walked over to the convertible.

"Melina told me about Kim's bad luck with the oven."

"Yeah man, something in the oven messed up and the kitchen started to fill with smoke. She had made a great casserole. It got ruined and that was the end of that."

"What a drag." Looking at the car, Tony said, "How come you have the top up?"

"Because of the rain."

"The rain? It only rains for a few seconds when it does."

"Yeah, but that's long enough to mess with Kim's hair."

"Right, I hadn't thought of that." After looking the car over, "This is just like the Caddy I had, very nice."

Once they were in the restaurant they took a table and ordered.

Kim said she was going to pay since she felt it was her fault that things went wrong. The rest objected and agreed that it would be unfair to her. Tony and Mate agreed to split the bill.

Kim conceded, "I know that stove is old, I just haven't wanted to spend the money to get a new one."

Mate told her, "Have no fear my dear, I will buy a new one."

Tony was amazed, "Well, I'll be."

"Really?" Kim asked Mate.

"I was lucky last week. We can look for one tomorrow."

Kim gave him a big kiss. Tony wasn't aware that he had done so well at the poker table. During the meal they discussed their plans until the guys were due to leave again.

Outside, two rednecks, Jim and Jack, walked past. "What'a ya think, Jack? You wan'a check out some of this Jap grub?"

"Sounds good to me." They sauntered into the restaurant and looked around the room before choosing a table along the wall opposite Kim and company. Their manner of dress and the dog tags they were wearing gave them the appearance of being from among the thousands of military stationed on the island.

The group at Kim's table was nearly finished with their meal and hadn't noticed the twosome. But the two men noticed Tony with Melina and Kim with Mate all right.

With a sneer on his face Jim remarked in a hushed voice, "What the fuck is that? Do you see that shit over there, Jack?"

Frowning, Jack said, "Yeah, what's the fuckin' world comin' to?"

"I bet I know who's drivin' the Cadidlyack ash tray outside." He nodded toward Mate.

Jack agreed, "Most likely."

Jim had a little ring in his left ear lobe. Not something allowed by the military. As he lit up one of his little cigars he noticed a wide wavy pink line throughout the color scheme of the walls that formed an occasional bow. As if just looking for something to complain about he picked up a pink cloth napkin with embroidered flowers from their table, "What's with all this pink shit?"

As Jack was looking through the menu, he asked, "What pink shit's that, Jim?"

He motioned around. "Look!"

Jack looked up and all around. He didn't really get it but to be agreeable he said, "Yeah, you're right."

With a half smile, Jim said as an aside, "Queers. This dump is for fagots."

"Yeah, fagamuffins," agreed Jack with a dumb grin.

In a lowered tone again as if speaking in confidence, Jim said, "You'd better be careful 'cus they like you."

Mimicking the gesture, Jack said, "And you'd better be careful because they like you too."

"They like us both." And with that they burst out laughing, disturbing everyone near them.

Tony and Mate looked over at them with a frown.

Jim noticed and looked back at them with a sneer as he drew Jack's attention to them. Jim looked at Mate, and used his lips to form the words, "Fuck you."

Tony said to Mate, "Just ignore them, and maybe they'll slither away."

Mate felt like responding, but he was held in check by the presence of Kim and Melina. "They're not at all cool, man."

Tony said, "They're obviously assholes." Because the ladies were talking between themselves they didn't know what the guys were talking about.

With a snicker, Jim and Jack returned to their menus.

As the foursome finished their meal, Kim asked, "Are we going to the Jolly Roger after work tonight so we can practice for the dance contest?"

They were all in agreement to that. After the bill was paid they left the restaurant and went to their cars; but Mate had a slight blush as he looked at the two men on his way out.

Jim and Jack had watched them go out. They looked at each other with a smug smile as Jim said, "I think I heard something about dancing later tonight. Did you?"

Jack agreed, "I sure did."

"Maybe later, huh? Could be interesting."

"Could be fun."

Jim added with a sly grin, "Maybe we'll get a chance to kick our heels up a bit, just a couple of good ol' boys havin' some good ol' fun." That was followed by more obnoxious laughter.

Outside Mate said to Tony, "Man, you know those assholes are look'n for trouble. I've seen 'em around. They're a pair of creeps."

Tony agreed, "They look like military. What do you think?"

"Maybe, they're wearing dog tags. I don't know, but I know they better not mess with me again, even if the women are with us. I hate that kind of shit."

"I'm with you, man," Tony said.

After saying goodbye to each other the two couples drove away.

When Tony and Melina were back in her apartment he asked her if she had heard the song, *'It Ain't Me, Babe'.* He told her he had heard it played on the radio before she met him at the Cup and Saucer earlier. She told him a friend had left a copy of the same Dylan album there.

He asked, "Can I play a couple of songs for you to see what you think of the words?"

"Okay, I'll make some tea; and I have some cheesecake to go with it."

After letting the stereo warm up he played, *'All I Really Want To Do,* is baby be friends with you.' He followed that with, *'It Ain't Me, Babe,* it ain't me you're a lookin' for.'

She came in from the kitchen with the tea and cake while the second song was playing. She sat on the couch next to him and waited for it to finish.

He said, "I like the sound of the song; his style is so good, but it is completely opposite to the way I feel. I want to be the one my woman is looking for. In declaring freedom the song also denies commitment and responsibility. Everyone wants freedom, but does it have to be at the expense of giving up one's responsibility?"

"I understand what you mean when you say you're not like that. But you know a lot more people are taking that attitude. I'm not that way either."

"When I heard it today it made me wonder if I was right or wrong."

"Well at least you're concerned about it, which is more than can be said for most men."

"I'll put on some other music. This cheesecake is good. What would you like to hear, Classical, Jazz, Afro-Cuban?"

"Put on one of the George Shearing albums." She whispered in his ear, "I feel like something soft and mellow," then lightly bit his ear lobe. "Did I make your tea hot enough?"

The sensation of her breath in his ear sent a chill through his body. "I love the way you do that. Yeah, you made it hot enough all right." He stacked on two albums, the second being Latin Escapade. He thought a touch of spice could enhance any further biting. He wasted no time getting back to the couch. As they were carried away by love and the music, the element of time dissolved. The two albums were finished before they were.

It was nearly seven o'clock when Melina leaped up from where they were lying, she said, "I have to get ready for work!" She gave him a kiss then hurried into the bathroom for a shower. He loved the sight of her nude body in motion. "Make yourself a snack; I'll grab something to eat at the club later," she added.

He went over to the stereo to switch on the radio to a program of classical music. Melina came out of the bathroom to get dressed. When she saw that he hadn't thought to put anything on she said to him, "Hon, if you don't put some clothes on, I'm going to want to go over there. Then I'll never make it to work. Please," she said with a pleading smile.

He was not sure which way she meant the please, but he reached for a bib apron draped over the back of a chair and put it on over his head. Pretending innocence he asked her, "Can you tie the back for me?"

"No way, you're going to have to manage that all by yourself." She disappeared into the bedroom to dress herself.

Tony took Melina to the Sleeping Lady and dropped her off. He didn't think he should go in to watch her. She agreed to that, so they arranged to meet in the lounge as before. It was a beautiful night. He drove over to the art museum to buy two pairs of tickets for Sunday's Balinese concert, then on into Waikiki to while away a couple of hours.

Chapter 8

RUMBLE

Later on at around ten o'clock, and after checking out some bars, Jim and Jack had found their way to the Jolly Roger. They went inside in anticipation of having some fun. The club was nearly full of couples who were there to practice for the dance contest on Saturday. The two men sat on stools at the bar as Jim looked around the room. "I don't see the punk that was drivin' that ash tray, do you?"

Jack was a little dense. He looked around, "Ash tray?"

"Jesus Christ! The convertible next to the Jap joint where we ate today."

"Oh yeah, okay."

"The dip shit who was drivin' it."

"I didn't see who was drivin' it."

"The darky who was sittin' with the Chinese broad."

"Oh yeah, she wasn't a bad looker."

"Never mind her. Do you see him and his buddy in here?"

"It's hard to tell for sure, Jim, this joint is so crowded."

"They might be in the head. Why don't you check it out while I order us a round?" He reached into his pocket to see how much money he had. "Okay?"

"Okay." Jack slid off the stool and walked to the back. His walk had just a hint of wobble in it. He didn't have as high a tolerance for drink as Jim did.

Jim ordered them each a whiskey with beer for a chaser.

Jack returned with no luck of a sighting. "Maybe . . . this is the wrong place," he said. Too much drink was causing him to slur his words.

Jim gulped down his whiskey, "This is the right place, all right. I heard 'em say its name. They're just not here yet."

Meanwhile, a young sailor at the end of the bar and facing him had caught Jim's attention. They had begun making eye contact with each other. A conversation was sure to follow.

Tony arrived at the Sleeping Lady lounge at around a quarter of eleven. The Mother Jean Singers had already left. The bright cleanup lights were on and the cleanup man was busy putting the chairs on the tables. Tony settled into a relaxed conversation with Mate and Kim. "You know, I think you stand a very good chance of winning that contest Saturday if you can work on some new steps."

Mate agreed, "That's my thought exactly. What do you think, Kim? Doesn't it sound like a good idea?"

"It sounds like a great idea. But you're going to have to help me out a whole lot, honey."

"I love the way you say that. Am I really that sweet?"

Tony interrupted, "All right, lover boy, don't get carried away with yourself. It's good that you have three nights to practice."

Mate said, "And that's just what we are going to start doing tonight; just as soon as our sweet things are ready to head over to the Jolly Roger."

Melina entered the lounge through the private door that connected it to the theater. She had a small bag containing her music tapes. "Hi, everybody. Hi, sweetheart." She gave Tony a kiss hello.

Tony was enamored by her presence. "I'm speechless."

Mate commented, "That's all right. I think I speak for both of us when I say you always look great."

"I concur with that," Tony agreed.

"All right you two." She sat on a stool between them and leaned against Tony. Kim seemed to be finished with her work so Melina asked her, "Are we all still going over to the jazz club to do some dancing?"

Kim said, "Just as soon as we can get me out of here." She came out from behind her bar with her purse and a sweater over her arm, "Okay, let's boogie."

Mate was all smiles. "Man do I feel hot tonight!"

They left for the Jolly Roger in separate cars.

The parking lot was full so they parked on the street about a block from the club.

After going inside, a hostess took them to a table that had just been vacated near the bandstand. The air was heavy with cigarette smoke and the dance floor was full.

At the bar Jim had been so absorbed in an exploratory conversation with the young sailor involving the things they had in common that he totally missed the arrival of Mate and Tony. Jack was sitting on the other side of Jim from the sailor, with his forehead lying on his folded arms and half asleep.

Back at the table the foursome ordered two sodas and two beers then went on to the dance floor. Mate wasted no time showing Kim the new steps he wanted them to work on. Tony and Melina were just enjoying dancing together.

After about twenty minutes of dancing Tony went to the men's room to relieve himself. There was someone in one of the stalls throwing up and coughing and making an awful sound. Tony was at a urinal when Jack came out of the stall to clean himself off. He looked up at himself in a discolored mirror over the sink and said, "I've looked worse." The mirror was opposite the urinal. When Tony turned and went to the other sink he didn't look directly at Jack so he didn't see his face. Jack was squinting into the mirror and half recognized Tony. Jack turned his head and watched as Tony went out the door. "Well, I'll be damned."

The band had taken a break but was back playing a slow dance tune. On the dance floor Tony and Melina were dancing cheek to cheek, kind of melting into one another. Mate was showing Kim some dance ideas in slow motion.

Over at the bar Jack was trying to get Jim's attention while Jim, with one hand on the sailor's thigh, was trying to ignore Jack. His voice was affected by having just been sick. "Listen, Jim," he almost coughed something up but swallowed it.

Jim frowned, "What the hell's wrong with you?" He turned to the sailor and smiled, "You'll have to excuse my friend here; he can't hold his liquor."

Jack tried again, "You know the guy you were looking for in here earlier?"

Jim had almost forgotten about that. "Yeah, did you see him?"

"No, but I just saw his buddy in the head."

Jim felt suddenly revived as he looked around the room. "No shit?" He spotted Mate dancing a slow dance with Kim. "I feel like dancing, don't you?" he said to no one in particular. He slid off the stool and walked toward the dance floor with Jack half-heartedly poking along after him. The sailor had a blank look on his face; he hadn't a clue to what was going on.

Tony and Mate were oblivious to anyone around them other than their partners. Once he was on the dance floor Jim walked over to Mate from behind and tapped him on the shoulder. "You don't mind if I cut in, do you, boy?"

Mate could hardly believe his eyes, "What in hell do you want, man?"

"I'm sure this gal would appreciate dancing with a man for a change," he said as he forced himself between them. Kim didn't understand what he was up to and became frightened.

Mate said, "Get the hell away from her." He attempted to grab Jim's arm to pull him away.

Tony let go of Melina and moved to help Mate just as Jim pushed against Mate's face with the palm of his hand. Jim was a lot stronger than Mate and pushed him away with little effort. His friend Jack was sitting on a chair at the edge of the dance floor just watching. He had another drink and was not feeling too well. One of the waitresses quickly told the bartender there was trouble, so he pressed the emergency button under the counter to summon the police.

Kim was having difficulty keeping away from Jim.

Mate lunged at Jim shouting, "I said get away from her."

The band stopped playing. As the other dancers tried to leave the dance floor, Kim got away from Jim. Both she and Melina held on to each other off to the side.

Jim had no trouble fending off Mate, brushing him aside so that he crashed into another couple. "What's the matter, boy?" Jim laughed, "Didn't yo' mama teach ya all how ta fight, boy?"

Tony and Mate began circling Jim trying to find an opening.

"What's wrong, boy, can't ya hold yer own? When we get through here, I've got somethin' for both of ya."

Mate was in front of Jim with Tony behind him. Tony dove for his legs as Mate jumped up to ram him in the chest. It completely threw Jim off balance, causing him to crash onto a table flattening it. When he scurried to get to his feet, he grabbed a fallen bottle and broke off the bottom by hitting it against a metal table leg. Tony and Mate had just gotten to their feet when Jim lunged at them. He swiped the jagged edge of the bottle at them barely missing Mate, but he caught Tony on his cheek just above his right lip. Immediately blood appeared. Someone called out, "He's been cut!" Someone else came up from behind Jim, putting an arm under Jim's armpit with the hand grabbing the back of Jim's neck while with his other hand he dug a thumbnail hard into the underside of Jim's wrist causing him to drop the bottle. It was Rob who had just come into the club with Chuck. He was an easy match for Jim.

Then suddenly, "All right, break it up!" Two shore patrols: the Navy's police and a pair of Marine MPs, billy clubs in hand, were standing around them. "Let's see some identification."

Tony was holding a dinner napkin against his cut cheek.

Jim complained to the SPs, "These two guys jumped me, then this guy joined 'em. I was only trying to defend myself.

You can ask my friend." But Jack had slipped away when he saw the police arrive.

"We'll see about that. Let's see some ID," the Marine MP insisted. Jim handed him an expired driver license from the state of Arkansas. "It says here on this expired license that your name is Jim Smith. Is that correct?"

"Yep."

Meanwhile the others were showing their driver licenses to the SPs.

Jim's license was the older type with no photograph. Seeing that Jim was wearing dog tags the MP wondered why he answered in the manner he did. "Let me see your military ID."

"I don't have any." Jim was growing a little nervous.

"And why is that?" the MP asked him.

"I'm not in the military."

Now seeing that he was dealing with a civilian, the MP said, "Would you mind taking off those dog tags so I can have a look at them?"

Seeing that he was surrounded by four armed military police with billy clubs in hand he could hardly say no. "Sure," but he was even more uneasy as he handed over the ID tags.

As soon as the MP saw the name on the tags he winked one eye at his partner who instantly drew his .45 caliber side arm pointing it at Jim. "Cuff him." After they handcuffed his wrists behind his back they searched him. This produced a switchblade knife with about a seven inch blade. "Quite a pig sticker," the MP said. He asked Jim, "How did you get hold of these military dog tags?"

Jim lied, "I found them."

"Well, if you did it was either at the bottom of the ocean or in a shark's belly." Then the Marine said to the SPs who had been talking to Tony, Mate, and Rob, "You should find this interesting. Remember the nude body of the sailor they found floating in the yacht harbor about a month ago? Or I should say what was left of him?"

One of the SPs said, "Yeah, they thought it might have been a shark that got him."

"These are his dog tags. I think we just caught ourselves a shark."

When the young sailor who had been talking to Jim heard this he quickly went outside and threw up in the parking lot.

Meanwhile the Honolulu police had arrived. Since Jim was a civilian the military handed him over to them with charges of disturbing the peace, masquerading as military, and suspicion of murder. Some of the club's customers had come forward with an account of what had just taken place, so no charges were pressed against Tony, Mate, or Rob.

One of the customers came over to Tony, "Hi, I work at the hospital. Can I see that cut?"

"You sure can."

"You're lucky; it doesn't appear to be a deep cut. I'll see if the bartender has a first aid kit. I'll be right back."

After Mate went over to Kim, Melina returned to Tony. She said, "Oh dear, is it very bad?"

"Someone is helping me; he doesn't think it's a deep cut. How is Kim taking all of this?"

"She's pretty upset, but Mate being with her will help a lot."

Tony said in amazement, "I can't believe what happened in here tonight. Who would have thought?"

"I'm still a little shaky myself," Melina admitted.

The customer returned with the first aid kit. "This should hold you until you can get to a doctor. Is it true that the police are holding that guy for murder?"

"That's right, of the sailor that was found in the yacht harbor a month ago."

Melina blurted out, "Oh my god, are you serious?!"

Tony said, "I'm serious."

She told him, "Now I'm going to be upset."

Chuck and Rob came over to them. "Tony, are you all right?"

"Yeah, I'll be okay. You know, you probably saved our lives. Thanks a million. Oh, excuse me; you two haven't met Melina before, have you? These are two of our shipmates, Rob here who saved us and our good buddy Chuck."

Chuck said, "I'm pleased to meet you, ma'am."

Rob added, "I can see that Tony is a very lucky guy."

Melina told them, "The pleasure is all mine. Thank you so much for your help."

Tony told her, "Also they went on a trip to Maui today."

Rob said, "That's why we didn't get here sooner." He asked Tony, "What was going on between you guys, anyway?"

"It's a long story which I will tell you later, but the short form is that the guy was a total asshole looking for a fight with somebody he thought he could beat."

Melina asked Tony, "Sweetheart, I really need to get out of here. Can we go home soon?"

"Good idea, let's see how Kim and Mate are doing."

The four of them went over to their table. Kim had been crying and Mate was holding her in his arms.

Melina asked her, "Do you think you can make it home okay?"

"I'm a lot better now. I would like to leave pretty soon though."

Mate said, "I don't see why we can't leave now."

Kim asked, "Tony dear, how bad is that cut?"

"Hopefully it's not too bad. I need to stop at a clinic on the way to Melina's. By the way Kim, these two lads are our shipmates, Rob and Chuck."

"I wish we could have met under better circumstances," Rob said to Kim.

"Thank you for helping Mate and Tony. They might have gotten killed if you hadn't come along."

Mate added, "I don't think he would have hesitated to do me in. He may have had that in mind for later on. I'll bet his switchblade knife has seen some serious use."

Mate and Kim returned to her apartment to nurture one another.

Tony and Melina drove to an emergency clinic. The doctor in attendance believed two stitches would be a good precaution to insure the healing. From there they returned to her place.

In the two days that followed, Mate and Kim worked on their dancing. Because Melina didn't have to be at work until late each day, she and Tony had more time to be together. Anytime someone asked him about the bandage on his cheek he would just say he had a mole removed.

The thought of the two couples going to the Jolly Roger after the ladies finished work caused them to have a feeling of great discomfort.

A DOLPHIN IN PARADISE

Friday morning Melina and Tony were up early to prepare for a trip on a high-speed boat to Maui until dark. The boat ride was exhilarating as the craft only skimmed the surface. They arrived at the island paradise after just over two hours. Once the craft settled down to a slow cruising speed it rode lower in the water. There were three locations where the craft could allow passengers to disembark. The first seemed a bit remote. There was a very small pier where Tony, Melina, and one other couple disembarked. The craft then continued on to its third and final stop; Lahaina, which was much more of a tourist's delight.

Once ashore the two couples had a brief conversation before going off in different directions. Melina and Tony were both carrying small bags containing the essentials. When Melina led Tony into the vegetation she told him, "Wait until you see the spot I've picked out for us."

"How much farther is it?"

"Just a little ways." After about five minutes into the underbrush they reached the edge bordering on a small, secluded cove. Pointing to its beach she said, "There it is."

It looked like something out of a dream. "Wow! What a neat spot." They carefully walked down to the beach with its silky smooth black sand. "Have you ever met any pirates here?"

"Not yet." They opened their bags, spread out a huge beach towel, and after bringing out the radio, Tony tuned in a station that had some of the more traditional Hawaiian music.

He asked her, "This seems very appropriate, don't you think?"

She just smiled. "It's so beautiful here. I think this is my most favorite place in the whole world."

As he finished emptying the bags, he took out her white bikini. "Here's your bathing suit."

"Oh good, I brought that just in case."

"In case what?"

"In case it gets cold, of course."

"You mean—"

"Isn't it obvious, with no one here but the two of us?"

"An excellent idea."

After they removed all their clothing, they carefully folded them and placed them as two pillows at one end of the towel. "Quick!" she said, "The lotion. We don't want to get a sunburn."

He had the bottle of lotion in his hand. "Where shall I start?" Hesitating as he looked at her, he said, "I don't think I can put this on you and remain calm."

It was becoming noticeable that her naked beauty was having an effect on him. "I see what you mean. Then I think we'll have to put it on ourselves. But I can't reach my upper back."

Just a little embarrassed, he said, "I think I can do that for you."

"You're sure?"

"Uh, yeah, . . . pretty sure."

"Anyway, let's go for a swim first." She leapt up and ran off toward the water.

As he watched her with great delight, he said, "Well, maybe not so sure." He quickly followed her into the calm water and swam about, feeling the sensation of his entire body touching nothing but water. That was until he caught up with her.

She saw him closing in on her. "Why do I feel like I'm being pursued by a dolphin?"

"Let's find out," he attempted to embrace her. She struggled, breaking free. Again he pursued her. She ducked under, and he followed. When she came up for air he came up beside her. Entwining himself around her like a vine he kissed her. They sank together, kissing and embracing one another. The need for air forced them back to the surface. After taking in some air they swam around each other as if in a water ballet. He said to her, "God is truly merciful. It seems he just let Adam and Eve back into Paradise."

"Yes, he truly is," she said. Both needing a rest, they slowly returned to their towel and laid down. "You'd better let me put some of this on your cut." She had produced a small bottle of alcohol and a cotton ball from the bag containing the food.

"Thanks." It was a sudden reminder of a place totally removed from their paradise.

She told him, "We'd better get some lotion on ourselves. The sun seems to work even faster here than it does at Waikiki." So they took turns with each other's back.

He was a bit worn down from the swim, and the heat of the sun was working on him. "I suddenly feel very lazy." He turned on to his stomach turning his head to one side facing her. She was lying on her back with her eyes closed against the bright sun, even with sunglasses to shade them. He noticed how her breasts seemed to melt into her chest when she was on her back. He wondered how he could be so lucky. It wasn't that she was so lovely to look at. That does help to keep the fires stoked. But she was really a good woman—intelligent and kind hearted. But he wasn't feeling a bond, maybe because they had only known each other barely two weeks out of the past five.

Between them the backs of their hands were lightly touching. They turned their hands and the fingertips teased one another. Without opening her eyes she asked, "Do you think Kim and Mate will still try to win the dance competition?"

"I don't know how Kim feels about it now, but when Mate attempts something important to him he's determined to make it. I think what has just happened to them is going to make him all the more determined."

She told him, "Last night Kim told me she realized that what happened was not because of her, but that the guy had targeted Mate from the beginning."

"I would have to agree with that."

"And she went on to tell me that even though the Jolly Roger has this very unpleasant experience connected with it, she can overcome it for him. She also happens to like the place very much."

"It really has become our club. Is there another place here as good?"

"Not for us," she said. Suddenly feeling amorous, she asked, "Do you feel ready for another dip?"

He thought, *Not really*, but answered, "Sure."

Once in the water she quickly engaged him in a game of tag. She pursued him, he pursued her, they both played hard to get, like two kittens playing. And like two kittens it was only a game until the pursuer was caught in a trap. She allowed him to catch her then entwined herself around him until he was sufficiently aroused. This time the activity borrowed from the dolphins was taken to completion. Now his energy was quite gone. He thought he was lazy before, now it was all he could do to keep himself from sinking to the bottom. She asked him, "Do you want to do it again?" almost as a dare.

In disbelief, he exclaimed, "What?"

"Do you want me to chase you or will you chase me?"

"Are you kidding? I hope you have some lifeguard training because you may have to 'take me in.'" He was only joking, of course.

"Oh, had enough? I thought you were a dolphin kind of guy."

"Well, even dolphins stop to eat, don't they?"

When they were in shallow enough water to walk she said, "Then you'll love what I brought for us to eat."

They were out of the water and walking on the beach back to their towel. He asked her, "What did you bring?"

"The main course is two small cans of sardines. I thought raw tuna would be nice, but I had no way to keep it cold." After sitting they reapplied the lotion to themselves as before along with another application of the alcohol to his cut. She began to set the food out between them on a small patterned cloth.

He commented, "That was such a trip. I've never made love while swimming before, have you?"

Teasing him, she said, "Now is that a question to ask a lady?"

"Sorry, another point for your side."

She leaned toward him, "Come here, hon." He leaned toward her as she said, "Another point for our side." She kissed him and said, "By the way, you make a very effective dolphin."

He blushed then laughed, "I love it when you talk dirty."

She laughed with him, "Don't let it go to your head now."

After they finished eating and after he found some soothing music on the radio, they drifted off into a relaxed sleep.

The ride back to Oahu in the last hours before the sunset was extraordinarily romantic. Again riding on the open after-deck Tony and Melina looked to the east with the color of everything changing as the sun neared the horizon. The islands took on an orange hue eventually becoming reddish. From tiny spots here and there along the coastline a bright light reflected back as if from so many mirrors. And the air became gradually cooler causing little goose bumps to form on their arms. The ride was at the same time earthy and surreal.

The boat unloaded its passengers at the pier next to the yacht harbor as the sun disappeared and night began.

Tony and Melina returned home in her car. After a shower and a quick bite to eat, Tony drove Melina to work. After so much activity and exposure to the sun she had hardly any energy left. Tony went off to do some errands and grocery shopping for Melina before returning to the Sleeping Lady.

On that night Melina was the third in line to perform so she took advantage of the opportunity to have a visit with Kim in the lounge. Melina had been telling Kim about their excursion to Maui. Kim was envious of all the fun they had been having, but she voiced a concern about one thing in particular, "I hope you've been careful."

"You mean . . . ?"

"Birth control, of course."

"It's not my time. It was over a week ago."

"How can you be sure?"

"I'm regular as clockwork. My period is due about midway into next week."

"Well, we'll know then, won't we?"

"Don't say that. Now that you mention it, what about you?"

"The pill."

"I remember you said you were going to stop using them."

"I changed my mind just before I met Mate. It was strange, but I just had a feeling I should wait."

Melina admitted, "I don't like the idea of having something mess with my hormones like that."

Kim's final comment on the subject was, "Well, it takes a whole lot of worry out of the most enjoyable thing in life."

"I guess I can't argue with that. Listen, I have to be back on the other side pretty soon. How are you and Mate feeling about tomorrow night's contest?"

"Well, we've thought about it a lot, and we've talked about it enough. And we've practiced for it one heck of a lot. I think we have a good chance. In fact, I believe we can win it."

"All right! That's all I need to hear. I'll see you later, darlin'." Melina returned to the burlesque hall.

Saturday morning arrived along with a light rain. It was midmorning when Tony and Melina were awakened from a sound asleep by her phone ringing. It was Mate. He was exited about that night and invited them out to lunch. They were to meet at Hook, Line, and Sinker around eleven o'clock.

Inside the seafood restaurant, while the foursome were waiting for their meal, Mate showed Tony a copy of the local newspaper. "Have you seen this?"

Tony read the article that included a small photograph of the troublemaker from the nightclub, Jim Smith. "Well, what do you know?"

"What's that, hon?" Melina asked.

Referring to the article, Tony told her, "Jim Smith, the guy we had the run in with? The paper says that the ID he showed the police wasn't his. The thumbprint on the driver's license didn't match his. They don't know who he is yet. They are waiting for his prints to go through the FBI files in Washington, D.C. Also the paper says that the real Jim Smith was reported missing four months ago."

Kim recalled, "When he stood between us I got a feeling off him that was evil. I hope they keep him in jail forever."

Mate said, "Well, if they tie him in with the sailor they found here and the guy missing in Arkansas he may end up in jail forever."

Kim said, "Let's talk about something more pleasant."

Melina agreed, "Amen to that."

They tried to distract themselves by eating their shrimp and crab salads. Tony asked Melina, "Do you want me to double back to the Sleeping Lady to pick you up after work tonight?"

"No, I'll be getting a ride over to the Jolly Roger with John, the driver who makes sure the dancers get home safely."

"Chuck and Rob said they would try to be there to give their support to boost spectator response."

Mate agreed, "Every bit helps."

Tony said, "This is a great place to eat." He looked at each of them, "You know, Hawaii is really starting to grow on me."

"You and me both," said Mate.

Kim told them, "I was lucky to get Linda to work for me tonight. She had almost arranged to be away with her boyfriend. So I'll work for her Monday night. That way they can still have two days away. Plus I won't lose any work."

Melina asked, "So what are you two doing this afternoon?"

Mate said, "I have a great pair of shoes for dancing that I left with a repair shop to put the right kind of heels on. I'll be picking those up."

Kim added, "I have all I need. Basically we're both going to rest up then be at the club around nine o'clock."

Tony said, "It sure sounds like you're the favorite to win tonight. Melina and I are going to take a stroll through a botanical garden until it gets dark."

When they finished their lunch they left in separate cars. Tony and Melina drove north through the middle of the island to one of the most beautiful of the botanical gardens. Once inside they strolled around for hours.

AND THE WINNERS ARE

After driving Melina to work, Tony went next door to listen to the Mother Jean Singers for a bit of spiritual inspiration before continuing on to the Jolly Roger.

Mate and Kim arrived at the Jolly Roger early enough to get a table next to the dance floor. Since they had a long evening ahead of them they conserved their energy by dancing through their steps at a slow tempo. Mate carefully observed the competition. When Tony arrived he joined them at their table.

The music had been disco until nine o'clock. At that time the band arrived and slowly set up their instruments for the evening. There was the usual screechy whistling sound as a microphone caused some feedback. Not long after that Rob and Chuck arrived. Mate and Kim's table wasn't big enough for six so they crowded their chairs in close around the table. The guys filled each other in on the latest events while Mate and Kim were on the dance floor. Once the band got going the room filled with their music.

Rob commented, "Mate and Kim are looking very good tonight. What do you think?"

Tony answered, "They've been practicing their tails off. They are up against some good dancers. It's going to be close."

Seated at one of the tables taking a rest was a pair of likely contenders in their mid-twenties. Also sitting with them was a girl of about eighteen who was the sister of the woman. She and Chuck had caught each other's attention. It took about fifteen minutes for him to get up enough courage to ask her, "Excuse me, would you like to dance?"

She looked at her sister who gave her a very subtle nod, then told him, "Sure." When she stood up she was only a few inches shorter than he was. She was an attractive girl with short brown hair and brown eyes. They danced a kind of rock and roll style, improvising as they went.

Tony remarked, "Hey, Chuck's doing all right. I didn't know he was a dancer."

Rob said, "Yes, he's a pretty sharp kid. He just needs some experience with life."

Kim sat down at the table to take a break while Mate went off to the men's room. "Isn't that our friend Chuck dancing over there?"

Rob answered, "That's him all right."

"They're not too bad. Who's the girl he's with?" she asked.

He pointed to her table and said, "She's with that couple over there."

"Do you think he'll want to be in the contest?"

"I don't think so. I don't think he's ready for that yet."

Tony told them, "Well, if he is he can have my place. I signed up for Melina and me a month ago for tonight, and we're not going to enter. Even if he doesn't win, it could be fun for them."

"Hmm, that's a thought. We can tell him that," Rob said. "I could be wrong, let's give him the choice."

Mate returned from the rest room, "Hey, I see my man Chuck out there. And he's lookin' good too. I didn't know he was into dancing."

"Neither did we," Tony admitted.

The piece ended, and the band made some adjustments before they began the next piece. Chuck took the girl back to her table then returned to his. He said, "Hi, Kim. Hi, Mate. How's it goin'?"

"Pretty good, thanks. Things seem to be going okay for you."

"Yes, I think so. That's a nice girl I just danced with. Her name is Mary. She's here for the first time with her sister. She just turned eighteen and will finish high school this June."

Kim said, "Well, you found out a lot. If you two want to enter the dance competition you can have Tony and Melina's place because Melina can't be here in time."

"We won't have a chance. There are some good dancers here."

Rob encouraged him, "Even so, it would be a good experience to mix it up with some of the best. And besides, you never know how things might turn out. Often in a race someone will come from the back to win."

"You really think so?" Chuck asked all of them.

Mate said, "Sure. Why not, kid. Give it all you've got. What have you got to lose but a little sweat! Wait a minute, did I just say all that?" Then he added, "As long as you don't beat us of course." Then he laughed and slapped Chuck on the back. "I'm just kiddin'. Go out there, and dance like there's no tomorrow."

Suddenly filled with courage, Chuck said, "I'll go over and ask her." And off he went. They were all watching him as subtly as possible. When they saw a big smile come over Chuck's face they knew she had agreed. When he returned to their table Tony took him over to where he had signed up. He made sure that Chuck and Mary could replace him and Melina. Then they returned to their table.

Tony informed the group, "It's all set; Chuck and Mary are now in the competition."

"All right, Chuck!" the group chimed in together.

Chuck said, "I feel nervous."

Mate said to him, "Listen, man, there's nothing to worry about. Come with me for a minute." He took Chuck over to a corner of the room where there was some open space. Mate was talking to him all the time. He gave Chuck a lot of pointers and showed him a few moves. "And the rest is up to your own creativity."

"That's it?"

"The rest is up to you. Now I would suggest you start dancing and practicing a bit with her instead of sitting with us. You don't have a lot of time. The main thing is to just be relaxed with it. Don't think of it as a competition. Just have fun."

"Thanks a lot, Mate. You're a real pal."

"Good luck, my man." They started to part when Mate said, "I nearly forgot."

"What's that?"

"When you dance with someone, dance to that person, and for that person. And your partner should do the same with you."

"Thanks again." Chuck returned to Mary's table and after a moment sat beside her talking quietly, imparting the advice from Mate.

Back at Mate's table, Tony was full of admiration. "Well, teacher, how did it go?"

"He's going to be just fine."

About an hour went by, then the leader of the band talked into the microphone. "Good evening to all of you, kats and kittens, out there in *boogie land*. It's time to show us what you can do. As you know it's that time again when we have our monthly dance competition." He pointed over to a large meter on the wall with numbers going from 0 to 10 and a needlelike pointer.

"Now you see this gismo here. My buddy brought this over from the mainland. Hollywood I think he said. He didn't say how he happened to acquire it. It's called an applause meter. So the way this is going to work is that once the competition begins we'll play a piece. Then my friend there," pointing to a waitress, "will hold her hand over each couple in turn, and each time you will applaud. Then of course the meter will go berserk giving us a reading for each. Since we have a lot of couples the six with the highest reading will dance again."

The leader continued, "At the end of the second round, the three couples with the highest reading will compete in the third and final round. The highest reading from the final round will give us our winning couple. Understood?" Loud applause, shouting, and whistling followed. "All right, we're going to play one piece to let you get warmed up before we begin. Competing couples only, please."

The music started again. With all the competitors on the floor there was not a lot of room to maneuver, but the more aggressive ones managed.

Eventually, the leader asked, "Is everybody ready?" The crowd expressed its readiness with a roar. The music took off like a rocket, and all the couples found themselves a spot. Chuck and Mary were holding their own making good use of their unlimited energy. Mate and Kim were very smooth in the execution of their moves.

The first round was over when the band stopped to uproarious applause. Like the man said, when the waitress held her hand over each couple the meter went berserk. One thing was for sure with Mate and Kim, Mary's sister and her friend, and Chuck and Mary, the needle of the meter went beyond its own numbers.

Tony was almost shouting to Rob through the noise, "Can you believe this?!"

Rob shouted back, "It's great!"

On the dance floor Mate told Chuck and Mary, "You're doing great, keep it up." The music took off again, and the six couples gave it their best.

At the end of the second round when the meter was read, Chuck and Mary were eliminated along with two other couples. Mary's sister and friend, one other couple, and Mate and Kim were the remaining competitors.

The band gave the couples a few minutes to take care of business. Tony asked Rob, "I think they're going to win, what do you think?"

Rob was cautious, "I don't know. One of the other couples is very good. Chuck should be very proud of himself."

"For sure," Tony agreed.

When the couples returned to the dance floor, the music took on a slower tempo encouraging a more creative performance from the dancers. Mate was in very good form, and it was apparent to Tony that Kim had been a willing student. True to Mate's style they danced to and for one another. Not long after they started dancing Tony watched only Mate and Kim. It was while he was concentrating on them that Melina was able to slip unnoticed into a chair behind him. She gave him a gentle nudge.

"Melina!"

She gave him a quick kiss hello, "How are they doing?"

"This is it."

She quietly watched with him.

The music stopped. Mate and Kim's performance was so unique that even before the waitress raised her hand over the dancers, the other two couples acted as though they had lost. When the applause came it was obvious that Kim and Mate had it even without the meter.

"Ladies and gentlemen, brothers and sisters, the winners for tonight!" As he spoke the bandleader shook Mate and Kim's hand. When the applause finally began to taper off he handed them a small plastic trophy with two pairs of gold colored shoes in miniature, a man's pair and a woman's pair, mounted on it. They were also given a certificate.

When Kim and Mate returned to their table they were both elated and extremely tired. Chuck and Mary came over to congratulate them. Mary told them, "You were just the best dancers I've ever seen. My sister thinks you were very good too."

Kim said to her, "Why, thank you, dear. Mate was my teacher. With out that it couldn't have happened."

Chuck told Kim, "He really helped us too."

Tony asked Mate, "Well, what do you think?"

"It sure feels good. Kim was my inspiration." Then to Chuck and Mary he said, "You know you two had me worried for a while there. You were dancin' up a storm."

Kim agreed, "They sure were."

Rob added, "You just watch them. They'll be winning this competition before you know it."

At that point Chuck introduced Mary to everyone. She told them, "Chuck was very good. He gave me some new ideas. You know there's a trend now for each person to sort of dance in their own little world, but I felt he was dancing with me. And that was nice."

Chuck responded, "I have Mate to thank for that. But Mary was so good to dance with."

Melina said sadly, "And I didn't get to see them dance."

They were all very tired so it wasn't long before they left, but not before Chuck made a date with Mary for the next day.

Tony asked Mate if he wanted to celebrate, but he had put so much of his feelings into his dancing that he was actually exhausted. So everyone just went home.

Because Melina had invited Kim and Mate to her place for their Sunday lunch, Melina and Tony were up early to begin preparations. Melina sent Tony off to get some things she would need from the food market.

Standing in front of a liquor store a few doors down from the market, Melina's friend Bruno was panhandling for spare change. Tony saw him from a distance and hoped he hadn't recognized Melina's car.

When he went back to her place Tony told her what he saw. "Also, he looked a little strung out."

"It sounds like he might be back on drugs. I wonder if he's still at his mother's place."

"Can she cope with him when he gets like that?"

"I doubt it; she's not in great shape herself. Her problem is poor health and alcohol."

The phone rang. It was Kim letting Melina know when they would arrive and to see if she needed anything. "Kim dear, I'm glad you called. Do you know that liquor store down at the corner of . . . Oh what's that street called? Close to the supermarket I always go to. . . . That's the one. Could you pick up a small bottle of that mix I like to use? . . . Great! See you soon."

Tony asked, "Why did you do that?"

"If Bruno is still there she'll see him. She'll talk to him, and then she'll tell me what's happening with him."

With displeasure apparent in his voice, he said, "I see."

"You have to remember, he did a lot to help me when I first came here. And if it becomes necessary I will try to help him. But if it's drugs then I can't do much, if anything."

"You're right, I'm sorry."

A little while later Kim and Mate arrived for lunch. After they all greeted each other, Tony and Mate stayed in the sitting room playing records while Kim went into the kitchen. "Here's the mix you asked for."

"Thanks, hon."

"You can't imagine what I saw outside the store."

"Bruno looking strung out on something?"

"Now how did you know that?"

"Tony saw him standing in front of the liquor store. I thought if he was still there you could give me a second opinion."

"Did he see Tony?"

"Tony didn't think so. He said Bruno looked like he was panhandling."

"He was standing so near the door we couldn't avoid him. Mate even gave him some money."

"How did he seem to you?"

"I talked to him only a second. I would say he just came down off of something and needs some more pretty soon, with no money to get it."

"Well, I'm not going to help him with that."

"And there's no reason why you should."

"You know how I feel about him."

"Yes, I know. Melina dear, there's only so much you can do to repay a person who has helped you."

"Yes, I know. You're a good friend, and I know you understand."

Meanwhile in the next room, Tony asked Mate, "So how does the new champ of Hawaii view the world of dance today?"

"Damn near with bloodshot eyes if it hadn't been for Kim's eye drops."

"The smoke gets pretty bad there. They're lookin' okay now."

"That's good because I figure I'll need 'em tonight to see those cats groovin' at the concert."

"I still can't get over Chuck last night. It was as if he suddenly came to life."

"Well, I would imagine the girl Mary had something to do with that. She was pretty nice."

"I think he has a date with her today. Hey, I just remembered something. Willy's lady friend's name is Mary too."

"Now there's a coincidence for you. Chuck's a good kid. He deserves to be with someone nice like that. And he could be a hell of a dancer if he set his mind to it."

"All he needs is a good teacher like you to show him the way. Have you ever thought of becoming a dance teacher, eventually?"

"The thought has passed through my mind a couple of times. I discovered a little while back that I enjoy showing people how to do things, any thing."

"Sounds to me like there's a teacher inside there somewhere."

"Time will tell."

Tony said, "You know, somebody told me something once. I don't know if it will ever sink in with me, but listen to this; if you have a destiny, you know, if you are destined to do or be something in particular, but your head has you going off in wrong directions, then sooner or later nature, or God, or whatever is guiding us, will trounce on you so hard that you'll either have to do that one thing you're meant to, or you'll die trying."

"I understand what that means. But you see I have some kind of a wall standing in my way. I'm not sure what it is, but I run right into it when I think of something like teaching."

"A wall named self-doubt, maybe?"

"That sounds like a good name to me."

"I've seen you, brother. I've seen you workin' on the *Lady*. I've seen you dance. And I've seen you with your woman. You can be or do whatever you set your mind to."

"You know, man, I know what you're saying is true. But sometimes I feel so scared and confused that I can't make a move."

Melina came into the sitting room. "Well, guys, why don't you sit at the table while Kim and I bring out the food?"

Mate said, "After last night I could eat a horse."

Kim told him, "Well, sweetheart, it's going to have to be a sea horse because Melina has cooked some lovely fish for us."

Since Melina and Kim were excellent cooks they had a very satisfying lunch on this, their last day together. They spent the afternoon enjoying good music and each other's company.

At seven o'clock they left for the concert at the museum and arrived early enough to get seats near the front. Willy with his friend Mary was there soon after. When they greeted one another, Mary informed them she would be flying to California in about two weeks to try her luck in San Francisco. So they were seeing her for the last time.

A portable dance floor had been placed on the ground in front of the raised area where the musicians were to perform.

As the program began, the leader of the gamelan orchestra described the instruments and the story the dancers would depict.

When the musicians began playing, the sound was at the same time unusual, spectacular, and beautiful. It began with subtle sounds like individual raindrops falling but quickly accelerated to dynamic crescendos. It moved back and forth between the two extremes in an almost fluid way.

About a minute into the music it stopped then started again with the same subtle sound as a female dancer appeared. Her dress and makeup were of another world, the ancient magical world of Bali. She was the Hindu princess Sita and moved in such a way as to appear to be floating over the floor. She talked with her eyes, the movement of her head, and her fingers. The movement of her body was a language in itself. It all stated that she was very feminine, innocent, vulnerable, and lost.

Then with loud crashing and banging, another dancer appeared as a demon. It tried to trick her into going with it to its kingdom. She would not go. So the demon forced her. The music was done in such a way that it seemed the dancer's movements were causing the sound.

A third dancer appeared as the Hindu hero, Rama. He proceeded to search for the princess. When he found her a battle ensued wherein the demon was subdued, and Sita was rescued.

The first dance concluded to applause from a very appreciative audience that was followed by an intermission.

Tony and his friends were quite excited by what they had just experienced. As dancers Melina and Mate were particularly moved.

Mate said to Melina, "That just gave me a whole new perspective on dance and how it can be used. How about you?"

She replied, "I had seen something like this when I was a girl, but I had forgotten how fantastic these dancers are. It gave me some ideas too. I just wish I had the right environment to try them in."

Tony and Willy had gone off to the rest room. Tony asked him, "How are things with you and Mary going?"

"All right so far. We're becoming good friends and that is nice. We've been playing and singing a bit at the Crosswinds."

"I haven't been there since I went with you. I had a very unusual experience the night I slept on the beach."

"Really? Good or bad?"

"It was okay, just very strange. How do you think Mary will do back on the mainland?"

"It's hard to say. She could do all right if she gets with the right people. It's hard to know with the music business. You can be hot today and cold tomorrow. For me, it's like a hobby. But for Mary, at least for now it's serious, do or die."

As they walked back to their seats, Tony asked, "How long before you'll see her again."

"That's not a sure thing. But this cruise winds up in May, in about seven or eight weeks. So I'll see how things look then."

After they sat down everyone quietly awaited the start of the next performance. The music began as it had before. It wasn't so much a musical piece as it was an accompaniment to the dancers. Even so the instruments had a fascinating sound. Tony looked forward to a performance for instruments only.

After the end of the concert the six friends walked to a nearby café for hot drinks and some conversation but not for too long as the couples wanted to spend these final moments together alone.

The final night before a couple is to be separated for a long period of time can be one of the most important times in their life together. It's reminiscent of someone going off to battle, not knowing if they will return.

After Tony and Melina returned to her place she placed candles throughout the apartment and burned incense. While she made tea, he warmed up the stereo then put on some romantic music. The atmosphere became so peaceful and warm. They sat opposite each other on a rug, recalling the good times they had shared. She poured his tea, then he poured hers. They put their arms through one another and drank the tea. They then kissed each other's forehead, eyes, lips, and so on into the night.

When the alarm clock went off at five a.m. they felt that they had been in a state of bliss for the past few hours. If Tony had not prepared himself mentally for that moment he would not have been able to return to the ship.

With Melina's help they made it to the *Lady* with time to spare. They sat in her car still bonded in their feelings. Soon that moment would only be a memory, and their feelings of love would be set aside to be kept in a special place until a later time, while the reality of the present took precedence.

Other cars had pulled into the area near the *Lady Explorer.* They were unloading their passengers who were returning to the ship. When Tony could delay no longer, he and Melina said their final words and kissed goodbye. He walked at a rapid pace up the gangplank followed closely by Mate. "Hey, man."

"Hey, man, yourself."

As they rounded the turn at the end of the last step and set foot on the deck of the *Lady*, he said, "Well, here we go again, Mate."

"Amen, here we go again."

Chapter 9

DESTINY

At lunch the first day, Tony discovered a letter in the crew's mail rack that had been there since Saturday. It was from Maureen. There was no longer any doubt about her pregnancy. She greatly appreciated his last letter to her. She had a new friend that she met at her acting school that had been very kind and helpful. He had just graduated from a university in New York and joined the teaching staff at her school. They had developed quite a rapport. She told Tony not to worry. There was a PS: Cliff had disappeared with no hint of his whereabouts. Tony just sat at his table astounded, "What a scene!"

About midmorning of the second day, the *Lady* encountered a bit of weather. It wasn't nearly as bad as the first storm she had encountered over five weeks before. After such an experience she was more than prepared. Most of the crew took it in their stride with only a few becoming seasick. Tony was kept busy in the sick-bay issuing motion sickness pills. More than rough seas, a very heavy rain was pelting her.

It was during the morning of the third day with the weather beginning to taper off that the first mate came into the sick-bay complaining of an earache. Because of it he'd been relieved of duty until the following day. Before leaving the sick-bay, he reminded Tony of their brief conversation at the time of their first interview. "I seem to recall you mentioned something about an acquaintance in Berlin. A lady I believe, that caused you to drop the *h* from your name."

Tony was impressed. "That's quite a memory, Mr. Jenkins, sir."

"I read a fair amount. I believe it helps to keep one's mind sharp."

"I love to read, but I haven't had much time for it lately."

"That is a pity."

"Not really, since I enjoy very much what has been causing me to not have the time."

"I see."

Tony asked him, "Anyway, getting back to Berlin and Europe in general, have you seen much of the world?"

"My lord, yes, I'd say most of it."

"Really, I have a lot of questions, if you don't mind, sir."

"Mind you, an awful lot of it has been by way of sea ports, which is not quite the same as what one might see as a result of traveling over land."

"I'm hoping to see as much of it as I can one day."

"That's quite a big undertaking, lad. May I ask, what is the driving force behind all of this?"

"I was in an acting school for some time. When I was finished with it I had to decide what to do next. In trying to portray the characters of different people I realized how little I knew about people. Of people outside the United States, I probably knew nothing. I felt so young and inexperienced, and then I had a kind of revelation."

"What, pray tell, was it?"

"To know of all men and to know of all lands is to know of thy self."

"That is profound. It could be a driving force all right."

"Well, obviously I can't learn of all men, but the more the better."

"Lad, you've set yourself quite a goal there."

"It's nearly time for lunch which means I'm going to have to close up shop here for today. My duties are in the chart room after lunch."

"I'll be here to see the doctor again in the morning. He will see if the inflammation has subsided. I would be pleased to continue our discussion at that time, if it's agreeable with you of course."

"I'll have my list of questions ready and waiting."

"Quite so, then."

"Good day, sir."

"And a good day to you as well, Mr. Lewis."

Later that evening some of the men were still in the crew's mess after finishing dinner. Tony, Chuck, and Willy were sitting at a table together when Mate and Rob came over with fresh trays of food. Rob greeted them, "How are you doing, guys?"

Tony said, "Considering I've just spent two nights back in my old bunk above a devout smoker, not bad."

Someone at the table said, "We were wondering what happened to you, two."

Mate said, "Looks like we almost missed chow."

Willy asked, "I heard there were some problems down in the engine room. Is that right?"

Rob replied, "Yes, one of the engines was acting up. They're the originals so they're both pretty old. They've been rebuilt a few times, but I don't think they're long for this world."

"That's a shame," Willy said. "I overheard the captain and the first mate talking today when I was working outside their office. Remember, right after the big storm we went through, the *Lady* was being repaired?"

Rob said, "Sure. Wasn't the upper boat deck damaged?"

"That's right. Since she was being taken out of duty for a few days, the engineers decided, because of her age and history, to put her in a dry dock just long enough to have a look at her bottom. We never heard the results."

Rob again, "Yes, that's right."

Willy continued, "Well, the results just came back from our home office in Washington, D.C. And that's what the captain and the first mate were talking about."

Tony interrupted, "Good grief, the suspense is killing me."

"I didn't hear all that they said, but I did hear words like 'extensive rust in the hull' and 'obsolete' which could only spell one thing."

Tony again, "I'm still dying over here."

Rob interpreted, "What this must mean is that the *Lady*'s days are numbered."

Mate added, "And the number is probably not a big one."

Tony groaned, "Man, I like this ship. She's been like a great big mother duck to all of us."

Willy continued, "If what we fear is true, and I'm sure we all love her, this is probably her last cruise."

Chuck was also moved, "And then what, Willy?"

"What else is there but the scrap heap?"

Rob added, "I read that the Japanese are buying up all the scrap metal they can get."

Mate asked, "Wouldn't it be ironic if part of her was turned into one of those little Japanese cars, or motorcycles?"

Tony was mortified, "You're going to make me throw up. Crap, what is Sparks going to do? This ship is his life."

Willy chided him, "We're only making a guess here, matey. I only heard those two things. Don't go over the side yet."

Tony informed them, "Well, I'm actually having a little chit-chat with Mr. Jenkins tomorrow in the sick-bay. I'll see what I can find out."

"If it's okay for him to tell you," said Rob.

The rain had finally given up its assault. There was a bright full moon lighting up the night. Tony had decided to walk about the open decks of the *Lady*. With the thought that her existence may be nearing an end, he felt like spending time alone exploring places on the ship both familiar and unfamiliar, places he had painted or helped to fix. While he was forward of the wheelhouse he looked at the inscription on the large brass bell:

U.S.N.

LADY *X*

1941

He touched the part of the *X* that was the gash from a bullet. He tried to go back in his mind to that time and imagine what it must have been like to be standing on the same spot then. He imagined how she must have looked crossing the Pacific Ocean from San Francisco Bay to Pearl Harbor with both engines running at nearly full speed—brand spanking new and as proud as any filly ready to enter a race.

Tony's imaginary vision faded when something caught his eye. The angle and brilliance of the moonlight were just right to enhance the outline of a small rectangle on the surface of the bulkhead below the wheelhouse. It was centered between two portholes just behind the ship's bell. On close inspection, there appeared to be lettering engraved on it, but there was so much paint covering it Tony couldn't be sure. He took out his bosun's knife and carefully peeled away layers of paint.

What he discovered was a brass plaque that was placed there in 1945 just prior to being retired from her naval service. It had been covered over innumerable times with paint and preservatives during the ship's sixteen years of floating storage in the mothball fleet. Then when she was refurbished it hadn't occurred to anyone to strip away the paint on an insignificant rectangle.

He removed enough to be able to read the lettering but even that much was very difficult with only his knife. To avoid scratching it would require paint remover. But what he read would remain in his memory forever.

```
* * * * * * * * * * * *
*            USS LADY              *
*   FOR DISTINGUISHED SERVICE      *
*      IN THE PACIFIC THEATER      *
*           1941 TO 1945           *
*      DEPARTMENT OF THE NAVY      *
* * * * * * * * * * * *
```

He sat there and contemplated the events and people that must have led up to receiving that plaque. He thought of the enormity, the tragedy, and in the end the glory of it all. He went up to the bow to sit with his feet dangling over the edge. The wind blew against him, but he could still hear the sound of the Pacific lapping at the ship's bow just as it had all those years ago.

At breakfast the following day Tony told his friends of his unbelievable find. He intended to bring it to the attention of the first mate when he saw him later that morning.

It was about ten o'clock when Mr. Jenkins arrived at the sick-bay for the examination of his ear. Dr. Christian saw that the inflammation was beginning to subside, but would see the first mate again the following morning. Before leaving, Mr. Jenkins continued the conversation of the previous day. There was an electric coffeepot in the room that Tony used to make some hot water for tea. He made a pot of tea for the two of them. Tony asked, "Would you care for some milk in your tea, sir?"

"I may. What tea is it?"

"Earl Grey, sir."

"Ah yes, the queen mother's favorite. Just a bit please."

Before Jenkins could get into the topic of world travel, Tony had a more pressing matter to discuss. Because Tony felt he and the first mate had a good rapport he decided to get right to the point. "I heard a rumor yesterday that I hope you can clear up for me."

"Why certainly, I only hope I can be of help."

"Remember the storm we went through a couple of months ago?"

The first mate took a drink from his tea as he recalled, "I'll never forget it."

"When the *Lady* was in dry dock right after that, the rumor is that there were some serious problems with the hull. What did the engineers find when they inspected her?"

Jenkins hesitated before answering, "I see. How did you hear about this?"

"One of the men overheard a conversation between you, sir, and the captain yesterday. But only bits and pieces."

"Well, I don't see any reason not to tell you the whole of it. Since the ship was originally refurbished independent of Coast and Geodetic Survey, we had not seen the ship's hull. It was an excellent opportunity to give it a close look with a critical eye."

Tony refilled Jenkins's tea, "So there was an inspection?"

"Oh yes. But the findings of the engineers were sent on to our headquarters in Washington, D.C., for appraisal."

"What happened then?"

"The captain received a report only this last Monday morning. The engineers found the rust on the ships hull to be rather extensive below the water line and recommended replacing most of the surface with new steel. They also recommended that the design of the hull be more compatible with use on the ocean. It was believed that the condition of the hull was mainly due to her lying at anchor for sixteen years while in floating storage unattended."

Tony had a feeling of relief, "That's good news then. She's going to be given a new lease on life."

"Not necessarily. Headquarters has made a decision about that. They determined that repairs would be too costly. Updating the engines and equipment, which are by modern standards obsolete, would also be too costly. They've decided to replace her with a purpose built, all electronic, state-of-the-art craft. It would include modern air-conditioned quarters for the crew and will even have a recreation room."

Tony's heart had already sunk into his stomach. "When will they make the switch?"

"The new craft had actually been in production for some time and is expected to be fully sea worthy one month after our return to our home port across from Alameda."

Thinking about Sparks, Tony asked, "What about the crew?"

"Those of the crew who wish to remain will simply move their gear to the new ship."

Tony was starting to feel detached from the conversation. "Has a name for it been picked yet?"

"The captain has seen a picture of the prototype, so he thinks an appropriate name would be the *Pelican*."

Tony was almost nauseated then and felt a great need to go out on deck. "I have to close up shop here. When I finish can I show you something I discovered last night? I think you'll find it profoundly interesting."

"Actually, I need to get back to my quarters for just a moment. Can I meet you?"

"Say twenty minutes at the front of the wheelhouse?"

"That would be just fine."

"Thank you, sir. I'll see you there."

"Right you are, then."

Once the first mate was gone Tony said to himself, "What a bummer. Oh *Lady, Lady, Lady.*" Then in disbelief, he said, "The *Pelican*? What kind of a stupid name is that?"

Tony was waiting when the first mate arrived at their meeting place. "So Mr. Lewis, what did you want to show me?"

Tony pointed behind the bell to the plaque. "Last night while the moon light was just so, I noticed this. I was barely able to tell that there were letters engraved in it. I could make out that it had five rows of something in it. I peeled some paint away with a knife. Have a look at what I found."

Mr. Jenkins moved closer. "You're certainly right about the lettering." He put on his reading glasses and began to read, "USS LADY . . . distinguished . . . 1941 to . . . Department of the Navy. Good Lord, Mr. Lewis! This is an amazing find, especially now. I don't think anyone knows about this."

Tony saw a glimmer of hope. "Sir, do you think she'll still get junked?"

Almost offended by the word, the first mate said, "I'll mention this to the captain. I'll see what his take is on the matter. Meanwhile I'll have the bosun get one of his men to remove the paint from the plaque, and give it a good polish as it deserves."

Tony was very pleased at that idea, "Thank you, sir."

"I'll let you know tomorrow what I learn from the captain."

"That would be great, sir. I'll see you then." As Mr. Jenkins was saying goodbye Tony had turned and was quickly making his way to the crew's mess. At lunch he hoped to tell his friends all that he had learned.

During the meal, all of Tony's friends had joined him, hoping to hear the result of his meeting with the first mate. He waited until they finished eating and were having coffee before beginning. Tony started out slowly, "I don't know if I have bad news or good news." He went on to tell them what the first mate told him followed by the result of showing Jenkins the plaque.

Willy said, "It's hard to figure out what all this means. I had a chance to see the plaque today. I have to tell you it was a very moving experience."

Mate and Chuck couldn't resist having a look. They had similar experiences. Rob would have to wait until after he finished his shift to see it.

Chuck said, "You're really lucky, Rob, because one of us will have it all shined up for you."

"I hope it's one of us," said Mate.

Willy said, "We have to be realistic about this. There may have been thousands of ships in our navy in the Second World War. Suppose all the survivors have a plaque like this?"

Rob said, "I've never seen one."

Willy added, "Come to think of it, neither have I."

Mate said, "We really need to wait to hear what the captain has to say about the plaque."

Tony added, "We wouldn't have seen this one if I hadn't found it just by chance."

Rob had to admit, "I'm sorry but I have to tell you that I wouldn't mind working in a modern engine room."

Willy added, "As for Sparks, he would have an air conditioned radio room instead of that little shack with its portable fan."

Tony felt beaten and admitted, "That's true. It's not that I think a state-of-the-art ship would be a bad thing. Obviously it wouldn't be. I know it seems I may have gone too far with this. I don't know why I've become so attached to the *Lady* in such a short time either. But the thought that she may get turned into a massive pile of scrap after all that she's been, and then probably turned into a Japanese who-knows-what, makes me sick."

Later on the bosun assigned someone to strip and polish the brass plaque. Because he wanted to be sure it wasn't damaged in the process, he gave the task to Willy. As Willy worked on it, something of the significance of it made its way into his feelings more and more. When he finished and walked away he noticed a sense of pride in being a part of the ship that he had not felt before. He stood far forward of the plaque and looked back at it. He spoke as if talking to the *Lady*, "You won't have to worry about it not being seen now, ol' girl." The only answer he heard in return was the sound of the sea being cut in two by her bow as it rose and fell.

After dinner Willy took his four friends to have a look at the plaque. Tony commented, "Willy, you did a beautiful job."

Chuck was awestruck. "It's so beautiful, it looks like it's made of gold." Otherwise they didn't say very much. Willy had to go below for something. Members of the ship's crew came by to see the plaque as word spread of its discovery. Mate had to go below to get ready for a card game he would join later in the crew's mess. Tony, Chuck, and Rob just sat on something and looked out to sea thinking their private thoughts. Eventually either because of the darkening sky or the increasing chill in the air they all left the bow and went inside.

The following morning after the doctor examined the healing of the cut on Tony's cheek he finished with Mr. Jenkins. He and Tony continued their discussion. Tony told him how great the plaque looked. Jenkins told Tony, "The captain was rather surprised when I told him of your find. He said that as far as he knew there was a remote chance that a historical preservation group may be interested in the *Lady Explorer.* He said that it would depend on the reason the ship was honored with the plaque."

Tony asked him, "How can we find that out?"

"When the mail plane makes its next pickup, the captain will send a letter of inquiry to the Department of the Navy as to the issuing of the plaque. We really won't know any more until we receive a reply."

"That could take forever."

"It could, except that the captain has an old friend in the department of records. So we may have a reply in a record breaking short time."

"Wow! That's great. That would be so fine if she were to wind up being preserved for posterity. Oh, I'm sorry. I just realized that I forgot to offer you some tea."

"That's quite all right. I know how this whole episode of the ship's fate has been weighing upon you. The doctor is giving me a final examination in a week's time. Perhaps you would be kind enough to share some of your European experiences with me then."

"I'd be glad to. Again I want to thank you for your help."

"You're quite welcome, I'm sure." And with that the first mate left the sick-bay to return to his duties.

A few days passed before Tony went up to the radio shack to engage Sparks in a conversation. He looked inside the hatch and found Sparks sitting at his little table transmitting the ship's position to a coast guard station in Alaska, the nearest to their present location. Tony waited for him to finish before greeting him. "USCGS *Lady Explorer,* over and out."

"Sparks, how's life in your ivory tower today?"

"Tony, come on in. How are you doing?"

"Just fine, thanks."

"Are you still keeping Mr. Jenkins busy?"

"So you heard about that?"

"Even though I'm stuck up here most of the time, there's not much that escapes me. This is information central, you know."

"How do you feel about the . . . about the . . . ? I can't even say the name. The *Pelican,* stupid name. You know something, Sparks? I figured this out yesterday, a pelican by any other name is still a bird, right?"

"Right."

"So the captain's going to give us the bird."

"Say, that's pretty good, Tone'."

"Anyway Sparks, how do you feel about all this rigamarole?"

"Well, Tone', say, you don't mind if I call you Tone', do you?"

"Not at all."

"When you've been around for a long time you learn to roll with the punches. I've been bouncing around out here on the water for a very long time. I've had two marriages go haywire because of it so I gave up on that."

"It sounds like you're thinking of calling it quits?"

"There's only one thing that worries me about retirement."

"What's that, Sparks?"

"Motionless sickness."

"Motionless sickness?"

"Yeah, you know. I've been movin' up and down with the water most of my life. I wonder if I can get used to solid ground that doesn't move around under me."

"I think I know the answer."

"What's that, Tone'?"

"California, live in California. Preferably near the San Andreas Fault. There's never a still moment, and you'll be a happy man."

"Tone', have you ever thought of going into real estate?"

With that they broke into laughter.

Sparks had a radio call to respond to so Tony said goodbye and climbed the ladder to the flying bridge, his other favorite spot on the *Lady*. As he often did to relax he laid on the enclosed deck. He closed his eyes until he was fully relaxed. When he opened his eyes a large bird gliding high above him caught his attention. It was flying so high that Tony couldn't make out its color. He wasn't sure but it looked like an albatross. It was following the ship. Long after seagulls have given up, the albatross continue to follow a ship for days longer. They look similar to gulls but are much larger, some with a wing span as much as six feet. Tony wondered what it must be like to be up there flying along so effortlessly and free.

He closed his eyes to see if he could visualize the experience, then he opened his eyes and slowly stood upright. He held his arms out like wings and danced about like an Indian ceremonial dancer. In his mind he became the albatross and felt the freedom of flight. He glided to the right, then over to the left. He dropped down and then swooped up. Looking far below he saw a little white ship, the *Lady Explorer*. He knew that if he patiently waited, his effort would be rewarded with the most important thing the ship had to offer him. When she dumped her garbage over the side it would be time for a feast.

And sure enough he saw the albatross glide down to the ship's wake. Like clockwork before and after mealtimes, or six times a day, the garbage was dumped over the side. And like the albatross it was time for Tony to eat.

The following Friday was the morning of the first mate's next appointment with the doctor. When it was completed he and Tony had another conversation. But first Tony made another pot of hot water for their tea. "Have a seat, Mr. Jenkins, the tea will be ready in a minute."

"Jolly good. I brought some biscuits."

"Now that was a good idea." Tony poured two cups of tea then sat down. He picked up his cup and said, "Here's to your health, sir."

Jenkins couldn't wait any longer. "I'm really keen to know what I can about life in Berlin. Since Germany was our adversary during the last war and Berlin was its cultural center, it has always been of great interest to me."

"To begin with, it's a very long and involved story, so I will skip all the interesting and intimate details. I'll give you the tip of the iceberg, the first few drops of rain before the storm, the first snowflake before the winter snow."

"You make it sound irresistible."

"At the beginning of my travels I had no real desire to go to Germany. Because of the actions of the Nazis I could not relate to the Germans at all. For me it wasn't even a thought. The irony is that although Berlin was not only a divided capital of a divided country, in time it became the capital of my life."

Now captivated, Jenkins said, "Please go on."

"It was November of '63 when I left San Francisco with about six hundred dollars, bound for India. I crossed America as cheaply as I could; sometimes hitchhiking. I got on a Yugoslav freighter in New York headed for Morocco, stopping first at Casablanca. The ship arrived at Casablanca on Christmas day. That was the beginning of one amazing experience after another. From Tangiers I made my way to Spain. After a few days at Algeciras, I hitchhiked eastward. The problem with that was that no one gave me a ride, so the first day I walked thirty miles carrying an extremely heavy backpack. I later found out that the American tradition of holding out your closed hand with the thumb pointing up was in Spain an obscene gesture. It's a wonder they didn't try to run me over."

"If I recall, in Europe one has to wave his arm up and down as though he's flagging down the traffic, isn't that right?"

"That's right. Well, after I made my way to Torremolinos on the Mediterranean Coast I stayed with an old friend of a friend, Frau Kornitzer. From there it starts. This lady was an expatriate from Berlin. She and her late husband had been intellectuals who fled before the Nazis got hold of them in 1933. She was a super nice woman, real people. She had several tiny cottages that she rented to tourists. Also staying there was a young German artist named Gobela. He was a physicist before escaping from East Germany. After spending some time as an engineer with Grundig, he left everything behind and was in Spain to develop himself as a painter. But that is another story."

The first mate made another pot of tea for the two of them.

"I never did figure out how many years it would take me to walk to India." Tony continued, "Because I needed to work as I traveled, they suggested that I try my luck in West Berlin. There was a lot of work available to foreigners as guest workers. They told me that West Berlin, surrounded as it was by East Germany, was like an island. It had become a symbol of freedom in Europe. Gobela gave me the addresses of a friend and his sister in West Berlin as well as a friend and his mother in East Berlin."

Dr. Christian interrupted them, "I'm sorry to disturb your conversation, but I'm expecting two other men in a few minutes for their checkup."

Mr. Jenkins apologized in return, "I'm terribly sorry, sir. I didn't realize . . ."

Tony told the first mate, "Mr. Jenkins, if you like we can continue after dinner today."

"A splendid idea. My office is rather cramped but we could carry on there."

"And then I could finish the story."

"Shall we say seven o'clock?"

"Seven o'clock it is, sir."

"Good day then."

"Good day, sir."

After lunch Tony did his work at the depth recorder until dinner. After that he arrived at the first mate's tiny office in time for their meeting.

Jenkins told him, "I very much appreciate you taking the time to share your story with me."

Tony settled into the only chair there was room for. "I find I like talking about it because it helps me to relive it, more so than thinking about it."

"Yes, I can see how it would. That accounts for why we avoid talking about unpleasant things."

Tony wondered aloud, "Let's see, where did I leave off?"

"Names of friends and relatives in Berlin I believe."

"Oh yes, thank you. I spent New Year's Eve in the good company of my new friends in Casa Kornitzer. I stayed on there nearly two weeks. Some places are hard to leave."

Jenkins asked, "Forgive me for interrupting here but wasn't President Kennedy assassinated at about that time?"

"Yes, a month and a half earlier."

"Oh, right you are then."

Tony continued his recollection. "I hitchhiked my way through Spain and France to Germany. That was an adventure in itself. It was beginning to become a very cold winter. Once I arrived in West Berlin I phoned a friend of Gobela's who happened to be a woman my age. She met me and took me back to her place. She told me I could sleep on a couch in the sitting room and have free access to the apartment until I was able to find my own apartment. Now this was someone who didn't know me. Of course Gobela had sent a letter of introduction ahead of me, and there was the one that I carried with me. Much later I found this kind of hospitality all through Germany."

"So I've heard. That seems to be more the case on the continent. I'm afraid that in England they are a bit more . . . conservative."

"Anyway, the next day I was taken to meet Christina, the sister of Gobela. When I introduced myself as Anthony Lewis she hesitated at first then responded with embarrassment, 'Oh, you mean Antony.' It was as if I had heard my name pronounced right for the first time. By the time I left Berlin five months later she had become the love of my life. And that's how I happened to drop the *h* from my name."

"That's extraordinary." Mr. Jenkins became so interested in Tony's story that he persuaded him to continue telling the entire drama, as the unfolding proved it to be.

In the week that followed they met for at least an hour each day or evening while Mr. Jenkins was given another portion of the story. The telling seemed to open a floodgate of past memories.

After finishing one of their sessions late one afternoon, Tony took a walk around the deck of the ship to quell a feeling of restlessness and longing. When he got to the stern it was in the twilight before dark. The wake trailing behind the ship was still visible but fading. He leaned on the rail and looked out to sea. It was like being on the rear platform of a time machine watching the present become the past in degrees.

He remembered standing on the balcony of the last train coach as it left the train station in West Berlin. Christina stood on the platform with little Mathias holding her hand. Tears filled her eyes as they looked at one another for the last time, while he remembered the feeling of holding her close and the sound of her voice filled with sadness. And as he held her for that last moment on the station platform, he remembered how she was when they experienced their first embrace, her love, her passion, and her joy. And when they were in that first embrace he remembered the faraway, forgotten place from where we all have come, a place that only God can describe.

He stared at the ship's wake as the image of Christina and her son grew smaller and smaller, until they were no more.

MOUNT ANTONY?

In the days that followed, time went by in an uneventful way except that Tony recorded a prior unknown undersea mountain. He was told that he could name it after himself. He called it Mount Antony, but unfortunately he didn't make a personal note of its longitude or latitude. Since it was under the sea no one would ever see it anyway.

The mail plane had come and gone. This time Tony didn't receive anything, but he sent a letter to Melina expressing his love.

Captain Reiger sent a letter of inquiry to the Navy's department of records as promised.

After dinner one evening, Willy and Tony were engaged in a conversation about life in general. Willy said, "I noticed that your roommate, George, spends most of his off time in bed?"

"Yeah, he's a special case. It wouldn't be as bad in there if he didn't listen to that lonely hearts elevator music on his little radio all the time."

Willy asked him, "How are you getting along, you know, with this cruise in general?"

"Okay, I find I'm doing a lot more thinking about things while we're out here. When I'm on land I'm too busy to think."

"It's that way with most of us. But when we're out here some guys keep busy with reading, studying, or hobbies. A few gamble too much. Most of those lose their money before their next paycheck."

"Yes, I've noticed that. Mate seems to win most of the time."

"He's been lucky so far. The thing that is really sad about the gamblers is that there are those who have no money left when they get back to their home port."

"That really is sad."

"And if they have a wife waiting for them it's a disaster."

"That's for sure. You know, Willy, I feel like I'm living two lives. When I'm on land I'm living life day to day, almost care free. Out here I'm recalling the past, looking at today, and wondering about the future. For example I can see that I fall in love too easily. It's almost as though I'm in love with love."

"Well, now, you may find this interesting. In India there was a writer philosopher named Sri Arobindo. Among other things he wrote of love. He referred to the Don Juan complex. That's love for its own sake."

"India again. Anyway, I wonder if that's what's going on with me."

Willy added, "I have to tell you, I'm hearing and seeing more of that attitude, especially in San Francisco and Berkeley."

Pete walked into the mess as though looking for someone. When he saw that whoever wasn't there he turned and left.

Tony commented, "Isn't it something? How easy it was for Chuck to get that jerk off his back?"

"Right, all he had to do was stand up to him."

"Once he knew what Pete was up to. Has he said anything about how things are between him and the girl he danced with?"

"Yes, it seems to be off to a good start. I know he sent her a letter with the last mail plane."

"That's cool. I hope the captain sent a letter to the Navy. I've got a feeling saving the *Lady* is going to be a long and difficult process."

The third Friday out Tony was just putting the finish to his story for Mr. Jenkins. "After I returned to Tangiers to catch a freighter back to the States, I swear this is true, the next one going that way that I could get on was the Slovenija. It was the same one that I had gone over on."

"Unbelievable."

"And that is the end of the story," Tony said with a sigh of relief.

"Good Lord, Mr. Lewis. You should put this into a book."

"I don't know. I can't stay in one place long enough to get a book started. If I did, I would make "*CHRISTINA*" the title. But I seem to be too busy doing things, to stop long enough to write a story."

MEANWHILE

Back on Oahu, Melina's period was two and a half weeks overdue from when she thought it would be. She had just returned from her doctor and was at Kim's place. Kim was putting together a light lunch for them both. Melina was not feeling good about the results and was telling Kim, "He told me that the tests show that I have all the signs of pregnancy."

"What kind of birth control did you say you used?"

"The rhythm method. It's based on a twenty-eight-day cycle, and I've always been regular," she was not her usual calm self. "I must have ovulated a week late. That would have put it right at the beginning of Tony's last visit here."

"If you're pregnant, do you want to have the baby?"

"It's not a question of wanting to; it's a question of can I? You know as well as I do that it would mean the end of my hope of a career in dance for at least the next two years, or maybe three or even four. And that's if everything goes okay, and there's a father around."

Kim asked, "Do you think Tony would stay with you and help you?"

"I don't know. He seems like a super guy. He's hooked on traveling, he says so himself. If I tell him I want to have his baby he might get scared and run off. Men are always doing that."

Kim put their lunch on the table and said, "Dear Melina, what are you going to do?"

Melina had picked up her knife to cut her sandwich in two. She carefully placed the knife on it and slowly began to cut. "I don't know." For a moment she contemplated the two halves as they fell away from each other. "I really don't know."

$$Chapter\ 10$$

LIKE A HOUSE OF CARDS

It was midmorning on the last day of the third survey cruise. The *Lady* was in the middle of a heat wave. The ship stood motionless to allow the crew to have a swim. The water was fairly calm with tiny waves lapping at her starboard side.

On the ship's stern a removable section of railing had been opened up so that a diving board could be set up. The air was hot and even though the broken clouds provided occasional shade, swimmers could still receive a serious burn from the piercing rays of the sun.

Gradually members of the crew made their way onto the deck at the stern of the ship. One of the men tried to find some music on his shortwave radio. George, wearing a Hawaiian shirt and a pair of cutoff jeans, settled on to a mat with his back resting against the cabin. He lit a little cigar. After a puff he began thumbing through his collection of girly magazines. Johnny got more static than music on his radio. Luckily he found some jazz just as Mate and Tony appeared carrying towels and ice water.

Tony remarked, "That's real nice. Isn't that West Coast jazz?"

Mate corrected him, "Sounds kind of like East Coast to me."

Johnny asked, "You got me. What's the difference?"

Tony explained, "It's like the difference between San Francisco and New York. One is mellow and cool while the other is intellectual and often up tight. I leave it to you to decide which is which."

Johnny looked perplexed. Mate caught a glimpse of George's magazine. Mate said, "Hey, my man. You should try to meet some real women; it'll change your life."

"I wish," remarked George with a half smile as he choked on some smoke.

Tony did an aside to Mate, "That wasn't a bad suggestion, if he's not too far gone."

As Tony rubbed suntan lotion on his arms and legs, he asked Mate, "Can you rub this stuff on my back? I can't reach it."

"Sure thing, I would appreciate it if you would do the same for me."

Tony said jokingly, "So as to enhance your tan, no doubt."

"Okay, funny man, how would you like me to pour this ice water on your lily white stomach? I'm trying to keep from getting a burn, pale face."

"Okay, take it easy, I'm just teasing you. And don't call me pale face; half of my ancestors were Cherokee Indians."

"Can I call you half pale then?"

"No, you can't." He handed the lotion to Mate. "Here you go, man, just a little bit, okay?"

As Mate took the lotion, "You never told me you were half Indian."

"I didn't? Maybe I forgot."

"That's cool with me, man." He briskly rubbed the lotion into Tony's back and shoulders. His mind wandered off, and he began remembering rubbing lotion into Kim's beautifully smooth skin. Unconsciously his rubbing became slow and sensuous.

"Hey, man, what are you doing back there? That's starting to feel too good."

Mate, as if awakened from a dream, quickly pulled his hands away, "Sorry, man, I was thinkin' about Kim."

Tony got the bottle of lotion back. "When you and Kim won the dance contest you both were great. Turn around." He started applying lotion to Mate's shoulders and back. "You weren't just the best dancers there; you were in a whole other league. What are you doing working on a ship anyway?"

"I don't know, maybe I'm trying to find myself."

Tony was still applying the lotion when he said, "When I was studying acting I used to spend time at the theater. I saw a lot of dancers there and met some of them. But only a few had something that's hard to describe. I would get a special feeling when I saw them dance, or even just walk. You've got that special something Mate. When you danced with Kim there was magic in your legs."

As Mate took the lotion back from Tony, he began applying it to his own legs. "You know, when I was in high school I was studying modern dance. The guys used to make fun of me and call me sissy."

"Yeah, I remember you mentioned that."

"Well, there were times when something would happen to me while I was dancing. It seemed kind of strange then, but I would feel like I was coming to life. As if my legs or even my whole body had been asleep and was waking up."

"That's great. I'm telling you, man, a dancer is what you are, and on the stage is where you belong, instead of floating around out here on the water. After you show the world how good you are you can open a school and teach."

"That all sounds really good, but at the same time the whole thing scares me. You know man, just before I signed on with the *Lady* I nearly started classes at the New York School of Modern Dance in San Francisco, but I chickened out. I needed time to think about it all."

"Thinking is what you're doing too much of, just go do it."

Chuck arrived on deck closely followed by Willy. Both were wearing bathing trunks and T-shirts. Chuck's trunks were orange with a small red and white Red Cross emblem near the bottom along with some other small symbols. When Tony and Mate greeted them Tony asked, "Chuck, I haven't seen you wear those before."

"Yeah, my others are torn."

"Isn't that a life-saving emblem?"

"It sure is, I took lifeguard training at my high school, and I was on the swimming team. I used to do lifeguard work during summer breaks."

"A lifeguard and on the swimming team. What was your best stroke?"

"The hundred meter free style."

"Man, you are amazing. You should talk more about yourself."

"I know, I've always been told I'm too quiet."

"How about diving? When I come off the high board I feel like I'm flying."

"With diving I would always mess up. So I stuck with swimming."

Mate commented, "I'm telling you, my friend, Chuck here is gonna turn some heads one day."

Rob arrived after everyone else. Chuck said to him, "Rob, I was afraid you were about to miss out on the swim."

As he laid his towel and a bottle of lotion on the deck, "I was called back to fix a problem with a generator."

Chuck went over to look at the makeshift diving board. He thought to himself, *I could have been a good diver, if I'd just practiced.*

"All looks clear from here!" The shout came from the shark lookout in the crow's nest at the top of the mast. "All looks clear from here!"

"Hey, Mate, isn't this lotion supposed to stay on even in the water?" Tony asked.

"That's what it said on the bottle the last time I read the label."

"Well then, let's go cool off."

With the all-clear signal, a line started to form at the diving board ending with Bill, Tony, Mate, and Rob. Since Chuck was already at the head of the line, he dove in first.

In his bright yellow bathing trunks with big red flowers Bill looked like someone who had drunk far too much beer and had far too little exercise. He asked Tony, "When we get back to Oahu, am I gonna see you and your buddy at that strip joint called the Sleepin' Lady?"

The overall quiet was overcome by shouting from the men as they dove off the board and splashed into the water.

"Yeah, that place has become like our home away from home."

Bill continued on, "I've seen you at one of the clubs on Hotel Street with a chick who looks just like one of them dancers at the Sleepin' Lady, a tall good lookin' babe. Man, wouldn't I like to get myself a taste of that chocolate pie."

As Tony started to turn red, and not from the sun, he said, "She *is* a dancer at the Sleeping Lady, a *real* dancer."

With a kind of half drunk manner, "Well, maybe with her clothes on, I didn't recognize her." He half choked into a sickening laugh. By this time the men in line ahead of them had dove into the water leaving only Bill, Tony, Mate, and Rob in line.

Tony gave Bill a nudge toward the edge and said, "In your condition do you think it's safe to go in for a swim?" Bill was too near the edge, he lost his balance and grabbed for Tony's arm causing Tony to lose his balance and grab for Mate's arm causing all three of them to go over the side with one huge splash. Rob was left standing with a half smile—half puzzled look on his face. By this time most of the men, including Chuck, were already making their way up the ship's side by way of rope ladders that hung from the deck in order to prepare for another dive.

Mate was a good swimmer. In need of some real exercise, he decided to swim out a ways from the ship to get a good workout.

Tony didn't care much for Bill, drunken bastard that he knew him to be. Still, he thought he should keep an eye on him just in case he couldn't make it back to the ladders on his own. But he was nowhere to be seen.

Suddenly Bill appeared at the surface coughing up water, flaying his arms all about, and shouting for help. Tony was about ten yards from Bill and began to swim toward him. Mate was over seventy-five yards from the ship when he heard the calls for help. He swam back as fast as he could to help. Still on deck, Chuck followed his instinct and training when he heard Bill's shouts and jumped into the water to help him.

Some men were climbing down the rope ladders to help pull the guys out of the water. Willy threw a life preserver their way with a line attached. Because of his training, Chuck knew to approach Bill from behind. He put an arm through one of Bill's armpits, then around his chest to the other armpit telling him, "Just stay loose. I'll take you in." Luckily Bill calmed down and cooperated as Chuck began to tow him while swimming toward the ship.

Just as Tony got close to them a shout rang out from the crow's nest, "Sharks! Sharks! About a hundred yards to the stern and headed this way!" Now everyone was shouting. The captain and bosun appeared on deck with a rifle. When Bill heard the word 'shark,' he panicked. He hit Chuck in the nose with a flaying elbow causing Chuck to lose his hold in pain as his nose started to bleed profusely. Tony struggled to get a hold on Bill from behind. No sooner did he get a hold on him than Bill seemed to be pulled right from his grasp. At that same moment Tony was pushed away by something powerful as he felt a sharp pain in his side. From the deck Willy shouted at Tony to take hold of the life preserver so he and Chuck could be pulled over to the ship.

At the railing Rob began shouting, "Chuck! Where's Chuck?!"

Tony looked in every direction but couldn't see Chuck. He put his hand to his side and felt a gash. He called out, "I can't see him. Chuck! Chuck! Where are you?! Chuck!"

Up on the deck Rob started to dive into the water to find Chuck but about four men held him back, "Don't be a fool! The sharks'll finish you off too." Rob just stared into the water in disbelief. There was no sign of either Bill or Chuck.

"Mate! What about Mate?!" He was swimming as fast as he could but there was a shark's dorsal fin cutting through the water toward him at a much faster speed. "Come on, Mate, hurry! There's one after you!" Although his feet were kicking rapidly, the shark caught Mate's right foot in its mouth. He screamed in agony, but the sound stopped as Mate was pulled under. With all his strength Mate twisted his body and pounded his fist into the shark's snout and eyes. A dark liquid came out of one of its eyes as the shark released its hold on him and swam away.

Mate appeared on the surface and struggled to swim. There was so much blood in the water that he couldn't see the condition of his foot. It had no feeling, and it didn't help him to swim.

Holding the life preserver with one hand, Tony swam in Mate's direction with the other. From the deck the bosun took great care not to hit the swimmers when he shot at the sharks. Mate got close enough for Tony to grab him. With one arm around Mate and a hand on the life preserver, Tony was pulled over to the rope ladders. As the men reached down for Mate and Tony, another shark appeared and was about to take after Mate's bloody foot when the bosun shot his rifle. Tony heard the bullet go past his ear before hitting the shark's head. He quickly looked at the bosun who nodded with a faint smile.

The crew managed to pull the two of them onto the deck. Mate's foot was mangled to above the ankle. Tony had a ten inch long gash above his waist that didn't appear to be deep. He was struggling to get his breath, "Where's Chuck?" He saw that Rob was still standing with his hands locked on the thin metal rail staring at the place where Chuck had disappeared, in a state of shock. "Oh god, no!" Tony struggled to get to his feet and quickly headed for the edge. He was stopped by two of the men who grabbed his arms.

Rob's eyes were filled with tears as he stared down at the water. He said to them, "He's gone, Chuck's gone."

Dr. Christian appeared with a stretcher accompanied by a junior officer. Three of the men put Mate, who was writhing in agony, onto the stretcher and carried him to the sick-bay as quickly as they could, accompanied by Tony.

An announcement came over the intercom, "All hands prepare to return to your duty stations at once. I repeat. All hands prepare to return to your duty stations at once."

In the sick-bay the doctor had stopped the bleeding the best he could. After injecting a local anesthetic, he cleaned and dressed Mate's mangled foot. Tony had tended to himself, putting a large bandage over his cut side. He was given the task of looking in the records for Mate's blood type so that the doctor could find volunteer blood donors to replace some of the blood he lost. The doctor gave Mate a shot that put him out then got on the telephone to the bridge, "Captain, sir, the condition of Mr. Jones's foot is critical. I don't know if it can be saved, but we must get him to the hospital at Pearl as fast as possible." There was a pause while he listened to the captain. He answered, "Very good, sir." After hanging up the phone, he said, "Mr. Lewis, I will need you to assist me with Mr. Jones?"

"Yes, sir. Will I have a chance to get into some clothes?"

"Of course, but return here as quickly as you can. You'll be with me until we get back to Pearl. The captain is going to radio for a seaplane to meet with us. It will take Mr. Jones to the hospital there. In the meantime the ship is going to return to port at maximum speed for as long as possible."

"Yes, sir. Lucky for us we're near the south end of our run and the islands." Tony looked at Mate who was in a deep sleep, and said, "He's not feeling any pain now."

Once Tony was in the privacy of his quarters he gave a prayer asking that Mate's foot be saved so he could dance again. After he cleaned and dressed he returned to the sick-bay. Mate had been placed on the only bed there was room for. Because of the sedative the doctor had given him, Mate was still asleep.

Meanwhile on the ship all hands were at their duty stations. Because the tragedy happened just before lunch, the men would have to take a meal break whenever they got an opportunity.

Since Bill and Chuck did not appear after a reasonable time they were presumed lost. The captain ordered that the U.S. flag be flown at half-staff from the main mast.

Rob was in such a state of emotional shock that the doctor wanted to give him a sedative. Rob refused in order to be able to assist the chief engineer get the *Lady* back to Pearl Harbor as fast as possible, so the doctor gave him something for depression.

The *Lady*'s course was set south-southwest in the direction of the Kauai Channel between the islands of Kauai and Oahu. The chief engineer had made preparations to run the engines at full speed. Rob was not sure how long the aging engines could hold up under the strain, but the chief was optimistic.

After doing all that they could for Mate's comfort, the doctor told Tony to take a break. He went to the crew's mess for a hot drink and a sandwich to take with him to the bow. When he got to the bow the ship had been at full speed for about half an hour. There was a rolling sea so an occasional wave would hit the bow sending a spray over it. In the mist caused by the spray he imagined Chuck's face. He remembered him dancing with Mary and having the time of his life. He remembered him exploring the rain forest, eyes filled with wonder, and he remembered an innocent kid who had the whole world ahead of him. He couldn't understand why life went the way it sometimes did. He had to stop thinking about it all, it was too depressing.

Pacing about the bow, Tony began to imagine how the *Lady* must have performed in action, going full speed into battle. There would have been an antiaircraft gun on the stern and bow for her defense. The Japanese would have done what they could to sink her. But they never did. Again Tony wondered why she was awarded the plaque. He stopped pacing and stood holding fast to the rail as she steamed ahead, proud that he had known her.

Willy appeared from behind him. "Look at her go, would ya, slicing the biggest ocean in the world right in two."

"Willy!"

"How's Mate doing? And how's his foot going to be after this?"

"The doctor doesn't know, but he doesn't hold a lot of hope for Mate's foot, it's so badly mangled. His only hope is surgery and soon at the hospital at Pearl."

Something caught Willy's eye causing him to look up. Seeing his expression Tony also glanced up. Neither of them had noticed the flag flying at half-staff until then. A heavy sadness came over them, and they fell silent for a moment. Willy's voice was full of emotion when he said, "By god, matey, I can't get over what's just happened to Chuck, and even old Bill. But especially dear sweet Chuck, I just can't fathom it. This has been such an unbelievable day. And Rob, is he going to be all right?"

"I sure hope so." Tony took a moment to regain his composure. "He's amazing. He's in emotional shock but insists on helping the chief engineer keep the *Lady* running at full speed until we contact the seaplane, or put in at Pearl."

"If anyone, he needs a long break."

"He's the best mechanic the chief has," Tony said.

"That's incredible. I'll be amazed if she can sustain full speed for very long."

"Keep your fingers crossed." Looking past Willy, Tony noticed a large sea bird perched on the ship's main mast. It was the same albatross that Tony had seen following the ship. Pointing to it he said, "Look there, Willy."

Willy turned to look just as the bird gracefully rose off its perch and flew away from the ship, "You know what they say about the albatross, don't you, lad?"

"No, what do they say?"

"Well, there are some who believe that the albatross have a special kinship to those of us who sail the seas. And there are those who believe that when a sailor is either buried at, or is lost at sea, that it is an albatross that shows him the way back to the creator."

Tony was speechless for a moment. "That's beautiful. I wonder if it is like that." After a pause, he said, "I have to get back to the sick-bay. If you know any good prayers—"

"I'll see what I can come up with, lad. God bless."

It was nearly sun set when the seaplane circled the ship before sitting down on the water. The very launch that Chuck had painstakingly prepared was readied to transport Mate to the plane. The doctor and Tony stood by as two of the crew placed Mate's stretcher into the launch. Willy joined the four of them before the ship's small crane lifted the launch on to the water.

Willy was at the helm of the launch as it took them to the plane. Once there they carefully lifted Mate's stretcher inside. After it was secured, the launch returned to the ship.

The plane's engines were given full throttle. In a matter of seconds it was airborne. The *Lady* continued on to Honolulu at her normal speed. Because she had been at full speed for over five hours she was expected to arrive in port quite ahead of schedule. After the evening meal most of the crew settled into preparing for their arrival. Because it was too late for Tony to send a radioed message ahead explaining the expected change in the arrival time, Kim and Melina would be at the *Lady*'s berth at the usual time.

TEARS

At Pearl Harbor the plane arrived at its docking area. A waiting ambulance rushed Mate to the emergency ward of the naval hospital. Altogether it had been eight hours from the shark's teeth to the surgeon's knife. Many more hours were needed to reconstruct Mate's foot.

Meanwhile the *Lady,* still more than a half day away from port, was experiencing a problem in the engine room. The chief engineer was on the phone to the captain. "There was a hell of a knock coming from engine number one. I had to shut it down Sir."

"I was afraid of this. What about engine number two?"

"She's running strong, Captain."

The captain asked, "Do you think it can get us back to port?"

"I'm not sure, sir, it could be close one way or the other."

"Very well then, I will have Sparks send a message to the coast guard alerting them, in case we need assistance." Being adrift on the sea without power was something every captain dreaded. "It's lucky for us that we have calm seas, should we become dead in the water, yah?"

"Yes sir, it's been a rather unlucky day so far. We're due for a change."

"Very good, chief, you and your men do the best you can."

"Aye, aye, sir."

So into the night and morning the chief engineer and Rob took turns standing by in the engine room listening for any sound coming from the remaining engine that would indicate trouble. They were like parents waiting for their sick infant to fall asleep.

In the early morning the *Lady* had just begun to skirt the northwestern coast of Oahu when an unusual sound and vibration began in engine number two. This followed a gradual decrease in lubricating oil pressure that became quite low. The chief contacted the bridge to notify the captain. After explaining the situation to the captain he suggested that if he slowed the engine just enough to keep the ship in motion she should last until help arrived. The captain agreed and had another message sent to the coast guard requesting a tow as soon as possible.

Most of the crew weren't aware of this situation, but when they went for breakfast they saw that the ship was going exceptionally slow. When an exhausted Rob came into the crew's mess Tony and Willy asked him what was going on. He explained about the overstressed engines and the call for a tow. "Right now, if we were at normal speed, we would be about two and a half to three hours out from our dock area, depending on the current along the way."

Willy asked him, "What are the currents likely to be like on this side of the island."

"I'm not sure, but the surveyors are bound to know."

Tony said, "Maybe I can find out."

Rob continued, "That's a good idea. At least the wind is westerly. That should keep us from getting too close to the island, if the engine quits before a tow reaches us."

Tony perked up, "I just had a wild idea! We have two launches ready for use, right?"

Willy agreed, "That's right, lad. What do you have in mind?"

"If the engine gives out before the tug arrives, we could use the launches to tow her just enough to keep her moving forward?"

Now Rob perked up. "That might just work. Wouldn't it be something if it did? I'll see what the chief thinks about it."

Rob relayed the idea to the chief engineer who took it up with the captain. The captain knew the pattern of the currents in their path and had determined the situation to be less than favorable. He called a meeting with the first mate, chief bosun, and chief engineer. The bosun was to have the two launches and heavy rope lines made ready and standing by. The chief engineer was to alert the bosun the moment he suspected that the engine was about to fail. The first mate would be in charge of the operation. He was to make the necessary calculations and guide the two launch crews by walkie-talkie. Their chances of going a considerable distance looked good. The only question was that of having enough gasoline for fuel.

Back in Honolulu, Melina and Kim were awakened by their alarm clocks. The night before, Kim had baked Mate's favorite chocolate cake with strawberries. After she had been up for a while Kim phoned Melina to see which car they should go in. Since Kim's was larger they decide to use hers.

"Melina dear, I'm so excited that Mate will be able to meet my mom and pop this time."

Melina had her phone propped between her head and shoulder while she attempted to make herself some tea. She admitted, "If I were you, I'd be scared to death."

"Well I am, a little. How about you, dear, have you changed your mind about ending the pregnancy?"

"Hon, I don't see how. I really don't have any choice if I'm to have a career."

"Are you going to tell Tony?"

"I don't know. I know I should, but I don't know how."

"Maybe something will come to you."

"I'm just so afraid that he's going to be either angry or hurt." She paused a moment before asking, "What time are you coming by?"

"I guess I'll pick you up around nine o'clock."

"If we get there the same time we did before, we should be okay. How did the cake turn out?"

"With the new oven Mate bought me, the cake looks lovely."

"That is so sweet of you." Melina admitted, "I've been so worried I haven't done anything special for Tony." She thought to herself, *What could be more special than a baby? Dear God, what am I going to do?* She stayed quiet for a moment.

Kim asked, "Are you all right, dear?"

"I could be better."

"Listen, dear, I'm nearly ready. I'll be over as soon as I can. We can have a little snack together and talk a bit before we go, all right?"

"Thanks, hon, I really appreciate that."

"See you soon."

"Bye."

Meanwhile the *Lady Explorer* was moving ahead under her own power with her two launches at the ready. The captain was on the bridge when he got a call from the radio room. It was Sparks, "Sir, we've just received word from the Navy's oceangoing tug, *Sandra Lee.* She's had us on her radar and is closing in on us at a distance of twenty miles."

"Very good, Sparks. Tell them that we are at minimum speed and hope to see them soon."

"Aye, aye, Captain."

The captain switched on the public address system. "This is your captain speaking. I have just received word that the oceangoing tug *Sandra Lee* is just about an hour from us. I wish to keep the two launches at the ready until we are actually in tow. Once we are under the control of the tug the launches are to be re-secured. I take this opportunity to thank all of you for a splendid job. Once the ship is in her berth we will return to our normal schedule. Again I thank you. That is all."

During that time Rob had been in the engine room, Willy had been part of the team seeing to the launches, and Tony had been in the sick-bay keeping it ready in the event of an emergency. Tony had been wondering how he would break the news of Mate's injuries to Kim. It wasn't going to be easy.

Near the dock where the *Lady* normally berthed, Melina and Kim sat in Kim's car among other waiting cars. Kim looked at her watch for about the tenth time in as many minutes. They arrived there half an hour earlier than the previous docking time of ten a.m. and had been there for an hour and a half when Kim said, "I have a bad feeling about this."

Melina agreed with her, "So do I."

The tug *Sandra Lee* with the *Lady Explorer* in tow became visible as they entered the channel.

Melina saw them first. "Look there, Kim. Isn't that boat pulling the *Lady* behind it?"

"I can't tell. It's too far away, dear." After a few more minutes, "You're right. But that's not their usual pilot boat; it's too big. Why is it towing them, what's happened?"

Ordinarily they would wait in the car until they caught sight of the guys about to come ashore. Because they both had an apprehensive feeling, they left the car and stood at the place where the gangplank would normally rest. They were arm in arm as they strained to see some sign of their men. Kim was the first to notice. "Isn't the American flag always at the top of that mast instead of at the middle?"

"I'm not sure but I think you're right, unless—"

"Unless someone has died!"

"Oh, my god! Maybe someone had an accident."

Kim's intuition was making her more apprehensive. The *Lady* being towed as she was made the image more ominous. Tony was standing by the rail on the starboard side near the portholes of the sick-bay. When he caught sight of the ladies he started to wave but not in his usual carefree excited way. When Melina first saw him she had a great sense of relief, until, "Why is he still wearing his work clothes?"

Kim was becoming nervous. "Where is Mate? Why can't he show himself?"

Melina was hopeful. "Maybe he's getting ready to meet us."

"Maybe you're right. Maybe I'm just being silly."

When it was obvious that the ship was about to be moored to the dock, Tony rushed below to his quarters for a quick change into his street clothes. By the time the gangplank was about to be lowered, Tony was standing at the gangway. His look was very serious as he looked into Kim's eyes then over to Melina. With his sea-bag hanging from one shoulder, he walked down the gangplank into their waiting arms. As he hugged them together he told them, "There's been a terrible accident."

Kim implored him, "Tony, where is Mate?"

He half lied to her, "He's all right; he's in the hospital at Pearl."

With tears filling her eyes, Kim wanted to know, "If he is all right, why is he in the hospital?"

Melina saw he was very restrained. "What happened, Tony?"

He was finding this very difficult. "Yesterday we were all having a swim. It was such a peaceful day." His eyes were beginning to look glazed as he remembered. "Right after a bunch of us fell in, Bill was having trouble swimming so Chuck,"—as soon as he said the name his voice started to break— "Chuck . . . Chuck got behind Bill . . . to bring him over to the rope ladders. That was okay until the lookout spotted sharks." Kim gasped at the word. "He hollered out a warning. Old Bill panicked smashing his elbow into Chuck's nose, so I got behind Bill to get a hold on him when something pushed me aside pulling him right out of my hands."

Melina became shaken by his account. "My God, Tony, what happened to them?"

Now half in tears, he said, "They're gone. Chuck's gone, Melina. Chuck's gone." Shaking his head, "They're . . . just gone."

Through her tears Kim pleaded with him, "What happened to Mate, Tony?! Please tell me, why is he in the hospital?!"

He forced himself to speak and tell her, "He was swimming far from the ship and was coming back to help when he was attacked."

"Oh god, oh my god!" Kim held on to Melina.

"It got a hold on his foot—"

"No!" Kim didn't want to believe her ears.

"We're hoping the doctors at the hospital can save it."

Kim was feeling very weak in her body but determined in her spirit, "Tony, can you drive us to the hospital in my car?"

"Yes."

Melina was holding Kim close to her. "Let's get there as fast as we can. I'll show you the way."

They got into the car and sped away with Tony at the wheel.

It didn't take them long to get to the hospital. Once they were inside at the main desk, Tony told the person behind the desk, "Jerry Jones, he would have been brought in last night."

After the clerk found his name, she said, "Yes, here he is. He's on the second floor. You'll have to check with the nurse in charge of that ward when you get there."

"Thanks." They took the elevator up to the second floor.

They went to the nurse's station. The male nurse told them, "Mr. Jones is sleeping. Are you relatives of his?"

Kim answered, "I'm his girlfriend."

The nurse suggested, "You probably should talk to his doctor. He's still in the ward. I'll see if I can get hold of him."

"Thank you." They sat in the tiny waiting room adjacent to the nurse's station.

After a few minutes a doctor came over to them. "Are you the friends of Mr. Jones?"

Tony answered for them, "Yes. I was with him when he was attacked. This is Kim, his girlfriend, and Melina, a good friend."

"I'm pleased to meet you." The doctor addressed Kim, "I'll tell you where things stand at the moment. The damage to his ankle and foot was severe, but luckily for Mr. Jones a specialist in reconstructive surgery of muscle tissue, tendons, and nerves, Dr. Igor Krasin is visiting with us for a short time. Dr. Krasin is quite optimistic of the chances for a complete repair. It's a miracle the shark didn't take Mr. Jones's foot. He said he put up quite a fight. We gave him a sedative so he would sleep for a while. Mr. Jones owes a debt of gratitude to the ship's doctor who treated him and did the blood transfusion."

"He needed a blood transfusion?" Kim was stunned.

"According to the report I received he had lost quite a bit."

Tony agreed telling Kim, "I work with Dr. Christian, the ship's doctor. He did everything possible to make sure Mate would be okay."

The doctor added, "If it hadn't of been for him, Mr. Jones might have lost the foot."

Kim shuddered at the thought. "Doctor, when will he wake up?"

"Once the sedative wears off; he should be awake by the evening meal. You could see him then but you might phone first just to be sure."

Tony asked, "How long do you think he'll be here?"

"We will keep him here under observation for the best part of a week. After that we will need to see him twice a week. Once the damaged area has healed there will be a period of physical therapy."

Kim asked the doctor, "How long could all of this take before he can return to California?"

The doctor answered, "If he remains in Hawaii it could take from two to three months. If he chooses to do the physical therapy in California he only needs to be here around six weeks."

Melina asked, "Doctor, will he regain full use of that foot?"

"It really is too soon to say but Dr. Krasin said that there is every reason to believe that he will. Once the healing has taken place the rest is up to Mr. Jones. Physical therapy for something like this is going to be hard work. And it will take some time. The key is to be patient and to persevere."

Willy unexpectedly appeared from the elevator along with Rob who was looking quite fatigued. Tony motioned them over telling the doctor, "These are Mate's friends from the ship."

"Mate?" the doctor asked.

"Sorry. It's Mr. Jones's nickname."

"Oh, I see."

Tony introduced them, "This is Willy."

Willy gave a nod and a smile. "How do you do, Doc.?"

"And Rob. Our ship was having serious engine trouble, and he helped to keep them running."

He only gave a nod. "Sir."

"Pleased to meet you both, I'm sure. I was just telling your friends the situation with Mr. Jones. They will have to fill you in because I have to get back to my other patients. I'm sure Mr. Jones will be very pleased to see all of you this evening, say after six."

They all looked at one another and seemed to be in agreement with the doctor's suggestion. Kim who had been making a strong effort to control her emotions said to the doctor, "Thank you so much, Doctor, for taking the time to speak with us." The rest expressed their thanks as well.

"Unfortunately I won't be here when you return because my shift will end at four o'clock. So I'll wish you a good day." He left to carry on with his work.

After the doctor had gone, Tony relayed the information to Willy and Rob. Kim and Melina were sitting together in the little waiting room. As tears began to fill her eyes, Kim told Melina, "This has all been too much for me. I don't think I'm going to be very good company today. Can we come back together tonight and in your car?"

"Sure, hon."

"I don't want to drive by myself," she began to cry.

Melina hugged and tried to comfort her.

They were all to return to the hospital at around six o'clock. Tony and Melina took Kim home in her car. From there they took Melina's car and headed for her apartment.

When Kim walked into her dining room she saw the chocolate cake that she had made for Mate. She sat at the table putting her head on her folded arms and broke into tears.

Willy and Rob were in a station wagon that Willy had rented. They drove to a church that Chuck had mentioned being a member of. Rob made arrangements for a special memorial service for Chuck for the following Wednesday. Rob had been experiencing an enormous amount of anxiety but had been suppressing it. Before leaving the church he sat near the altar in front of an imposing statue of the crucifix. At first he just sat looking up at it. He contemplated his friendship with Chuck—someone who had been like a younger brother, with so much potential. As his emotions began to surface past the barrier he had placed over them, he knelt before the crucifix and began to cry. It became uncontrollable sobbing. The time, the place—all were forgotten. Afterward he felt as though he had been washed clean all through himself. He was also feeling an overwhelming sense of love surrounding him. When he stood to leave he felt clear, and he sensed a strength that he had forgotten.

Willy had been sitting in the car waiting patiently. When Rob got in he said to Willy, "I need to let Chuck's friend, Mary, know what happened."

Willy sensed a change in Rob. He asked, "How do you figure on finding her?"

"First we get permission from the captain to look through his things for an address or phone number."

"Are you going to be okay looking through Chuck's things?"

"I'm not sure yet. If I can't, would you mind doing it?"

"I don't mind. We don't have much to go by other than her first name, do we?"

Rob said, "It's not the sort of thing he would have hidden away. It should be easy to find, like in his wallet."

"You're right. Why don't we grab a bite to eat and head back to the ship for a look?"

"That's fine with me," agreed Rob.

Before Tony and Melina went to her place they stopped at a drugstore to pick up some bandage material for his side. A short time later they arrived at Melina's. She put together a lunch while Tony changed his bandage.

Melina asked him, "Can I see that?"

"It'll be okay," he reassured her.

"That looks awful. What did that?"

"I'm not sure but it felt like it might have been the edge of the shark's fin. They can be pretty abrasive."

The thought of how close he came to being eaten alive stirred a sudden sense of emotion in her. She hugged him without saying anything. After a moment she stopped hugging him and said, "Be sure to put some alcohol on it, hon."

"Thanks, sweetheart, you're so good to me."

She touched her finger to his face. "The cut on your cheek has completely healed."

He took her finger and kissed the tip. "Yes, there's just a faint line left."

"That will grow fainter."

They were both beginning to feel amorous, but she resisted the feeling and went back into the kitchen. She was anxious because of her pregnancy and the fact that he still didn't know. She placed their lunch on the little table in the kitchen. "It's ready." They sat facing each other but ate quietly at first, both lost in their own thoughts.

Tony was again feeling a bit numbed by the events. "You know, this has been the screwiest two days I think any of us has experienced. I'm not sure I'm all here yet."

"I understand. I only hope Kim doesn't have a breakdown. You know, she was going to have Mate meet her parents this week."

"No kidding? That's a real bummer. I have to tell you, it had to have been a miracle that saved his foot. A shark that size can take off a leg without even trying, let alone a foot."

"And poor Chuck. The girl he danced with, didn't he have a date with her?"

"Yeah, the day after the contest. But I never asked him anything about her. Rob might know something."

"She needs to know. And this happened to him while he was trying to save someone else?"

"If he hadn't jumped in to save old Bill, he might still be with us."

"In which case you might not be with us."

He hadn't considered that probability. He had an uncomfortable feeling. "You're right, I hadn't thought of that."

"I hope Mary won't be too hurt. She was a very nice girl."

That comment made him depressed again. "I'll ask Rob about her, if we see him at the hospital later." Tony admitted, "You know, right now I don't feel up to much."

"I understand. In a little while I'm going to go over to Kim's to see if I can somehow be of help to her."

"I think that's a great idea." He was overcome by a need to be nurtured. "Can we lie down for a bit before you go?"

"Of course, hon."

After Willy and Rob had finished with their meal they returned to the *Lady* to find something that could lead them to Mary. The captain was still away at the Coast Guard station turning in his accident and mechanical failure reports. After Rob and Willy explained the unusual circumstances to the first mate he gave permission for them to make a limited search while one of the ship's watch accompanied them.

When Rob first saw Chuck's clothing he had a surge of anxiety that was quickly replaced by a feeling of love like that of a man for a younger brother. A piece of paper with Mary's phone number and address was found in Chuck's wallet. This was all they needed. They showed their find to Mr. Jenkins, copied the information from it, and returned the paper to the wallet. After they gathered some of their own things from their quarters they left the ship and headed for the nearest pay phone.

The number turned out to be that of an apartment Mary shared with her older sister. The sister was home but not Mary. Rob explained what had happened. The sister told Rob that although Mary had just met Chuck, she had grown quite fond of him and was very much looking forward to his return to the island that week. She was expecting to hear from him that day. Mary was sure to be sick at heart by the news. Both Rob and the sister felt it best if she broke the news to Mary. Also she was sure that Mary would want to attend the memorial service, so Rob could count on them both being there. The sister was shocked to hear what had happened to Mate, adding that he was an incredible dancer.

When Melina arrived at Kim's she saw that Kim had been crying since they brought her home. Kim hadn't eaten since that morning so Melina made her a light lunch. She suggested that Kim phone her parents to tell them of the events. After Kim had something to eat she began to feel a little stronger. She telephoned her parents who were very sorry for Mate and asked if there was any way they could be of help. Later in the week they could visit Mate in the hospital if it was all right with him.

A little later on Melina phoned Tony to tell him that after Kim was ready to leave she would drive Kim over and pick him up for their trip to the hospital to see Mate. Before leaving, Tony was to phone to make sure that Mate was awake.

It was nearly six when the three of them arrived at the hospital in Melina's car. Once inside they quickly made their way to Mate's ward. He had just finished eating and was sitting up in bed with pillows behind his back to prop him up.

Tony and Melina waited a few minutes before going in so that Kim could be alone with him. Even though he was still very tired and feeling the after effects of the drugs he'd been given, he felt a flow of energy fill his body when he first saw her. When she leaned over to kiss him he realized the state that Kim was in. He couldn't help but feel extreme sorrow for her, then for the two of them as a couple. So much had gone through his mind about his life, and the future he had hoped to include her in. He wasn't feeling very sure about the future usefulness of his foot, and therefore himself.

She openly cried but managed to smile as she repeated the encouraging words of the doctor. Words he'd heard but not with the urgency and added strength of another's love sharing his ordeal. He was so moved by her words and her presence that he went from delight to sorrow, to hope, and determination in a matter of a few moments. Mate was also moved by her parents' offer to be of help and really looked forward to meeting them.

Tony and Melina entered Mate's room. Melina gave him a gentle hug. She and Tony sat on the opposite side of the bed to Kim. Mate and Kim were holding tight to each other's hand.

Mate said to them, "You know, so much has gone through my mind beginning with the moment the shark nailed me. I must have gone through my whole life. I wondered, 'Why did I this? Why didn't I that?' And now, having you here," he squeezed Kim's hand tighter, "means so much to me."

Melina told him, "We all love you, hon."

Tony added, "God is smiling on you, brother."

Mate agreed, "He must be. By all the rules I should be shark shit by now."

Kim cringed, "Oh, don't say that, sweetheart."

"I'm serious," he continued. "Having you here and especially Kim has helped me so much. I feel like I could take on the world. Except that I feel pretty tired, so I may have to wait until tomorrow." He gave a healthy smile.

Jokingly Tony said, "Now there you go, putting things off until tomorrow."

Mate, with a half laugh and a smile, said, "You've got me there, brother." They laughed together and the sense of sadness lifted from the room.

Kim felt a great sense of relief seeing his mood swing upward. "It's so good to hear you laugh."

Becoming more serious, Tony said, "According to Dr. Krasin the ball is pretty much in your court. It's up to you, my man."

"I know. He was talking to me today before they put me out. He also reminded me of someone. Have you heard of

Django Reinhardt, the French gypsy guitarist? The last two fingers of his left hand were badly deformed by a fire?"

Tony answered, "Sure I do. The violinist Stephan Grappelli used to play with him."

Melina added, "And the Spanish guitarist Rodrigo who composed the fantastic concerto that Gil Evans and Miles Davis recorded?"

Tony said, "Yes, a beautiful piece of music, and he was blind."

Kim remembered, "A friend of mine used to listen to Japanese koto music. It was so beautiful and would make me feel so relaxed. The musician's name was Kimio Eto, he was blind too."

"And the list goes on," Mate said.

Melina added, "So many great artists have overcome handicaps, struggling so much harder because of them to become among the best at their art."

Mate said, "When that shark bit into me, the pain was unbelievable. But more than hurt, I was pissed off. I beat my fist into its eye until it quit. I've decided that's what I have to do to that part of me that becomes afraid and wants to give up."

Tony agreed, "Right on, man."

Melina told him, "Mate, with patience, perseverance, and your strength you can be the best there is."

Mate replied, "Thanks, Melina, those are great words."

It was at that point that Willy and Rob arrived on Mate's floor. The nurse in charge told them that they would have to wait until Mate's other visitors came out since there was a limit of four visitors at a time. She went to Mate's room to inform them that he had two other visitors and about the limit.

Tony saw who they were and suggested that Kim might be able to ride with them so that she could stay longer with Mate.

Tony and Melina said good night to them followed by a brief conversation with Rob and Willy. Rob told them of his luck in finding Mary and about the memorial service Wednesday at two in the afternoon. Since Willy could take Kim home after their visit, Tony and Melina left the hospital.

Once they were in the car, Melina asked him, "Hon, can we stop on the way for dinner? I'm feeling so tired."

"Sure thing, love. Are you all right?"

"Basically, but I'm really going to have to rest up tomorrow so I can go to work." Melina was actually quite drained of energy. She leaned against the doorpost. The events and her anxiety over her pregnancy were weighing her down.

Tony was also very tired. "I've noticed a small Chinese place on the way. We can stop there." He looked at her and wondered why she was leaning against the door and not him.

"That would be lovely. I don't know how Kim is going to be able to work tomorrow night. This whole scene has really knocked her out."

"I'm sure we'd all like to wake up and find this was a bad dream."

She agreed, "That's for sure."

They spent very little time eating before returning to her place. There was a note pinned to her door. It was from Bruno.

The note said that he needed to talk to her and that it was important. She told Tony that she had no idea what it could be about. When they were inside they each showered and prepared for bed. Melina was already beginning to drift off to sleep when Tony finished his shower. As he slipped into bed beside her she simply whispered, "Good night, hon."

"Good night," he said as he kissed her lightly on the cheek. He was extremely tired too but he did not fall asleep so quickly. He sensed that she was avoiding any kind of sensual contact with him and thought that it was probably due to the stress and tragic events. He understood and accepted this even though he felt a need to be close and nurtured. So he contented himself by merely snuggling up to her.

They slept soundly until around seven the next morning. Tony was awakened by the unsettling sound of Melina in the bathroom throwing up. Afterward she went into the kitchen for a glass of ice cold water. He put on a robe and went into the kitchen.

Still wearing her nightgown, Melina was sitting at the little table with one hand on the glass of water and her head resting on the other.

He took her robe from the back of the bathroom door and placed it around her shoulders. He sat to her side facing her. "Melina, are you okay?"

Without taking her gaze from the glass, she said, "No."

He was afraid it could be something serious, so he asked, "What is it?"

She was finding it very hard to tell him. With a look on her face that was a mixture of despair and an attempt to smile, she said, "I'm pregnant." She looked up at him.

He looked confused. He wanted to smile. Wasn't it great news? But her state was confusing him.

Looking back at the glass of water, she repeated, "I'm pregnant."

"That's great, isn't it?" He wondered aloud, "Unless there are complications."

"Complications? What about my career as a dancer? That's a big complication."

"What do you mean?"

"What I mean is that if I have a baby, your baby, now, there is no dance career. Not for a long time, if ever."

He didn't say anything. He was considering the implications of her words. "This sounds as though you don't want to have the baby, our baby."

She looked away from him. "I can't. Want doesn't even enter into it."

"It does for me. Do you want to have it?"

She gave him her honest answer, "I don't know."

They both grew silent. He had an empty feeling inside as he sat back in his chair. "I see." After a pause he asked, "I guess you've given this some thought. What do you plan to do?"

"What can I do but get an abortion."

He had a sharp pain as though someone had just run a knife into his heart. "Oh god, no."

There were tears in her eyes and despair in her heart. "What can I do, Tony? What can I do?"

He took hold of the hand that had been holding the glass. "Marry me. Let's get married. I'll get a job here."

"You'll be lucky if you find any work here." She continued while he dried the tears from her eyes with a napkin. "They don't give jobs to people that are from the mainland anymore."

With a renewed feeling of hope he encouraged her, "Then return to San Francisco with me."

"Tony, I love you. But I'm not taking a chance marrying you until after I know you really well."

He let her hand slowly slip from his. "Have the child and leave it with me. I'll raise it on my own if I have to."

"While you travel all over the world?"

"Of course not, I'll stay here and work if I can. If not, it's back to California."

"Tony, dearest, it's not only after the baby is born. It's being pregnant and carrying it. I won't be able to work as a dancer. And I wouldn't be able to afterward for a while, altogether for nearly a year."

He felt as though there was nothing he could do to change things for the better. He felt useless. He and Melina had created another life. The ultimate human act and it was going to be eliminated as a kind of inconvenience. "Melina, you seem to have made up your mind before now."

Having told him she had a sense of relief. Her voice had gained an air of determination, "When I decided on a career in dance I decided then that there would be no children until much later, maybe after I am ready to teach."

"What about birth control?" He didn't want their relationship to sound like something out of one of Dr. Christian's textbooks, but, "You told me you were using the rhythm method and that we didn't need anything else. What happened with that?"

"Something went wrong. I must have ovulated late, like about a week."

He was beginning to feel nauseous. He got up from the table and walked slowly to the bathroom. He had the sensation to throw up, but nothing came up except some fluid. Looking into the mirror he wished he hadn't. He cleaned his teeth and rinsed his mouth, threw cold water on his face, combed his hair, and went into the bedroom to dress.

He returned to the kitchen and kissed Melina on her forehead. "Sweetheart," he hesitated a moment, "I'm feeling kind of lost. Adrift, like a sailboat when there is no wind. So I'm going to leave now. I need to go somewhere where I can think about all of this."

He knelt down beside her chair to give her a hug. Her eyes filled with tears as did his when he kissed her lightly on her lips. He stood holding her hand. He let it slip from his and left her apartment. Despite her self-assuredness she broke down and began sobbing. She felt an enormous sense of loss.

Once outside he became aware of the early morning sunlight. He walked without any real direction at first. After a half hour of walking and thinking he saw a bus stop that he was familiar with. He caught a bus to the beach area. When he was there he wandered about until he found the little café where he ran into Willy the day they went up to the Crosswinds. Inside he ordered breakfast and just sat staring blankly out the window.

After he had eaten he went to one of the large grassy areas near the beach and walked about. There was a strong breeze blowing. He lay on the soft grass and closed his eyes. Filling his lungs with the clean air and feeling the warmth of the sun on his face and arms, he slowly became rejuvenated. He recalled the time Melina surprised him with her dance and how stirred it made him; how absolutely overpowering his need for her became. Just the remembering stirred his passions. For either of them to resort to birth control at that point would have been like holding up one's hand to stop a speeding locomotive.

He believed that everything had a reason, even mistakes, if only to learn a lesson. But he believed that she was pregnant because they were to raise a child together and not to just learn a lesson. He knew he could be wrong, for he often was.

He opened his eyes and looked up at the fluttering palms at the tops of the coconut trees as they swayed in their own kind of dance with the wind. But when the wind was done the trees would stand relaxed. One thing about an island in the ocean, there was almost always some amount of wind. In his mind he wondered if man was like the trees and woman like the wind.

He was reminded of the Crosswinds and thought a trip up there would be a good idea. But he was afraid he might miss the memorial service for Chuck the next afternoon. Maybe he would go after that. He closed his eyes again and unintentionally drifted off to sleep.

After Kim finished her lunch she gave Melina a call to see if she wanted to accompany her to visit Mate. Melina was still upset from the morning and was about to phone in sick at the Sleeping Lady. She told Kim how the news and her decision had affected Tony. Kim was very sorry to hear the result.

Oddly enough Kim had decided to return to work as usual since Mate was in such good spirits and since they were going to need the money. She put the cake she had made for Mate into a round container and headed for the hospital.

On her way to the hospital Kim stopped at a bookseller to get him the latest issue of *Down Beat* magazine. At a flower stall she bought a bouquet of flowers for him.

When Kim arrived at the hospital she went to Mate's room. "How are you feeling, darling?"

Mate was just delighted. "Sugar, you are lookin' fantastic."

She handed him the magazine and flowers. "Remember the cake I made for you?" She removed it from its container and placed it on the special table beside his bed.

"Now doesn't that look yummy?"

"I made it the night before last. It should still be good."

"Well, I'm ready for it, dove."

She put a piece of cake on a small dessert plate for him. "I was worried that the strawberries might not last, but they seem okay."

"Sweetheart, you're the greatest." He took a bite of the cake. "This is fantastic."

"Oh, I'm so glad you like it. Any more news?"

"The ship's captain was in to see me earlier. He said I'm not to worry. The department is taking care of everything. They will send all of my belongings to wherever I want. The hospital will take care of me until I'm ready to be on my own. And that in the meantime I'll be eligible for disability."

"Really? Well, that's good news, darling. When shall I have my parents come to meet you?"

As soon as she asked he got a scared feeling, one that was all too familiar. He had been holding her hand since he finished his cake. His grip on her hand tightened a little as he said, "Anytime they like."

"Good, I'll talk to them after I leave."

"You know, sugar, I may be out of here in a week. I'm going to have to decide where I'm going to stay."

"Well, you're going to stay with me, aren't you?"

"I was afraid that wouldn't be all right."

"Oh, it's all right. You better not even think of staying anywhere else."

As he struggled to pull her to him, he said, "My kind'a gal."

"Oh, Mate!" She nearly lost her balance as one foot came off the floor. They were having a good kiss when Willy and Rob appeared in the doorway totally unexpected.

Willy was the first to speak, "Well, now, it looks as though the patient is feeling much better today." Kim jerked back as if from an electric shock.

Rob added, "Perhaps he'll be sailin' back with the ship after all."

Mate was quite surprised, "Well, if it isn't the crew from the good ship *Lady Explorer*."

Kim was a bit embarrassed. "Hi, it's good to see you."

Willy said to Mate, "There's no need in askin' how you are." Jokingly he told Kim, "If this seaman gives you any trouble, ma'am, just give us the word, and we'll put him right."

Mate corrected him, "Ex-seaman, if you don't mind."

"Then you won't be goin' back with the *Lady*?"

"Yes, but not that *Lady*. I'll still be here when you come through on the next cruise."

Rob told Mate, "You need to fill us in on the latest news."

And so he did.

Tony knew he should phone Melina, but he couldn't bring himself to do it. Later in the evening he found himself wandering into the lounge next to the Sleeping Lady. He thought he might see Melina. Not expecting to find Kim there he was surprised to see her behind the counter, and looking so well. "Kim! I thought you were going to be off tonight?" He sat on one of the stools.

"Mate is in such good spirits that it's made me feel so much better. So here I am. Did you see him today?"

"No. I was going to but I've been so bummed out I didn't think it would be good for him."

She was sympathetic, "Would you like something to drink?"

He took a moment to consider, "A soda would be fine, thanks."

"You know, a visit with Mate might help you out. Willy and Rob were there."

"Yeah?"

"Melina told me you two were having a serious disagreement."

"Has she come in to work yet?"

Kim felt sorry for him. "No, dear, she called in sick."

That had him worried. "Is she all right?"

"Well, yes and no." Kim wanted to help them both.

"What do you mean?"

A cocktail waitress came to the counter. "Kim, I need a scotch and soda, a brandy, and a rum and soda."

"Tony, you'll have to excuse me for a minute."

He became aware of the music for the first time. The group had been on a break. It was so refreshing to hear them again after a month away. If anything, he needed food for his soul. He listened while Kim made the drinks. It all reminded him of the first time he and Mate came in. Even with the smell of the smoke and alcohol ever present, he closed his eyes and pretended he was in a church. Mother Jean would sometimes call out "Amen," or someone else would call out "Hallelujah," and the mood would be complete. It was what he needed.

After Kim gave the drinks to the waitress she returned to Tony. "Melina's feeling pretty bummed out too. She thought she knew what to do, but now she's not sure."

"I have to tell you that I'm really against abortion."

"For any reason?" she asked.

"No, but for this reason I am."

"I understand how you feel."

"What about you?" he asked.

"I'm against it in most cases, but in some I can see how it could be necessary."

"Like when?"

"Like when a father gets his own daughter pregnant or when a girl or woman is raped, or if the doctors know that a baby is going to be horribly deformed."

This was making him depressed. "There's just no easy way out of this. There doesn't seem to be anything I can do." He looked down at his drink, watching the last bit of ice melt.

Kim was very serious. "There is one thing you can do."

He saw a ray of hope. "What's that?"

She controlled her emotions as she said, "Just let it go."

Oh god, oh god, he thought to himself. "I can't. I mean, I don't think I can."

Kim put her hand on his. "Why don't you go see her? She is suffering too. Even more than you are. The final decision will be hers. Just accept that."

He gave a long sigh. "I can accept that the choice is hers, I just can't accept the choice she's made."

"Tony, why don't you take my car and go see her?"

"If I do, how will you get home?"

"I can take a taxi."

"Instead of that I'll take a taxi over now. Thanks for trying to help us, Kim. I'll see you tomorrow at the church, okay?" He gave Kim a kiss on the cheek and left the lounge.

Kim picked up the phone from under the counter and dialed Melina's number. She let it ring several times, but there was no answer.

The drive over seemed to take forever. During that time he thought about all their moments together. They had only been together about thirteen days in the last two months, yet it seemed like so much longer.

After the cab arrived Tony got out and paid the driver. When it pulled away from the curb Tony looked up at Melina's apartment. It looked a bit dark except for a faint light coming through the dining room window. He went up the front steps and knocked on the door. There was no response. He knocked again. Still there was no response. Thinking that she may be asleep he put his face close to the door and softly called her name as he knocked, "Melina . . . Melina. It's Tony. Can you let me in?"

A light came on in the living room, followed by the sound of the lock opening. When the door opened Tony could see that Melina had been crying a lot, and she looked very worn down.

Her voice sounded frail, "Tony, where have you been?" When he took her in his arms and held her close she said, "I was afraid you were never coming back."

He touched his cheek to hers, still moist from her tears, "I'm sorry love, I'm feeling so lost." They kissed then she took his hand as they slowly walked back to the bedroom where they comforted one another through the night until they fell asleep.

The day of the memorial service for Chuck was a beautiful warm day with white clouds drifting across the blue sky. Rob and Willy had arrived early to be sure the flowers they ordered had been delivered. They arranged them near the altar with a photograph of Chuck, Rob, and Tony taken together in the rain forest. It was a good picture showing Chuck doing something he loved. Following the service there was to be coffee, tea, and cake served in the garden behind the chapel.

By two o'clock everyone had arrived and was seated. Kim came with Tony and Melina. Mary was there with her sister. Captain Reiger, Mr. Jenkins, the chief bosun, Sparks, and a few of the crew were there also. Pete was absent.

The pastor performed a moving service that was for men lost at sea. This was followed by a few words of eulogy from Rob. At first he was unable to speak. Seeing Mary there, with tear filled eyes, had moved him greatly. He took a moment to calm himself before beginning:

"As most of you know I was very close to Chuck. In the three months that I knew him we had become like brothers. He had many good qualities and was a very unique young man. He possessed a kind of innocence that was often mistaken for being naive." Looking at the bosun, he continued, "And he had a goodness of heart that made it easy for others to take advantage of him." Again he paused to quell a touch of anger. "And so it was that he sacrificed his own life in an effort to save another. He will be greatly missed by all of us." After he finished, Rob sat near Willy in the front row.

The pastor again stood at the podium. "I would ask each of you to pray for the soul of the departed. After which we can all gather in the garden. Let us pray: *Holy Father, please accept the soul of our dear brother Charles Thomas into your glorious house. Glory be to thee, the one Almighty God. Amen.*"

After the service everyone went into the garden. Kim and Melina were consoling Mary. She told them, "You know, I had only known Chuck for two days, really. But there was something so special about him that I felt as though I had known him for ages. All of the things that his friend said about him, I was aware of." Her eyes again became glazed. "I only hope that I can be fortunate enough to meet someone like him again."

Mr. Jenkins had been trying to catch Tony's eye. He went over to Tony. "Excuse me, can I have a word with you?"

"Sure. What is it, sir?" They walked away from the others.

"It's the most extraordinary thing. Remember, I told you about the captain's friend in the department of records?"

"Yes, I do."

"Well, as I expected he did come up with something in a short time. The *Lady,* designed to assist small seaplanes, was built and launched at a shipyard in Sausalito, California, in the fall of 1941. She joined the Pacific fleet at Pearl Harbor on December 6th of that year. She received minor damage during the Japanese attack the next day. She was later converted to service PT boats. Still later she was reassigned to serve in the Philippines. There is no record after March 11th of 1942."

"So he was able to find her. What else did he find out?"

"That's what is so extraordinary. That is where the record ends. But even more extraordinary than that, the ship's diary for December 6th, prior to seventeen hundred hours is missing."

"Missing? And nothing after March 11th?"

"The date did bring something to mind. It could be a coincidence, but because the Japanese were about to take the Philippines in March of 1942, General MacArthur was removed from Corregidor by four PT boats and taken to Mindanao where B-17s were waiting to fly him to Australia. An extremely secret operation at the time. The friend told the captain that if she were involved in any secret activities the records would be classified and out of reach and would therefore account for the record ending as it does."

"That could be it, but how to find out? And why the day before the Japanese attack as well?"

"Who can say? In any case, unless someone with a secret clearance does the search we may never find out the story behind the awarding of the plaque."

"Damn." He felt a sense of defeat.

"I'm sorry, lad."

"Thanks for trying. Mr. Jenkins, what do you think is going to happen to the *Lady*?"

"You may not know that since Tuesday she's been having her engines repaired for the final charting and return home. From past experience I would expect that after we've transferred on to the new survey ship, she will be put up for auction. That whole process could take some time. Someone will buy her even if it's only for scrap."

"So, is there much time left?" Tony asked.

"That's difficult to say for sure. It all depends on who, when, and if. You know, that sort of thing."

"An educated guess?"

"Oh, a year or so before a possible dismantle."

Tony reiterated, "I just dread the thought of her winding up in a Japanese scrap heap."

"Unless you come up with something to substantiate the issuing of the plaque, that's assuming that the reason for the awarding was something extraordinary. If not, then she will undoubtedly end up as scrap."

"Listen, sir, I just had an idea. What if we were to find a

member of the crew from *Lady X* who was aboard her at the end of the war, or from the beginning?"

"You do come up with some good ones, I must admit, Mr. Lewis."

"Well, what do you think?"

"How are you at finding a needle in a haystack?"

"I've never tried."

"Sorry, I'm being facetious. You know, I believe that anything is possible no matter how improbable."

Tony was beginning to have a sense of excitement. "I could start by putting an ad in the newspapers."

"Not a bad idea. You might start with the major ones that make their way into the rural areas of the country."

"You know, Mr. Jenkins, I was feeling pretty hopeless minutes ago, but now I feel downright inspired."

"Well, I wish you and your friends all the luck you'll need to see this through. And if I can think of anything that might be of help to your cause I will let you know."

"Thank you, sir."

After they shook hands Jenkins left with the rest of the men from the ship. Tony went over to talk to Willy and Rob about the recent news and his idea. On his way Kim stopped him to tell him that she needed to go home in order to prepare for work. He arranged to meet with the guys at the hospital after he took Melina to work.

After Tony and Melina took Kim home they went to the Japanese udon house for some dinner. This time the place was nearly empty so they sat next to the only tropical fish tank there. Once they had ordered, Tony's attention was drawn to the fish.

He said, "See how that one with all the plumage intimidates the others?"

"That's a bahamis fish."

"What did you call it?"

"A bahamis fish, they're always doing that." Placing her hand on his, she said, "Hon, something has been going through my mind all day. It's the realization that if I have your baby and live with you, I'll probably have one baby after another."

"Even with the pill?"

"They are fine until you forget one, then it's a different story."

The waitress brought their first course. Melina asked her, "How are your little girls doing?"

"Oh, okay, thank you. One of them has a cough though."

"I'm sorry to hear that."

"My sister is looking after them. We're hoping that her sister doesn't get one too."

"I hope she's better soon."

"Thank you." She returned to the kitchen.

They began eating. Melina was using chop sticks without any help from Tony this time.

He said, "You're doing all right with those things now."

"I've been practicing at home."

Thinking of the waitress, he said, "It must be hard for a woman to raise children on her own."

"It is, and there are so many mothers trying to do it."

"And some fathers too, I'm sure. Melina, I think I understand how having a baby would be for you now. And I know that the final decision will be yours. And I accept that."

"That is very good of you."

The waitress arrived with the rest of their meal.

"Thank you." He continued, "But my feeling about abortion seems to come from very deep and remains unchanged."

"Sweetheart, we need to talk this out, but talking about it while eating is not a good idea. Can we wait till later?"

"Of course, I'm sorry, love."

After dinner they drove to her place so she could get ready for work. While she was in the shower he was in the sitting room listening to some LPs with his shoes off.

She called out to him, "Tony? Tony?"

He got up from the couch and went toward the bathroom,

"Yes, love?"

"Can you scrub my back? I can't seem to bend my arm back far enough for some reason."

"Sure, I'd love to." But when he realized he could get the long sleeves of his shirt wet, he said, "Hold on a sec." He took off his shirt which left him with a bare chest. He removed his socks before going into the wet bathroom. "Okay, here I am."

She handed him a scrub brush. "Here, hon, just scrub up and down."

As familiar as he had become with her unclad body he still found her to be perfection itself. "Melina, you look good enough to eat."

"Good enough to wash will do for now." After he had soaped up the brush, he gave her back a hardy scrubbing. It was a bit too hardy for her liking. "Ouch! Easy does it." She shied away from the coarseness of the brush.

He got soap on his trousers and in the worst place. "Oh, brother. Melina, how come you keep moving away?"

"It's that brush, I never realized how stiff it could be."

"Look at my pants, they're a mess."

"You should have taken them off."

"What would the neighbors think?" He tried to reposition himself with one foot on the floor and the other on the shower floor so he could scrub her back more gently. But the foot on the floor slipped. "Whoa!" He lost his balance and grabbed for the shower curtain on his way down, taking it with him. He ended up lying flat on his back on the bathroom floor.

Melina just looked down at him and laughed. Then they were both laughing. She said, "Those pants are a mess. Why don't you let me help you take them off?"

"You know, you're absolutely right." He unfastened them.

She had to step out of the shower to take hold of the cuffs and pull them off.

Looking up at her was an inspiration that was more than any man could hope to experience.

With a mischievous smile she asked, "Shall I help you up?"

"I think you already have."

She began kissing his chest, his throat, his chin, his face, his eyes, and last of all, his lips. It wasn't long before they were making love. The urgency of the moment determined that the floor of the bathroom would have to do. By the time they were finished they were both in need of another shower so they squeezed into the shower together. Fortunately there was no need to scrub her back this time.

After Tony dropped Melina off at the Sleeping Lady he excused himself then drove her car to the hospital to meet up with the guys in Mate's room. When he arrived they had been there for the past hour.

Mate said to him, "Hey, brother. We were afraid you weren't going to make it tonight."

"How's everything, guys? Listen, I had a real brainstorm today."

Willy asked him, "Has the captain received any word about the plaque yet?"

"That's what I want to talk to you about." Tony described the conversation with Jenkins.

Mate said, "What a bummer."

Tony went on, "That's when I had this great idea. I'm going to put an ad in the major American newspapers, an ad that asks for anyone who was part of the crew of *Lady X* from 1941 to 1945 to contact me."

Willy agreed, "That is a great idea. Altogether there could be a fair number of men who crewed on her sometime in that three and a half year period."

Mate agreed too, "A great idea, man. Go for it."

"Mr. Jenkins thinks the *Lady* will be sold in auction and be at a scrap yard in about a year after she gets back to her home port in Oakland and the crew has transferred to the new ship."

Willy said, "So that gives us just about a year from now to come up with something, or someone."

Rob said, "It looks like a crewman is about our only hope."

Tony added, "That, and some proof."

Mate asked Tony a question, "When the *Lady* leaves here Monday, are you still leaving with her?"

There followed a moment of awkward silence that was broken by Willy. "I didn't know you were thinking of quitting the ship."

A surprised Rob added, "Neither did I."

Tony was not prepared for this question. "I'm not planning on quitting the ship. But I might have to."

Willy asked the natural question, "What about all this business of finding some way to save the ship from the scrap heap?"

"That won't change. It's just that if I do stay here I'll have to do what I can from here, or from San Francisco if I'm there. I've only signed on for this cruise and wasn't planning to sign on afterward."

Rob asked him, "What's going to keep you here before the end of this cruise."

"In a word—Melina."

Willy said, "I'm sure we can all relate to that with no problem. But why can't you wait until your contract is finished when the ship arrives back in Oakland? You can place the ads you mentioned giving an address here, or anywhere for that matter, then fly back here?"

Tony said, "It's a little more complicated than that."

Mate encouraged Tony, "Go ahead, tell them what's happening."

Tony struggled with his response, "She's pregnant, and—"

Willy said, "I don't see that as a problem. Crewmen's wives or girlfriends often get pregnant. They don't quit their ship because of it."

"You didn't let me finish. That's not the only complicated part. She wants an abortion, and I don't. We're having a real struggle over this now. The *Lady* leaves in five days. It doesn't look like this is going to be resolved by then. I'm hoping it will so I can go back with the ship."

Willy was nodding his head in agreement. It was quiet as the men thought about what he just said.

Tony started to look through the window toward the ocean at the night, but only saw his reflection looking back at him.

Later Tony said good night to them and left the hospital alone. He pulled out of the parking lot and instead of going east toward Honolulu he headed north and drove without any particular direction. He was lost in thought, just wandering. Nothing was making any sense to him, at least not in a way that he would like it to. Deep down he was too much of an idealist, seeing the world only through his own eyes.

He had to return to where Melina was working and didn't want to. He didn't want to see her stripping for an audience, especially that kind of audience. He respected her determination to dance, even admired her for it. But he would rather she didn't strip to earn her living. She said she couldn't be a dancer in Hawaii, but here she was pursuing her career. He wondered how other dancers dealt with that. He had to agree with her when she said that if they married they would have one child after another. The two of them were too inclined to let their passions of the moment take control over reason. He knew that would put an end to her hopes of being a professional dancer. He didn't want to admit it, but he could see how this pregnancy could represent the beginning of a disaster for her. He turned the car around and headed south for the Sleeping Lady.

Chapter 11

A DEAD END STREET
BY ANY OTHER NAME

Tony pulled into the parking lot of the Sleeping Lady where he left the car. After showing his ID, he went through the main entrance like the usual customers. He didn't want to attract attention to himself. This was the first time he had been there since the one other time when he was thrown out. He found it to be just as unpleasant as before—smoky and smelling of spilled beer. The room was dimly lit, so the spilling of drinks was inevitable, especially by drunks.

The area near the stage was crowded. Tony sat as close as he could get, but he was still about twenty feet away. A waitress wasted no time in getting to him. He ordered a beer and waited for Melina to come on. The next dancer was one he hadn't seen before. She was very attractive but not a good dancer. What she did couldn't really be called dancing. She just moved about the stage in a very organized kind of routine. But when she finished she was thrown a fair amount of money. The same jugglers that he had seen before followed her performance. They used the band's drummer to good effect. When they were done the band left the stage.

Recorded music started to come from speakers above the stage. Tony knew that it meant Melina was about to appear. Two men who were sitting directly in front of him were talking loud enough for him to understand what they were saying. He had tuned them out, but his ears perked up when he heard one of them say, "Hey, man. Remember the broad I was tellin' you about?"

The other guy was a little more drunk than his friend. "No, wish one wus dat?"

"The mulatto babe, man."

"Oh yeah, so?"

"I think she's gettin' ready to come out, 'cus the group always leaves first."

Nodding his head, the other one said, "Tha'z nice."

Sure enough, with the enchanting music that she preferred, Melina appeared on the stage wearing the same costume as before. With the lighting, her music, her costume, and her dancing, Melina was a definite show stopper. The combination was overpowering. At that moment she was a seductress without equal. Except that Tony also saw her as the person carrying their child.

Tony could still hear the men in front of him, "Hey, man, that mask is too much."

"Yeah, she's my kind'a bitch, man."

"Don't be stupid. What would you know 'bout somethin' like that?"

Tony was restraining himself, trying to be cool. He didn't want to make a scene while she was on stage. The two didn't say much for a few minutes except for the occasional "Umm," or "Oh shit," they were so engrossed, watching her strip.

Tony had a sense of relief when her act finished, and she picked up the money thrown on to the stage.

The drunk said to his friend, "D' ya think she fucks?"

"Sure, they all do."

"How wud'ju know?"

"I know."

Melina left the stage.

The last guy to speak continued, "Why do you think they strip?"

"'Cus they like it?"

"Nah, it's just to get up a little business."

Referring to Melina, "Ya mean she's sellin' it?"

"Sure. In fact, I might just get me some a that tonight."

Tony tightly wrapped a cloth napkin around his right hand then tapped the shoulder of the guy doing the bragging. "Hey, buddy, what did you just say?"

The guy turned around with a surly look on his face. "Yeah? Wha'da **you** want?"

With all the pent-up frustration and anger that Tony had been experiencing, he took his tightly wrapped fist and hit the guy in the mouth so hard that he fell across the table causing it to collapse. The guy's drunken friend just looked down at him with a dumbfounded expression. "Hey, what the—"

Back stage Melina heard a crashing sound out front. She peeked through the curtain just in time to see Tony looking down at the guy.

This time the dim lighting worked in his favor. He quickly moved away from there before the bouncer could tell who did what.

Melina said to herself, "My god, what has he done?"

In the confusion he slipped out the exit and into the lounge next door. Once his adrenalin rush had subsided he became calmer.

Even though he was trying to be very composed Kim could tell that something had excited him. "Tony, hi." She asked him, "Is it hot outside tonight?"

He slid on to a stool. As he did he noticed pain in his knuckles. "No. Why?"

"Because you're sweating. What have you been up to?"

"I'll tell you if you promise not to tell anybody."

Putting a glass of his favorite drink in front of him, she said, "All right, I promise."

"I just slugged an asshole in the mouth."

"You what?!"

"This bastard was saying some very nasty crap about Melina."

"When? And where?"

"Just now, next door."

"Oh my god. Did anyone see you?"

"I don't think so; it's pretty dark in there."

"That's the second time you've been over there and that's the second time you've gotten into it with somebody."

"There are some real creeps who hang out in there."

"You're going to have to stop going in there. Otherwise you could get Melina fired if the owner connects the two of you."

Tony had a faint smile as he thought that might not be a bad idea.

Kim said, "I know what you're thinking, just forget it. She needs that job."

"Listen, Kim, can you give Melina these keys? Tell her my stomach's feeling strange. Maybe something I ate. Okay?"

"If that's what you want."

"I think I should sleep on the ship tonight. Just between you and me, Kim, I'm so confused I don't know if I'm comin' or goin'. I'm afraid if I see her I'll change my mind."

"Okay, good luck."

He left through the main door.

Almost on his heels Melina appeared from the employee door that connected the theater to the lounge. She was wearing a kind of jumpsuit.

"Kim, have you seen Tony? You can't believe what I just saw."

Kim laid the car keys on the counter in front of Melina. "He was just here and asked me to give you these keys. He said his stomach was feeling strange, like maybe something he ate."

"More like something he hit," Melina said with a tone of annoyance in her voice. "If he gets in a beef every time he's next door he's going to get me fired."

"What happened?"

"I'm not sure. I heard a crashing sound so I looked through the curtain. I saw a smashed table with some guy lying in the middle of it, and there was Tony running off. I don't think anyone saw that it was Tony. At least I hope not."

Kim told her, "He seemed pretty worked up. He said that this guy was saying some very nasty things about you, and that he slugged the guy in the mouth."

Melina was trying not to become emotional. "Oh, Kim, what am I going to do? I like him a lot."

"Do you love him?"

"Yes, I do, but not enough."

"Not enough for what, hon?"

Melina admitted, "Not enough to give up my career for."

"Do you want some advice?"

"You're my best friend, Kim. You know me better than anyone. I don't know what to do."

"You have to decide between your work in burlesque or a life with Tony. With him you can't have both. The decision is for you to make, no one else. If it's to be him then get out of strip clubs. He knows you should be a dancer, but not here. Otherwise you'll have to drop him." Kim had to stop talking for a minute to make some drinks for customers.

Melina was having difficulty being honest with herself. She knew Kim had cut to the heart of the issue. She had begun to look forward to the sensation she got when she stripped for men. She was very sensual and it was the one time she could express her sensuality. And she enjoyed being desired. Because she found the work fulfilling in this way and because any other kind of dance work for a woman who looked more Negro than not was nonexistent on the islands, she had easily lost the drive she once had for the career in dance that she had wanted. As time passed by she did not want to admit that her desired career of modern dance was becoming just a pipe dream.

Kim had completed the drinks. "Okay, I'm back."

Lost in thought, Melina was slow to respond, "Kim, you know I don't want to leave these islands. Where else can I get work?"

"In Hawaii? For dancing? Nowhere else except at one of the other strip clubs and this is the best one."

"It's as if I've danced myself into a dead-end street."

"Dear, you have to face the fact that to pursue a dance career you're going to have to leave these islands anyway."

"I know. I've been putting that off as long as possible, hoping that a miracle will come along to change things so I won't have to leave."

"Melina, dear, so many of us who have chosen to live here are waiting for that miracle. It may only happen in our dreams." Melina knew Kim was right. The girl who worked in the dressing room appeared from the employee door looking for Melina.

"Excuse me, suga', you're on in fifteen minutes."

"Thanks, hon. Well, Kim, I have to get back to work. Did Tony say he was going back to his ship tonight?"

"Yes, he did." She watched as Melina, with a worried expression on her face, quietly turned and left through the same door. While it was open the sound of drunken laughter could be heard coming from the other side. Kim felt lucky not to work in there.

Tony was lying in his bunk. One of the pipes directly over him had a photograph taped to it, facing downward. It was not the usual pinup one would expect to find in a men's dormitory. Instead it was a picture of a tree similar to a cypress. The tree was jutting out from an island of black rocks in a placid lake. Far in the distance was a range of both high and low cliffs. The colors were a soothing green, dark slate gray, and sky blue. The whole image was reflected off the water. It was an esthetic and serene picture from one of the Japanese islands. Often, while lying in bed, he would imagine that he was either lying under the tree or leisurely paddling along in a canoe. This time he was floating in the water on his back with his arms outstretched and very relaxed. He concentrated his whole being on that. He became more relaxed and at ease than he had been in a long time.

Early the following morning, he was wakened by Willy tapping on his foot. "Tony. A good morning to you, lad. The watch told us you were aboard."

Tony was slow to come fully awake. "Hey, how are you doing? I needed to sleep here, away from things last night."

"Rob and I are going to brunch. It's the only meal they're having this time in port except for cold cuts in the afternoon. Why don't you join us?"

"Okay, I could sure use something to eat."

"After chow we're driving up to the Crosswinds. You're welcome to come along, lad."

"I'll see how I feel after I eat. But it does sound like a good idea."

After Tony showered and dressed, he joined the others in the crew's mess. Placing his tray of food on their table, he said, "I'm feeling pretty good after a good night's sleep, how about you two?"

Rob answered, "Yep, there's nothing like a good night's sleep. Willy said he invited you to come with us. What do you think?"

"You know, when I went there before, I had a very far-out dream."

Willy said, "You mentioned that at the last concert."

"Why don't I tell you about it on the way to the Crosswinds?"

Willy was pleased. "Great, I've got old Nelly outside all fueled up and ready to go. We can leave after we eat. Oh, by the way, have you checked your mail yet? There was a letter for you."

"No, I completely forgot. Also I need to make a phone call first."

Tony had a letter from Maureen waiting for him. Next he phoned Melina to let her know he was going with the guys up to the Crosswinds. She had wanted to see him and talk about what happened the night before. He told her he needed to be away from everything for a day to clear his head and that he would phone her the next day. She unhappily agreed.

Once they were in the car and on their way Tony opened the letter. Maureen was over two months pregnant and it had become apparent to the people in her office and at the acting school. As for the relationship with her teacher it had become a bit more serious. She said she was growing very fond of him. Absentmindedly Tony said, "Life just goes on."

Rob asked, "What was that?"

"Oh, I was thinking out loud. In my letter, my last girlfriend is pregnant and has a new boyfriend."

Rob and Willy looked at each other with a frown. "Your ex-girlfriend is pregnant too?"

Tony said, "Yes." When he saw their expression, he explained, "Wait a minute, it isn't mine. She was raped by a friend she let crash at her place."

Rob asked, "Some friend. And where were you?"

"At that moment? Somewhere in the north Pacific Ocean."

Willy said, "Phew, you had us worried for a moment there."

"I guess it did sound a little . . . suspicious," Tony admitted.

Willy jokingly said, "Just a bit, lad, just a bit."

They were making good time and had nearly passed over the mountain range when Rob remembered, "Hey, Ton', weren't you going to tell us about a dream you had up here?"

"That's right. It was related to that really heavy storm we went through our first month out."

Willy recalled, "That's when I very nearly got my head bashed in, thanks to old Bill, rest his soul."

"Well, the night I slept on the beach, near the Crosswinds—"

Willy interrupted, "I remember that night."

"Right, anyway I had a dream that was incredibly real. So real, in fact, that I'm still not sure it was just a dream."

"What do you mean?" Rob asked.

Tony went on to retell the whole experience including his rescue by the dolphin.

When Tony finished the story Willy said, "That's amazing. That's one of the best sea stories I've heard in a long while."

Rob was equally amazed, "You actually heard the men in the galley beating on the bulkheads; and a whirlpool in reverse saved you from the shark?" This gave him an unpleasant reminder of Chuck's fate.

Willy added, "You even heard old Neptune laughing at you **after** you woke up!?"

Tony said, "It really scared me, I'll tell you that."

Rob was truly impressed, "As if that wasn't enough, you went in to wash off and nearly drowned except for the kindness of a dolphin."

"That's right; I swear it's all true."

Willy observed, "You know, lad, you must have a charmed life."

After they arrived at the Crosswinds it was still too early for the coffeehouse to open. After they bought some cool drinks and potato chips at the little store, they just relaxed in the area in back of the coffeehouse. Rob had a book on backpacking to read, and Willy was putting a couple of new strings on his guitar. After tuning it he would also have his concertina to practice on.

Tony ventured off toward the water to explore the tide pools. He walked along a path that eventually led to a narrow beach with tide pools at both ends. At one end he found a good place to throw down his bag. Thinking he would like to go in for a swim, he stripped down to his shorts.

As he walked toward the water's edge he had an overwhelming urge to run. One thing about always wearing shoes is that it makes one a tenderfoot, so he began by running slowly and carefully.

After finding this a bit awkward he ignored the tenderness of his feet and ran as fast as he could with the dry sand absorbing most of his effort. When he ran along the edge of the water, with its gentle waves rolling in and out, his feet came down on hard sand, then water, then sand again, and so on. Using only his nostrils his breathing was deep and controlled. There was a fresh feeling of energy flowing through the muscles of his whole body, especially his legs.

He imagined how a horse must feel while running at the water's edge or anywhere. He felt so strong, solid, and so unstoppable. How grand it must feel to be a horse and to just run, and run, and run. When he reached the end of the beach he dove into the surf.

WITH A LITTLE HELP FROM A FRIEND

Melina was lying in bed staring up at the ceiling, imagining grotesque faces in the patterns formed in the plaster. Her lower abdomen felt cramped. She was depressed and wished she wasn't pregnant. When the phone rang she didn't want to answer it. But when she thought it might be Tony or Kim she reached across the bed to pick up the phone.

The broken voice at the other end asked, "Mel?"

Not recognizing the voice right away Melina asked, "Who is this?"

"Bruno."

"Bruno? What's wrong with your voice?"

"I'm a little under the weather, man."

"Really? So am I."

"Listen, baby, I was hopin' you could help me out a little."

"Kim saw you about a month ago. She said you looked kind of hung over."

"What does she know? I just need a little help, that's all."

"I could use a little help myself. I thought your mom was helping you out?"

"I think Mom's about to check out, man."

"What do you mean?"

"She's been real sick for a while, man. For the last week she hasn't eaten much at all, you know. Her friend Max was by this morning. He thought she might be on her way out then. So he called an ambulance, you know. One came, right? And took her away. I don't even know which hospital they took her to."

"Gee, I'm sorry to hear that. What are you going to do with yourself now?"

"I don't know what to do, Mel. I don't have any bread, man. I sold my board a while back so that bread's gone."

"I can help you with a little money, but you'll have to pay me back."

"That's cool with me, baby, but if somethin' happens to my mom this apartment's history."

"I'm sorry I can't help you with that. I've got some problems myself."

He thought she was just trying to put him off. "Now what kind'a problems could a good-lookin' babe like you have, man?"

"Well, for one thing, I'm pregnant. And if I have a baby, what's going to happen to my dance career?"

"Are you still goin' on about your career? What's wrong with dancin' in the clubs? I thought that was your career, man?"

"I mean a career in modern dance, Bruno. Haven't we talked about this before?"

"Yeah, sure, I know. That's your scene, and that's cool with me. But you're makin' such a big deal over bein' pregnant, man."

"It is a big deal. Also there isn't just me."

"Yeah, right. So who's the lucky father?"

"You met him once in the drugstore when we were picking up a prescription for you a couple of months ago."

He was quiet as he tried to remember. "Oh yeah, that skinny guy you were talkin' to. Is he the stud?"

"He wants me to have the baby."

"And you don't, right?" Bruno saw this as a golden opportunity for him. "It needn't be a big deal, you know?"

"What do you mean?"

Bruno was beginning to feel somewhat revived. "You're a healthy woman, right?"

"Most of the time, I make sure I have enough exercise."

"Right, a career dancer has to keep in good shape."

Melina was curious. "What are you getting at, Bruno?"

"Only that you are probably going to have a strong healthy little kid that will undoubtedly be the first of many." He hit the nail on the head.

"That's what I'm afraid of. And he's against an abortion."

"So you'll have a baby. Unless—"

"Unless what?"

"Unless you have a miscarriage."

"That's always possible, but it's just as likely not to happen."

"Mel, how would it be for you if it did happen?"

"I hate to admit it but it would be a great relief."

"How would Mr. Right feel if you had a miscarriage?"

"He would probably be relieved too."

"Listen, baby, I know a sure way to bring on a miscarriage undetected, but it will cost about a hundred dollars." Melina didn't say anything. "How long have you been pregnant?" His future was looking brighter.

She was so unsure of what to do. "One month."

"No problem, babe." He thought to himself, *This is going to be so easy.* He continued, "You won't lose it right away. It'll take a day or two, just like the real thing, man. Your boyfriend won't know the difference either. No one will."

"I don't know, Bruno."

"What about your career in dance? You could go to L.A. and be a main attraction, with all those rich clowns followin' you around like little puppy dogs, lickin' your—" he smiled to himself, "boots."

She asked him, "What's involved?"

He explained the process he was going to go through, leaving out some of the more unpleasant aspects.

She hardly believed she was saying, "What do I have to do?"

"Are you still getting off work at eleven tonight?"

She was now resigned to this course of action. "Yes. Listen, Bruno, no one is to know about this, all right?"

"Hey, it's cool with me. Here is what you need to do, baby. You know where my mom's apartment is, right?"

"Sure, it's between my place and the Sleeping Lady."

"Cool, because I'm broke, and I have to purchase some items. I need you to drop off some cash at my mom's on your way to work."

"On my way to work?"

"Yeah, because on your way home from work you're going to swing by here again and pick me up to take me to your pad. That's where I'm going to help you fix your problem." The word "fix" had a special meaning for him.

She hesitated for a moment. "How much will I need?"

"Just the hundred."

"Hold on a minute, I need to see how much I have." She went to her purse. She realized that if she didn't have the cash it couldn't be done that night. She knew that it had to be then, while Tony was away. She returned to the phone, "I have it, but a hundred in cash will leave me with only twenty dollars."

"Don't worry, baby, you'll pick up some more bread at work. What time will you be by here?"

"Is seven thirty all right?" She was feeling a sense of urgency now, bordering on desperation, to get it over with.

"Too cool, I'll be standing out front."

"Okay, Bruno, I'll see you there."

"Later, baby." He hung up the phone and said to himself, "Man, I can't believe how easy that was." He found a piece of scratch paper by the phone and dialed a number from it. When a female voice answered at the other end Bruno said, "Jewel, baby . . . Yeah, it's Bruno . . . Really . . . Dig this, I just had a change of luck . . . That's right. Are you going to be there around eight? . . . Yeah? How's your stock? . . . All right. Dig ya later."

The sun had set so the Crosswinds coffeehouse was open. Tony was nursing a large mug of hot apple cider that he found to be refreshing no matter what the weather. Rob was still into his book, and Willy was scanning the notice board. The place was relatively quiet except for some modern jazz coming over the sound system.

Meantime a girl stepped onto the stage. She looked to be Hawaiian or Oriental or both with long black hair and dressed similar to an American-Indian from the southwestern U.S.

She had a dulcimer that she accompanied herself with as she performed song versions of her poetry. Her voice was like magic. When she sang, all conversations stopped. She seemed to have a very angelic way about her, even when she walked. She was a temporary relief for the uneasiness that Tony was feeling deep within his self.

Melina had been nervous and apprehensive all night. It had even affected her performance. During the breaks between her performances she stayed in the dressing room instead of going next door to visit. Kim was busy as usual for a Friday night so she had been too preoccupied to worry.

When Melina finished work she drove in her car straight for Bruno's. He was waiting in front of his mother's place just like he was when Melina dropped off the money. After Bruno got into her car he said, "Don't worry, baby, I have everything we need." In the dark car she didn't see the sly smile on his face.

They arrived at her place in no time. Melina had been quiet. As Bruno followed Melina to her front door he was afraid she might change her mind, but he was reassured after she said, "I want to get this over with as fast as possible."

"The deed is as good as done." Once they were inside he put his bag on the kitchen counter, took out some canned beet juice, a box of mustard powder, a tiny jar of turpentine, and a pint of gin. Out of a smaller bag he took out a tiny container, an eyedropper, and a syringe. He instructed Melina, "Get a hot bath ready then soak in it for thirty minutes."

While the tub was filling she removed her clothes and put on her robe. Into the bath Bruno poured the box of mustard powder. He stirred it in as if he were making a huge vat full of some bizarre concoction. "Okay," he said, "the bath is ready. But first I'll give you the drink." Using the eyedropper he carefully added a measured amount of turpentine to half a jar of beet juice. He handed her the glass, "Here, drink this."

She drank it, "I like beets but this stuff is awful."

He gave her the remaining beet juice, "You can chase it with this." After she had the last drink, he said, "Okay, now lay in the hot bath as long as you can."

She took off the robe and climbed into the bath, "It's too hot!"

"It has to be to work. It'll feel like it's burning you but that's the mustard. You have to be completely covered."

"Bruno, this is awful."

"Just a little longer."

Meanwhile it had been a long night at the Crosswinds. Tony was missing Melina and wanted to see her. The coffeehouse was about to close for the night. He thought she might be home from work and, he hoped, in a good mood. If it was all right with Melina he could stay the night with her, if he could catch a ride back with someone. He decided to phone her.

When Melina couldn't take another minute, she said, "I have to get out." She climbed out of the tub and dried off. Putting on her robe she asked, "Why do I feel like I have a sunburn?"

"Like I said, it's the mustard. I have to give you a small injection before you drink the gin. After that you'll go to bed."

"What's in the injection? It's not a drug, is it?"

He lied when he said, "Nah, it's a kind of herb. Something Jewel, the chick who put me onto this stuff, put together that has to go directly into the blood. When it connects with the other stuff it will trigger the miscarriage." He didn't mention an additive, codeine, which is made from opium. It's very addictive when injected into a vein. He needed as many customers as he could get so he could afford to support his own habit. He prepared the syringe as she rolled up the left sleeve of her robe. He tied off her arm and rubbed alcohol onto the chosen spot.

It was eleven forty-five when Tony was able to use the only pay phone inside the building. It had been busy for a half hour. He put a dime into the slot, dialed the number, and waited.

Melina's phone couldn't ring because Bruno had turned off the bell earlier. With the syringe in his hand he carefully inserted the needle into a vein, and released the tie. He pressed the plunger down to the hilt.

Tony listened as the line rang and rang. There was no answer. He hung up, deciding to try again later.

Bruno waited a few seconds before he withdrew the syringe and disposed of it in the trash. "All you have to do now, Mel, is drink this pint of gin and go to bed."

Melina began to feel very strange after he released the tie from her arm. She felt as though she was flying through a cloud. She half whispered, "It's so . . peaceful up here."

Bruno helped her over to her bed so she could sit on it. He handed her the gin, "Down the hatch, baby."

She took the open bottle in her hand and looked at him through very hazy eyes, almost seeing double. To her, Bruno looked like some kind of murky demon. She thought, *You bastard.* She got about halfway through the pint then fell back onto the bed. Bruno lifted her head up and helped her swallow the rest of the gin. After she became unconscious he collected all of the things he had brought, put them into a bag and left.

Because the coffeehouse had been closed for a while, Tony used a pay phone outside to try Melina's number again. There was still no answer. "Where can she be?" he wondered aloud. "Oh well, maybe she doesn't want to be alone and is spending the night with Kim."

Willy had retired to sleep in his station wagon. Rob had gone off to sleep on the beach, so Tony decided to do the same. He was able to find his way by moonlight to where he had gone before, but on higher ground. He laid out the sleeping bag borrowed from Willy, got undressed and crawled into the bag. After wriggling his body about to adjust the sand under the bag, he got comfortable and eventually fell asleep.

As he slept, he dreamed: *He seemed to be in the middle of a dark place like a cave or a tunnel. At one end there was a golden light with beautiful music playing and faint images of people dancing. At the other end it was almost dark. People were crawling around and moaning as if in agony. He was stuck to the middle as if connected by a tube. He felt in danger and helpless, as if something was coming to kill him. There was a murky liquid slowly making its way toward him, and he was unable to move away from it. Closer and closer it came. He knew it was deadly because he could sense the death it contained. When it touched his naked body, . . .* he awoke from his sleep with a start.

"Whoa!" His eyes were wide open and staring up at the stars. "What was that?" Despite the warmth of his sleeping bag he had a chill. He rubbed his upper arms as one would in the cold, closed his eyes, and eventually went back to sleep.

In the morning when he awoke he just lay there a while contemplating the events leading up to then and the dream from last night. He knew that if he and Melina were to have any kind of future together he was going to have to remain in Hawaii when the *Lady* left. And that meant leaving the ship. Since it was Friday it was his last chance to do so. He unzipped the sleeping bag and got dressed. He rolled up the bag and took it with him as he looked for Willy's station wagon. Willy wasn't there, but Tony found him sitting at one of the tables behind the store drinking coffee and reading a newspaper. Tony greeted him, "Good morning. Any good news there?"

Looking up from his paper, "Hey, Tony. No, nothing new, this is yesterday's paper and local at that. It's kind of interesting though. What about you, any wild dreams?"

"Not wild as much as strange," and he went on to describe his dream as best as he could remember.

Willy remarked, "That was a pretty heavy dream. I don't know a lot about the meanings of dreams, but it sounds as though there's something going on with that one."

"When were you and Rob planning on going back to the ship?"

"Not any special time. Why?"

Tony didn't want to tell him that he was planning on leaving the ship. He was afraid Willy would talk him out of it. "I just remembered some business I have to take care of."

"Well, I was going to wait to see what you and Rob wanted to do. Have any idea where he went to sleep?"

"Not exactly. You know, I don't want you two to cut your scene out here short just because of me. I think I should just catch the local bus back."

"Hey, whatever you want to do. I'm just having a relaxing week off before we head back home."

That word 'home' always had a nice feeling to it even if he wasn't quite sure where it was. "What have you heard from Mary?"

"I got a letter from her a couple of days ago. She looked up the contacts you and I gave her and met another woman singer at one of the Sunday hoots in North Beach. She is staying at the woman's place temporarily. It's in Sausalito."

"That's where my friend Brite lives. He has a houseboat right off the main street up at the end of the waterfront."

"That's right, she said she met a friend of yours that you had given her the name of. I think she's going to be all right there. I hope she's still around when I get back."

"You know something Willy, at the north end of that part of the bay is where the *Lady* was built."

"That's right, I forgot about that."

"The shipyard is long gone. To look at the area you wouldn't even guess it was ever there. I know a woman who worked in that shipyard during the war. The women who worked those jobs were nicknamed Rosie the Riveter."

"I remember that. Because most of the men were away fighting the war, the war industries were using women workers to keep the war machine supplied."

"Exactly, if it weren't for all those women, who knows how the war might have turned out." Tony put his hand first in one pocket then another pulling out a half dollar. "Can you change this? I need a dime for the phone."

Willy took some coins from a pocket. "Sure, here ya go. Are you going to use the phone outside the front of the store?"

"Yeah, I want to see if Melina is home yet."

Willy took the fifty-cent piece Tony gave him out of his pocket and handed it back to Tony. "Would you mind getting me a pack of Camels and some Juicy Fruit gum at the store?"

"No problem. That's without filters, right?"

"You got that right, laddie."

Tony went around to the pay phone. He put the dime in the coin slot and dialed Melina's number. Again it just rang and rang. Thinking out loud he said, "Man. I wish I had Kim's number, she must be there." Then with a smile, he continued, "Wait until she hears I'm staying. Boy, will she be surprised." He went into the store to buy the cigarettes and chewing gum. When he returned to Willy he laid out the goods in front of him along with a nickel change, "Here ya go, man."

"Thanks, lad. Did you make your call?"

"Yes, but there was no answer. There wasn't any last night either."

"What do you suppose?"

"I think she must be at Kim's."

"You mean you hope she is at Kim's."

"What do you mean, man?"

"Easy now, she seems to me like one hell of a woman. Now don't get me wrong, it's good havin' you along with us, but don't you think you ought to be with her making her feel glad you are?"

Tony mulled that over in his mind about half a second. "I know you're right. I guess I don't want to see it that way."

"Listen, Tony, you're both very good people. It's just that there are a lot of jerks out there that aren't so good. And I'll bet you my last nickel here that they'll follow her around like a pack of hungry dogs if given half a chance."

Tony agreed, "You're right again. I'm catching the next bus back." He got up from the table and said, "Say goodbye to Rob for me."

Willy said, "Maybe we'll see you at the hospital tomorrow when we visit Mate."

"Maybe so. Ciao!"

"Ciao!"

Tony went into the store to check the bus schedule. Luckily for him he wouldn't have to wait long for the next one into Honolulu.

Because of all the stops, the bus ride took a long time. In Honolulu he transferred to a bus going to the ship's docking area.

It was noon when he finally arrived there. Walking from the street to the *Lady* seemed to take a lot longer than usual, maybe because he was going to quit. Something he never thought he would do.

After he made his way up the gangplank, he asked the crewman standing watch at the gangway if the skipper was on board.

The crewman replied, "No, Mr. Jenkins is the officer of the day today. You'll find him in the exec's office."

"Thanks." Ironically it seemed just like the day he had signed on. He walked down the passage until he came to the next passage and the captain's cabin. But the odors of fresh paint and diesel exhaust were missing. The door to the office was open slightly. The first mate was concentrating on some paper work. A very hesitant Tony said, "Excuse me, Mr. Jenkins."

"Good Lord! Mr. Lewis, you gave me a start. How have you been, lad?"

"Very well, thank you, sir. And how have you been, sir."

"Not bad, actually, once I got over my cough. Well, to what do we owe this occasion?"

"Well, sir, I feel very awkward over what I'm about to request."

"Good heavens, lad, what seems to be the matter?"

"I need to leave the ship, sir."

"Not an unusual request at this port, I daresay."

"Mr. Jenkins, please, sir. I'm sure this is not the usual reason I have. Allow me to be honest about this."

"You have my full attention."

"Over the period of our stays here I have become involved with one of the local women."

Mr. Jenkins seemed a little uncomfortable as he said, "I think I've seen her, the woman who accompanied you at the church service?"

"Yes sir, her name is Melina."

"A striking woman, if I dare say so myself."

"Well, to make a long story short I've gotten her pregnant and this is causing her a great deal of anxiety and stress. She wants an abortion and I'm against them, in general."

"I say, that's quite a predicament all right. And I suppose you feel a pressing need to stay by her side during this traumatic period?"

"Sir, I couldn't have put it in better words."

"And what of your pursuit of the history of *Lady X*?"

"I still intend to go through with that."

"There is one other option."

"What do you mean, sir?"

"You needn't resign from the good ship *Lady Explorer*."

"I still don't understand."

"If you were to take a leave of absence while under extreme personal circumstances you would be able to rejoin the USC&GS service once your circumstances have been resolved. Meanwhile you would remain in good standing with the service. If you were to quit at this port at this time it is doubtful that you would ever be considered for reemployment."

"I see. How do I get the leave of absence?"

"We can fill out the necessary paperwork now. I would suggest making it effective this Sunday midnight prior to our sailing with the tide Monday. The engines are due to be tested tomorrow, and if all goes well we can leave according to schedule. That would give you time to gather your personal effects. You could even stay on board and make use of the ship's facilities until Monday if necessary."

"You're a good man, Henry Jenkins, sir. Let's do that, just as you suggested."

"Good choice. Just allow me a moment to put together the proper forms for the application."

"Application?"

"Not to worry, the matter will be complete with my signature of approval, in the captain's absence of course." After he had put together the forms he motioned Tony over to the same little desk where he had filled in the application for work on the *Lady.* "You can fill out everything right there."

"Déjà vu."

Jenkins agreed, "Yes, it is. Do you want to take a moment to reconsider? This will go out with tonight's mail."

"No, let's get it over with."

After Tony had some lunch in the ship's mess, he went to his quarters to put the remainder of his things in a box to pick up later, and a bag to take with him. In the process he came across a matchbook with Kim's phone number written in it. He realized that he still hadn't made contact with Melina so he was still not certain where he was going to take his things. He started to leave through the cabin door when he remembered something he almost forgot. He went over to his bunk and stood on the lower one to reach up to the overhead pipes. He took down his picture of the tree on the island and put it in a book in his box.

When he stepped out onto the deck and walked slowly down the gangplank, he could smell the rich aroma of the island. He realized how easily one could take such things for granted. He was reminded of how so many of the good things in life are taken for granted. Walking toward a bank of pay phones he thought of the most important thing of all that many people took for granted: their very life and the events that surround it.

At the phones he tried Melina's number. There was still no answer. Next he tried the number he found for Kim.

She answered, "Hello."

He was so glad to finally get through to someone, "Kim, this is Tony. I just found your phone number on the ship. Is Melina there?"

"I haven't seen her since the night before last. We were very busy last night, but I know that she did work last night."

"I phoned her number several times last night and today but she doesn't answer."

"Maybe she turned off the bell and doesn't know you're calling her. She has done that in the past, to sleep, and forgot to turn it back on."

"I bet that's what happened. Are you going to the hospital to see Mate?"

"I was just getting ready to leave when you phoned."

"I was going to go over to Melina's now, but maybe I should let her sleep. She must have been really tired. Can you swing by the *Lady* to pick me up on your way to Mate, and drop me off at Melina's after that?"

"Sure, Mate would like to see you anyway. I'll pick you up in about fifteen to twenty minutes."

"That would be great."

Tony figured that since he was getting a ride he may as well take the box with his things in it. He returned to the ship to retrieve the box.

When Kim arrived, Tony was near the curb sitting on a bus stop bench with his bag and box at his side. Kim pulled up next to him. When he opened the back door she asked him, "What's all of that?"

He put the things in, closed the door, and got into the front. "I've taken a leave of absence."

"Can you do that?"

"I'll tell you on the way." So off they drove to the hospital while he told her of his plan to stay on the island.

She responded with, "I hope you know what you are doing. It's not going to be easy for you to find a job here. The natives don't like Howlies, that's what they call whites. And the locals don't believe mainland people stay here very long. They get bored with the place, not much to do that's different and because the place is so small. So locals only want to hire locals."

Useful information too late, he thought. "Where were you this morning?"

"What do you mean?"

"Before I took my leave of absence. Anyway, I have to try. Otherwise what can I do?"

"Well, good luck is all I can say."

"Here we are." Kim left the car in the parking lot, and they went into the hospital.

Mate was sitting in a wheelchair with the repaired leg jutting straight out on a support. He was by a window looking out at the harbor. When he saw their reflection in the glass and without turning to look at them he said, "Isn't this view somethin' else?"

They walked over to him. Kim put a hand on his shoulder and gave him a kiss on the cheek. "Hi, sweetheart, look who I found."

Mate asked Tony, "Hey, my man, what have you been up to?"

Kim and Tony sat on a pair of chairs that they moved near Mate. "You mean other than maybe becoming a father?"

"Congratulations." Looking over at Kim, he said, "I heard about that, do you mean there's more?"

"I've taken a leave of absence from the *Lady*, and I'm going to stay here and live happily ever after."

"Sounds more like you've taken a leave of your senses. Sorry, I just couldn't pass that one by. Well, welcome aboard, laddie."

"That reminds me. Willy and Rob will be by to see you tomorrow. Well, that's all the news so I guess I'll leave now."

"Wait a minute. How did you get here?"

"With this lovely young lady."

"So how are you going to leave now?"

Tony thought a moment. "Good point."

Kim protested, "Will you two stop? Sweetheart, my mother and father will be here to see you right after your lunch tomorrow." She sat a bag on the tall table beside his bed. "Here are the things you asked me to get you."

"Thanks, dove. Don't worry, when your parents are here I'll be Mr. Wonderful personified."

Tony commented, "That I would like to see."

"My man, they are going to let me out of here sometime Sunday. Kim is taking me over to see the *Lady* off on Monday morning. Why don't you come along?"

"I'm going to miss her, you know. I can't let her go without saying goodbye. Sure, I'll go."

An hour passed before Kim and Tony left the hospital. They drove straight over to Melina's. Kim went to the door with Tony. He pushed the doorbell a few times without a response.

Kim observed, "That is her car parked in front. Let's try knocking." They knocked and knocked, but still no response. She said, "You know, I'm having a bad feeling about this."

Tony agreed, "Me too. Now I'm worried."

Kim said, "I have a key Melina gave me for an emergency." She took the ring of keys from her purse and inserted the one with the letter *M* etched into it. The door opened, then Tony went in first.

He noticed something in the air. "What's that smell?" They both headed for the bedroom. The smell was very strong now and foul. Melina was sprawled across her bed with her robe half off. Her head was hanging over one side, and below it was a dried puddle of vomit. "Melina!"

"Oh god." Kim tried to feel her pulse. "Her pulse is very weak."

"Kim, we need to get her to a doctor."

Kim dug in her purse and took out a card. She handed it to Tony saying, "This has the number of our doctor. Give him a call and when you contact him give me the phone." While Tony was doing that Kim looked Melina over for signs of what might have happened to her. She saw a bruise on her left arm around from the elbow. Looking more closely she could see a tiny puncture mark over a vein. She said to herself, "Something tells me Bruno's been here." She got a fresh robe from the closet and put it on Melina making sure to cover her arms.

Tony came back with the phone, "I have the doctor on the phone."

She took the phone. "Thanks . . . Dr. Lim, this is Kim . . . That's right. I have an emergency, Doctor. It's Melina. She's unconscious, maybe since late last night. Except that she has been throwing up . . . Yes, I think so . . . Can you come to her apartment right away? . . . Yes, that's right, the same place . . . Very good. Thank you, Doctor." She hung up the phone, "He'll be here in about ten minutes."

Puzzled by something she said, Tony asked, "The doctor's been here before?"

"Yes, it was for Bruno. He had overdosed."

"Good ol' Bruno. I had forgotten about him." Tony couldn't remember ever feeling so worried. He put his hand on Melina's forehead. It was cool and clammy. He felt a little helpless. "Kim, isn't there anything we can do for Melina before the doctor gets here?"

"Maybe wipe her face with a damp cloth and cover her with a blanket. I've put a fresh robe on her. I'll clean up the mess by the bed." She added, "I checked the phone, and the bell had been turned off."

"Why would she turn off the bell?" he asked.

"I don't know."

"There's something odd about the bathroom. The tub is full of yellow water and smells like mustard. I can't figure that out."

"Mustard? I don't know. That sounds strange. But leave it for the doctor to look at."

He went back into the bathroom to soak a washcloth with warm water, then used it to wipe Melina's face and neck.

Kim got up from the floor. "Why am I smelling paint? Would you mind giving this a second scrub with soapy water? You can use the dishwashing liquid from the kitchen sink."

When Tony came back with a pan of soapy water, Kim went into the kitchen to throw what she had cleaned from the rug into the trash. When she opened it she immediately saw the syringe that Bruno had left behind. She just stared down at it wondering what to do. She opened a cupboard where she knew Melina kept empty jars and took one out. She carefully put the syringe into the jar, and the jar into a small paper bag. She went back into the bedroom and put the bag into her purse, with not a word to Tony about her find.

There was a knock at the door. Kim said, "That must be the doctor. I'll let him in." Tony continued cleaning the rug. By the time she reached the door she had the paper bag back out of her purse. As the doctor entered the living room Kim handed him the bag. "Dr. Lim, I'm glad you could come on such short notice." Before the doctor could reply she said in a half whisper, "There's a needle mark on her left arm, and I found this in the trash. I think Bruno may have been here."

The doctor looked into the bag and saw the syringe in the narrow jar. The doctor's voice had a serious tone, "I see. Where is she?"

"In here, Doctor." Kim led him into the bedroom.

Tony had just finished the cleaning and thought he smelled paint thinner. He stood looking a bit puzzled, "Doctor, it's so good to see you. I'm Tony Lewis, a close friend of Melina's."

"Pleased to meet you, Mr. Lewis." He immediately began to check her over. While checking her vital signs he leaned near her face to sample her breath. He could smell the odor of gin. "Do you know if she had been drinking gin last night?"

Both Tony and Kim responded with, "Gin?" Kim added, "She isn't a drinker, a glass of wine now and again with a meal, but no gin."

Tony couldn't understand, "Why would she be drinking gin?"

The doctor informed them, "Well, there's a distinct odor of gin on her breath. I'm surprised you didn't notice." Then to distract Tony the doctor asked him, "Do you think you could find a clean towel and a glass of drinking water for me?"

"Yes sir, I think I know where the towels are."

When Tony was out of the room, the doctor examined Melina's left arm. He told Kim in a soft voice, "She's definitely been injected with something and my guess is that it came from the item in the jar. I'll test the residue of its contents back in my office." He continued with another observation, "I didn't find any other marks of any kind on her."

"Doctor, I need to tell you something. Melina is pregnant."

"My god." The doctor began to see the pieces fall into place. "Mr. Lewis?"

"Yes, and he wants to keep it," Kim informed him.

"And she doesn't?" more as a supposition than a question.

Kim said to him, "You might also want to take a look in the bathroom at the bath. It's half full of yellowish water that smells like mustard."

"Did you say mustard?" the doctor asked.

Tony came in with a glass of water and a towel. "Here are the things you asked for, sir."

"Thank you." He poured some of the water onto the towel then wiped Melina's closed eyes. Again he opened each eye, this time he directed the light from a tiny flashlight into first one, then the other. He was looking at the fluid in her eyes. He didn't reveal what he saw or suspected. "Let's take a quick look at that bath water, and then I'll see if I can bring her around."

In the bathroom he looked at the water, dipped a finger into it and smelled it. "You're right about the mustard smell."

Tony asked him, "What do you make of all this, sir?"

The doctor had been adding up all the clues, but he didn't think it would be a good idea to tell Tony yet, "It's difficult to say really." He looked through the medicine cabinet over the sink.

They followed the doctor back into the bedroom. They had left Melina lying on her back with her head on a pillow. The doctor held smelling salts under her nose. Melina began to stir.

Feeling a sense of relief, Kim said, "Look! She's coming to."

Filled with hope, Tony asked, "Is she going to be all right?"

The doctor gave it another try, "I don't believe she was unconscious but rather passed out." Melina began a barely discernible moan.

Tony saw a ray of hope. "It's working. Do you think she's going to have a nasty hangover?"

"Most certainly. I'm going to give you a prescription for her."

Kim said to the doctor, "You need to give it to him because I have to get to work. Oh, that reminds me. The club doesn't know Melina can't work tonight. I need to phone them."

Melina was trying to talk in a garbled way, "What . . . happened . . . to me? Bruno . . . that bas . . . What happen . . ." She choked and coughed. "Oh . . . my head."

The doctor tried to get her to respond, "Melina, Melina, look at me. It's Dr. Lim. You've been very sick, but you are going to get better. Can you hear me? Mr. Lewis is going to get some medicine for you, and I want you to take it. He's going to be looking after you. Do you understand me?"

Melina tried very hard to speak, "Yes, . . . Doctor."

"Good, don't try to talk any more." The doctor said, "She probably won't be able to work for a few days."

Kim told him, "Since she's going to miss tonight and tomorrow she'll be due back at work in four days on Tuesday."

"Fine, I want to see her in my office Monday afternoon, let's say two o'clock, for a thorough exam."

Tony said, "I'll be sure she's there, Doctor."

Kim told the doctor, "Since we're leaving at the same time I'll go down to the car with you."

The doctor wrote out a list of things for Tony to do for Melina then and the next day. "Can you get this prescription filled tonight?"

"Sure, I'll use Melina's car. But where is the drugstore?"

The doctor told him how to find it. The pharmacy turned out to be the same one where Tony first saw Bruno. The doctor then checked Melina one last time. "I'm sure she's in good hands. It was a pleasure to meet you, Mr. Lewis."

"Thank you for all your help, sir. I'll phone you if something goes wrong. Otherwise we'll see you Monday."

While they were talking Kim telephoned the Sleeping Lady to inform them that Melina was very ill and wouldn't be able to return to work until Tuesday. When the doctor left, Kim followed him out as she said, "Don't worry, Tony, Melina's going to be okay. I'll phone you later tonight."

Tony just said, "Bye," then gave a big sigh.

When they got to their cars Kim asked the doctor, "What do you think happened to her?"

"Well, the mustard bath and probable large amount of gin would indicate something if combined with either a small amount of turpentine or paint thinner given in a glass full of beet juice."

"There was an empty jar of beet juice in the trash. I thought I smelled paint. But what are all of those things for?"

"To induce a miscarriage, it's an old and risky remedy. Only the strongest are able to endure it. If you hadn't told me she was pregnant I would be very puzzled. But why the injection?"

Kim thought she might have an idea. "Melina probably asked Bruno to help her find a solution to her problem, and I wouldn't put it past Bruno to trick her into taking a drug."

"As soon as I get back to my office I'll test the contents of the syringe." The doctor got into his car and drove away.

Kim had barely enough time to drive home to change into something for work.

Later on, Tony returned from the pharmacy and the market where he bought the things the doctor suggested for Melina to eat. He spent the time trying to make her comfortable and make her something to eat when she felt able. He changed her bed sheets and blanket, then he busied himself by straightening her bedroom and kitchen. He wondered why she said Bruno's name, but he respected her condition and so didn't question her. Eventually he became so tired that he couldn't stay awake any longer. He got into the bed beside Melina and fell asleep. It wasn't until the next day that she was able to talk to him.

Chapter 12

NOW WHAT?

Outside, Saturday was just another typically beautiful Hawaiian day, but inside something ugly had entered Tony's life. Not yet aware of what had really taken place in Melina's apartment or why, he could think of nothing else as he tried to figure it all out. However, almost from the moment he saw Melina on the bed looking like death he sensed a connection with the pregnancy. Because his greatest fear was an attempted abortion, he pushed it out of his mind as far away as he could and searched for any other logical answer. He wasn't finding any.

The night before, Dr. Lim didn't have an opportunity to test the residue in the syringe until rather late. But he phoned Kim first thing in the morning to tell her of his finding. He phoned in a prescription at the same pharmacy for Kim to pick up and take over to Melina's.

Tony was in the kitchen making a light meal for Melina when there was a knock at the door. He answered it and was pleased to see Kim. Then upon seeing the familiar little white paper bag she was holding, he asked, "Dear Kim, what have you got there?"

"Hi, the doctor phoned me this morning and said I should get right over here with this. How is Melina feeling?"

"A bit better but she's having an aching feeling all through her body."

As they walked to the bedroom, Kim said, "The medicine I brought will probably help that. Did you get any sleep?"

"Not much, and I was really tired." He leaned over Melina and said softly, "Sweetheart, Kim is here." After a moment he hurried back into the kitchen to keep something from burning.

When Melina opened her eyes and saw Kim she began to cry. Kim hugged her and began to cry too. She half whispered into Melina's ear, "Dear, sweetheart, what have you been up to?"

Melina asked in a half whisper, "Does he know?"

Kim said, "I don't think so, but the doctor and I have it pretty well figured out." She dabbed at her tears with a tissue. "Did you try to—"

Melina cut her off with, "Yes."

"Dr. Lim wants you in for a full physical at two o'clock Monday. You should know then how you are."

Melina stopped crying. She frowned as she recalled, "But Tony's ship leaves that morning," she coughed momentarily, "to take him back to the mainland."

"I have a couple of surprises for you. Do you remember having an injection the night before last?"

"I can barely remember, but I think so."

"Well, you did and it contained codeine."

"Codeine?!" She coughed again, "That bastard."

"Our lovely friend, Bruno?"

"Yes. Oh my god."

"I thought so."

She was afraid to ask, "What's the other surprise?"

Tony appeared from the kitchen with a tray of food for Melina. "Did I hear something about a surprise?"

Kim said to him, "I was about to tell Melina about your latest decision, but it would be better if you told her."

Melina slowly sat up so Tony could put the tray on her lap. He gave her a glass of water, "Kim has some more medicine for you to take first." Kim opened the little container giving one tablet to Melina. She put it in her mouth and was about to follow it with the water when Tony said, "I've quit the ship." Melina again coughed bringing up the tablet and water. "'Quit' is not the right word." He wiped away the spilled water. "Actually I've taken a leave of absence, so I can stay here with you until you've had the baby and beyond. They're going to be scrapping the *Lady* after she gets back to her home port. I thought you would be surprised, and happy."

But instead of looking happy Melina was looking at Kim with a confused and worried expression. She had been speechless until then. "I don't know what to say. I wish you would have said something to me about it first."

"I know I was kind of off on a tangent Wednesday night. I probably shouldn't have hit that jerk. But I couldn't help myself. I tried to phone you after you would have been home from work Thursday night but your phone just rang and rang with no answer. And I tried Friday too."

Kim told Melina, "The bell on your phone was turned off."

"It was? I don't remember turning it off."

Tony continued, "Because Friday was the last day I could turn in an application I had to decide then one way or the other. So I took a chance."

Kim told Melina, "I told him he was going to have trouble finding a job here."

"That's true, hon, unless you do the kind of work no one else wants to do or can do."

Tony told them with determination, "I'm going to start looking after you're feeling better."

"Listen, my parents are going to meet Mate for the first time at the hospital today after lunch, so I need to get over there. Remember, he gets out tomorrow and will be staying at my apartment."

Melina said, "You two are moving pretty fast. I hope everything works out."

Kim admitted, "I am a little worried."

Tony suggested, "I can meet you at the hospital to help you with Mate if you give me a time."

"I don't know if you'll need to but I'll let you know before I go to work later."

Melina had a sudden sharp pain in her abdomen, "Ohh!"

Tony asked, "What's wrong, love?"

Melina was clutching her stomach. "I'm having an awful pain in my stomach."

Kim looked concerned, "Melina, you need to get on the phone to Dr. Lim, and tell him what you're feeling."

Tony looked at a card the doctor gave him then picked up the phone and dialed the doctor's office number. There was no answer but an answering service told Tony that it would relay his message when the doctor checked with them as he often did on Saturday. "He wasn't in so I left a message."

Melina strained to speak, "I'm sorry, Kim, I can't do anything. I'm just going to lie here until Dr. Lim phones. Thanks for all your help. And good luck with your parents meeting Mate."

"I would stay longer, but I really have to get going. I'm picking up my parents and taking them over." She kissed Melina and Tony goodbye then left.

Melina told Tony, "She is so sweet. I sure hope her mom and dad like Mate."

"He's a likable guy. I think it's going to work out fine. Melina, if you're strong enough, I need to talk to you about what happened to you. I don't really know very much."

She was quiet. She was not ready to tell him and would rather not tell him at all. "Would you mind if we don't talk about it right now? My stomach is hurting so much." Just then the phone rang.

Tony answered it, "Hello . . . Dr. Lim . . . Yes, just a moment." He handed the phone to Melina.

"Dr. Lim? . . . Better, but I'm having very sharp pains in my lower stomach . . . Yes. I took one about half an hour ago . . . Okay . . . All right . . . Yes, we will . . . Thank you . . . Bye, bye." Then she told Tony, "He's coming over and will be here in about fifteen minutes."

Tony went into the kitchen. "I'll clean up the breakfast things. Can I get you something?"

Melina just lay still holding her stomach. "Thanks, hon. Some ice water would be good."

"Ice water it is."

"You're a dear."

Talking from the kitchen, "You know, Kim and I were very worried when we found you. You looked like you might not still be alive."

Melina said, "That must have been awful for you."

"It sure was. We were surprised when the doctor figured you had drunk a lot of gin. We didn't think you drank the stuff."

"I don't drink gin as a rule."

Tony continued, "He also said that instead of unconscious you probably passed out."

"The doctor said that?"

"Yes. Some smelling salts brought you right out of it."

Tony came out of the kitchen with the ice water. "But it was gin, right?"

She took the water and drank it slowly. "I'm afraid so. This cold water is nice."

"And you don't want to talk about it now?"

She wanted to wait until after her exam on Monday to tell him. "It's a little complicated, and I'd rather not go into it now."

"Okay." He returned to the kitchen feeling frustrated. He wanted to know what happened.

She asked him, "Have you seen the silver dancing shoes you gave me?"

He had difficulty hearing her. "What's that?"

"The silver shoes you gave me."

"I'll look for them when I finish in here."

"You might look under the bed, hon."

About twenty minutes later, after finishing the dishes, Tony looked under her bed. "Here they are. I found them." He stood up and handed them to her.

"Oh, thank you." She gave him a light kiss. After wiping the silver chain and shoes she hung them from around her neck. She asked him, "Where is the one I got for you?"

He suddenly felt uncomfortable. "It's in my duffel bag. I haven't gotten around to taking it out since I packed all my gear together."

"I thought you would always want to wear it."

"I like it a lot, really."

The doorbell rang. "That must be Dr. Lim." Tony opened the door; the doctor came in with a concerned expression.

Meanwhile Kim had just arrived at the hospital with her parents. In Mate's room Kim was standing near Mate while her parents sat near his bed in the only two chairs in the room. After Kim introduced them there was an awkward silence as everyone waited for someone else to speak first.

Mate kind of stumbled into, "Sir, your daughter is one of the finest"—he hesitated as he caught himself about to say women—"and one of the kindest people I have ever known."

Kim's father replied, "Mr. Jones, you must excuse me for what I'm about to say."

Kim had been holding Mate's hand. It tightened as she thought, *Oh my God. What is he going to say?*

Her father continued, "Before we left our home in South Korea our town was being attacked by the North Koreans with the help of the Chinese army. The American army was retreating to the southern coast so they could be evacuated by ship. We might never have escaped alive if it had not been for an American soldier. They were all rushing to escape to the south. He must have seen Kim and her mother holding on to each other through a broken window of our house. He hurried to the window and shouted in Korean, 'Come on. Get out! They are right behind us. They're burning everything.' I had just come from another room when he saw me. 'Come on! I'll help you,' he shouted. So we just left everything and ran out the door as he stood by with a machine gun at the ready." He took an emotional breath.

"We walked as fast as we could; we couldn't run very well. There was gunfire all around us, and total confusion. I looked back to see the soldier. I wanted to thank him," he hesitated as he was moved by emotion, "but he was lying on the ground and not moving. He had been shot by a sniper from a window in one of the buildings. Another soldier told me he was dead. We owe our lives to him. I'm telling you this story because he was a dark man like you."

Kim's mother was nodding her head and crying at the memory of that tragic time in their lives.

Kim was also crying. "Dad, you never told me that part of the story before."

Mate was dumbstruck. All he could say was, "Wow."

Later that afternoon Willy and Rob arrived at the hospital. They were in Mate's room. Rob said to Mate, "You're looking pretty good there, my friend."

Willy added, "Yeah, there seems to be something different about you, almost a glow."

Mate suggested, "Well, there could be a couple of things helping that along. One is I'm getting out of here tomorrow afternoon. And the other is Kim and her parents. I just met them. I was really scared they weren't going to like me."

Rob asked him, "So how did it go?"

Mate related the story Kim's father told him.

Willy was very moved. "That is amazing."

Rob was equally affected. "That just goes to show you one never can tell how things are going to go. So what happened after that?"

"We talked about my foot and my hopes and plans for the future. They know that I'll be staying at Kim's until I've recovered enough to return to the mainland. Also her father said that I would always be welcome in their home. It was a far-out visit. I just can't get over it."

Willy agreed, "That is fabulous all right. What else is new?"

"With me? That's pretty much been it. Have you seen Tony though?"

Willy again, "Yeah, he went with us to the Crosswinds Thursday and came back on his own on Friday. He had gotten into a fight with one of the customers where Melina works the night before he went with us. He was pretty concerned with the way things were going for them."

"Well, then I've got some news for you. He's quit the *Lady.*"

Willy admitted, "I was afraid he might do that."

"You've got to be kidding," responded Rob.

"He's taken a leave of absence. That's the official term. That way he can return to the new survey ship if he doesn't wait too long. So in a way, it's not quitting. I guess it's more like just taking some time off."

Rob said, "I didn't know you could do that during a cruise."

"Basically it's because Melina is expecting. He wants to stay here with her until they decide what to do next."

Rob commented, "That's as good a reason as any."

"But there's more; yesterday afternoon he and Kim found Melina unconscious in her apartment. When the doctor arrived he was able to bring her to. But they don't know what was wrong with her."

Willy exclaimed, "Good grief, man, that's a whole lot of somethin' you're telling us. I can't guess what all of this means. I think our friend Tony is in for some heavy times."

"It sure looks that way, all right." agreed Rob.

"Where is he now?" asked Willy.

"Kim told me that when she left Melina's today he was there waiting for the doctor because Melina was having some severe lower abdominal pains."

Rob suggested, "It sounds as though she might be losing the baby."

Willy said, "My god in heaven, what a predicament. We're going to the chapel tomorrow, right, Rob?"

"Yes, we are. I think I know what you're getting at. They could use some prayers, couldn't they?" Rob asked.

"They certainly could," agreed a very concerned Willy.

Mate said, "I'm going to be stuck here until around five o'clock in the afternoon. Otherwise, I'd like to be there with you."

Willy informed him, "Well, my dear friend, you can pray from anywhere, can't you."

Mate admitted, "Well, I'm just not used to it."

Rob asked him, "What about the time the shark had a hold on your foot, did you pray then?"

"No, I was too scared and too busy cussing to think of it. But I probably should have."

Rob told him, "Well, I did a prayer for you then. It was too late for me to do one for Chuck."

Willy looked at Rob for a moment. He hadn't mentioned Chuck's name since the church service.

The sun was just setting. Tony was alone in Melina's car on an errand to the pharmacy and to a food market. He took the opportunity to drive a little and catch a breath of air. He had the car radio on and was listening to jazz. Miles Davis was playing a forlorn Spanish piece by Rodrigo.

His driving had taken on the nature of wandering aimlessly as he began to ponder the past; his likes and motivations that had brought him to this moment, and all the influences from other people. He believed traveling to be his forte for the moment—to be on the move exploring places and people, and thereby discovering his self. He had related his realization to Mr. Jenkins, along with his determination to explore the greatest school of learning—the world.

Without realizing it he had driven to Waikiki. He parked the car, walked across the street to the nearly deserted beach and sat on the sand. The sun had set leaving the western sky almost glowing orange, with peach colored rays shooting up past clouds along the horizon. Thinking about nothing his mind was completely quiet. He was just savoring the moment, feeling the vibration of God, as it were. As his thoughts returned and darkness approached, he became restless.

When he crossed the street to return to the car he saw Cheryl, the waitress from the Ocean Breeze, standing at the curb. A man was opening the door of his Corvette for her to get in. They gave one another a special smile as they drove away. With all that had been happening Tony had forgotten about her. He returned to the car then drove to a market. The music on the radio seemed far away now as his thoughts became filled with the confusion of the past few days.

During the time that Tony was gone, Melina was going through mental distress over what she had done, what Tony had done, and what Bruno had put into that syringe. The doctor told her that he needed to know everything she had consumed. What could explain the strange sensations she had been having in her body? She knew that if Bruno was desperate enough for money he could do almost anything. She felt anger and pity for him at the same time. She worried about Tony staying with her. He wouldn't want her to dance at the club, and she didn't think he would find work. Also she was afraid she would only get pregnant again. Before she met him life had been going along just fine, and it was simpler.

Tony let himself into Melina's apartment and took the things he bought into the kitchen. He put some things into the refrigerator then went into the bedroom. "How are you feeling, love?"

"I'm aching, and I'm bored. You were gone a long time."

"Yeah, I went for a little drive. Would you like me to make you something to eat?"

"Were you able to get the fish?"

"They just happened to have two left of the kind you wanted."

"Oh good, do you think you could cook them?"

"Sure, the same way you do them?"

"That will be too complicated. Just fry them in a pan with a little oil."

He was starting to lighten up a little. "Can I make you some mint tea, madam?"

She was beginning to warm up as well. "You're too sweet. Did you get the prescription?"

"Oh, I forgot it."

"You forgot to get it?"

"No, I left it in the grocery bag." He returned to the kitchen. From one of the larger bags he withdrew a small white bag. He poured a glass of water then took it and the medicine into the bedroom. "Here we are, and a glass of water if you need it."

"Thank you. You really are an angel, you know."

He sat on the bed next to her. "Yeah, sure."

"No, really, I'm serious. Have you ever done anything bad?"

"Probably." He wondered what she meant by bad. He lay back on the bed as he tried to remember. "Well, now that I think of it, when I was very young—"

"What was it? Come on, tell me."

"I think I was in first or second grade at the time. I took a small pack of cookies from a grocery store shelf and kept them."

"Is that it? Nothing else?"

"Let me think." The mind has a way of rejecting what it cannot accept. "Let me think." In an instant of no thought a hidden memory emerged. He was on the stern of the *Lady* waiting for his turn to dive into the water. Because he was very annoyed with old Bill's insulting remarks about Melina he gave him a nudge toward the edge. Bill lost his balance and grabbed

Tony's arm. Tony lost his balance and grabbed Mate's arm. Mate also lost his balance causing them all to fall over the side into the water. Because Bill went into the water unprepared to do so he must have swallowed a lot of water. He was down too long and came up gasping for air. Chuck was again on deck and thought that Bill might be drowning. He dove back into the water to save him. Because of that nudge two men were dead and another nearly lost a foot.

Tony rolled on to his side facing away from Melina and stared at the wall. A look of distress was on his face as a shudder coursed through his body.

Melina was not prepared for this. "What is happening to you? Tony? Tony? What's wrong?"

"I can't tell you." He swallowed with difficulty, "I can't tell anyone."

That night Tony was so distraught that he hardly slept.

After a late breakfast Tony took Melina for a drive to the park where he had bought her pendant. This was her first venture out from her apartment since she had become so ill. Tony drove more carefully than usual.

Once they were in the park they walked arm in arm but Melina walked as little as necessary sitting whenever she felt the need. Because it was Sunday there were more people in the park than on other days. It was also the best day for craftsmen to ply their trade. So it was no surprise that they should again come across the gold and silversmith, Bill Younge. Tony was hoping he would be there.

They were walking so carefully that Bill couldn't help but notice them. "Hello there. I haven't seen either of you in a while. How are you?"

Melina tried not to sound too weak as she talked to him. "Well, I have been very sick, and this is my first day out to get some exercise."

"Oh, I'm sorry to hear that." Then he smiled. "I see you're both wearing the pieces I made."

As Melina sat on Bill's only chair, she said, "Yes, we really love them."

Tony added, "They have a special feeling about them." He asked Bill, "Have you seen the symbol of yin and yang together?"

Bill took a pad of paper and a pencil and drew the symbol. "Do you mean this?"

"Yes, that's it. I was thinking of having you make a pendant where the symbol splits in two so we each can wear a half."

Melina was surprised. "What a nice idea, hon."

Bill reached into the bottom of his display case and withdrew a thick binder. It contained photos and drawings of his work. He opened it to a photo of a pendant on a woman's neck. It had the very symbol Tony asked him about. "Are you thinking of something like this?"

"Yes, just like that," Tony answered him. "But smaller, almost as small as a dime."

Melina asked them, "Can I see that?" Bill handed the binder to her. "That's very nice, Bill. Could you make one for us in gold with one half white and the other half black?"

"Any way you want it," he told her. He asked Tony, "How soon would you need it?"

Tony noticed his use of the word "need," instead of the word "want." Could Bill sense a disharmony between them? Tony had thought that he was an unusual person when he first met him. "How long will it take you to do it for us?"

"I can have it for you the day after tomorrow."

Tony looked at Melina. She gave him a faint but warm smile. He told Bill, "That would be great." They were about to leave when Tony asked Bill, "Do you mind if I ask where you're from?"

Bill answered, "Not at all. I'm from California."

"Far out, so am I. What part?"

"Fairfax. That's in Marin County."

"You're kidding me. I'm from San Francisco, across the Golden Gate from you."

"I thought you might be from California. I've been here for a while though, I needed a change."

"Yeah, I can dig that. This place and the Bay Area are as different as night and day. Listen, I need to help a friend leave the hospital today. We can talk more when I pick up the pendant. Do you want a deposit?"

"Half would be all right."

"Okay." Tony paid him. "Ciao!" Tony and Melina slowly walked back to the car.

Melina said to him, "It's such a small world, really."

"The silversmith and I were practically neighbors. How are you feeling your first day out?"

"Weak, but I am feeling better. It is so nice being in the park. Coming here was a good idea. Thank you, hon."

"I thought the exercise would be good for you. Would you like to take a short outing before you see Dr. Lim?"

"Maybe, doesn't the *Lady Explorer* leave tomorrow?"

Tony replied, "Yes, and for the last time."

"We could all see her off together. Let's see how I feel then."

"I hope you feel up to it because it's going to be an important moment for all of us, including the *Lady*."

After Tony took Melina home he drove on to Kim's place where Kim was waiting for him to accompany her to the hospital. Tony was going along just in case Kim needed his help.

When they arrived at the hospital and Mate's floor, Mate was ready to leave and was practicing the use of his crutches.

"Well hello. I was beginning to think I might have to walk home." Mate was in good spirits, happy to finally be leaving. He had been confined to the hospital room ever since he was taken off the *Lady*. "You know, I would almost be willing to walk there on these crutches just to get out of here."

Tony teased him as he pushed the wheelchair over to him, "Yeah, sure. If the truth be known you're in a big hurry because you have a date tonight."

Mate settled into the wheelchair. "Well, that too."

Kim reassured Mate, "Don't worry, sweetheart, everything at home is ready for you."

He looked over at Tony and gave him a wink. "You know, I could do with a bit of exercise." And at that Tony gave him a wink.

Tony asked him, "My man, do you suppose, after you've had sufficient exercise of course, that you would be up to seeing the *Lady* off tomorrow. Say around ten a.m.?"

"Wild dolphins couldn't keep me away."

Kim added, "We've been looking forward to seeing her off, haven't we, darling?"

"That we have, my dove."

Tony had a hold on Mate's wheelchair, "Shall we go, sir?"

Mate gave his room the final once-over and said, "By all means, my good man." After they were outside the building Mate said, "Man, smell that air. Isn't it great to be alive?"

Kim carried a bag of Mate's belongings and his medicines while Tony pushed the wheelchair to the car. Once there, Kim held open a front door while Tony helped Mate into the car.

When Tony was sure that Mate had settled in at Kim's he phoned Melina to see if she needed anything.

After picking up some things at the market, he returned to Melina's. With her help he cooked a dinner for them both. She was not strong enough to do it on her own, at least not yet.

They had not made love since before her attempted miscarriage. She was still in no condition to even consider it, and Tony knew he should wait until she initiated any form of affection beyond hugging and kissing. They spent the remainder of the evening reading and listening to LPs of more soothing music. Tony would occasionally read a poem to her. And so the evening passed quietly with each of them becoming more relaxed.

It was Monday morning. Kim and Melina's cars were parked as near as possible to the *Lady Explorer*. The ship's reworked diesel engines had been ticking over smoothly since the early morning. She was as ready as she would ever be to make her final voyage. As originally planned the ship was to spend the first part of the return journey completing the survey run. There had still been no word concerning the awarding of the plaque.

Melina was standing beside Kim's car while Tony helped Mate out of her car and into his wheelchair. Tony said to Mate, "You know, man, I just had the strangest feeling that I should be on that ship."

Mate looked up at him with the wisest look Tony had ever seen on his generally carefree face. "It's too late now, my man. She's going on without you, and you know it." Something about that comment resonated deep within Tony.

On the main deck of the *Lady*, Rob and Willy were asking the captain, "Permission to go ashore, sir?" Captain Reiger looked puzzled. Willy nodded toward their friends on the dock.

The captain said, "Permission granted, but be quick about it."

"Aye, aye, sir." They hurried down the gangway to the foursome on the dock. Shaking their hands and patting the men on the back, Willy said, "Well lads, you're going to be sorely missed."

Rob said, "I don't suppose we'll be seeing the two of you again any time soon."

As the two were hugging the ladies goodbye, both Tony and Mate were trying to maintain dry eyes. Mate told them, "You better get back up there or she'll leave without you."

"So long and good luck."

"So long and good luck to you too."

Willy and Rob hurried back up the gangplank. Tony couldn't resist the urge. He left the three behind and ran up the gangplank behind the others. He went to the captain, "Sir, I want to apologize to you for leaving the ship this way, but I felt I had no other choice."

The captain replied, "Mr. Jenkins explained your situation to me. It is regrettable, but I do understand."

"Thank you, sir." He went over to the rail and strained to look up, looking for the first mate on the flying bridge.

The pilot boat *Jenny Girl* had come alongside and a crewman had thrown a line to the bow of the *Lady Explorer.* The captain told Tony, "You had better go ashore, Mr. Lewis. And good luck to you."

Again he thanked the captain, "I was hoping to say goodbye to the first mate, sir."

Knowing that Tony was on the main deck below, Henry Jenkins leaned over the rail of the flying bridge to see him. He called down to Tony, "Mr. Lewis. And so ends another story, hey lad? Good luck to you."

Calling up to Mr. Jenkins, Tony said, "So it seems, sir. Thank you for all you've done." He dashed forward to touch the bell, saying softly, "So long, old girl. Good luck." The line from the pilot boat was secured and the *Lady* strained at her mooring lines.

The captain had gone up to the flying bridge. He called down to Tony, "Mr. Lewis. You must leave now." Tony went quickly down the gangplank. The captain ordered, "Raise the gangplank, and cast away all lines." No sooner had Tony stepped off the plank than it was lifted off the dock and just as quickly secured to the rail. As the mooring lines were disconnected from the dock's bollards, the line from the pilot boat was tightened and quickly rose out from the water's surface, weeping water as it did so. The *Lady* was slowly pulled away from her dock. The two were not to come into contact ever again.

On the flying bridge, a crewman was at the upper helm. Mr. Jenkins said to him, "Steady as she goes, helmsman. We'll be under our own power soon enough."

The captain looked toward the open sea, "It looks to be a fine day, Mr. Jenkins."

"Aye, that it does Captain."

"Just between you and me, Number One, it wouldn't be a bad idea to keep our fingers crossed. We have yet a long way to go, and we're short four damned good men."

"Right you are, sir." Jenkins was moved by emotion, he looked away from the captain and toward the shore. The *Lady* seemed to glide along her way. The images on the dock grew smaller, then fainter and fainter, until they were gone.

Tony, Melina, Mate, and Kim had stood at the dock's edge until the *Lady* had gone out of sight. After all the waving and shouting goodbye to the familiar faces they would catch a glimpse of, they had become quiet. They all sensed the end of something, and in the few moments that followed they sensed a depth of meaning that seemed beyond them.

Back at the cars Mate brought them out of their quiet, "Well, there's only one thing to do at a time like this. Let's eat."

They were all feeling a bit hungry so following Mate's suggestion they ended up going to Hook, Line, and Sinker for a seafood lunch. Later in the evening they planned to get back together for dinner at Kim's apartment.

After lunch Tony took Melina for her checkup with Dr. Lim. Tony sat in the waiting room while the doctor took Melina into his examination room. "First of all, you are going to have to be perfectly honest with me."

"I will, Dr. Lim." She was curious and fearful about what he may have discovered.

Because the doctor had known Melina for most of her time in Hawaii he was more personal with her than he might otherwise have been. "I'm going to be perfectly frank with you. As far as I can tell, you made a foolish attempt at an abortion. And if you used the assistance of your friend Bruno, that was just as foolish. I did the best I could to determine the content of what remained in the hypodermic syringe Kim found in the waste basket of your kitchen."

Melina couldn't believe her ears. "There was a syringe in my kitchen?"

"Yes, apparently discarded in the trash. I found it to contain traces of codeine." The doctor showed her a typed report where he had entered the information.

She thought there must have been a mistake. "What else did you find in it?" Bruno had told her of a special ingredient, an herb, to trigger a miscarriage, the ingredient his friend said to use. "Doctor, could there be a mistake'?"

The doctor was surprised at her question. "That was the only ingredient I could determine, but that is enough. Codeine is highly addictive. I had to prescribe the medication I did to counteract its after effect."

"Then he lied to me."

"You must tell me all you know so that I can deal with your condition correctly."

So for the next few minutes Melina told Dr. Lim what she had been going through since she found that she was pregnant, and the way in which she had dealt with it.

The doctor had heard similar stories all too often, but he was mildly shocked to hear this account coming from Melina, a person he had always thought well of. As a doctor he devoted his every thought to either repairing life or saving it. The act of having an abortion for the sake of convenience was something he found appalling. "I shall be very much surprised if the life that you wanted to extinguish has survived such an attack. I'm going to need some samples from you that I will have tested to determine whether you are still pregnant."

The doctor's last remark left her feeling at fault and unsure. "When will you know for sure, Doctor?"

"Tomorrow, give me a call around two. But there are still two matters that I want to touch on with you."

"I'm so grateful for your help. What else can I tell you?"

"What about your friend Bruno? What do you plan to do about him?"

"I'm not sure what you mean."

"You should press charges against him. Maybe you would rather I did it for you."

Melina was confused again. "I don't know. I don't want to hurt him. He was only trying to help me."

The doctor was almost angry. "You don't want to hurt him? Good Lord, Melina. You could have died from what he did under the guise of helping you. The only effect the codeine would have had on the fetus would be to make it addicted as well as you. He was obviously attempting to accomplish two tasks with a single effort. The second could only be to addict you."

Why hadn't this occurred to her before now? She couldn't believe she had been so naive. "I guess you're right. I'm going to have to give this some thought."

The doctor was not going to let her get out of taking some action so easily. "When you phone me we can discuss your decision again. Now, about the second matter."

Melina is beginning to feel uneasy, "Yes, Dr. Lim?"

"The young man who brought you here, does he know about all of this?"

She began to feel cornered. "He only knows that I was pregnant and that he was the father."

"And that's all?"

"Yes, I think so." Feeling guilty, she began to cry and added, "He was glad that I was pregnant."

"Melina, it's interesting and sad that you gave me the last two answers in the past tense. The test results won't be back until tomorrow."

Again confused and fearful, she asked, "Do you mean it might still be alive?"

"It may not only be alive, but now it may also be damaged."

She had a strained look on her face when she repeated, "Damaged, in what way?"

The doctor set his compassion aside when he described the possibilities to her. "There is a good probability of chemical damage from the turpentine and vast amount of alcohol in your system and an even greater probability of neurological damage. There could also be long term effects that don't manifest themselves until later in life. If the fetus has survived it could become a severely handicapped individual. As I said at the beginning, what you have done was very foolish."

Melina was stunned. She realized that she might have made matters worse, beyond her wildest dreams.

Out in the waiting room Tony thought the exam must have been thorough since it was taking so long. When Melina came out of the exam room she looked very distressed. She told Tony, "The doctor took some samples that he will have tested. He won't have the results until tomorrow. He will phone me when he gets them back."

"You're not looking well. Did he say anything about how you are?"

"I'm just depressed, I'll be okay."

"After I take you home I'm going to look for work." He thought this might be good news to her.

Melina was feeling as though she was about to become trapped.

After leaving Melina at home, Tony drove to places he'd noticed along the marinas and docks where boats were repaired. At first they seemed interested, until he told them that he was from the mainland, then they seemed to go cold. They all told him the same thing, that they wanted someone with this or that kind of experience.

After trying the few boat repair businesses he stopped at a café. He had a milk shake while he looked through the Help Wanted section of the local news paper. The only thing he saw that he knew how to do was a dishwashing job on Hotel Street. *No way,* he thought to himself. *There's got to be something else. Maybe in tomorrow's paper.* When he was back in the car he drove around town hoping to get some new ideas.

Later that evening Tony and Melina were at Kim's for dinner. The feeling of the event was completely different from what it had been in times past, but then so much had happened in the past month. Kim was talking to Tony, "If they're advertising in the paper, it's probably because no one has been there to ask for a job as a dishwasher."

Mate added, "In other words, no one wants the damned job."

Kim again, "I wouldn't want it, but I would do it if I had to. You just have to apply where you'd like to work."

"That's basically what I did with the boat repair places. I don't know a lot of different things, but if someone shows me how, I can usually do the work okay."

Melina was just listening and not saying much. Inside she was feeling kind of disjointed. They had all been sitting in the living room. Kim needed to finish getting dinner ready. She asked Melina, "Why don't you come in the kitchen and give me a hand with the salad?"

"I'd love to," Melina answered. "I haven't done any cooking in a while. Tony has been spoiling me."

Once they were in the kitchen, Kim asked her, "How are things going between you two?"

As Melina began to sort out the salad ingredients she told Kim, "Okay. We've been more like brother and sister since you two found me."

Kim was tending to a special Korean soup. "How much does he know about what really happened to you?"

"Nothing that I know of but I think he might suspect that I did something that I shouldn't have. I think he's too polite to ask at this point."

Kim wondered how Tony would take the news when and if he found out what Melina was really up to. "Have you gotten any word from Dr. Lim about," patting her stomach, "your condition?"

"I'm to phone him tomorrow at two o'clock so he can tell me the results of some tests. He told me some pretty scary things when I was there for my first checkup today."

"What kind of scary things?" Kim asked.

"Like how the baby could end up being damaged and handicapped. Also he found traces of codeine in the syringe that was left in my waste basket."

"What do you think Bruno was up to with that stuff?"

"I wish I knew, but the doctor thinks he was up to something other than helping me."

"Maybe he wants to make you a customer of his. Melina, dear, are you going to tell Tony about any of this?"

Melina had a confused, almost pained look on her face. "I don't know what to do. I'm afraid I really screwed up. I was hoping to make things better; instead I've only made everything worse."

"I would have to agree with that. So what is next, my dear?"

Melina said, "First I want to find out if I'm still pregnant. I hope I'm not, especially after what Dr. Lim told me."

"I see, so you haven't changed your mind at all." Kim didn't like what Melina had resorted to but she was her friend and would stand by her no matter what, except for one thing. "Bruno is a bastard, you know, and should be put away for what he did without telling you."

"I don't know, Kim, he helped me so much in the past."

"Wake up, woman!" The men in the next room looked at each other, surprised by Kim's raised voice. Melina was taken aback as well. "What do you need to have happen before you realize that he is just a loser drug addict? If you let him he will drag you down with him. He almost killed you. Now I'm getting upset. I don't want to mess up this dinner."

"I'm sorry, Kim, I know you're right. It's just so hard for me to—"

Mate had been sitting on the couch talking with Tony. He called out toward the kitchen, "Hey, what's going on in there? Need some help?"

Tony got up from the couch and was about to go in the kitchen when Kim said, "No, we're okay but we're just about ready to start with soup and salad. Why don't you move over to the table?"

The rest of the evening was spent enjoying one of Kim's excellent meals and good conversation among friends.

The following day Tony went out looking for work. At two p.m. Melina phoned Dr. Lim for the results of her tests. The doctor had been talking and was saying to her, "I think you would probably say you are lucky."

"You don't know what a relief it is to hear the results."

"You have undoubtedly lost what remained of the fetus, but you could still experience some bleeding. Keep me informed if you do. The prescription I put through to your pharmacy should be sufficient for now."

"Thank you so much, Doctor."

"What about the matter we discussed. Have you given it anymore thought?"

"Do you mean Bruno?"

"Yes."

"My friend Kim agrees with you. She gave me a good scolding. I know he's sick, but I guess you should do what you think is best. Is there a place he can go to that will help him?"

"I'm not sure of the most recent developments, but I will look into that."

"It would be so good if he could be cured."

"I'll see what I can find out and then I'll let you know."

"Thank you again, Doctor. Goodbye."

After a tiring search Tony still had no prospects for work; he was feeling frustrated and inadequate. The money he had saved wasn't going to last very long without a job. He didn't know what he would do if his money ran out. He wouldn't let himself live off of Melina. He believed a baby was on the way, so he had to find work. At least he had managed to start sending letters off to the major American newspapers. Little by little he hoped to contact most of them. Using the return address of his parents in California he was asking to be contacted by anyone who was a crew member of the torpedo boat tender *Lady X* during the war in the Pacific from 1941 to 1945. And especially if they had knowledge of any special circumstances she may have been involved in, that could have led to the issuing of the plaque.

Melina was returning to work that night in the cocktail lounge, so Tony had to get back to her place in time to drive her to work.

Melina was again feeling a bit weak so she had phoned the club to tell them that she would begin work the following day. When Tony arrived she explained the situation to him. He sat on the couch next to her, kissing her on the cheek he told her, "I'm glad you're not going to work tonight because I didn't want to spend the evening without you."

"You're too sweet."

"Did you find out today if the baby is okay?"

Melina felt like a mouse that had just been cornered by a cat. She didn't know what to say to break the news to him gently so she just said, "I'm sorry, hon, I have bad news for you. I've had a miscarriage; there isn't a baby anymore."

Tony was stunned by this news. "You had a miscarriage?"

"Yes."

"Did the doctor say how or why it happened?"

She didn't answer him and started to feel uncomfortable.

Now all of the images of Melina on her bed when he and Kim found her Friday afternoon went through Tony's mind. "It must have been caused by whatever you did the Thursday night before we found you, don't you think?"

He was getting too close for comfort. "What do you mean?"

"I mean, whatever you did the night before that made you so sick, must have triggered it. By the way, what was all that yellow water in the bath tub from?"

Trying to be vague Melina answered, "Yellow water in the bath tub? I don't know. It's hard to remember anything from that night."

"Can you remember anything from the time you left work?"

"It's kind of foggy."

"So you don't remember anything?"

She insisted, "It's very hard."

Tony got the feeling that she was not being completely honest with him. A suspicion was aroused that he had not wanted to recognize. He stood up and began to walk about. He asked the next question only to see how she would respond, "If I ask Bruno do you suppose he could remember?"

She was stunned, and nearly bolted when she said, "What?!"

He sat on the chair opposite her. "After we found you I thought I heard Kim talking to herself saying that she bet Bruno had been here."

Melina felt completely trapped. She was looking down at the floor, avoiding his eyes.

"After Dr. Lim brought you to, you said Bruno's name. Why did you say his name? Was he here with you?"

"Don't ask me that."

"He was here!"

"Don't ask me anymore, please."

"What were you two up to that you can't talk about it?" Again she said nothing. Then it dawned on him. "Oh god, oh my god. Of course, how could I have been so dumb?"

Melina began to cry. "What are you thinking?"

"You didn't want to have our baby so you found a way to have a miscarriage, didn't you?"

Now she was sobbing. "Tony, I didn't know what to do."

"So you found someone else who did, good old Bruno."

Melina's pendant of miniature dancing shoes was hanging from her neck. She squeezed them with one hand. Sobbing heavily, she appealed to him, "Oh god, I'm sorry. I'm so sorry, but I can't give up dance. I can't, not yet. Can't you see that?"

"Then why let yourself get pregnant? And then have to kill an innocent baby?"

Through her sorrow anger welled up. She would have slapped him if he weren't sitting so far from her. "I didn't get pregnant on my own. You don't have to act as if you weren't responsible. It took both of us to make that baby, not just me. What about your responsibility in not getting me pregnant. Have you thought of that?"

She was absolutely right and he knew it. He was just as much at fault for putting her in this predicament. He grew silent for a moment thinking over what she just said. Then he admitted, "You're right, you're so very right. I guess I'm blinded by my own wants. I wanted you and our child. Nothing else mattered, and that's not right. What you want hasn't mattered to me as much as what I want." He hesitated a moment. "Actually, that's not entirely true. I do believe you should be a dancer, but something better than a burlesque dancer. I do believe that. And I don't think it can happen here on these islands." He was silent for a moment. "I'm sorry I said that about killing an innocent baby. That wasn't fair to you."

Her anger had stopped the tears. She had become overwhelmed and very tired. "Tony, I'm feeling so drained by everything. I just want to lie down and not think about any of this."

"Maybe I should leave. Maybe I can stay with—"

"I'm not asking that, if you could just leave me alone for a while. You can take my car. I need to rest and just be with myself for a while."

"Sure, I can go for a drive up to the Crosswinds and maybe sleep on the beach."

"You don't have to do that, but if you want to, it's okay."

He went over to her and gave her a hug. "I'm sorry; I seem to have a knack for thinking of myself first."

"You're not alone there, hon, we all have that knack."

"I'm not sure what I'll do yet, but I'm sure I'm going to do a lot of thinking. Maybe I'll visit with Mate a while. I'll phone you in the morning to see if you need anything."

"Don't forget I'm going to work tomorrow. I need to be there before five o'clock."

"I won't forget." He put some things into a backpack. "Oh, I'll need a sleeping bag. Do you have one?"

"Just take a couple of my blankets and a pillow, if you want. They should be enough. "

After about fifteen minutes he had all he needed tucked under one arm. She had gone to her bed to lie down so he went to her to kiss her goodbye. "I haven't told you, you're looking beau—"

"Don't say it. Please, just get into the car and go somewhere."

Tony went to Kim's to hash things over with his good friend, Mate.

Mate was astounded by the details Tony told him. "And I thought I was the one that all the bad shit happens to. And the *Lady* has gone! So that option is out. What are you going to do with your sorry self now, man?"

"Right at this moment I haven't got a clue, but I know I need to find a job."

"From what I hear your chances are not good."

"Yeah, but tomorrow is another day."

"Either that or the rest of today."

Tony looked puzzled. "What's that?"

"I don't know, it just came to me."

"But it does make sense. The way things look to me, I had a job, I had a girlfriend, and I had room and board while on board."

"Amen, brother."

"Even what I left behind in the old country ain't there no mo'."

"It's beginning to sound to me like you are feeling detached."

"More like cut adrift. I'm feeling like I need to head up to the Crosswinds. You know, sleep on the beach where I had those far-out dreams. Maybe something will come to me."

"Maybe so, man. If that is what you think will happen then it probably will. You know, like when you pray for something. Did I just say that?"

Tony answered him with, "It didn't sound like your words, but it did sound like your voice."

"You know, man, ever since that bastard tried to have me for lunch I've been noticing a change taking place in my feelings."

"What kind of change?"

"Like when it looks as though you might be dead in less than a minute, you wonder what's next."

"So maybe tomorrow isn't just the rest of today, maybe each day is a whole new start," suggested Tony.

"Maybe for some, but for some others I've known it's just the same ol' shit, day after day."

"That sounds too much like slow death. It's not for me. I want each day to be a beginning, not just more of the end."

"Yeah, you got that right." Mate stood on his good leg and without his crutches he attempted to stand unaided. As soon as he put weight on his right foot a sharp pain shot up from it. "Oh shit!" He lost his balance and fell to the floor knocking over a potted plant. "God damn it, mutha jumper!"

Tony leapt to his aid. "Easy does it, man. Are you all right?" He put a hand under Mate's armpit. "Let me help you up."

Mate pushed Tony's hands away. "Don't help me. I'll get up on my own." He scooted over to a cushy armchair and pulled himself onto it. "Not being able to use this foot yet is really gettin' to me, man."

"Listen, Mate, I'm driving up to the Crosswinds in a minute, but before I go I have to tell you something." Tony became uneasy.

"What, that I'm stupid?"

Tony grimaced, "Not you. More than likely, it's me. Something has been eating at me since I remembered it a couple of days ago: That last day on the *Lady* when everyone was swimming."

"I'll never forget it." An event he would rather forget.

"Old Bill was standing in front of me, and you were behind me waiting your turn to dive in."

"Okay, I get the picture."

"Bill had been razzing me about Melina. After he said something pretty nasty I nudged him to the edge causing him to lose his balance and fall in."

"And if I remember right he grabbed you, then you grabbed me, and we all fell in."

"Exactly."

"Exactly what?"

"Don't you see?"

"See what?"

"It was my fault."

"I still don't see what you're getting at. Unless you mean that all the shit that happened after that was your fault."

"It was my fault."

"How do you figure that? You didn't know those sharks would be waiting for us, did you?"

"Of course not."

"And we were all going to be in the water anyway. You just made it happen a few seconds sooner, that's all."

"Yes, but because the way Bill fell in he must have swallowed a lot of water. Remember he came to the surface gasping for air and calling for help."

"In the condition he was in, and I should add, was usually in that's probably the way he would have come up anyway. All I can say about him is that the shark that got him, probably still regrets it. So don't go blaming yourself."

"What about Chuck? He was at his prime."

"Listen, Tony, a lot of really good people have died in their prime. No one knows for sure why."

"I can't stop thinking that if I hadn't pushed Bill none of the other things would of happened."

Mate told him, "I've given all of this a lot of thought, don't think I haven't. And I've come to the conclusion that it was all meant to be. We can't change any of it so let's just let it be."

Chapter 13

THE END BEGINS

It was after dark when Tony arrived at the Crosswinds. He parked Melina's car in a space that was under a light so it would be safe all night.

When he walked into the coffeehouse he was greeted by singing. On the little stage a black man in his late fifties was playing a slide guitar on his lap and singing the blues. An attendant behind the counter told Tony that the musician was blind and from New Orleans, Louisiana, "His name is Joseph Brown. He said he was a neighbor of Louis Armstrong's family."

The musician was wearing dark glasses so Tony hadn't noticed that he was blind. Tony sat facing the stage and thought to himself, *He sure knows how to play the blues.* The way the musician moved the slide on the strings gave color to the sadness he was singing. Any listener couldn't help but be drawn into the mood of the piece.

There was a man sitting about two stools away from Tony. Between songs he would talk to the waiter behind the counter. Tony overheard their conversation and learned that the man was a merchant seaman. His freighter was to leave the next day for Guam, then Japan and the Orient, before returning to California.

When Tony had the opportunity he asked the man, "Excuse me, did I hear you say that you are a seaman?"

The man answered him, "Yes, that's right. Why do you ask?"

"Well, I've been working for U.S. Coast and Geodetic Survey for the past three months between here and the Aleutian Islands. But now I'm out of work."

"I'm familiar with them. But I thought their crews finished up at the port of origin."

Tony answered but he didn't want to go into details, "That's right, except in my case."

"Are you looking for a job on another ship?"

"The thought has been occurring to me."

The man asked, "Do you have your seaman's papers with you?"

"I don't have any. The survey ship I was on didn't require them so the coast guard won't give any to the men who have served on USCGS ships."

"Sounds like a conflict between services to me."

"Probably, so what can I do? Oh, by the way, my name is Tony."

"Pleased to meet you, my name is Leopold." They shook hands. "It's not as difficult as one might think. You first have to find a captain who will hire you. Get a letter from him to that effect and take it to the coast guard. They will issue temporary seaman's papers to you."

"That's it?" Tony couldn't believe how simple this all sounded.

"Pretty much, but the catch is finding a captain at an American port who will do that. Once on the ship you would have to agree to join the seaman's union. Of course if it's a foreign ship, you just get a job on it and sail away. Then you might wind up at a foreign port at the end of the voyage."

Tony detected a stirring in his feelings. He took a deep breath before saying, "That sounds interesting." Then he asked, "If I want to go to the Orient but don't have the money for a ticket then I could work my way there?"

"You could give it a try. Your chances of it happening that way are fifty, fifty."

Tony was re-inspired. "And I could earn some money on the way."

"That depends on the captain and your agreement. You could end up earning only your passage with no pay in exchange for your work. I'm a union man myself, but the trip I've signed on is only as far as Singapore."

"Why is that?" Tony asked.

"After I get off the ship I'm taking a trip over to Indonesia, to the island of Java. The ship will go on to India to unload and load cargo before returning to Singapore and then the States. I'll pick it up again at Singapore then finish up at San Pedro in California."

"That sounds far out. What's happening in Indonesia?"

"I belong to a spiritual brotherhood that began there just before the war."

"A spiritual brotherhood, you mean a religion?"

"It's not considered a religion, people from different religions belong to it, and they worship God together."

Tony asked, "People from different religions worshiping God together. How can that be? One of the biggest things wrong with the world is that the different religions won't align themselves with each other, so they just coexist."

Leopold answered, "It is unusual, and you're right about the organized religions coexisting, at least most of the time. People can unite on a spiritual level, and until this brotherhood came about it was never done; at least not to my knowledge."

"Does that only happen there?"

"No, it's been slowly spreading throughout the world, but the center is on Java near Jakarta, and the man who began the brotherhood lives at the center. I thought that since this ship was going to pass so close I should try to join her crew, and so I did."

"Pretty lucky," Tony said. "You know, my friend, you've given me a whole lot of new ideas. If I ever want to check out this brotherhood how do I find it?"

Leopold took a napkin from under his drink and began writing on it. "I'll just put what I know on this for you."

"That's great. I don't know if I'll ever go there, but if I do I can check it out."

Leopold handed him the napkin. "Here you go, this bit here is a simple map with the location of the center in Cilandak. It's not hard to find."

Tony looked at the map. There was an unfamiliar word written on it. "What is Subud, the name of the road?"

"It's the name of the brotherhood. Anyone in the area knows about it."

"Thanks a lot. Where do you live when you're not on a ship?"

"I have a little house in San Pedro, California."

Tony exclaimed, "Another Californian! Sorry but I seem to keep running into people from California."

"Probably because there are so many of us."

"Do you get your ships from San Pedro?"

Leopold answered with a light chuckle, "Yeah, most of them. So I don't have far to drive to work."

Tony laughed, "Yeah, right." The conversation went on for a little while longer. The main thing that had taken place for Tony was that he discovered a way to carry on, to continue traveling. Here was a way for him to expand his experience and learn more about life and himself.

As the night wore on Leopold returned to his ship. Just before closing time Tony had a very brief conversation with the musician about his guitar and his technique with the glass slide he used. Tony had always been fascinated with that style of playing.

After the Crosswinds closed, he made his way through the semidarkness to a place above the beach where he could put his bedroll. Despite his uneasiness during the day and the conflict with Melina, he was feeling peaceful and quiet. As he laid there waiting to fall asleep he mulled over the concept of people of differing and sometimes opposing religions actually worshiping together, and the potential effect that could have on civilization—unimaginable. As he began to drift off to sleep he wondered how his friends Willy and Rob were doing and if the *Lady* was making it back okay.

Tony had picked a good spot to place his bedroll because he didn't awake until around eight o'clock. He got his stuff together and returned up the hill. Melina's car was as he left it. He went into the little store to buy some food and get change for the telephone.

After Tony finished eating on the back patio he placed a phone call to Maureen in San Francisco. He got a recording that told him her phone number had been changed, then it gave him the new number. When he dialed it, a man answered, "Hello."

"Hello, is Maureen there?" Tony asked.

Sounding a little suspicious the man asked, "Who is this?"

"Tony, who's this?" he asked, annoyed.

"Just a minute," followed by murmuring in the background.

"Hello, Tony?" It was Maureen's unmistakable voice.

"Maureen, how are you doing?"

"Great, I'm getting bigger every day."

"Wow! It's still hard for me to picture you with a baby."

"It might help if I send a picture. We just took some, I'll send you a couple."

"There might be a problem, I'm not with the ship anymore."

"What happened, Tony?"

"It's a very long and complicated story."

"My intuition tells me there's a woman in the story."

"That's a good first guess."

"Knowing you it wasn't that hard."

"Speaking of, who's the guy who answered the phone?"

"I told you about him, my new teacher at the acting school."

"Oh, yeah." He thought to himself, *Her teacher?*

"Well, we've moved in together."

A feeling of sadness came over him, "Far out, how's it going?"

Smiling at her lover, "Just peachy."

Tony thought, *Yuck!* Then he said, "That's great. When are you expecting?"

"Early October. I haven't had any complications so far."

"Do you think you might keep the baby?"

"Our plan is still to have it adopted."

Tony thought to himself, *What does this guy have to do with it?* Tony was having mixed feelings, especially discomfort. "Listen, I think my time is about to run out so I'll say goodbye and wish you well."

She had a sudden feeling of desperation. "Tony, wait. When are you coming back to the city?" Her friend was frowning.

"I don't know, love." *Now why did I say love?* "You're going to have to use your intuition on this one. Right now, it's anybody's guess."

"You always were a bit of a mystery man."

"It's not intentional."

She tried to hide her sadness, "I know. Good luck to you, Tony."

"Good luck to you too, Maureen." The phones clicked off. He had an uncomfortable empty feeling that lingered awhile.

AT LAST

Later that morning Tony was checking for available work at the boat repair yards among the docks and warehouses. Whatever else may develop Tony needed money to support his self. Out of all the places he checked, one could use him. They wanted him to begin work the next day at six o'clock, and he was delighted. He thought this might be a sign that he was meant to stay on the island after all. He phoned Melina to give her the good news. She didn't sound as pleased as he thought she would.

It was nearly noon when he remembered that the silversmith, Bill Younge, had a finished pendant waiting for him, so he drove to the park where he knew the man would be. He picked up the pendant and drove to Melina's thinking that he might make a lunch for them both. When he arrived he found that she had already eaten and that she was starting to prepare for work. She was also in fairly good spirits.

He began making a lunch for himself as he talked, "Remember the girlfriend I told you about in San Francisco?"

Melina was in the bathroom working on her makeup. "The one who got raped and pregnant?"

Tony found it interesting how the memory picks some aspects over others. "That's the one. Well, I called her this morning, and she is doing just fine. Got herself a new boyfriend and a new place to live. She sounded contented as can be." He began to eat his lunch.

"And that bothers you?"

He thought, *Women and their intuition,* then said, "Kind of, it's just odd how things turn out sometimes. There she is with a baby that I believe she wants to keep and her boyfriend doesn't." Then under his breath he said, "And here I am with someone who doesn't want a baby and probably doesn't want me either."

"What was that last part, hon?"

He finished eating and moved to the living room. "Oh, nothing important, I was just thinking out loud. Are you in the lounge tonight or the other side?" He didn't want to identify it by name and thereby acknowledge its existence.

"I'm in the lounge with Kim from five to eleven, our usual shift."

"With the Mother Jean Singers. How long have they been there?"

"I don't know. It's been a while though." She came out of the bathroom. She was wearing only a sheer bra and lace panties. He experienced a rush of desire he had nearly forgotten could happen.

"Wow! You do look good." He was starting to feel like his old self again. They say it just takes the right woman.

"I'm feeling a lot better."

He got up from the couch and went over to her. "It's been so long since we—"

She quickly took some clothes from their hangers, saying, "And it's going to be a little longer because I really don't want to be late my first day back."

Ah, that old familiar frustration, he thought to himself. *Isn't it amazing how practical women can be at times?* Then he said, "Do you want me to take you, then pick you up after work?"

"If you don't mind, hon?"

Reaching in his pocket, he said, "I nearly forgot. I picked up our pendant, or is it pendants, today."

"From the silversmith? Oh good."

Pulling the small clear plastic envelope out of his pocket, he said, "Yes, here they are, a white one for you and a black one for me." Each had its own chain. He put one around her neck and the other around his. Then he went close to her so they could put the two half circles together. And as they did so he kissed her. Her response was hesitant at first then she began to kiss him back. Both their temperatures increased rapidly. The recent experience of the attempted miscarriage flashed across her memory, and she jumped back from him with a start.

"What's the matter?"

"I'm sorry, hon, but something very unpleasant just came to my mind. Can you take me to work pretty soon?"

"Whenever you're ready, sweetheart."

As soon as she was dressed and ready, they got into her car and drove to the Sleeping Lady.

Once there, they both went inside. All of the employees had heard of her illness and expressed their sympathies when they each saw her. She felt so good to be back to work and in the company of so many familiar faces. Kim had also just arrived and was beginning to prepare things behind her bar. "Well, hi you two. Are you feeling okay?"

"Hi," Tony said.

"Hi, hon," Melina said, leaning across the bar to give Kim a kiss on the cheek. "I'm feeling a lot better, but I'll see how the night goes. I might feel a little weak later."

"Well, sit down on something every chance you get, dear," Kim suggested. "Aren't you both wearing something new around your necks?"

Melina said, "Yes, Tony just got these from the silversmith in the park. You remember? Anyway they fit together to make a symbol of harmony."

Kim observed, "You know, that same symbol is on the Korean flag. They're very nice. Tony, can I make you something to drink?"

"Sure, just a soda please."

"With a cherry in it?"

"Please," Tony answered as Melina began to make sure all of the tables were ready. He asked Kim, "How's Mate feeling today?"

As Kim handed him the drink, she said, "I think he's feeling kind of down but doesn't want to let on. Not being able to stand on both feet is getting to him. I take him in every day now for his physical therapy, but it's going to be a slow process because of the nerve damage, and now atrophy of some of the muscles."

"I'll go see him. What is he doing for dinner?"

"Before I leave for work I make something for him that he can heat up later."

"I'll give him a call before I go over to see if he needs something. Or maybe I can take him somewhere."

Kim was pleased, "That would be nice."

Tony told her, "I nearly forgot to tell you, I got a job."

"You're joking."

"No, really, I start in the morning."

With a big smile on her face, she asked, "Doing what?"

"Working in a boat repair yard down by the docks."

"That's great."

"Melina didn't seem to be very impressed when I told her."

"Did you ask her why? . . . You should."

"Good advice. I think I will."

Melina sat on the stool next to Tony. "I thought I heard my name?"

He wanted to change the subject, "Your name is in the air. Since the return of their star all are relieved."

"Well, knock me over with a feather. But I did hear the word 'advice' so maybe we can talk about whatever it was later if now isn't a good time."

"Sorry, love, I was just trying to make light of a touchy subject. Listen, I'm going to pay Mate a visit and maybe do something together. Would you mind if I left in a little bit?"

"No, not at all, it would be good for both of you to do something together. Besides, it could get boring here for you with nothing to do."

Tony told them, "I'll go phone him to see what he's up to, excuse me." He slid off the stool, kissed Melina on the cheek, and walked back toward the rest rooms where the pay phones were located.

Kim asked Melina, "What's going on with you two?"

Melina answered, "I don't know, hon, my feelings have gone through a big change since what happened. I mainly just want to be on my own for a while. But now I'm feeling responsible for Tony, especially since he went and quit his ship and then can't find work. That was until today, did he tell you the news?"

"Yes, he said you didn't seem so pleased about it."

"I am, and I'm not. I was hoping he would get discouraged."

Kim looked confused, "Discouraged?"

"I'm sorry, but I'm being honest with you. I only wish I could be as honest with him."

"I think you should be. He suspects that something is odd, you know, not like it was before the miscarriage."

"We are going to have to talk this thing out. The other thing is that if he gets a job that lasts a while then he could get his own place to live in. Maybe share with someone if he has to." Just then two couples came in looking for a table. "Excuse me, I have some customers."

Tony returned to the lounge and his stool. "Well, it's a good thing I caught him when I did. He was about ready to heat up some food. I'm going to take him out for a while, maybe catch a good flick."

Kim was very pleased. "Oh, good, I'm so glad. Sitting around all day is not good for anyone." She took her car keys out of her purse and handed them to Tony. "Why don't you take my car? I don't think Mate will be comfortable in Melina's beetle."

"That's a good idea. Don't worry; I'll take good care of him." He said goodbye to Kim and Melina then left to pick up Mate.

Tony was taking Mate to Hook, Line, and Sinker for a seafood meal when Mate asked him, "Have things between you and Melina changed much since yesterday?"

Tony told him, "You know how you get a feeling when things aren't happening?"

"Yeah, man, I sure do."

"Well, that's the feeling I'm getting."

"Want some feedback?" Mate asked.

"Sure, if it will help me figure out what's going on."

"I could give it to you in a nutshell, but I'm afraid that would be too painful. So here is the long form. Stop me if you don't agree."

"Okay dealer, hit me."

"The primary factor is that Melina wants a career in dancing, legitimate dancing. Not this burlesque jive, right?"

"Right so far."

"Even so, any dancer has to have a slender, well toned body, right?"

"Right again, and you know she has that."

"Have you ever seen a dancer after three months of pregnancy still dancing?"

"No, I don't think I have."

"Correct. And that's because there aren't any. Another factor is that dancers, unless they are established in a certain locality, need to have the freedom to travel anywhere to follow opportunities. Have you noticed any dancers hauling their kids around with them following a one night stand, then another, and another?"

"How would I know?"

"Don't bother to check. You won't find any. If you do then you'll probably find a selfish parent and some screwed up kids."

"Anything else?"

"There sure is, brother. The only dancers who are likely to be supporting a boyfriend are alcoholics and druggies whose boyfriends are also users." Tony was taken aback by that remark. He looked over at Mate a little longer than he should, causing the car to drift toward the right. Mate exclaimed, "Look out!"

Tony turned his head around just in time to avoid hitting an open car door and attendant arm. "Thanks for the warning."

"Which one?" Mate asked.

"Both, and thanks for softening me up before clobbering me with the last bit of info."

"You're welcome, I really appreciate you both. Your friendship has been a groove."

"You gave me the long form. What's the short form?"

"I hesitate to say."

"If this was a game of five-card-stud I'd say hit me with the last card."

Mate looked at Tony with one of his most sincere expressions. "You are close to overstaying your welcome."

Tony felt a sharp pain in his heart. "Oh, man. You know, I've suspected that but haven't wanted to see or admit it." But still clinging, he asked, "Mate, do you really think so?"

"That's the way it looks from here, brother."

Tony began to feel like a little boy who had gotten himself lost. He just looked straight ahead at the road for a bit. Then for no apparent reason a feeling of wellbeing came over him as if from out of nowhere. He looked over at Mate who was quietly looking out the door window at the sights going by. Tony welcomed the feeling of calm that had come into him. There was something about knowing, even bad news that helped one to begin to cope. "Thanks, thanks a lot. I'm glad you told me all that."

Mate had gotten lost in his own thoughts for a moment and missed Tony's last words. He turned his head away from the window catching a glimpse of the restaurant ahead through the windshield, "There it is. Man, I'm so hungry I could eat a whale."

Jokingly, Tony suggested, "If you pick up the check."

Mate reminded him, "But you invited me, right?"

After dinner they went to one of their favorite movies, a Japanese slice'em up with Mifune. After the film, Tony drove Mate home. He helped him out of the car and into Kim's apartment.

Mate told Tony, "Don't be late for work tomorrow."

Tony replied, "Man, I can't wait to start."

"All right, my man, see you later."

"Later, man."

Tony had just enough time to get back to the club before the women finished work. He told Kim what a good time he and Mate had. She was grateful to hear that.

When Melina was ready to leave Tony drove her home. On the way she told him how being back to work went. "It was so good to be back, but by the end I was exhausted. What time are you getting up in the morning?"

Tony parked in front of her apartment as he answered, "I have to be at work by six so four thirty might be a good time for me to wake up."

As they got out of the car she said, "That's not going to leave you much time for sleep, hon."

"Nearly five hours is enough for me, sometimes."

Sounding a little disappointed, she said, "We won't have much time to talk."

Or much else, he thought to himself. After going inside, they cautiously sat on opposite ends of the couch. After a long pause Tony told her, "I think you would agree that my being here has become, well, more than you expected. If that's the case, I'm sorry."

Melina couldn't believe what she just heard him say. She had an overwhelming sense of relief. "Oh yes, to be honest it has. Everything seems to have happened too quickly. I have been totally unprepared for the way things have developed."

"Well, thanks to the observation of our friend Mate I've just been made aware of this today. I guess it was because I needed to see things differently, that I did."

She moved a little closer to him and took his hand in hers. "Tony, dearest, we have begun living like a married couple. I am not ready for marriage, and I don't believe you are either."

He couldn't disagree with that. "You're right, I'm not. When I let myself think about it, I'm really not ready."

Melina admitted, "I feel responsible for a lot of what has happened with us."

He also admitted to her, "A lot of responsibility rests with me too. We had some good times."

"We had some wonderful times and may have more. This is not a farewell speech." She let go of his hand in order to gesture with hers. "It's just that I have to have my freedom, my space, and my privacy. I have begun to feel obligated to you. And I'm just not ready for all of that."

Tony took her hand in his, "Melina, believe me, I understand, I have a little of those same needs. It's just not so total with me."

He sensed uneasiness in her hand when she added, "It's not easy for me to say this, but I have to tell you. When it comes to making love at the present, after the experience of my miscarriage, I'm feeling almost sexless."

That's not good news, he thought. He said to her, "I'm glad you told me, you certainly don't look sexless."

With her free hand she stroked the back of his. There was a gentle smile on her face when she said, "I'll take that as a compliment."

He felt sad as he looked deep into her eyes. He couldn't help wondering what happened when pairs of eyes looked into each other. Were they looking into the soul? He must have been reaching beyond her mind when he said, "I want to kiss you. If I could I would kiss your soul."

Almost in a whisper she told him, "But you have, many times."

They moved closer together and slowly, carefully began kissing. Not just on the lips, but on the cheeks, the eyes, the ears, the hair, and so on.

It was four thirty when Melina's alarm clock woke Tony from a deep sleep. The night before, Melina and Tony felt closer than they had for some time. Instead of driving him to work, Melina had him take her car for his first day.

Tony arrived a few minutes early at the boatyard: 'Jerry's Boat Repairs and Restorations.' He found Jerry, the owner and foreman, who introduced him to two other workers: Frank and Mark. No one was especially friendly, just businesslike. The boss told Tony he might need him one or two weeks. He gave him the tools he would need for the day's work. The work reminded him of his first day aboard the *Lady Explorer.* The job that Jerry gave him was scraping and chipping barnacles and paint from the hull of a large commercial fishing boat. Jerry and the others would be working on the restoration of an old schooner. Scraping the bottom of the fishing boat meant a lot of overhead work for Tony who had to stand or lie under the hull. It also meant that he would end up with paint chips and debris all over him.

By his lunch break Tony's arms felt like they were ready to fall off. While on his break, Tony checked out the schooner. It was constructed of wood and seemed to be fairly old with a beautiful design. It had been neglected for a long time and was in need of a lot of work. Jerry's brother came to work late, and joined the crew working on the schooner. Tony thought that if he could get in on the schooner repairs he could be there for some time. After his break he asked Jerry about his chances.

Jerry told him, "The fishing boat job came to us at the last minute. I was too short handed to take it on. That's why I brought you in. I'll see how you do, but you'll be with that hull until it's scraped, prepped, and painted. Now if that's not all right with you . . ."

"No, everything is fine. I just thought I'd ask."

Three o'clock was quitting time. After Tony cleaned up he said goodbye to the guys and left. Leopold, the merchant seaman he met at the Crosswinds, had given Tony the location of some shipping agents that handled foreign ships. On his way back to Melina's he stopped in at one but there was no sign of a crewman being needed. He decided to go to an agent each day after work.

When Tony arrived at Melina's there was only enough time for a quick shower before taking her to work. At his new job he had heard about a small rooming house within walking distance of the boatyard. After a brief visit with Melina and Kim he drove over to the rooming house to check it out.

There was a room available on the second floor with a view of the harbor. There was a parlor and kitchen on the main floor that was shared along with the bathrooms. He decided to rent the room and move into it the next day after work. With a job and his own place to live in, he felt more independent than he had in months.

Because his first day at work had really burned him out, Tony spent the rest of the evening reading and resting. Melina had arranged for Kim to take her home after they finished work at eleven. By nine o'clock Tony had fallen asleep on the couch with a book in his hand. When Melina came home he awoke just long enough to tell her about the room, then he fell back to sleep in her bed.

The following day was Friday. Melina was going to need her car before Tony was free for the day. She arranged for Kim to drive her to the boatyard around noon so she could pick it up, and still have time to lunch with Tony.

Tony had taken his duffel bag and a box of his things with him to work. When it was time for his hour lunch break he met with Melina at the entrance to the yard and took her to a small diner near the docks. It was converted from an old streetcar that someone had brought over from the mainland after the war. Inside they sat in a small booth by a window. After ordering milk shakes and hamburgers, they had a quiet conversation.

Expressing her relief, Melina told him, "I'm so grateful that you got a place of your own."

He agreed, "Yeah, now we can just take life as it happens."

She added, "Also, we'll appreciate each other more."

He thought, *I haven't had a problem appreciating her so far.* Then he said, "I see you're wearing your half of the yin yang symbol. Mine is in my bag, I didn't want to mess it up at work."

Taking one of his hands in hers and looking at his fingers, she asked him, "How is the work going, hon?"

"It's two things for sure; very dirty and very tiring. I shouldn't complain, if they didn't need someone to do the dirty work I wouldn't be there."

"How long is the job supposed to be for?"

"At first, Jerry, that's the boss, hired me for one week, but yesterday he said he might need me for another week."

"That's still not very long."

"I asked if I could get in on the restoration work they're doing on an old schooner. Jerry said we'd talk about it after the fishing boat is finished. He didn't seem to like it when I asked."

"Are there any other chances for work?"

"Not that I'm aware of. But I'm going to a different shipping agent each day after work, to check on incoming ships."

"You've changed your mind about going back to California, haven't you?"

"I'm just putting it off for a while. I need the answers to questions that haven't occurred to me before now."

"I don't think that's odd at all. I need some answers too, but I'm going to have to find them where I happen to be."

Again he noticed that women tend to be more practical than men, but sometimes too practical. He continued, "On the other hand, I know I'm going to miss my pal Mate. I've only known him for a little over three months, but so much has gone on that it seems more like half my life."

She agreed, "A lot has happened all right."

"Melina, what do you think? What will happen with Mate if he ends up unable to use his foot, especially for dancing?"

"Well, I know Kim thinks the world of him and will stick by him through anything. She's going to give him a lot of moral support when he needs it. And I've noticed that Mate is very resilient."

"You're right about that. I guess the process is just going to take a long time." He looked at the clock near the register. "I have to get back to work in a minute."

"I'm ready," she said with a smile.

When they left she drove him back to the yard. They kissed goodbye. He took his things out of her car and left them near the office.

About an hour before quitting time Jerry asked Tony if he could work the next day, his regular day off. Tony agreed since he needed the extra income. After quitting time Tony carried his duffel bag and box to the rooming house that was a few blocks away.

Inside his room he gave it a careful check. It was sparsely furnished but had a double bed and a sink. It was about twice the size of his last room in San Francisco's North Beach. That cost him seven and a half dollars a week because it included a sink. This one was costing him twelve dollars a week. "Looks like I'm moving up," he said to himself. He plopped down on the bed and gave it the bounce test. "This'll work." He put some of his things in a chest of drawers before going downstairs.

He used a pay phone that hung on the wall near the kitchen to phone Melina.

He told her that he was spending the night getting acquainted with his new place and surrounding neighborhood. He arranged to meet with her at the Sleeping Lady the following night.

His trek around his neighborhood proved to be uninteresting. Aside from a couple of bars, a gas station, and a liquor store he did find a small market where he could buy groceries.

The next five days were uneventful and fairly routine. Tony and Melina's relationship became one of dating when it was convenient, which Melina was more comfortable with. From Tuesday on it was Melina's week to dance in the burlesque hall. Tony stayed away from that side so he wouldn't get her into trouble. He was spending a lot of time on his own traveling around the island by bus and writing some poetry when inspired.

Also by that time he had mailed off so many ads related to the USS *Lady X* for the personal columns of newspapers that he had lost count. Mate became able to stand on his injured foot with only a feeling of discomfort. He became more optimistic and worked hard on his physical therapy exercises.

Because of Tony's success at finding work and a place of his own, he became lax in his efforts to find a ship to the Orient. Thursday marked the beginning of Tony's second week at the boatyard. When he began work that morning, Jerry introduced him to a new worker who would be helping him. His name was Bobby. He was around twenty and was glad to have the work even though, as he said, it wasn't his thing. They weren't able to have much of a conversation because they were using electric sanders that made a lot of noise.

Just before quitting time Jerry called Tony into his office. Jerry asked him, "What did you think of Bobby? He's a good kid, huh?"

Tony said, "Yeah, he doesn't seem too keen on the work, but I think he'll do all right."

"I didn't want to tell you at first because I didn't want it to influence your opinion, but Bobby is my son-in-law."

Tony repeated, "Your son-in-law?"

"Yeah," the boss continued, "they've been married two years now and are havin' a tough time."

"I'm sorry to hear that."

"Yeah, so, Tony, you remember when I hired you I said it would be for a week, and actually that was a week ago today."

"That's right, last Thursday. And you said you might need me another week, and I asked you about getting in on the—"

Jerry cut him short, handing him a check that he took from under a notepad. "You put in a good week kid, even got in an extra day. But I don't have enough work to keep you on. You understand."

Tony had an enormous empty feeling inside his chest that suddenly seemed to become filled with cigarette ashes. "Yeah, sure, I understand." After he took the check, Jerry extended his hand and they shook hands. Tony thought to himself, *Always that friendly handshake, even when they stick it to ya.*

When he left the office he didn't feel like he was all there. He took a short bus ride to the area where some of the shipping agents were. The third one that he went to told him to return the next day because they might have more information on a possible opening. He figured that he was just in for another letdown.

Tony returned to his rooming house not wanting to talk to anyone. He showered then just lay on his bed. In his hand he held the small black half of the yin yang pendant thinking how ironic it all was. Even though he and Melina loved one another they could not commit to each other: He would have to stop traveling in order to live in Hawaii where there was no work for him; and she would have to give up dancing in Hawaii where she really wanted to live. He looked out the window through a light mist at the harbor named Pearl and contemplated what lay beyond to the west.

The next morning Tony returned to the agent who asked him to. The agent informed him of a Norwegian freighter named *Vietnam* that was due in sometime Monday. It had a crewman who needed medical attention. The ship would probably need a replacement. After spending one full day unloading and taking on new cargo, the ship would be sailing for Japan Tuesday evening. Its final port before making its return run would be Bangkok, Thailand.

It was an opportunity too good to miss. He filled out the necessary paperwork. If all was agreeable with the captain he would even receive a decent wage for the run. Tony left the shipping office filled with renewed hope.

He made his way to the post office to send off a batch of ads to newspapers. He had informed his parents in California about the ads so they would be prepared for any responses. They could inform him during his occasional phone calls to them. From the post office he caught a bus over to Kim's for a visit with Mate.

Mate had just returned from a session with his physical therapist and was feeling pretty good. Tony told him of the recent developments. Mate responded with, "That is so far out, man. It has all the signs of something meant to be."

"I hope you're right. The job on the ship is not a sure thing."

Mate suggested, "Well, if all else fails maybe you could become a passenger on it."

Jokingly, Tony said, "Trying to get rid of me, huh, so you can have all the women to yourself?"

"Well, I am feeling a lot better, you know."

"I've got a feeling you're one bird who's found his nest."

"You could put it that way. Not to change the subject but have you had any word on those newspaper ads you're sending all over the place?"

"Not so far, it's probably too soon."

Mate asked, "How do you find them? And doesn't it cost you?"

"It was a problem at first. I went to the main library where I got addresses from the mainland newspapers themselves. The librarian suggested I go to the newspaper office here for more addresses. It had a whole slew of them. I send money orders with the ads for a little more than the standard charges here just in case. I figure it won't be much more."

"That's pretty amazing. I sure hope it works, and we can save the old girl."

Just then Kim came into the room with freshly brewed tea and a coffee for Mate. "Who's an old girl?"

Mate said, "We were just discussing the fate of the *Lady*. Tony is the main man who's trying to save her from the melting pot."

Kim replied, "From what Mate has told me about the plaque and what is known about her history, it all sounds to me like there might be something in her past worth finding out."

Tony informed her, "The main problem is that a lot of her records were classified as secret. And what's even stranger is that most of December the 6th, the day before the Japanese hit Pearl Harbor, is missing from the ship's diary."

Kim asked, "The day before?"

"Yes, it goes something like this: She left San Francisco Bay where she was built and headed for Hawaii to join the Pacific fleet. She arrived at Pearl in the late evening on the sixth of December, whereupon the captain gave the crew shore leave for the weekend until Monday the eighth. But for Saturday there is no record before he gave the crew leave."

Kim responded with, "You know, I've been a bartender in a few other places around the island. One thing about bartenders is that people love to tell us their problems."

Mate chimed in, "Don't we, though?"

She continued, "The war ended only twenty years ago so there are still a lot of people around who were here then. One thing I've heard from more than one person is that our military had broken the Japanese code before December 7th of '41, and that our military commanders couldn't do anything to reveal that fact. And didn't right up to the end."

Mate again, "I vaguely remember hearing something like that."

"So have I." Then Tony said, "If that's true then we, the U.S., knew a lot that we never let on to anyone."

Kim answered that with, "You can be sure of that. For example that's how the U.S. military knew where Yamamoto was when they shot down his plane, killing him."

Tony was puzzled, "Yamamoto?"

Kim replied, "The admiral who headed the attack on Pearl Harbor."

Tony almost lit up. "My god! Do you think they, I mean we, knew Pearl was about to be attacked?"

"That is the question a lot of people would like answered."

"What a mixed up scene. If I can just find someone who was part of the crew back then, I know I can rescue the *Lady* from—"

Mate interrupted him, "From becoming a hubcap on one of those little Japanese cars!"

"Exactly."

The phone rang. It was Melina asking Kim if she or Mate had heard from Tony. Kim answered, "He's here paying us a visit." Then to Tony, "It's Melina, do you want to talk to her?"

"Sure." Kim handed him the phone. "Hi . . .Fine . . .Me too . . .Listen, so much has happened since I last saw you. I got a ship . . .Yeah, I'd rather tell it all to you in person . . .I know you are . . .I'll catch a bus over . . .I'll leave here in a few minutes . . .I love you, bye." He hung up.

Mate said, "Give her a kiss hello for me."

Tony joked, "I haven't seen her in so long that I just might kiss her hello for a whole lot of people."

Kim asked him, "Did she know you might be leaving the islands soon?"

"No, but she knows I've been waiting for a ship to the Orient. She doesn't know I lost my job either, come to think of it."

"Then you're going to have a lot to tell her. Since you might be leaving soon, things are going to look different to her."

Mate added, "My man, what if she says, 'Don't leave'?"

Tony had a look of uncertainty about him. He didn't have an answer for that one. But he knew he would probably stay.

Tony wasted no time making his way to Melina's. When she opened the door for him the first words out of her mouth were, "When are you leaving?"

As they embraced in the doorway he just whispered in her ear, "I don't know for sure yet, but it could be Monday or Tuesday."

She guided him over to the couch. "Tell me what's been going on since I last saw you."

He told her what happened with his job, then with the shipping agents. "This Norwegian freighter is due here Monday night and will leave the next evening."

They had been sitting side by side, holding hands as he talked. She didn't say anything for a moment, and then, "Most of today has gone, so that only leaves three more days before you leave here." Her hold on his hand tightened momentarily.

He took in a breath and said, "Yeah, I'm afraid so."

She detected an air of uncertainty in his voice. She looked into his eyes and asked him, "You love me, don't you?"

Without giving her question any thought his instant response was, "Yes."

"And because you love me, you would give up anything I asked you to, wouldn't you?"

"I'm not sure but probably."

Tears were beginning to appear in her eyes as she said, "In a little while I'm going to ask you to give up something very dear to you, for me. But first I want you to make love to me as if it were our first time."

He couldn't imagine what she would ask him to give up if not his desire to travel. But at this moment he might agree to it.

He had no difficulty in imagining them together for the first time. They were both exploring each other's senses with a fresh innocence and curiosity seeking only to give the other comfort and pleasure.

Quite some time had passed. After their lovemaking they had fallen asleep. Melina was the first to wake. She showered then began to fix a meal for them both. She would have to leave for work in about an hour. Tony woke and showered while she was cooking. Afterward they sat together at the little table in the kitchen eating their dinner. Tony said to her, "You said you were going to ask me to give up something."

She told him, "It will be better if you finish eating first."

So about twenty minutes later when they had both finished he said, "Okay, I'm ready." He was sure she would ask him to give up traveling and was just being dramatic.

Again she looked straight into his eyes. Again tears began to form in hers as she said to him, "You are going to have to give me up."

He was stunned. He was not ready for that at all. His whole body felt as though it were just slammed by a giant board. He was speechless. He couldn't look at her but instead stared at his plate, which he didn't see. He felt an incredible emptiness. Then he realized that she was talking to him. He looked across at her and listened to her words.

"Don't you see? If we're together, neither of us is going to do what we need to in order to complete this part of our life."

He felt as though he was going to cry as one does from profound frustration. He got up from the table and walked quietly to the couch and laid down. He placed one arm on his chest and his other hand over his closed eyes.

Melina didn't know what to make of his reaction. She expected him to give her an argument of some kind but not a response like this. She looked at him laying there and said, "I'm sorry, hon, but I do think this is best for us both."

He thought to himself that if she had told him this when he arrived instead of having them make love, it would have been so much better for him. But instead it was as though his love and need for her had been reinforced. He knew then he had to let her go before he became destroyed.

Melina drove Tony back to his room on her way to work. They barely spoke along the way.

The time just slipped away as he lay on his bed in the dark. He looked out of his window at the lights from far away; reflecting off the water and shimmering through the night air.

It was noon the following day. Kim was on the phone to Melina. "What did you do to Tony last night?"

"What do you mean?"

"He came by here a little while ago in the same convertible he rented before. The one he took us in to the aquarium and beach."

"Really? What's wrong with that?"

"Well, he acted odd when I asked about you, and told me I would have to ask you. He took Mate for a drive up to the

Crosswinds. They don't expect to be back until late. Did you two have some kind of argument?"

"No, in fact we made love as if for the first time. It was really beautiful."

"So I guess he's going to stay here then?"

"Then later I told him to give me up for good."

"You what?!"

"It's the best thing for both of us, really."

"But after you made love like never before? Don't you realize that the guy is completely gone on you?"

"I think he's great, and when we make love it's as if I'm taken to a different world. But I want to stay here. And he can't, not really."

Meanwhile, as the open convertible moved leisurely up the eastern coastline and mellow music was coming through the car radio, a cool late afternoon breeze was blowing in from the ocean.

Tony asked Mate, "This car must have been built for a drive like this, wouldn't you agree?"

Mate answered faking an English accent, "I don't get out much these days as you know, but I would have to agree. On the other hand, if my memory serves me correctly, a certain '52 Cadillac convertible could really do this run in style."

Tony copied the accent, "I'll concede to that, old boy. How long before you're on your feet and walking without a crutch, then?"

"It's hard to say, my good fellow. It may be some time yet." Then in his natural manner, "I'm workin' on it."

Also speaking naturally, Tony said, "Since I'm probably leaving in just over two days, I want to take you and Kim, and Melina to the Jolly Roger one night for a farewell get-together. How would you feel about that?"

Mate was quiet for a moment. Tony looked at him thinking that maybe it wasn't such a good idea. Then Mate had a sly look on his face when he said, "I guess if no one asks me to dance it will be okay. But if some sweet young thing does, how can I not oblige her?"

"Good point."

"Hey, man, is there any good food at this joint you're takin' me to?"

"You know I'm not sure. If I haven't eaten beforehand I just grab something at the store, but it closes at sunset."

Mate reminded him, "I need to eat something substantial."

"If we get there early enough we can buy some food in the store and put something together. How does that sound?"

"That sounds cool, man. I wish I could go down and have a look at the place where you had those wild experiences."

"You can, with your crutches you can go far enough along the path to see it from a distance."

"I'm willing to give it a try."

"Good, that'll give us something to do until dark. That's when they make the switch from one setup to the other. Things don't really start happening in the coffeehouse until later."

When the Crosswinds appeared in front of them, Tony said, "There it is."

Mate had his head back looking up at the unusual cloud patterns in the late afternoon sky. He looked ahead at the old building. "I can see why you like to come up here. This area is kind of far out."

After Tony parked the car they went into the store. Mate was managing very well with his crutches. They bought a variety of things then took them to the patio at the back of the building. The view of the ocean was great from there. Mate said, "This place really has a nice feeling to it."

"Yeah, it's great. It's going to be getting dark in about an hour so as soon as we finish eating we'll take a walk on the path."

Mate tapped his wooden crutches. "With a little help from my friends here."

They had gone some distance when the path began to have abrupt drops of about a foot every so often. Mate had to stop at the first one. Tony pointed ahead to a small beach, "That's the area where I like to sleep."

Mate asked, "Is that where the dolphin pushed you ashore?"

"No, that was in a small cove farther on. You can't see it from here."

Mate again asked, "Didn't you tell me you weren't wearing a bathing suit when that happened?"

"That's right. After the dolphin left and I realized it wasn't a shark I felt relieved and stupid."

"Stupid?"

"Because I let myself lose control. When I realized that I was drifting farther from shore and couldn't get back on my own I really thought I might become fish bait. Then the dolphin showed up with me thinking that it was a shark."

Mate gave a chuckle, "With no bathing suit you're lucky some fish didn't take a bite."

"I never thought of that," Tony said with a frown.

Mate realized that the sun had set. "Hey, it's about to get dark."

"Sorry, man, I completely forgot. You lead the way, and I'll follow."

So they made their way back with no problem. After they were inside the Crosswinds, Tony checked out the notes and posters on the bulletin board. Mate ordered a large coffee with whipped crème then sat at a table facing the little stage.

Some time passed. Tony was reading a small book of poetry to himself. Mate was reading an out of date issue of *Down Beat* magazine and was deep into an article about Charley Parker. Talking more to himself, Mate said, "Bird was too much, man. The kat was somethin' else."

Not looking up from his book but nodding his head, Tony just commented, "Really."

"And he died too soon, man. Imagine if the kat was still blowin' today."

Tony asked, "I wonder if Bird and Shankar could have grooved together?"

"I don't know, man. They're both deep into improvisation."

Tony pondered, "But coming from different places within themselves. Or were they?"

Mate suggested, "If Bird was still here and Shankar wanted to, they could work something out."

Tony was looking at Mate intently. "Just imagine what that could be like. With those two grooving together it would be so out of sight that the world might spin right off its axis."

Mate just said, "Damn!" After a moment of deep consideration, they both returned to their books.

More time had passed. The room had been filling with people. It was a mixed crowd. Tony thought it might be because it was Saturday night. Tony soon saw why the place was filling. The blind musician Tony had seen there before came into the room with a woman who was also blind. They entered with the aid of a friend. The man was carrying his guitar case while the third person was carrying two smaller cases. At first they sat at a small table near the stage that had been reserved for them. After they had a snack and coffee they went onto the stage.

It was just big enough to hold two chairs and some instrument cases. And there was no microphone.

Mate had been quietly watching them. He asked Tony, "Have you seen these people before?"

"The man was playing and singing the last time I was here. He's really good. But I haven't seen the woman before."

JOSEPH AN MARY

Once they were seated the couple took the instruments from their cases. The man had an all wood Dobro guitar while the woman had a concertina and a small cymbal on a stand with a pedal. After they tuned their instruments the man spoke to the audience. His voice had the timbre of age and experience. "Ladies and gentlemen, good evening. Thank you for coming here tonight. We are Joseph and Mary Brown. We come from New Orleans and we are going to sing the blues for you. We hope you like it."

As they began with their first song, *'Oh God, What Can I Do Without You?'* it became apparent that everyone was in for a very special evening. One after another, the songs and the performance were awe inspiring. Her voice was just as affective as his. The combination of guitar, concertina, and cymbal created a voice that was unparalleled by anything that Mate had ever heard. He became fascinated by the couple and inspired.

While the couple were taking a break, Mate admitted to Tony, "You know I've been feeling pretty sorry for myself in the last couple of weeks. But after seeing these two . . . He's been blind since, what did you tell me, his twenties? And she said she's been blind all her life. They not only play and sing in a way that blows my mind, but here they are all the way from Louisiana, and you know they ain't stoppin' here. Hell, they'll probably wind up performing in Japan next."

"It wouldn't surprise me. In fact, they might even get there before I do."

"Listen, man, I've decided that when I get the use of my foot back, and I will get it back,—"

"God willing."

"—Okay, God willing. I'm going to work out until I get my chops back, then I'm going to dance like there's no tomorrow."

"Amen to that, brother. I know you can do it. And if I remember right, that's the advice you gave to Chuck before he and Mary danced in the contest."

"You're right. And he did just that. They almost made it into the final round." Mate was suddenly filled with sadness. "Damn, I sure wish the kid was still here with us."

"I figure he's moved on to a place where the music is even sweeter than it is here tonight."

Mate agreed, "I believe you're right, brother."

"After I leave Hawaii I don't know when I'll have an address, but when it looks like I'll be somewhere long enough I'll write you. I want you to keep me posted on what's going on with you."

"I will, but I'm not into writing long letters. A card now and then would be cool with me."

"That's cool with me too. How are you feeling now?"

"I'm feeling really tired. It's been a long day, but I want to hear these two some more. This is food for my soul."

"And mine."

Joseph and Mary Brown returned to the stage to play their last set. When they finished, Mate went over to thank them for being such an inspiration to him. The woman told him that they would be performing again at the museum a week from then on Sunday and that he should tell his friends. Also they were going to perform in Tokyo at an international sacred music conference in less than a month. Mate found all this information overwhelming.

The night had grown cool so Tony put the convertible top up. Mate fell asleep during the drive back, and Tony didn't wake him until they reached Kim's.

Tony walked with him to the door in case he needed help. Kim was already there waiting and just a bit worried. After the guys told what an amazing experience they had she wished she could have gone with them. Tony excused himself and drove back to his rooming house. A gas station near by stayed open all night, so he arranged to leave the car there where it would be safe until morning.

After an undisturbed sleep Tony woke up at around eight. He showered then made breakfast in the communal kitchen. There was no one else around except a big fluffy cat that seemed to like him. It was talking to him and purring. It just plopped down by his feet obviously waiting to be petted. Tony stroked the cat's chest with his shoeless foot. There was an empty saucer on the floor, apparently for the cat. Tony put some milk in the dish that temporarily distracted the cat.

After he finished with his breakfast Tony used the pay phone to call Melina, but there was no answer. He phoned Kim and invited her and Mate for lunch at the udon house. Tony told Kim he was unable to reach Melina. Kim told him that Melina was very tired when she finished work the night before and may have turned off the bell on her phone. She told him, "You need to phone her every so often. When she wakes up she'll turn the bell back on."

The thought of her turning off the phone's bell caused him to feel a bit apprehensive. He gave it another try. This time the phone stopped ringing as a voice at the other end said, "Hello."

"Melina?"

"Tony!"

"Wow! Did I just go through a number."

"What do you mean?"

"I tried to call you a little while ago, but there was no answer. Kim told me your bell might be off and that's what triggered it."

She understood the reference all too well. "I'm sorry, hon. I was just so burned out by the end of work last night that I didn't want anything to wake me before I just woke on my own."

"I can dig that."

"So what's happening?"

"I thought I'd take us all—you, me, Mate, and Kim—to lunch at the udon place."

"Well I'm hungry, and I don't have to be to work until Tuesday. When do you want to go?"

"How does two hours from now sound?"

"That's good because I need some time to get ready."

"Great, I'll be by to pick you up."

"Oh, that's right, you have that beautiful convertible you had before."

"Yes, and it's great. I'll phone Kim and let her know what's going on."

Near the end of a satisfying meal at the udon restaurant, Tony asked the group as a whole, "It might seem a little awkward but I could find out tomorrow that I'm leaving here the next day, bound for the Orient."

Mate replied, "That's weird, man."

Kim added, "And it's a little scary."

At first Melina found the information encouraging and tried not to let it show. However, she became aware of an underlying apprehension of loss.

Tony continued, "So I thought that tonight we could have a farewell something or other at the Jolly Roger."

Being facetious, Mate said, "How about calling it a wake? You know, since we could be seeing you for the last time."

Tony again, "Unless I come back to haunt you. Anyway, I know it's more of a place for dancing, but it just seems like the most appropriate place to celebrate having known each other."

Melina asked him, "But you won't know for sure that you are leaving until tomorrow?"

"That's right."

Mate asked, "What if you don't get the job on the ship and don't leave?"

Kim said, "That's a good question. You must have read my mind."

Tony reassured them, "I'll rent a surfboard, find a friendly dolphin, and have it tow me across the ocean."

Melina suggested, "Make sure it's a male dolphin."

Mate found that very funny. With a laugh he said, "Right on, Melina."

Glad that she was expressing some humor, Tony said, "But seriously, I'll get something eventually. Then I'll just have to invite you all to another farewell night out."

Mate agreed, "I can dig that."

Tony asked them, "So what do you think, should we do that tonight?"

Mate was still too inspired to be bothered about being in a dance club. "I'm all for it. But I can't promise to go more than one dance. How about you, dove?"

Kim was amazed by Mate's enthusiasm. "If that's okay with you."

Tony looked at Melina. "How do you feel about it?"

"Wild horses couldn't keep me away."

"Fantastic! How would all of you feel about a little drive up and around the windward side of the island?"

Kim said, "As long as we can be home with enough time to grab a bite and to freshen up before we go to the Jolly Roger."

Melina agreed, "A drive might be relaxing."

It was a beautiful afternoon as they drove up the east coast of Oahu with the ocean to their right. Melina was beside Tony leaning against him. Kim and Mate were in the backseat with Mate keeping his right leg stretched out. There was some soft jazz playing on the radio. Tony was feeling lethargic when he said, "This is so surreal, I feel like I'm in a time machine and just went back in time."

Mate agreed, "Man, you got that right. We have been in this moment before."

Melina said in a voice so light she was barely heard in the backseat, "Except that was at the beginning."

No one said anything for a while after that.

Much later in Melina's apartment, Tony was relaxing on a couch. Melina was in her kitchen making a snack for them prior to freshening up and changing clothes. Because he was so devastated after the last time, Tony had decided not to make love with Melina before going away. He was treating their time together as if it were at the beginning of their acquaintance rather than at the end: full of potential and promise, instead of bad memories and disenchantment. He sensed that Melina might be making the best of the moment as well.

After Tony and Melina picked up Mate and Kim they drove to the Jolly Roger arriving before eight. When they went inside the club's disc jockey must have been on his break because there was no music playing. Also the customers seemed pretty relaxed. "Table for four?" a waitress they didn't recognize asked them.

"Yes, please," Tony answered.

It had been well over a month since they had been there. But it wasn't long before they began to feel at home. Another waitress, one who was very familiar with them, came to their table to take their order. "Hi, I haven't seen you all in ages." When she saw a pair of crutches leaning against the wall by their table she asked, "Do those belong to one of you?"

Mate answered, "Yes, they're mine."

Remembering that Mate and Kim had won the dance contest before the last one, she exclaimed, "Yours?! What happened?"

Mate explained, "About three weeks ago I had a run in with a big hungry shark."

"Oh my god! You're kidding!"

Kim reassured her, "He's telling you the truth, all right."

The waitress said, "I hope it's going to be okay."

Mate again, "I'll be off it for a while."

The waitress again, "You know, about four weeks ago there was something on the news about a ship's crew being attacked by sharks, way up north of here."

Tony said, "That was us."

"That's horrible. I am so sorry to hear that. Would you like a little more time? I can come back to take your order?"

Mate said, "Well, I'm ready."

Tony looked at the others then said to the waitress, "I think we're ready."

While they were ordering drinks and some food for Mate, the disc jockey returned from his break. He recognized Mate whom he had a conversation with the first time Mate came to the club. He put on a record he remembered Mate had asked for back then. "Here's an old favorite. Okay, brother, get out there and shake that thing."

Mate heard him but wasn't paying attention until he heard the music. He looked up and over at the DJ who was looking directly at him. The DJ pointed to him and smiled. Mate experienced an instant moment of truth. In the first second he felt frozen to the spot. But a new spirit in Mate took over. He reached for his crutches and said to Kim, "Come on, dove, they're playing my song."

Kim looked at him in disbelief. "What?!"

"Time to boogie. Come on, girl, I need someone to dance with."

She knew Mate too well to argue. She looked at Melina as she got up to follow him. "Dear God."

Melina looked over at a surprised Tony. "Let's dance, hon."

Tony stood up and extended a hand to Melina. "May I have this dance?" With that they became the only couples on the floor.

The unusual sight of a man with crutches on the dance floor attracted some attention.

Mate had pretty well mastered the use of his crutches but certainly not for this purpose. He was able to drag his right foot along without it hurting as long as he didn't put any weight on it. He took it slow and easy at first. Kim was dancing ever so slowly opposite him although the music was fast. She was so afraid he would hurt himself.

Tony and Melina were dancing at about half the beat of the music's rhythm. Most of the regular customers recognized Mate and were watching him, along with the surprised DJ. You had to be a dancer to understand what Mate was experiencing.

There was a powerful feeling in his chest and torso that seemed to produce an energy of its own. That energy went into his arms, legs, and neck. Now he was moving about as only one on crutches could conjure up. They were still the only two couples on the floor when the song finished. It was quickly followed by a second. Other couples, instead of only watching, were joining them.

The lyrics to the second song seemed so appropriate that someone could imagine that Mate had written them: 'The sadness is gone, and I'm so happy. I'm so happy. With your love, the sadness is gone and I'm so happy, I'm so happy.'

Kim was full of pride for Mate. He had managed to dance through three pieces. Quite an achievement but the crutches were really causing his armpits to hurt. And there was an irritating blister that had developed. When he saw the waitress put his food on their table he took the opportunity to have a rest. He and Kim returned to their table followed by Tony and Melina.

As they sat down Kim said to Mate, "Sweetheart, I was so afraid you might fall."

Sitting beside her, Mate took her hand in his, "So was I, dove. Thanks for being there with me."

When Tony and Melina sat down, he told Mate, "I'm glad there's no contest tonight. You probably want to give it a shot."

Mate disagreed, "I would have to let that pass." Then with a grin, he added, "At least for this week."

Melina asked him, "How did it feel, hon, being on the dance floor?"

Mate answered, "What a scene. It was a lot of things at the same time. It was strange, scary, and fun at the same time. I lost my balance once and almost fell."

Kim squeezed his hand saying, "Really? I didn't even notice."

Mate again, "It was the greatest challenge I ever had. But I have to admit, I sure was glad to see my food arrive. You don't know what those crutches do to my armpits." They all made an understanding frown at that last revelation.

Tony said, "Speaking of food, I'm getting hungry myself." He motioned for the waitress to come back to their table. When she did he ordered a special Hawaiian desert for all of them.

As the evening wore on Tony noticed that the special feeling Melina used to give him was gone. When they danced together the other things were there, her special personality, her uniqueness, and her beauty, but the magic between them was missing. This gave him a feeling of sadness that he hid.

Mate asked him, "My man, what are your plans for tomorrow?"

"Well, first off I'm giving the shipping agent a call to see what he's heard. And then I'll just take it from there. At some point I'll return the car."

"So you've got to be ready to leave at a moment's notice?" asked Mate.

"It could happen that way. But from what the agent told me, the ship's due in tomorrow. Then I'll meet the captain or whoever does the hiring. That's when I find out what's happening, if anything. The ship leaves the next evening heading west."

Listening to the two of them talk, Melina had a matter-of-fact feeling of being somewhat disconnected. But beneath that was another feeling. She had always had a deep belief that she would be abandoned, and soon she would.

There came a moment when, without it being mentioned, they felt it was time to leave the club. As Tony drove them home he promised each that he would phone them the next day when he finally learned his fate.

Monday morning brought the usual hustle and bustle sounds outside the rooming house. Before returning the car Tony made a phone call to the agent. "Yes, Mr. Lewis. I've been expecting your call. The ship will be tying up at dock number seven by the warehouse area I told you about; around eleven thirty this morning. You will be able to go aboard at noon for an interview with the captain. You need to come by my office to pick up the paperwork and a pass that will get you past the guards at the dock."

"I'll be at your office right after I return a car rental."

The agent continued, "Good, remember I told you the ship is Norwegian. But it has a mainly Chinese crew except for the department heads and their assistants. It's one of the Norwegian assistants who has taken ill. Depending on the nature of his illness and after he has recovered, he would normally be flown to the port the ship is to arrive at next; in which case you would be relieved."

"I understand. That's the standard procedure, isn't it?"

"Yes, that's right."

Tony asked the agent, "Do you know which department the crewman is from?"

"Yes, luckily for you it's to do with the maintenance of the ship."

"No kidding?"

"So your chances of getting on are very good."

"Great!"

"So I'll see you shortly then?"

"It could be in just under an hour."

"Very good, I'll see you then."

"Thank you."

The car rental agency was not far from the shipping office so after he returned the car, Tony made his way to the office.

Inside, the agent's office was drab with two framed photographs of cargo ships hanging on a wall along with a wooden company logo. A couple of filing cabinets stood along another wall. The walls looked as though they should have been repainted long ago.

The casually dressed agent sat behind a cluttered desk. "Mr. Lewis, I believe I told you the ship is named *Vietnam*."

Tony was sitting opposite the man's desk. "Yes, that's right."

"I believe the ship belonged to the French originally."

Tony remarked, "Just like the country."

The agent didn't seem to get the gist of his comment. "Something like that. In any case the Norwegians are a fair bunch of people. If you do a good job they might just keep you on even if the crewman rejoins the ship later."

"Do you think so?"

"I know it to have happened once or twice." He handed Tony a sealed envelope with the same company logo on it. "Here are your papers, including a note to the captain. I hope you brought your passport with you?"

"Yes, I have it." He took the envelope and shook the agent's hand. "Thank you so much. I'd better get going; I don't want to be late."

"Good luck, Mr. Lewis. If for any reason you aren't taken on, get back to me because this kind of situation comes up every now and then."

"Thank you, I will."

After a short bus ride Tony arrived at the warehouse area and had no trouble finding dock number seven. With the help of his pass the guards let him onto the dock. And there she was, with the name *Vietnam* painted on her stern and the name Oslo painted below that. It was not very impressive though. She looked to be an ex-liberty ship, another veteran of World War II. Also she looked barely maintained. Tony thought it could be a modern version of a tramp steamer, a cargo ship with an open schedule. Walking up the gangplank he sensed an event was repeating itself.

Again there was the unpleasant odor of diesel exhaust. One of the crew took him to a cabin marked *Capitaine*. Inside was a bearded, middle-aged man of medium build. When he addressed Tony his English had a Norwegian accent. "May I do something for you?"

"Hello, sir. My name is Antony Lewis. The shipping agent sent—"

The man extended his hand to shake Tony's. "Yah, so, Mr. Lewis, I am happy to meet with you. I am Captain Olsen, Jon Olsen. Do you have some papers and your passport?"

Tony handed him the envelope along with his passport. "Yes sir, the papers are in here."

The captain opened the envelope and examined the two pages it contained. "So, I see you have experience, but for a short time only."

Tony began to feel discouraged. "Yes sir, I was on a survey ship with the American government. More recently I've done some work in a boat rebuilding business here in Hawaii."

"I see. Have you known the agent who sent you a long time?"

"Not long, sir."

"So I see. He recommended you, you know. You must have impressed him."

"I think he is familiar with the government agency I sailed with, sir. They have a good reputation."

There was a crashing sound outside the porthole behind the captain that startled both of them. The captain jumped to his feet and peered through the glass. "Please excuse me." He left the cabin and went on deck. Tony could hear angry shouting in Norwegian, followed by Chinese.

The captain returned looking a bit flustered and muttered something in Norwegian Tony didn't understand, but he thought he detected something resembling the word "stupid" in the mix.

Again seated the captain reviewed Tony's papers. "So, yah, if we can use you, can you begin tomorrow morning?"

"Yes sir." Tony began to feel very encouraged.

"But I must warn you, Mr. Lewis. If your work is not satisfactory you will become a paying passenger, and the fare to Japan will be four hundred and fifty dollars. On the other hand, you will receive wages equal to the man you are replacing. So, what do you think? Does this still interest you?"

Tony took a moment to think this through then agreed, "Yes sir, it does."

"Very good then." Extending his hand to Tony he said, "Welcome aboard, Mr. Lewis." After they shook hands he picked up the phone on his desk and spoke into it in Norwegian. Afterward he said, "There will be a crewman here in a moment to show you to your quarters, and to introduce you to your department. But first you may take lunch with the crew. I hope you are hungry."

"Yes, thank you, sir."

"As there is not much time, after you have eaten you will make the necessary preparations for beginning work tomorrow. Your department will begin at eight o'clock in the morning. I realize you will have business to attend to ashore. After your lunch you will not need to be on board longer than an hour."

"Yes, I do have a number of things to take care of, sir."

"I would suggest that you are here one hour early. We are sailing to Yokohama as the sun goes down. We will be there one day to unload and load, like here. From there it is not yet clear." At this point a crewman arrived to show Tony around the ship.

As soon as he had left the ship and warehouse area, Tony used a pay phone to contact his friends. They had arranged a dinner at Kim's. After that Melina wanted him to stay his last night with her.

After returning to his rooming house he packed his sea-bag full, and what was left he put into another bag. He wrote two short letters: one to his parents and another to Maureen. He said goodbye to the landlady and Fluffy the cat.

Because he was to change buses by the post office he was able to mail his letters, getting there just before closing time. When he arrived at Kim's he saw Melina's VW parked in front. He could hear soft music coming from the apartment. He felt sad knowing he might not see any of them for a long time, if ever again.

It was Melina who opened the door for him. She was wearing the same outfit she wore when he first met her. He had seen her in it a couple of times since then, but this time it made a special impression on him. She gave him an inspiring kiss that caused him to momentarily lose his balance.

Watching from the couch, Mate said, "Meanwhile, back on the planet Earth, a dinner has been prepared for the guest of honor."

Tony looked at Mate as he entered the room. "Hey, champ, what's happenin'?"

"At the moment, you are. So tell us what happened today."

So with all three of them sitting around him Tony told them the events of the day. When he finished, Kim responded with, "My god, Tony, the whole time you didn't know how it was going to turn out until the captain said, 'Welcome aboard'?"

"I had one or two hopeful moments, but you're right, I never knew until that point what to expect."

Melina had one arm through Tony's, and held his hand as if she didn't want to let go of him.

Mate said, "Well, you stayed with it, and you got it."

"You know, when I was in Dr. Lim's office waiting for Melina, there was a magazine that had an interview with Akira Kurosawa, the Japanese film maker. He said that through all his work one thought he never forgot was that patience and fortitude are invincible."

Mate said, "And that's exactly where I'm at right now."

Melina spoke for the first time, "I think we can all benefit from the practice of that belief."

Kim said, "I'm sure we can. We are going to miss you, Tony. So to thwart off our sad hearts let's make for some happy stomachs. Dinner should be ready any minute." She got up and went into the kitchen. "Melina, can you give me a hand?"

During the meal Tony and Mate reminisced about the good ship *Lady Explorer*, her crew, and their hope of saving her from the scrap heap. Tony spoke of how he had grown attached to different places on the island. He didn't need to mention his attachment to Melina. There was a strong feeling in the air that he was leaving for good.

When they finished the meal, Kim presented Tony with a cake she had made for him. On the top there was a big broken heart that a ship had just passed through. Also there were three palm trees growing out of one half of the heart and one growing out of the other half, causing it to also resemble an island. On the half with the three trees were the words, "We will miss you." Tony was very moved.

"That sure says a lot. It's a beautiful cake, Kim." He gave her a kiss on the cheek, "Thank you. It's a shame to eat it."

"I nearly forgot," as Kim recalled, "the ice cream." She went to the refrigerator then returned with a container of triple flavored ice cream.

Tony didn't feel like leaving such a mellow gathering of friends, but the reality of getting up at five o'clock the next morning was weighing on him. "Kim, let me help you with the dishes, then I'm going to have to leave."

Kim said to him, "Don't you worry about the dishes." Then speaking softly into one ear she said to him, "You and Melina enjoy what little time you have left together."

"Thank you, dear. You've been a good friend to both of us." After a few more minutes he and Melina were ready to leave. "Mate, we're leaving."

Mate was up on his crutches. "Didn't you say your ship sails at sunset?"

Tony answered, "Just a few minutes before. But it could leave the dock any time before that. The sailing time is when it leaves the harbor."

"Melina doesn't start work till eight and Kim has someone who can fill in for her at the beginning of her shift. So we are going to see your ship off. Let me have the phone number of the agent. Maybe we can get the last minute details from him."

"Great, if you want to go to the dock you'll need passes. Ask him about that too. Here's his card, you can have it."

Melina said, "We'll figure something out."

Mate tried to give Tony a hug and nearly lost his balance. "Well, my man, let me hear from you now and again. I also want to know what happens to the *Lady*."

"I will."

Kim gave him a hug and a kiss on the cheek. Her eyes were beginning to water. "Goodbye, Tony."

"Goodbye, you two."

Mate and Kim stood in the doorway waving goodbye, as Tony and Melina got into her car and drove slowly away.

Because Melina's apartment was not far from Kim's they reached her place in no time. Once inside her apartment Melina went into the kitchen to make some soothing mint tea for the two of them while Tony waited on the couch.

At one point Melina was standing at the sink rinsing the tea pot when a voice came to her mind for the first time in years. She was transported back to her family kitchen when she was twelve: *Her father was seated at the kitchen table finishing another beer and watching as Melina washed the dinner dishes. He said to her, "Hey, sugar, fetch a beer out'a the fridge for your dad, would ya, hon?" She dutifully got another beer for him and took it to the table. The image began to fade, but she remembered the following morning. He went to work, never to return home. She waited day after day for him, never knowing what happened to him.* Tears formed in her eyes as she recalled the loss and the pain. "Daddy," she said in a half whisper, "why didn't you come back?"

The kettle was whistling. She poured the hot water onto the leaves in the teapot. As she brewed the tea she became more composed. She took a tray with the tea pot, cups, and some little cookies into the living room and placed them on the coffee table near Tony. She sat beside him. Her eyes again began to tear. When he saw this he leaned toward her to kiss the tears from the corners of her eyes. "Don't be sad," he said to her. They were holding each other then. She said to him, "I just remembered something from so long ago. When I was a girl, my father left us without a word, and never came back." She looked into his eyes, and at that moment she was not sure who she was, and she was not sure what she wanted of him.

"And now I'm leaving you too," he said.

"I don't know why I'm feeling so terribly sad. I didn't think I was going to." They hugged each other for so long that it seemed as though they would melt into one another. Then in her softest voice she asked him, "Tony, would you mind if we just lie in bed together for a while?"

"Of course not."

They undressed and lay on the bed just under the top covering. At first they cuddled for the longest time. Then with an unspoken understanding between them he entered her. They were joined together as one body with neither of them moving, and would remain so until the next morning.

During their sleep he had a dream:

He was a cloaked pilgrim standing at the entrance to a great domed temple. At the center of the temple was a radiant altar. The dome had a subtle peek above the altar and had become transparent. Looking up through the dome he could see far out beyond this world, in the direction of the source of the radiance. Still standing only at the entrance to the temple his dream ended.

When they woke it was because Melina's alarm clock was sounding its wakeup call. Tony felt inspired by the dream but the inspiration quickly faded as he got out of bed and prepared to leave. The first thing he did was to arrange for a taxi to pick him up at six thirty.

While Tony was getting ready Melina put together a light breakfast for him but only some tea for herself. He told her about his dream, then she told him that she had the most peaceful and deep sleep she could recall.

After he finished eating, they were able to have a quiet moment together before the taxi was due to arrive. When it did they embraced and kissed goodbye. He loaded his two bags into the taxi and left for the docks.

Once Tony was aboard the ship he changed into his work clothes. A crewman he would be working with suggested that Tony wait in the crew's dining room until eight o'clock when they would begin work. Some of the crew were having their breakfast; Tony only had tea and pastries while he waited.

Just before it was time to begin work the same crewman, whose name was Paul, took Tony to meet with the chief bosun. Both Tony and Paul were to be the bosun's assistants, just as Pete had been on the *Lady Explorer*. Tony was to spend his first day aboard assisting Paul in order to learn his work. The job of the two of them was to supervise the deck crew in the minor repair and painting of the ship. The Chinese deck crew had been hired on at the port of Singapore, and their English was minimal but useful.

Tony spent the remainder of the day going to every area of the ship, where he was shown the work to be done and met all of the crew. Afterward he had dinner in the crew's mess with his work partner, Paul, who wanted to hear all about America.

Because the hour had grown late, Tony was on the upper deck waiting for a sign of Kim's car. He was leaning on the railing enjoying a pipe full of tobacco. The ship was no longer tied to the dock but was several yards out waiting for its pilot boat. Its space at the dock was already taken by another cargo ship preparing to unload.

Tony saw the pilot boat approaching in the distance. He looked back toward the dock and saw Kim's car pull up to the gate.

The three got out of the car and went through the gate. Tony was afraid that they might go to the wrong ship. But instead of that they quickly walked to an open space along the edge of the dock and began waving and calling out.

Tony responded by shouting back to them, "Hey! I'm up here!"

Melina was holding a lei that she brought for him. "There he is. Hey! I want you to write me!"

Not sure what she said, he hollered back, "I can't hear you!"

Mate answered for her shouting with more force, "She said she wants you to write her, and so do we!"

"I will, but I'll have to mail it from Japan!"

Melina was extremely disappointed when she said to Kim, "What do I do with this lei?"

Kim said to her, "I could be wrong but I think tradition would have you throw it onto the water after your loved one."

Melina agreed, "I think you're right."

The pilot boat had positioned itself just ahead of the ship's bow. The *Vietnam* was under her own power with the captain on the bridge.

Tony could feel the ship begin to move. He waved his arms and called to them, "We're leaving!" The freighter quietly followed as the pilot led the way out of the harbor.

Melina had tears in her eyes. Without a word, she threw the lei onto the water in the direction of the departing ship. She wondered if she would ever see Tony again. Only her intuition was a clue to the answer.

Mate spoke in a tone that even the two ladies could barely hear, "Well, my man, I guess I'll see you later."

When it was obvious that the ship was well on its way the three were somber as they walked back to their car. The feeling was universal that something had just come to an end.

The ship moved to find its course. The wake it left behind was the only evidence that it had been there. It had the appearance of a road much traveled, with its mist looking like imaginary dust settling to the surface.

When the wake nearest the ship's exit began to fade, Tony moved to the bow of the ship. As she started to rise and fall upon the rolling surface of the open sea, he leaned over the rail as far as he could to look down at the water being cut by the bow.

Ahead of the ship, the golden hues that were being created by the sun setting on the ocean, combined with the colors of the broken clouds above the horizon, to create a spectacular sight that was truly overwhelming.

He became transfixed to the spot until it was so dark that he could barely find his way.

Meanwhile

She's heading home for the last time.

THE END

of

Book 1

About the Author

Mursalin Machado was born in Santa Cruz, on the central coast of California in 1938. He has traveled throughout North America, Northern Greenland, Europe, northern Africa, the Middle East, Asia, Indonesia and the Pacific islands. He has taught middle school in India; worked as a merchant seaman in the Pacific, as a counselor to emotionally disturbed teenagers in England, and became a certified Hypnotherapist in California. His background includes music and art with four years in community theater and seventeen in the film industry. His writing began with stage plays and poetry.

The author believes that the experience he gained from meeting people throughout the world, has been the most beneficial, generating the inspiration for his writing.